WOUNDED LION

Part 5 of The Pride of Lions

ANTOINETTE GEORGE

The Granville Legacy: Set Two

THE PRIDE OF LIONS

Nicholas de Bresancourt was an aristocratic but penniless refugee of the bloody French Revolution from which he'd escaped as a four-year-old orphan, thanks to Francis Granville and his friends. Nicky had lost everything: family, estate and fortune, and grew up hating those responsible in France for ending countless innocent lives on the guillotine and then Bonaparte, whose megalomania had put his country through so much further upheaval and war. With no other means to support himself or earn a living, and his pride refusing to allow him to accept the charity of his wealthy adoptive family, Nicky has joined the British army, keen to serve and help end the interminable war in Europe.

With Francis as a mentor, Nicky has matured into a charismatic, capable man and a clever fighter, as well as a lover of many women. He is also trilingual, thanks to growing up and being educated at an English school with a Spanish step-mother and French step-father. He is therefore ideal material to work undercover and put his talents to use on behalf of his adopted country. First, as an agent liaising with the Spanish rebels and guerrillas as the British endeavoured to drive the French out of Spain during the Peninsular War, and then as a full-blown spy for an anonymous Whitehall Department and Wellington, on the trail of a dangerous and ruthless French agent operating in both Spain and France: a man with a long-standing, personal vendetta against The Shadow, the man he suspected had caused the death of his father.

PART 5: WOUNDED LION

England, 1816.

He was still not totally healed from his injuries received at Waterloo, but he'd looked death in the face and miraculously survived. Bona-parte is no longer a threat so Nicky and the wider Granville family were looking forward to a happy and peaceful future. Except... Miles Ashcroft was worried. The spymaster knew Frederick Bernheim had also survived and was out there, somewhere, possibly now in England. Deranged and obsessed with revenge against Nicky, The Shadow, and the people who were responsible for his father's death twenty-five years before. A death, he claimed, that had changed the course of his life.

As Ashcroft had feared, a fiendish plot and trap was sprung and everyone was caught up in it. A terrifying, nightmarish scenario that could only have been conceived by someone as crazed as Bernheim. Even Ashcroft, Ricky Ambrose and Jack had been sucked in, and some of the family's retainers and servants, but they hadn't hesitated to help, even at risk of their own lives.

Can the family survive? Will they all meet a grisly fate or can the rescue party save everyone in time? And if they do come out of it alive, at what cost will it be to all involved? Facing a pack of starving lions would traumatise most people, and when someone literally looks death in the face, it tends to make them reassess their life... their past and their future... but sometimes the trauma can have a much deeper impact...

Historical Landscape

Dear Readers,

If you're following the continuing saga of the life and times of Francis Granville, I hope you're going to enjoy this sequel story about Nicholas de Bresancourt, Duke of Valenciennes, adopted son of Edouard and Carlotta de Mornay. The twisting and turning plot is full of even more adventure and drama, love, passion, steam, fascinating characters (some new and some familiar) and of course, a really evil villain! And lions.... Rawwwwr!

But it's also based on what I think is a fascinating period of history, both English and European. If you aren't very familiar with this era, its revolutions and wars, or it's been too long since you were at school (!), I thought I'd give you a brief overview which will help put the events in the story into perspective. There are a couple of maps here as well (in case your geography is also a bit hazy) to help you understand what was going on in Spain while the British army was there, and then back to southern England and northern France where of course the main characters have their roots.

Historical enemies down the centuries, probably since William the Conqueror invaded England back in 1066, and the English controlled part of France during the Hundred Years War in the Middle Ages...

during the 1700s, Britain and France were yet again involved in significant wars both in Europe and far from their shores. From the beginning of the century in 1704 when John Churchill, Duke of Marlborough, (the ancestor of Winston Churchill), resoundingly defeated the forces of French King Louis XIV and his allies at Blenheim, the old rivalry continued unabated. Both nations vied with each other for supremacy as they sought to either influence who ruled the various countries of Europe, or colonise new territories around the globe, in North America, Africa and the Far East, seeking both power and influence as well as new trading opportunities.

By this time, Great Britain, or more specifically the all-powerful British East India Company, controlled large areas of the Indian sub-continent as it expanded its commercial interests across south-east Asia. Army units fought various wars in alliance with local rulers until eventually, the decisive battle between the British and the French at Wandiwash in 1760 cleared the way for Britain to become the main European power in India and it became a springboard for further expansion of trade and influence throughout that part of the world, all the way down to Australia where the first convicts landed from a small fleet of British ships in Botany Bay in 1788. A penal colony was subsequently set up near there and thus began the colonisation of Australia by the British (who incidentally just beat the French to it; they landed in Botany Bay 6 days before the French expedition arrived.)

Although a British commanded army continued to have a significant presence in India after 1760 and be involved in local battles well into the 19th century, the focus of the British and French animosity turned west and both countries became embroiled in the American Revolutionary War from 1775-83.

France's help was a major contribution towards the United States' eventual victory and resulting independence. However, as a cost of participation in the war, France accumulated over 1 billion *livres* in debt, which significantly strained the nations finances. The French government's failure to control spending compounded many other growing social problems and led to serious unrest in the nation which eventually culminated in the Revolution in 1789.

Thereafter, while Britain came to terms with the loss of its American colonies, France was in turmoil and descending into anarchy.

At the start of 1791, the other monarchies in Europe became concerned at the serious Revolution happening on their doorsteps and they considered whether they should intervene: either in support of King Louis XVI, to prevent the spread of revolutionary fervour across the continent to their own countries, or to take advantage of the chaos in France to expand their own borders. By 1792, France found itself at war with its neighbours and after a series of small victories, a series of defeats followed and this downturn allowed the radical Jacobins to rise to power and impose the Reign of Terror. This inevitably led to Louis XVI and Marie Antoinette, along with large swathes of the French aristocracy and upper classes, meeting a grisly end on the guillotine. Tens of thousands were either executed or murdered across France in under a year during this most bloody period of French history.

From 1794, the war situation turned again and improved dramatically for the French. A hitherto unknown officer from Corsica, one Napoleon Bonaparte, had been rapidly rising through the ranks. Appointed Brigadier General in 1793 at the age of only 24, he began his first full campaign in Italy in April 1796. Within a year, French armies under Bonaparte were overwhelming their enemies and one by one the European states sued for peace.

By the start of 1800, Britain was becoming ever more alone in its successful resistance to Bonaparte. Its maritime supremacy was of growing importance as a series of naval victories secured control of the Mediterranean while it endeavoured to blockade France by sea. There was a brief peace and break in hostilities in 1802, but inevitably it didn't last.

Bonaparte's star continued to rise, he was an extremely capable military general and his victories made him increasingly popular in France where he continued to consolidate his own political power. In 1804, he was crowned Emperor Napoleon I as his armies continued their conquest of Europe. However, at sea, Britain reigned supreme and Nelson's famous victory at Trafalgar in 1805 decimated the French and allied Spanish navies and prevented a potential invasion of England itself.

Fuming and frustrated by the old enemy across the Channel and hoping to isolate and weaken Britain economically, as she was trying to do to France through her naval blockade, in 1806 in retaliation, Bonaparte introduced and tried to enforce his 'Continental System'. This was a large-scale embargo on British trade, and even the post, which forbade the import of British goods into any European countries allied with or dependent upon France. But it was ineffectual as smuggling became rife and trade simply continued through Portugal, Spain and Russia, much to his irritation. As a result, Bonaparte launched an invasion of Portugal, the only remaining British ally in continental Europe. After occupying Lisbon in November 1807, he seized the opportunity to turn against his former ally, deposed the reigning Spanish royal family and declared his brother King of Spain in 1808. The Spanish and Portuguese revolted, and Britain supported them, and so began the Peninsular War.

Bonaparte did well when he was in direct charge, but problems and losses followed his departure from Spain to re-focus his attention on subjugating and controlling central and eastern Europe, leaving his Marshals to run the campaign. He severely underestimated how much manpower would be needed, and the effort in Spain was a drain on that as well as money and prestige, and ultimately failed. Especially once an able British commander, Sir Arthur Wellesley, was put in total charge of the British army, supported by the Portuguese and Spanish rebels and ruthless guerrillas. Wellesley had recently arrived after a victorious tour of duty in India. His success in the Peninsular War saw him elevated to become Duke of Wellington and eventually the two opposing military leaders faced each other at the epic Battle of Waterloo in 1815. After that, Europe enjoyed nearly a century of relative peace and prosperity.

Against this background, England in 1812 was itself experiencing a difficult year.

The war against Bonaparte and the French seemed never-ending and was a constant drain on the country's finances. In particular, action in the Peninsula was at a critical point as Wellington's fortunes continued to ebb and flow in his efforts to push the French out of Spain and back into France. In Europe, meanwhile, Napoleon's ego had made him cast his eyes east and the French were now marching on Russia. There seemed to be no stopping his megalomania. On the domestic front, the Government continuously watched public feeling, wary of radicals who sought social change and in May, to the shock of the country, the Prime Minister, Spencer Perceval, was assassinated in Parliament, in the lobby of the House of Commons. And if all that wasn't enough, tensions with the new United States caused an outbreak of hostilities between the two nations in June, known as the War of 1812 (which actually lasted until early 1815) with Britain subsequently having to defend its colonies in Canada from American incursion.

And the middle of 1812 is where Pride of Lions starts. So read on and find out what Nicky, Francis and their eccentric family and friends get up to as their tale continues some 20 years on from where Behind the Shadow finished in 1792...

Apologies for the boring history lesson, I trust it hasn't sent you to sleep! But I hope you move on and enjoy the fiction story now as much as I enjoyed writing it. And if by chance you are interested in little historical anecdotes related to events in my books, keep an eye on the blog on my website where I occasionally write further musings: https://antoinettegeorge.com/blog/

Antoinette…

Channel Coasts of England & France,
1790-1816

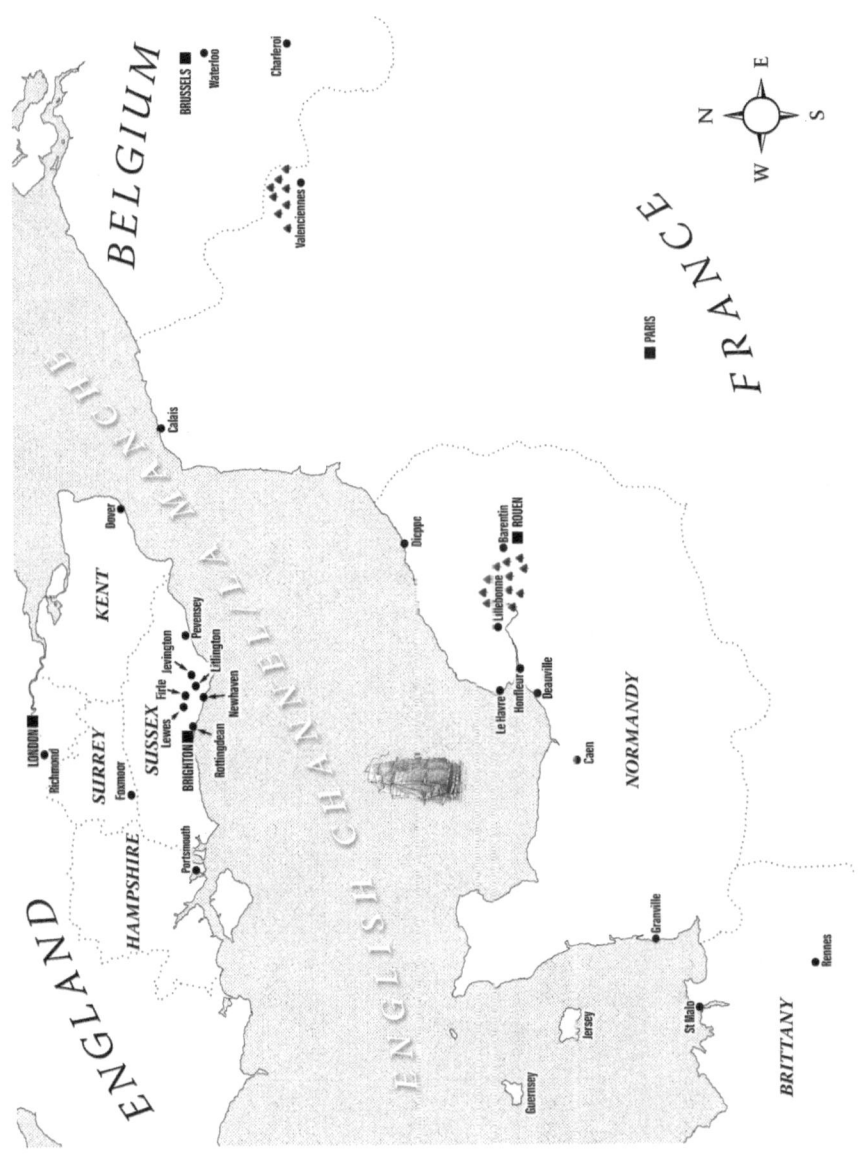

BELGIUM

BRUSSELS ■
Waterloo ●

Charleroi ●

Valenciennes ▲

FRANCE

PARIS ■

N
E
S
W

ENGLAND

LA MANCHE

Calais ●

Dover ●

KENT

Dieppe ●

Lillebonne ● Barentin
● ROUEN ■

Pevensey ●
Lewington
Firle Lewington
Littington
SUSSEX Newhaven
Lewes
BRIGHTON ■
Rottingdean

Le Havre ●
Honfleur ●
Deauville ●

SURREY
LONDON ■
Richmond ●

Exmoor ●

HAMPSHIRE

Portsmouth ●

ENGLISH CHANNEL

NORMANDY

Caen ●

Granville ●

Guernsey

Jersey

St Malo ●

Rennes ●

BRITTANY

Southern France, Spain & Portugal with the Main Battle Sites of the Peninsular War

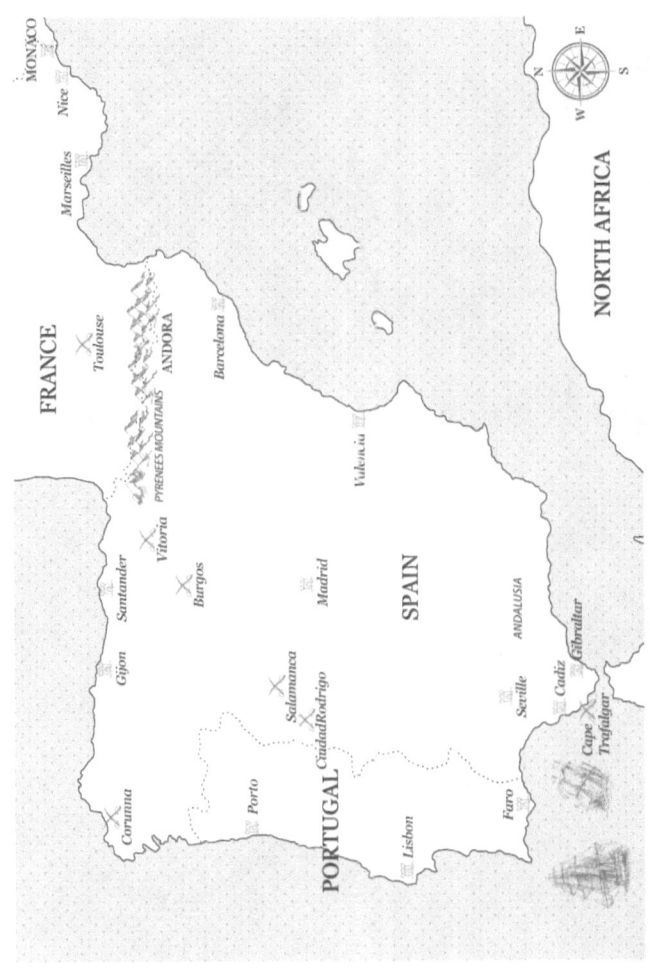

Chapter One

Seven people were being held in several damp, cold, rat-infested cellar rooms under a dilapidated, old farmhouse in the remote countryside near Richmond. They'd been taken there, one by one, as they'd arrived. They were all tightly bound with their hands behind them, especially the men, blindfolded and gagged with rags stuffed in their mouths and they each had a black sack over their heads to muffle any sounds. Their captor didn't want them to know who else was there, and he wanted them all to sit and stew for hours, in isolation and worry, wondering where they were, how long they'd been there, who had taken them and why, and what was going to happen to them next.

Frederick Bernheim was a master of torture and playing mind games, and softening up his prisoners in anticipation of extracting information from them. He'd watched and learned from the best.

Daisy was a simple farm girl. She was very plain, not very intelligent and certainly couldn't read or write more than her name and a few basic words, and her original job had been as a lowly housemaid in the lovely country house, cleaning out the fireplaces, scrubbing floors, dealing with chamber pots and a variety of other dirty and menial tasks. She didn't mind, it was paid employment, and she dutifully sent her meagre wages home to help her parents care for and feed her many brothers and sisters as she had room and board where she worked. She had grown to care for little Charles de Mornay as she toiled away in the Baron's home at Arlington, trying to mother him as she helped clean the house. She would chase him round and tickle him with her feather duster, or bring him treats from the cook in the kitchen, or tell him silly scary stories, just like she'd done with her own siblings. She felt sorry for him and tried to give him something else in his life other than books and the unrelenting company of his sad, scarred father, the reclusive and solitary man who simply couldn't get over the death of his wife who had tragically died giving birth to Charlie, the son he'd wanted so much. The Baron spent his life ensconced in his study, never wanting to go out, except occasionally to London to stay with his sister and her family there. His much older daughter and adopted son lived with the Baron's sister's family in London, in somewhere called May-Fair, most of the time, although his adopted son, who all the housemaids swooned over, had been away in the army fighting Boney for years, and then he and the Baron's daughter had married and moved to a house around the corner in May-Fair, not far away at all.

That little Charlie was completely happy with his books and his father, Daisy couldn't comprehend, but she still tried to mother him, in her own caring way. He reminded her of her little brothers, except they were all scallywags, running amok in the fields, wild and dirty, and could neither read nor write properly either, let alone read an actual book. Charlie had never got dirty in his whole life unless he inadvertently spilled ink on himself or his hands, and even that was a rare occurrence.

When Lady Elise had come to stay, things started to change and she encouraged Charlie outside. He still didn't want to run about much but she taught him to draw and paint, and he'd go walking in the fields and sit and draw pictures of butterflies and flowers, and she'd taken him riding on a little pony or down to the local village in a small gig with Daisy in tow sometimes, and even down to the coast on days out where he threw pebbles into the sea and laughed at the circling gulls. And then Lady Elise had married the Baron and he wasn't so sad anymore; he started to smile again, and laugh, and then they went off to France for the summer and she'd had a baby when they came back. After what had happened to his first wife, the Baron had been worried sick until the baby arrived safely and he saw Lady Elise was fine, and now he smiled all the time and the household was a happy place again. They went to London more often now where the Baroness had a house, coincidentally along the same street as the Baron's daughter and step-son in May-Fair, and they lived there now, whenever they stayed in Town and the Baroness offered Daisy the position of nursery-maid to baby Harry, since the housekeeper said how caring she'd been of little Charlie, and Daisy had been as pleased as punch with her promotion.

So, Daisy went to London with them to stay in the Baroness's old house between Hyde Park and Green Park. London was a big city and it scared her more than a bit. So many people, so many carriages and horses driving everywhere, so much noise. But she took her position seriously and cared for her little charge like a precious treasure and she liked nothing more than wheeling him in his pram around Hyde Park, at the end of the street, as the grass and trees and bushes reminded her of home. She met other nurserymaids there with their charges, and, being just a simple young girl, liked nothing better than to chatter and gossip and that is what she did. Every afternoon, unless it was raining or very cold and the Baroness wouldn't let her or the precious baby outside.

Daisy couldn't really remember how she'd been attacked and bundled into the coach with the baby screaming his head off, it was all a blur. All she remembered was hearing the Baroness's cry as she was thrown in after her, and then someone hit her on the head and she knew nothing after that and she'd woken up in some cold, damp place which made her shiver and her head still hurt. She couldn't see and she couldn't move. She thought she'd fallen into a strange nightmare and would wake up soon, she didn't understand anything. She lay back against the cold wall and went back to sleep, unbothered by the vermin that ran over her feet, it was something she'd grown up with in the ramshackle farm cottage they all lived in.

Elise was frightened and her head hurt. She berated herself over and over; hadn't Eddie told her NEVER to go out without her little pistol, that was why he'd patiently spent hours and hours teaching her to shoot. It was what he'd warned her about so seriously, the threat from decades before that had come back to haunt all the family from the man called Bernheim. She'd heard the entire amazing story and family history from Eddie, and Cat had talked to her about it during the previous summer at Valenciennes. It was almost unbelievable, like some far-fetched, romantic adventure novel from the circulating library, but it was all so long ago, back in the time of the Revolution in France, before Bonaparte had even appeared on the scene. Jack had said he'd killed Bernheim in Nice the previous autumn, although Eddie had said that was now wrong, but she still didn't really think she and Eddie were in any danger; they had nothing to do with Nicky's life now, even if it was hair-raising at times. They lived quite happily down at Arlington and only came to London occasionally to visit the family, or so Eddie could go to business meetings with Francis, and she could shop and gossip with Cat who she liked immensely. Another woman with a brain, rather like Eddie's daughter, Bella, of whom she was also extremely fond, or Richard Ambrose's wife, Sophy, who was a secret writer of gothic novels and very amusing. Women like the old Dowager who she'd loved and respected so much and who had been responsible, in her well-meaning, interfering way, for introducing her to Eddie... the most wonderful thing that had ever happened to her.

But she'd been foolish, like the worst ninny at Almack's. She'd been wrong and Eddie had been right, as usual, and her heart cried out for her treasured little son, wondering what had become of him.

She vaguely remembered being hustled off the street as she heard her baby cry, and tumbled into a dark coach and momentarily seeing a terrified Daisy there, protectively cuddling little Harry, and then

4

someone had hit her on the head and she knew nothing after that. Now she was bundled up like a parcel, where she knew not, and she was on her own. That this had to do with Bernheim, she was positive; why else would she be kidnapped like this? Eddie was comfortably off, as was she in her own right, and they wanted for nothing, but they weren't like the ducal Granvilles in their mansion in Berkeley Square, and they lived quietly out of choice, so if anyone were to be kidnapped for ransom, it would be one of them, certainly not her. But she wasn't going to give in to her fear, she needed to be strong... and then all the anguished emotions that she lived with started to creep into her mind.

Elise loved Edouard de Mornay very much, passionately, more than she believed she could ever feel for a man. He was her entire world. It had started slowly as he was such a reserved individual, and when she'd first met him he'd been withdrawn and remote, obviously still mourning his wife, Carlotta, the woman everyone said he'd loved to distraction. So they'd simply become friends. They talked a lot, discussed politics and science and books, and dined together more and more often. They went to plays and concerts and visited museums and galleries, always discussing what they saw and finding so much in common. He treated her as an equal, just like he did the other women in his family, and found nothing odd in her intelligence. They battled over the chessboard, much to his pleasure, and a variety of card games. She couldn't beat him, but she was a better player than the Dowager and pushed him hard. Their friendship grew and so did her attraction to him. He wasn't like the other men she'd met over the years, and there had been quite a few as she wasn't an unattractive woman by any means with her blonde hair and hazel eyes. Some men wanted a wealthy widow to supplement their lack of fortune, others another mother for their motherless children, but all had run a mile when they discovered she had a brain and forthright opinions, and expected to be treated with some respect and equality, and believed women did have views and thoughts worth listening to.

Finally, after months of seeing him in London, she accepted his invitation to go down to stay at Arlington and was introduced to his young son. It was rather indelicate since there was no chaperone there other than the housekeeper, along with a handful of servants, but

Eddie hadn't socialised with the local neighbouring gentry for years and kept to himself, so no one knew and she was a mature widow who wouldn't see forty again, she told herself, not some young and innocent, unmarried girl, and so threw caution to the wind. She went back again, and again, and again, and she became more and more fond of him. And then one day he kissed her goodbye. It had knocked her for six and she suspected even he'd seemed a bit bemused at something that had started as a gentle brush of the lips to her cheek and had gradually advanced each time they greeted or bade farewell to each other, to something a bit more than that. However, it hadn't progressed beyond soft and chaste, lips to lips, until they went to stay with his family at Firle for Christmas. To her pleasure, he kissed her again when she arrived, what she thought was a proper kiss, but THEN, much more deeply and quite passionately, the whole works... under the mistletoe when they got back from church on Christmas Eve, and suddenly everything changed. She'd never been kissed like that in her life, certainly not by her elderly husband who had barely touched her and treated her more like a daughter, or any of her other erstwhile suitors, and it had stunned her. He seemed slightly stunned too, but then he'd done it again, and again, and she'd been amazed at what a passionate man he was, she'd simply had no idea. He touched her, he caressed her as they kissed and she felt her body come alive as she responded to his expertise. And she loved it and discovered she had a deep well of sensuality inside her too, and she'd never known or realised it existed... and it seemed the more he kissed her, the more he wanted to... more and more frequently and more and more passionately. One thing had led to another and one night at Arlington, just after they'd returned to Eddie's country home from Firle where they'd been celebrating Christmas and the New Year, completely overwhelmed by everything, they got carried away and she let him make love to her... and that was it. She was completely smitten and realised, as she lay in the dawn half-light, wrapped in his arms, arms that were taut and lithely muscled like his chest, that she'd never been aware of, after a night that had left her speechless, that she'd tumbled headlong in love with him.

He'd told her how fond he was of her, how much he cared for her, how much he wanted to make love to her, how much he now enjoyed making love to her; he told her how beautiful she was, how special she was, he loved her intelligence and sense of humour; he talked to her seductively in French when they were alone or in bed; he teased her gently, he was so romantic and devastatingly charming now their relationship was on another footing; he told her everything, except that he loved her. And that was her cross. He was still in love with his dead wife. Carlotta, the perfect woman.

There were paintings of her everywhere in the house at Arlington and Elise had to admit to herself, the woman had been a real beauty. Masses of long dark hair and flashing eyes, rather like Bella she thought, except Bella had her father's and aunt's green eyes. Many of the pictures were of Carlotta in Spanish dress with a stunning ruby *peineta*, or comb, under a lace mantilla, and she wore other rubies around her neck and in her ears. She looked stunning, exciting and exotic, and Elise felt plain and dowdy in comparison.

If it had just been that, she could have lived with it; after all, the woman was long dead she told herself, but she had more angst to grapple with. Carlotta had been feisty, and a very brave and determined woman. Although the daughter of Spanish nobility, she'd been a dancer apparently, and Cat had reminisced one day to Elise about how wonderful it was to watch her do the flamenco, and how entranced Eddie had been with her and how passionately she'd loved him and had virtually seduced him when they'd first met, and then brought him out of himself when they'd married. Cat had had no idea how her innocent reminiscences about how she'd met Francis at the same time as Eddie had met Carlotta, with various laughing comments about their relationship as she'd chattered on, had been like a hot knife twisting in Elise's heart. Compared to Carlotta, Elise was a nun. Carlotta had also gone into the Fortress at Rouen and risked her life to help Eddie's parents and sisters escape. She'd risked her life to go back and rescue Cat and Nicky... and then when she'd been quite heavily pregnant with Bella, instead of staying at home with the Dowager as any other normal woman would, she'd gone chasing off to France with Cat to help rescue Francis who'd been captured by Bernheim's father and tortured terribly for The Shadow's fortune. And she hadn't even simply waited outside, she'd gone into the Fortress and confronted the man with a pistol, just to help Cat. It was all too much for the quiet Elise; how could she ever live up to a woman like that? Seductive, beautiful, determined and brave.

And now here SHE was, Lady Invisible and Boring, on her own, drawn into the mysterious web of revenge and hatred that involved the family she'd unwittingly married into. She wasn't a brave woman, well she didn't know if she was or not, had never needed to know. But she was damned if she wasn't going to be as brave as Carlotta had been. If Carlotta could face terrible danger, so could she. Elise also decided, if she ever escaped from wherever she was, she was going to change her attitude to some things in her life. Cat and Bella had taken her shopping in Paris while they'd been at Valenciennes and encouraged her to buy all sorts of disgraceful under-garments and accessories which they were also purchasing for themselves for after they'd had their babies and got their figures back to normality; or rather they were for their husbands' benefit, as Cat had laughingly said. Elise had been quite shocked at it all, especially at a middle-aged and apparently respectable woman like the Duchess of Firle, even if she was a slightly eccentric French woman, but Cat had merely said she still felt like she was thirty, so did Francis, so she was going to grow old disgracefully with him and enjoy herself as there wasn't much else to do at their age, and reading in bed was soooo boring!

Elise had gone bright red at that remark but Bella had merely giggled and said she needed to produce a pride of lions, whatever that meant, and what she had bought had made Elise's eyes nearly come out on stalks, not to mention venturing into one or two other of the little back street shops they'd investigated, never mind purchase anything in them. A sedate relationship was something both of these two women definitely DIDN'T have with their respective husbands. So she'd been coerced to buy all manner of wicked undergarments and seductive clothes and they were all still packed away in boxes at the back of her armoire and she was too embarrassed to even let her maid see them, never mind put them on. But now, she decided, perhaps she would, and see what effect that had on her husband. She would seduce him like his first wife apparently had. If it was the last thing she did,

Elise wanted to hear him say he loved her, and she was now going to go to any length to achieve that aim and she needed to find some reading matter to instruct herself on the subject. But she had to escape from this prison she was in first, and find her precious infant. Nothing else mattered. And so, with nothing else to do other than wait for her captors to come and get her and do their worst, and she would fight them tooth and nail she decided, for they were only men, most of whom were simpletons in her opinion, she settled back to plan how she would seduce her husband.

After a while, somehow Elise sensed that wherever she was, there was someone else there as well... but she couldn't hear anything except scrabbling noises and she shuddered; rats or mice? Could she hear something else? She couldn't decide and maybe it was her captor, she'd no idea. She decided to lie quietly and pretend to still be unconscious and just listen and continue to think.

Edouard de Mornay's head was reeling, and not just from the pain in his temple where he'd been knocked out cold. All sorts of thoughts were going round in his clever, forensic brain. The first was how good he felt in some very bizarre way. For once, he'd been treated as a normal man, not a helpless, limping, scarred cripple, as he was bound tightly as if they thought he was as dangerous and strong as Francis and Nicky, and his mind turned and he wondered if he'd been taken along with the other two men as part of Bernheim's plotting. For he was absolutely certain this was Bernheim's doing.

They'd all been waiting for it to happen ever since Ashcroft had told them he hadn't died from Jack's knife in his back after all, and then had been seen in England. Quite why he'd been taken as well, Eddie was still mulling over, but for once in his life he was in the same mess as his brother-in-law and adopted son, not just a bit player or follower in their adventures. For a while, he sat and put himself in Bernheim's place and theorised about what he might be up to. Inevitably, his thoughts then took him to his headstrong sister, Cat, the wife of The Shadow and the woman who had killed Bernheim's father, and he shivered; and then there was Bella, his daughter, Nicky's wife, who had apparently seduced Bernheim and helped her husband escape, mainly with Jack's assistance. The more he theorised, the more he thought they were ALL targets for Bernheim's revenge. Well, except him, or maybe not? He'd been there in Rouen fortress and had helped Francis escape, and killed Dupont, and had been the originator of the clever plot to rescue his family... so he supposed he WAS a part of it if Bernheim wanted to take his revenge to the limit; but how on earth would he know any of that? He'd not been seen by anyone when they'd got his parents, sisters and Nicky out, his role was to collect the escapees from outside the Fortress and squirrel them away to the safety of Francis's ship and await him and the others there. And the second time, only Bernheim, and briefly Dupont had seen him there, and they were most assuredly dead before he left. It was an unsolvable mystery to him.

Eddie's mind continued to turn and he wondered where he was, who else was there and why Bernheim simply hadn't killed him? That was what worried him. Why wasn't he dead? If Bernheim wanted The Shadow's treasure or the Valenciennes gold, taking Eddie wasn't going to persuade Francis or Nicky, no matter how dear he was to them, and he'd die before he revealed their secrets, though Eddie knew deep down both the men would give up everything if it came to saving HIS life. No, he decided, threatening Cat and Bella was the key to the other men, or if not their wives, their children. His mind turned, and he wondered if that was what was going on? It made sense. Bernheim's father had got nowhere torturing Francis, and Bernheim had got nowhere torturing Nicky... so maybe he was going to try another tack? Maybe he'd taken Cat and Bella? And therefore, maybe, that was why Bernheim had also taken him, so he wouldn't be out there to raise a hue and cry or come to their rescue; that was the only thing Eddie could think of. But what of Elise, his wife? Surely she had nothing to do with any of it, but what would they do about her? She would know he was missing, and would soon discover the others were, so what would she do? Oh God, Eddie suddenly wondered, had they taken her as well?

Round and round his mind went, analysing possibilities and theories, dismissing some and considering others, and he didn't like the conclusions he came to. He wondered where he was. He felt the damp earth floor beneath him. It was cold and the air was stuffy, not that he could breathe properly with a sack of some sort over his head. He concluded he was probably in a cellar. He lay quietly for a while and tried to listen, but all he could make out was scrabbling noises: vermin. He shuddered and struggled to sit up. The pain in his arthritic, shattered pelvis lanced through him but he persevered; it focussed his mind if nothing else, and eventually pure grit and determination got him upright. The effort had him sweating and panting but he dismissed it, for once not even thinking about the laudanum he sometimes took to dull the pain when it got really bad. He listened for what seemed like an age and then he thought he could make out footsteps and some muffled voices, and the bang of another door somewhere nearby, and then silence. It happened again a while later, and then a third time, and then the silence became unbroken.

He had to think, he told himself. Who would notice they were gone? What would they do? The servants? He doubted they would do anything quickly, merely assuming he and Elise had decided to go out. What about Jack? And Ashcroft? Ashcroft. Ashcroft was the answer. But how would he know? Was Jack home from school yet? He would know to go to Ashcroft for help if he suspected something wasn't right. But, and critically, Eddie was sure Ashcroft was watching them; if not him, then Francis and Nicky. The man had eyes everywhere, how else would he have found out about Bernheim down in Sussex? Eddie had immense respect for Ashcroft; he was the one man whose intelligence matched his own and they'd struck up a strong friendship since the previous summer in Valenciennes; Ashcroft had also quietly called on him for assistance on the odd occasion. Enemy ciphers and coded messages they were having difficulty untangling, especially if they were probably in French and had come from France where plots were still thick. These had quietly arrived on his doorstep, wherever he was, via a courier, for him to grapple with when Ashcroft discovered he had a knack for it. The man always seemed to know whether he was in Town or at Arlington. Eyes everywhere.

Round and round Eddie's mind whirled until he was exhausted with it all. And then he thought of Elise.

'The Widow of Hertford Street', as the family had originally called her, had crept under the hard shell of grief he'd wrapped himself in when his beloved Carlotta had died. He hadn't been able to face the world again without her at his side, encouraging and pushing him to forget his scarred face, disability and limp when they went out and about, and demanding and passionate in bed at night, saying she couldn't care less about his scars and injured body, he could still love and satisfy her as well as any man, if not better, because HE was perfect in her eyes. She'd built his ego and he felt he could conquer the world if she was with him. When she died, it all came tumbling down.

Elise was the complete antithesis of his Spanish love. Where Carlotta was fiery, loving, short-tempered, passionate, demanding and darkly beautiful... Elise was calm, caring, even-tempered, quiet, reserved and patient... and lovely in her classically English blonde way; in fact quite beautiful when she was dressed up to go out and socialise, as he'd discovered once he'd started to go out and about in Society again with her as his companion. And she had a brain, some very strong and forthright opinions, and a wry, cutting sense of humour. She was certainly a match for Francis's droll witticisms and their teasing banter and arguments about how women would run the country and fight in the army one day, sail ships and explore, ride race-horses, work in banks and the City, own and run factories, and a host of other activities only men currently did, all amused the family no end. When she teamed up with Cat and Bella to torment Francis on the subject, he'd run from the room in playful horror. Carlotta, on the other hand, had been streetwise, but not intelligent. Girls weren't educated in Spanish aristocratic families, other than learning to read and write along with a bit of basic history, geography and simple sums, but that was it. They were taught to sew, play the piano, paint and draw, and other ladylike pursuits. When she'd run away from home to escape being sequestered in a convent because she'd been callously seduced and made pregnant, she'd lost the child but survived on her wits, her dancing... and her body.

Eddie knew what she'd been, and why, and he hadn't cared, he was so infatuated and beguiled by her. But sometimes, very occasionally, when she'd driven him to groaning, exhausted ecstasy in bed at night with her technique and sensual demands, he couldn't help but think about the other men she'd done the same things to, and who had taught her... and how much she'd charged for her services. He couldn't help it. But Elise was the opposite. She was completely ignorant in matters concerning sex.

She'd spent her life growing up and caring for her widowed, scholarly father in a small country village and when his health failed, he married her off to an old academic friend to ensure she'd be taken care of. His friend had done his duty but hardly touched her, other than their wedding night and a few times after, very quick and basic interludes he'd gathered. The man was more like a second father to her, and she'd ended up caring for him, too, when he became ill and finally died. Eddie suspected that was one of the reasons he'd taken a wife at that late stage in his life. So Elise had been a comfortably-off widow but with virtually no experience of men at all and all the ones who had sought her company or her hand since, had either been obvious fortune-hunters, had bored her rigid or run a mile from her sharp intelligence and scathing wit.

When he first kissed her at Arlington, Eddie realised how inexperienced she was and backed off, not wanting to jeopardise the close friendship they had, despite feeling a surprising connection between them; but then he found he yearned to do it again, and again; so he did, progressing bit by slow bit towards her mouth and enticing lips, finally throwing caution to the winds at Christmas. She learned quickly and her enthusiasm and passion had amazed him, and that had been the start of it. Celibate for years and not bothered about taking a mistress, despite Francis's endless nagging to the contrary, saying it was unnatural, he wasn't a monk and Carlotta wouldn't want him to be like that, it was like a breached dam. The more he kissed and then caressed her, the more he wanted her. They went back to Arlington the first week of January after spending Christmas and the New Year at Firle with the family, and he decided to talk to her about their formerly platonic relationship, not sure what sort of turn it had now taken.

She had gone to bed early one evening, pleading a headache, and Eddie had sat with a decanter of port in his study and mulled over his life and where it was going. He was very fond of Elise and they'd become very close. They had so much in common and she and Charlie got on very well. And when she was in London, and he was alone at Arlington, he missed her… more and more. He realised he missed having a woman in his life, missed the companionship and someone to talk to… and now he'd opened Pandora's Box, he missed having a woman in his bed again. He wondered if he should propose? Would she want to give up her independence and marry him? Did she care for him enough? She seemed to, and they got on so well, and she wasn't repulsed by his kisses and caresses; quite the contrary it seemed. Or would she prefer a discreet affair, which would allow her to retain her independence? At the end of the day, would she want to marry and tie herself to a scarred cripple?

So, he'd wandered up to bed in the early hours, still mulling over his thoughts, but on limping slowly past Elise's room he noticed her light was still on. In concern to see if she was all right, or needed anything, he knocked politely on her door. She let him in and he was confronted by the sight of her with her long blonde hair loosely flowing down her back and in her nightdress and comfortable dressing robe. The room was only bathed in the light of a couple of candles and she appeared to have been sitting, reading, in front of a low fire. He didn't know what came over him, but without a word, he'd simply pulled her into his arms and kissed her, hungrily. She didn't object, didn't say a word and just gave herself up to his passion. Her dressing robe fell to the floor, and then her nightdress and everything went from there.

They ended up in bed and it was like making love to an innocent. When he started to kiss her up and down her body, entranced by her soft, pale, creamy skin, and then between her legs with its sparse covering of soft blonde fluff which aroused him beyond belief, she froze in appalled shock, and he had to gentle, reassure and explain to her until she relaxed again. When he entered her, she was so hot and tight, he thought his head would blow off, and then she climaxed with an agonised wail of abandoned pleasure and the look of amazement on her face was a picture. And that was when he knew he had to marry her. He wanted her all to himself, all the time and forever; he didn't want an affair, he didn't want anyone else to have her and teach her how to love. He made love to her for the rest of the night, unable to get enough of her and she responded to him, lost in a welter of passionate abandon that astonished her and him. The following morning he asked her to marry him and she accepted. They were going to wait until Nicky returned from France as Eddie wanted him to be there and be his Best Man, but events overtook them when Elise discovered she was pregnant, probably from that first stunning night when he'd not been thinking straight or sensibly about any sort of consequences, which he had after that, being the careful and considerate man he normally was, and so they'd had to bring the wedding forward and were married quietly at the little church in Firle at Easter.

Since then, their life had carried on much as it had before, except he made love to her constantly, night after night, quietly and intensely, like she was his port in a storm; he taught her how to let go of her inhibitions and enjoy the act of love with him in different ways, the long, barren, celibate years now in his past; and then their little son had been born and he thought his life was now complete.

Eddie just sat in his dark captivity and reflected on the woman who was now at the epicentre of his life and wondered how she'd managed it. He hardly thought about Carlotta anymore, at least not constantly, sometimes not for days at a time… and never at night. And as he mulled it over, he realised Elise had never once, not in all the time he'd known her, ever, ever mentioned his scars or his limp or disability. It was as if they simply didn't exist. If she went out, she didn't demand he accompany her, unlike Carlotta had sometimes, forcing him to socialise and telling him people didn't care about how he looked. Elise, on the other hand, just left it to him, merely asking if he would care to go with her, and he invariably did. Nor did she seduce him in bed or ask him to make love to her, it was always down to him; not that she didn't enjoy it, she did. When she let go of herself, she was passionate and sensual and loving, wanting to do whatever he asked of her to please him, not that that was anything unconventional or distasteful, he was always mindful of her innocence. But conversely, sometimes he wanted more from her, felt she was holding back somehow, and he wondered why that bothered him. In all other respects, she was the perfect wife and mother and he couldn't contemplate life without her. Couldn't contemplate life without her? His mind turned; what if she was there? What if Bernheim had got her? Eddie shook with fear; he couldn't bear to lose her, she was everything to him… he loved her so much…

When had that happened? When had she supplanted Carlotta in his heart and soul? Not that Carlotta wouldn't always have a place in his heart, but she was gone and his life had moved on. Elise was his world now and he couldn't face the thought of her dying as well. He thought it would truly kill him, and under the thick cloth around his eyes, tears welled up and trickled down his handsome, scarred face.

Chapter Two

C at was in shock and deeply, coldly angry, which made her head throb more than ever. How could she have let herself be taken like this? It was the bastard, Bernheim. He'd finally caught up with them, and her, despite all her precautions. She wriggled in her bonds, trying to decide if her little pistol in its holster on her calf was still there, but her ankles were tied and she suspected it had gone. She tried to feel further up her leg, on her thigh. That was where her stiletto was but was that still there? She didn't know. Maybe if they'd found her pistol they wouldn't have explored further up her leg? She wriggled around and finally managed to sit herself up, wondering if she was alone. She had a feeling there was someone near her, but she had no idea who. However, no one spoke so she continued to sit and seethe.

So this was how Francis had felt, Cat realised, when Bernheim had taken him all those years ago... and Nicky in the cellar in Nice. She'd made Francis tell her every detail, nagging and railing at him until he'd given in. But still, she wondered what else her husband had got up to, early on in his mysterious life before she'd married him. She knew there was much, much more. Some things so terrible he didn't want to admit to them, even to her. Maybe especially to her. She knew he was capable of them, deep down he was an extremely ruthless, hard and very dangerous man; she hadn't lived with him for so long without feeling it, knowing it, despite how he always played the fool and the charming, sensual, consummate lover. But she knew underneath it all, he was a good man and if he had killed or done some terrible things, he must have had reason. She suspected he'd been a proper pirate, knowing the man he was, he simply wouldn't have been satisfied with plying goods back and forth across the Channel, he was too restless, too ambitious, never happy to settle for the ordinary.

But that was neither here nor there now; it made no difference to her who he'd been or what he'd done, she still loved him, passionately, had always loved him from when she first saw him again in Reynard's gypsy camp. He was the only man who had ever got the better of her and no other man had ever come near him nor affected her like he did, not even Ricky Ambrose, that handsome scoundrel, his oldest friend. And if they'd taken her, she was sure they'd taken Francis. Except this time, she wasn't free to rescue him. But she was damned if she was going to lie there like a parcel and give in. He wouldn't, and neither would she. She wasn't a mere woman, men were fools, well most of them, and she'd find a way to escape and go and rescue Francis or her name wasn't Marie-Catherine Granville. Having decided that, Cat felt much better; she told herself she'd killed Bernheim's father and she decided she would kill his son, and put an end to this nemesis in their lives once and for all; all it needed was a woman to sort everything out.

Across the dirty floor of the dark cellar room, Bella lay trussed up like another parcel in petticoats. She was angry and frightened and couldn't decide which was worse. She was angry with herself for being taken, when she'd gone to such lengths to take care of herself. Always going everywhere in her own carriage, taking a groom to follow her when she went shopping and carrying around a pistol on her leg and a small dagger down her corset. Yet still, here she was. She had a feeling her pistol had gone, but she could feel the dagger pressing against her flesh below her cleavage and it gave her some comfort. The worst of her anger, however, was directed at her own frailty and yet again she railed at her lack of courage to kill Bernheim when she'd had the chance. But never again, she just knew if she had the chance once more, she'd plunge her dagger into his black heart without a thought.

She was also terribly, terribly frightened. She alone, apart from Jack and Nicky, knew what Bernheim was like, but only she had experienced him at his depraved worst. The thought of confronting the man again made her blood freeze and her stomach churn, and if he touched her, she didn't think she could bear it. Was that what he wanted? Was that why she was there and not dead in a gutter? She assumed he'd gone after Nicky again and some terrible premonition, just like she'd had before where he was concerned, told her he'd been taken, just as she had. She'd seen what Bernheim had done to him before, but he was still only just recovered from his injuries at Waterloo. His shattered arm would never be as strong as it had been so she didn't think he'd be able to sustain any sort of torture that Bernheim had in mind for him, and it was too terrible to contemplate as the haunting picture of him dangling in chains in Bernheim's cellar in Nice filled her mind once more.

As Bella lay in the dirt, her agonised thoughts turned to her aunt and uncle again, and the hairs on her neck stood on end as her premonition of something terrible took hold. Uncle Francis was The Shadow, Ashcroft had warned him and Nicky that Bernheim was out for revenge on one or both of them, and so it stood to reason that if Bernheim was indeed in London, he'd go after both men. Her stomach roiled and she felt even sicker. He'd never get away with it, she was sure. This was London. Her aunt would move heaven and earth to find them, her and Ashcroft... and Jack. Jack was due home from Eton any time and she wondered what he would do when he found her and Nicky missing. He'd go straight to Berkeley Square, she knew, and then there'd be a hue and cry and sooner or later they'd be found and either her aunt or Jack would kill Bernheim, she was sure of it. If they could get to him before she did. She felt immensely reassured, told herself she'd survived Bernheim's depravities once before, so she could do it again if it meant buying time for Nicky or Uncle Francis.

Uncle Francis had been a second father to her and her love for Nicky was so all-encompassing she'd do anything to save him… him and her uncle.

In the meantime, Bella wondered where she was. In the cellar of some London house no doubt, Bernheim seemed to like cellars and she could feel a cold, damp dirt floor beneath her bound hands behind her. She had a strange feeling she wasn't alone but had no idea if she was being watched or who was there, wherever 'there' was. So she lay quietly and pretended she was still unconscious.

Francis decided the lump on his head had affected his mind. He was more worried about Bubbles than what had happened to him. Visions of the brainless, giant white fluffy dog snarling and growling, attacking and biting his assailants were the last things he could remember before he'd taken another heavy blow to his head and passed out. He decided to get the dog a harem, if the not-so-lazy hound had managed to survive its brutal beating, it was the least he deserved… and a permanent supply of cream pastries and roast chicken, and Francis would have laughed if he didn't have something stuffed in his mouth.

How many of them had there been? He tried shaking his head to remember, but it hurt too much and as he struggled to sit up, his body ached from the beating it had taken. So much for feeling twenty-five or thirty, he thought to himself; he felt ninety and decrepit. He had a feeling there were five or six of them, but it didn't matter. They'd got him and Ashcroft had been right, expect the unexpected, and he should have taken more care. Walking by himself in the shady glades of the park with a lumbering mound of fluff wasn't exactly sensible when a lunatic was out to get him. His brain engaged itself and Francis started to think rationally.

Was he alone or had Bernheim got Nicky too? Bernheim wanted them both, so it made sense and he had a very bad feeling. He hadn't had a feeling like it since Benjy had brought him the note from Reynard to say his Uncle Gerard had been taken by Edgar Bernheim, twenty-five years before. But he knew it well, it had warned him countless times of trouble ahead when he'd been trying to avoid the Revenue men, the militia, the French or British navy, or other pirates; a sort of sixth sense. The question was, where were they and where was Nicky? He was trussed up good and proper and could barely move. He couldn't see or speak so he would just have to sit and wait for Bernheim to make his move. He knew what the man wanted and as far as he was concerned, he could have every last guinea he had… but just as he'd sensed with the man's father, he didn't trust this Bernheim one bit either… and he suspected that even if he did tell him where The Shadow's fortune was, he'd still be killed. Therefore, he'd have to play for time until he was rescued, or he could escape. But could he play for time? He was in his fifties, not his twenties or even his thirties, and he didn't know how much of Bernheim's nastiness he could endure. Nevertheless, he was going to have to, and he would have to persuade Bernheim to focus on him. Nicky wasn't up to it and as soon as Bernheim saw his arm or the scars on his body, he'd work on them and not even Nicky would be able to withstand that if he survived at all. So Francis braced himself for he knew not what, feeling the scars on his lower back tingle as if to remind him of what might be ahead. It was a daunting prospect.

He knew deep down they'd come and find him and Nicky; he also knew Ashcroft was having the pair of them watched, that's why subconsciously he'd been lax about taking more care. He and Ashcroft were still playing footsie with each other, but Ashcroft was a good and clever man and he trusted him implicitly now. If anyone could save them, he knew Ashcroft would… he just hoped Ashcroft could keep Cat out of it. Once she realised he'd been taken she would stop at nothing to find and rescue him, he knew that, and it was much too dangerous. She needed locking up for her own protection; however, hopefully, Eddie's common sense would prevail and he'd take her in hand. Some hope, Francis tried to laugh again as he thought of his beloved, headstrong and volatile wife who took no notice of anyone, least of all him.

In the meantime, he wondered where he was. He could barely move he was tied up so tightly, but he could feel a cold, dirt floor under his hands so that suggested a cellar as it was also chilly, musty and damp. He shuffled himself backwards, waiting for someone to say something, but all was silent, so he assumed he was alone and he kept shuffling until eventually, he backed up against a cold, damp wall. He leaned against it and tried to relax, wondering what the time was, how long he'd been there and when Bernheim would come for him.

He waited and waited and his mind inevitably wandered. His earlier humour, a desperate attempt to distract himself from the gravity of his situation, had dissipated, and long-ago, buried memories had surfaced, nightmares of what he'd gone through with Bernheim's father. The sack over his head was the worst; he hated being blind-folded even now, though he'd never admit it to anyone, especially to Cat, when they'd indulged in silly bedroom games over the years or played party games with their children. Edgar Bernheim and Pierre Dupont had put a sack on his head when they'd caught him in Rouen Fortress, and he'd been beaten and strung up so his shoulders dislo-cated; he'd been disoriented and unable to see, for hours on end, or was it days? He still could barely remember. He did remember feeling the heat of the brazier and the hot iron as they'd waved it in front of his blind face, taunting him... until he'd felt it on his back, sizzling and burning his flesh, and the smell and the pain had been beyond descrip-tion. The fires of hell on earth. That was something he'd never, ever, forget. Even today, twenty-five years later, the healed wounds still ached sometimes and the scarred skin itched and pulled.

Francis leaned his head back against the wall and as his scarred back continued to tingle, he prayed Ashcroft would find them quickly.

At first, Nicky thought he was having another of his nightmares, but then he realised the ache in his head was real and he wasn't asleep. But it was still the nightmare, all over again. A chilly, damp room - he was lying on a cold, dirty floor, he could feel that under his bound hands; and he thought he heard the vermin again, except now at least he had his boots on so they weren't nibbling at his bare toes. But he couldn't see, and the horror of all that returned. He'd thought he'd conquered his fear, but it was back, in spaces, and he shuddered. He'd no idea where he was or what Bernheim intended, as for sure he'd fallen into the bastard's hands again. His shattered arm was hurting, pulled back where his wrists and upper arms were tightly bound behind him; it still wasn't strong and it wouldn't take much for the bones to break again and the muscles tear, he realised that, and he doubted Benjy could mend them a second time. He didn't want to contemplate the consequences. Then he thought of how he'd barely survived his play-fighting and wrestling with Jack; he wasn't as fit and strong as he'd been in Nice because of his Waterloo injuries; he'd no idea if he was properly healed inside, never mind his heart... and the consequences of that were terrifying.

Bernheim, his nemesis. Well, this would be the end of it. The man could have his gold, if he wanted it that much, at least Nicky knew where it was now - sitting by the compost heaps in Francis's gardens at Firle. Bernheim could have his fortune to boot, everything, he didn't care. All he wanted was to get back to Bella and his children. If they didn't have any money again, he wasn't bothered now, he'd been there before and they could all go to the Americas and start again. Open a *Lion D'Or* there perhaps. The words of the Dowager went round in his head and he'd long ago acknowledged the truth of them... all the money in the world couldn't make you happy if you didn't have anyone to share it with. Well, Bernheim could go and drown in it all, if it would buy his life.

But then Nicky thought about what else Bernheim had wanted to know down in that cellar in Nice. The information about his work for Ashcroft and Wellington was now irrelevant, but The Shadow was another matter. Francis! Nicky blanched under the sack over his head. Had Bernheim taken him as well? Was he here too? He shook himself, he really wasn't thinking clearly... and then he thought of Ashcroft and he berated himself. He was worse than Jack, he at least should have known better; expect the unexpected. What on earth made him think Jack wouldn't be home that evening? He might be distracted by serving maids, petticoats and ale, for a few hours, even a night, to cele-brate a short break away from school, but they wouldn't keep him away from home when the family were expecting him, and what had made him think Bella wouldn't want to spend the evening *en famille* with Jack as they'd planned? His brain was in his breeches, as Bella sometimes laughingly told him, and as Francis also had when he'd been sixteen or seventeen. He was appalled at himself. He was in his thirties, not thirteen, but he simply couldn't help how much he loved and lusted after Bella. She would distract a saint and he was as far from one of those as humanly possible, and this was where his distraction had got him.

But all that was water under the bridge now. He still had to deal with Bernheim. Would the man let him go if he signed over all his money? Nicky thought, imagining how he could negotiate his way out of wherever he was to take Bernheim to it… and realised it was a forlorn hope. The man wanted him dead, just as much as Nicky wanted to kill him. Well, for sure, before this was finished, one of them would end up in their coffin. And he had to protect Francis. None of this was his fault, he'd never even met Frederick Bernheim, but Francis would hand over The Shadow's treasure without blinking, and plenty more of his fortune, if he thought it would serve any purpose… but then Bernheim would kill him too, and Nicky wasn't going to allow that. He had to think; he had to come up with a plan.

Just as Francis had done, if he but knew it, Nicky levered himself up to a sitting position with a painful groan and shuffled himself backwards until he was up against a wall. He leaned back and listened for any sound but could hear nothing, so settled himself down to wait, and started to think.

Ashcroft. He was the answer. Nicky was sure Ashcroft was keeping an eye on him and Francis, he knew how the crafty spymaster operated. If he and Francis had disappeared, Ashcroft would soon know about it and be moving heaven and earth to find them and come to their rescue. Bella and Cat would be on his back for sure, not to mention Jack. He and Francis had to be in London somewhere, Nicky was sure he hadn't been unconscious that long as he wasn't particularly hungry or thirsty or needing to relieve himself, a sure sign of passing time. Ashcroft had eyes everywhere and a bottomless pit of gold to buy information from whatever sources were necessary; Ashcroft didn't care if it got him what he wanted to know. Nicky trusted him absolutely, even more than Francis did... and Ashcroft wanted Bernheim for himself as well, Nicky knew, on behalf of all those dead former agents. People thought Miles Ashcroft was a cold, heartless man, only concerned with King and Country, but Nicky suspected he had emotions somewhere inside and revenge was one of them. Besides, any man who adopted a scruff of a mutt like Nelson and mollycoddled him to the nth degree, couldn't be totally without feeling.

Nicky dropped his head back against the wall to wait. He fought his fear of the darkness and tried not to think of dangling in chains; of tongueless, brutal Turkish guards, Chinamen with needles, or a barbed cat o'nine tails. He just needed to hold out until Ashcroft came. He'd done it before, he just prayed he could do it again and save Francis to boot. And then he'd kill Bernheim and HE wouldn't miss his black heart.

Chapter Three

Bernheim looked at his pocket watch and smiled to himself as he tossed off the last of his wine and pushed his empty plate to one side. It had all gone perfectly to plan. His captives were stewing in the dank cellars and the lions were hungry and waiting. He had intended to leave the prisoners to a long night of isolated torment, but the lions were starting to fight each other and he didn't want them to kill one of their number and feast on it and then lose interest in their human banquet. Therefore, he decided a preliminary midnight feast was in order.

It had taken him months of searching to find the perfect location and prepare it. Somewhere deserted where no one would note the comings and goings nor hear the noise. A house with plenty of cellar space to imprison his captives. A set of outbuildings large and potentially secure enough to house the lions and he'd had to order the caging carefully so as not to arouse suspicion. The lions had been brought to Tilbury, one by one, and sent down the river to Richmond and then quietly overland to their deserted destination to await their two-legged prey. They'd been fed chickens and some live goats, but never quite enough to dissipate their hunger. Any enquiries about them during their transport had been met with a reply they were to replenish the famous ones kept in the Tower of London.

All those involved in the plan and preparation had since disappeared. Bernheim never took any chances. If he could pay plenty of money to find people to do his dirty work, someone could pay them more to loosen their tongues. He'd done it in Spain and plenty of times before, except in Spain the wretched de Bresancourt had interfered and he'd lost the Rothschild gold; but now, he would get his hands on the Valenciennes gold instead, not to mention The Shadow's hoard. And when he'd done with them all, his hired help, a motley assortment of venal brigands and thugs, they would disappear as well. He'd decided to burn down the virtually derelict farm and outbuildings when he'd finished, and them with it, and the fire would destroy any other human remains or corpses, including the lions. There'd be nothing left to evidence what had transpired there.

In the meantime, he'd also found a suitable replacement for Mustapha - a silent, giant Sikh from India who hated the British and didn't like women either. His name was Ajeet, which apparently meant invincible and unconquerable. He was perfect. And he'd also picked up another Arab, Abdul, a fiery Moslem who hated Christians and had worked for a desert Sheikh and was familiar with big cats. That was where some of the lions had come from at a considerable cost, but he'd been so enamoured of his fiendish plan for the painful demise of his enemy, he'd have paid anything. He'd decided to keep both men. He needed servants and they'd already both proved their worth when dispensing with his earlier hired help, and a bodyguard was always useful when travelling, with another to look after the home he would live in, wherever he decided to settle. For some reason, the Arab had decided Bernheim wasn't a pious Christian, not that he'd ever been remotely religious in any way, and Bernheim hadn't bothered to ask why presuming it might have to do with his dark hair and eyes. However, as long as the man was happy to work for him and do his dirty work, for which he was being well rewarded, Bernheim was content.

Bernheim rang a small bell on the table and the Sikh appeared, bowed and picked up the plate and refilled the glass. He took the plate away and returned quickly and waited, arms crossed, immobile, for further instructions; standing big and silent, his black turban and garb the same colour as his pitiless dark eyes and beard. He had a large, curved, razor-sharp knife in the wide sash around his waist and a larger curved sword hanging against his leg. He was a true giant, nearly seven foot tall, and a daunting sight.

"Find Abdul, get the men, take the prisoners to the barn. You know what to do with them... then come and inform me when everything is ready."

"Yes, Master," the Sikh bowed and disappeared and Bernheim sat back, lit himself a cheroot and continued to sip his wine.

Chapter Four

Outside the farm gates, six men were discussing in whispers
what to do. Jack and Alfie were about to creep inside the
gates and reconnoitre up around the house when they
heard a commotion so they all quickly ducked back down, out of sight.

They watched in alarm as a group of burly men came out holding
lanterns and started tugging seven people, one by one, out of the
house towards the barn. One woman, the first to appear, dressed in the
black outfit of a servant, was so distressed, the men pulling her along
gave up and one simply hit her on the side of the head and as she
tottered on her feet, slung her over his shoulder like a sack of potatoes
and carried her off. The other six, bound tightly with black sacks over
their heads and shoulders, were dragged along roughly but none said
a word as they came out the farmhouse and then disappeared into the
large, dark farm buildings. The lions had obviously been dozing or
asleep, but with the commotion had woken up and were growling and
roaring. Ashcroft stared, completely horrified, as the bound people
froze when they heard the sound but still none made any noise. The
women simply pulled their shoulders back resolutely and the men,
including the limping one, just tried to shrug away from their guards.

When they'd all disappeared into the spacious barn, Ashcroft turned to the group. "They must be gagged underneath those sacks. I wonder if they know who's there, that it's all of them? That utter bastard; what do you think, Ambrose?"

"Oh, for God's sake, Miles, we're not at a social function now, observing the niceties, call me Ricky. I've no idea what to think, other than utter horror, but they must be scared out of their wits. I am, and I'm not in there with those snarling beasts. Those women have some backbone, I'll give them that, not that I'd expect anything else given who they're married to. The first one must be the nursery maid, poor girl," he tutted sympathetically.

"Quite," muttered Ashcroft. "How many of the guards did you count? It was a bit hard to see from here in the darkness. I wish the moon would come out again but I made it nineteen, including that Indian giant who brought up the rear. Four who went ahead with the lanterns, funny looking sort, that one in the front, did you think he was an Arab by his clothes? There were two each on the prisoners, and then the giant. Did you recognise Bernheim, Jack?"

"No, Sir. He definitely wasn't there. You can't mistake him: tall bastard, black hair, slender but strong, if you get my drift, a bit like His Lordship here," Jack cocked his head in Ricky's direction.

"Are you inferring I look like that misbegotten French cretin? Really, whatever next!"

"Oh, do be quiet," tutted Benjy crossly. "Enough of your nonsense, we know you can be sensible when you choose." He had no time for deference or politeness given the fraught situation which frightened the life out of him, and he'd known Richard Ambrose for years, so spoke to him as he would speak to Francis, his former master when they were alone.

"So, he's still inside the farmhouse. Unfortunate. I wonder how many others there are with him? I don't like the odds, I have to say, and as for that Indian, a Sikh if I'm not mistaken. I came across one or two of them when I was stationed out there. Nasty, very nasty, if they're not on your side."

"Rubbish. They're mostly just riffraff, didn't you see them? Deal with them in minutes, what? Even that giant."

"I wouldn't be so sure," muttered Jack. "They looked a bunch of brutal thugs to me."

"Not as brutish or nasty as what's in some cage in there. I've seen enough. They're not feeding MY friends to any damn lions," and Ricky rose to his feet, bristling with cold fury at what he'd witnessed, ready to go and do battle. He had a pistol in one hand, one tucked in his waistband and his rapier in his right hand.

"Just a moment," Ashcroft grasped his arm. "We have to think carefully. We don't know what's going on in there and nothing will start without Bernheim, that's for sure. Now then, there's six of us until the cavalry or the coach arrives, so we must think tactically. We can't all just barge in, an element of surprise is needed from all sides and then they might think there's more of us than there are at present; catch them by surprise, and if a couple of us are overcome on one side, the others might have a chance. I suggest you shoot as many guards as you are able and take down the rest as best you can, and if you can release any of the captives while you're about it, so much the better. Unless they've had their hands up Bella and Cat's skirts, they've got weapons secreted there, remember?" Ashcroft looked at Jack and Benjy knowingly and Ricky's eyebrows raised. "Therefore, I suggest two of you work your way round the back to the left and find a way in, two to the right, and two of us will wait until Bernheim has gone in and we'll enter by the main doorway. I'll do that; are you with me, Ricky? Jack, you and Alfie go left, Benjy, you and Fred go right."

"Sounds like the second Battle of Waterloo strategy," commented Ricky facetiously. "Where's the Duke and Blücher for their opinion on the battle plan?"

"WILL you be quiet! How the hell does Francis put up with you? Have you always been like this or does it come from associating with him too much?"

"Well, you did say we came from the same nest..." Ricky's mouth curled in a sarcastic smile.

"God help me," muttered Ashcroft.

"My old governess, down to earth northern woman, don't y'know, she always told me he helps those who help themselves... aha!" whispered Ricky abruptly, "Look, our Indian giant is going back to the farmhouse. I wonder if he's gone to get Bernheim?"

"Quick, you four, now's your chance. Off you go, be careful and God speed," Ashcroft nodded at the four men.

"They're dead men," whispered Jack, and with Alfie on his heels, the two youths silently disappeared.

"Come on Fred, it's been a while since I stuck my scissors into something other than broadcloth," and Benjy and Fred crept off in the other direction.

"It's you and me, Miles," grinned Ricky, "the deranged and a popinjay, an incomparable pair, don't you agree?"

"Can I ask you something?" Ashcroft whispered to Ricky as they crouched, waiting for someone to come out of the farmhouse. "You've known Francis since you were young boys at school, right?"

"Yessssss?"

"So, how come you never went smuggling with him? I would have thought it was right up your street; you're a complete lunatic, just like him. Didn't you fancy being The Shadow's right-hand-man?"

Ricky answered with the complete truth. "He never asked me. Apart from which, I'd never be anyone's second-in-command, not even Francis's. I'm my own man, always have been. We spent our youth always trying to outdo each other, though we did have the odd moment together here and there, but he wouldn't follow me any more than I would follow him, and you can't have two captains of a smuggling or any other ship, now can you?"

"Interesting," Ashcroft narrowed his eyes as he looked at Ricky. "You hide it well."

"Hide what?" enquired Ricky airily.

"You're a complex and dangerous man under all that foppery and facetiousness."

"You're a fine one to talk; sarcasm is your middle name."

"I don't try to hide what I am."

"Neither do I, actually. I can't be doing with all this violence, so fatiguing, and it plays havoc with my wardrobe. I don't indulge now, of course, I have my family to consider, and do try and mind the law. However, years ago, back in the day, if someone wanted to challenge me to a duel, that was their problem. I just got on with it then would go back to my valet. Mind you, family or no family, no one insults or threatens me and mine without repercussions, even now. I just repercuss differently."

"How many men have you killed?"

"No idea. Ask Francis, he was usually my second, unless he was otherwise occupied, of course." That was another thing that was now explained, thought Ricky.

"You don't even know how many men you've killed? Did you kill them deliberately, or did they succumb to their injuries?"

"I shoot to kill, quicksticks, and never miss. Kill them before they take a pot shot at me. I don't want to end up being ministered to by some sawbones, they might cut off an important bit of me."

"What about when you fight with a sword?"

"Depends on how much I dislike the fellow's cravat."

"I give in," Ashcroft sighed, but suddenly a light appeared from the front of the farmhouse and a hard hand grasped Ashcroft's arm, not the soft hand of a fop.

"Look. Is that him?" whispered Ricky.

He and Ashcroft watched as the big Sikh preceded his master out of the door, holding a lantern aloft, and they set off towards the barn; Bernheim, immaculately dressed and fiddling with his jacket and cuffs as if he was off to a High Society function, not some barbaric horror spectacle.

"He's wearing a rapier," whispered Ricky again. "He's mine. Never mind his cravat, I reeeally don't like his waistcoat," he muttered venomously.

"Listen to me, Ricky," replied Ashcroft quietly, a serious tone to his voice, "don't forget what Jack said; don't trust him a single inch, whatever you do. He's no gentleman despite his appearance and has no morals or scruples whatsoever. I'd shoot him if I was you, but you'll have to queue up behind me."

"Done," seethed Ricky. "Come on, I don't like the sounds coming out of that barn…"

Chapter Five

Ricky told his wife afterwards he'd never forget the scenes he watched that night as he and Ashcroft crept towards the barn and peered in through some gaps in the old, timbered walls. They gave him vivid and terrifying nightmares for months on end.

The six captives were seated on upright chairs, tied to the backs. The chairs were spread around in a semicircle and facing what appeared to be a small arena encircled by bales of straw and high caging. Six lions were prowling around inside it, snarling and taunting each other. It was obvious they weren't happy. The seventh prisoner, the maid, was standing, being held up between two men on one side, next to the caging. She was obviously shivering with terror and couldn't stand by herself. Behind each captive on their chair, two burly guards were standing and one of them each held a knife in his hand. Between each set of two guards, standing slightly further back, were three further guards, and a swarthy Arab appeared to be keeping an eye on the patrolling lions. Bernheim was obviously not taking any chances that his captives would escape or cause trouble. The whole interior was lit by lanterns on the walls and more lanterns were hanging from hooks on ceiling beams. It was a frightening, eerie spectacle. A bizarre parody of a circus.

Ashcroft and Ricky looked at each other in dismay. "We can't barge in, they're as like to slit their throats at the sight of us," whispered Ashcroft. "Look at all those guards. Why the hell are they standing like that, one of each pair with a knife? Anyway, there's two guards to each of them so that's what we've got to deal with before we even start to release any of the captives."

"Nasty, very nasty," muttered Ricky. "What do you suggest?" he was almost speechless and shocked to the depths of his soul. He was watching Francis closely, out of his mind with worry as to how to save him and his family with just six of them in a somewhat ramshackle rescue party, against such overwhelming odds. "And what the hell is that stench?" Ricky grimaced.

"Lion dung," and Ashcroft shuddered as he whispered, pulling a face. "Not that much from what I can see, so they can't have been in there for long. They must have kept them caged separately in another barn or farm building."

Bernheim moved forward, cleared his throat and started to speak. "Good evening, and welcome to my little *cirque*," he lisped, his cold, sibilant voice making the hairs on Ricky's neck stand up. "No doubt you have already gathered what the main attraction is this evening, even if you can't see them yet. *Naturellement*, in Paris, we have already introduced something more exotic than just horses, acrobats and clowns to our entertainments... and just so you know, as I'm sure you must be SO thrilled to hear... there are six of them and they are a touch hungry." Around the outside of the vast barn, Benjy and Fred shuddered as they watched and listened, just as Ashcroft and Ricky did the same.

Bernheim raised his hand and one of the guards behind each chair reached round their captive, snaked a hand under the sacks, grappled and pulled the rags out of their mouths.

A stream of angry, gutter French poured out of Cat's mouth as she swore terribly at Bernheim. "You fucking, eeevil bastard, you'll never get away with this. I'm going to kill you, just like I did your fucking father..." and she continued to swear at him, her temper getting the better of the disdainful reserve she'd been trying to maintain.

Ricky watched Francis's body jerk as he recognised Cat's voice, something he obviously hadn't expected to hear, and his heart went out to his old friend.

"Ah, good evening, Your Grace; how delightful to meet you at last. I've heard SO much about you."

"Let her go. I'll give you whatever you want," Francis grated. "So help me, you'll rot in hell for this pantomime you've concocted."

"Ah, Your Grace; charmed, I'm sure. Your reputation precedes you." Ashcroft wasn't sure precisely which reputation Bernheim was referring to: the Ducal one or that of The Shadow.

"It's ME you want. You can have it all, every cursed golden piece. Let them go and I'll tell you where it is," Nicky rasped. "It's got nothing to do with them, this is between you and me."

"Ah, *Le Lion de Valenciennes*. A slightly different approach to when we last met. I seem to recall you told me then you had no money and didn't know where the Valenciennes treasure was; quite an extraordinary *volte-face* wouldn't you say?"

"I found it last year, after Waterloo, by freak accident; but you can have it, all of it. As I just said, it's cursed, and I hope it kills you, just like it did my father."

"Really? How distressing for him, but I actually doubt that. So, it does exist then, the gold? Simply delightful."

"Let them go and I'll take you to where it's hidden. You'll never find it otherwise. It took ME years and as I just said, then it was only by accident."

"What a tempting offer..."

It was too much for Bella, Bernheim's hateful sarcasm playing games with them all. "Noooooo, Nicky, don't trust him, don't tell him anything!"

"BELLAAA?!" Nicky's heart nearly stopped. "You're here? Nooooo, oh please God..."

Francis swore roundly. "Let the women go, I told you, you can have it all..." his voice sounded grim.

"You bastard, why have you brought them? It's us you want, especially me. What sort of a man are you?" Nicky's tone echoed Francis.

"Ah, I would like to say a very clever one, wouldn't you agree, Baron?"

"EDDIEEE?" Francis blanched under his sack.

"Don't listen to him, Francis; don't do or say anything. He'll never get away with it, help must be on its way, it HAS to be."

"I wouldn't bank on it, Citoyens. No one knows where you are or what is going on."

"They'll find us, of course they will. This is England. You can't expect a whole family such as we are to disappear without an enormous hue and cry going up," Elise declared in withering tones. "And WE, are NOT Citizens, or Citoyens. WE are the best of what is English, and civilised. We don't cower before sans-culottes, or any insane Frenchman, for that is what you are. Insane, as bad as Bonaparte to think he could better US. Our people don't want to cut our heads off, we have more sense, nor do we wish to enslave Europe."

"Elise? Noooooo..." Eddie sounded distraught. "I hoped they'd leave you alone."

"Well, now you know, you're all here. All present and correct. The Duke and Duchess of Firle; Le Duc et La Duchesse de Valenciennes et Le Baron et La Baronesse de Mornay... ah, and someone else... l'hors d'oeuvres, très bien..." Bernheim spoke in both French and English, which was surprisingly good, as Ashcroft, crouched outside, noted in surprise.

Fortunately, Daisy didn't understand French or she might have fainted if she'd realised he was obviously referring to her, but five, then six people outside did, as Jack rapidly translated for Alfie, and Ricky and Ashcroft gasped softly as they watched and realised, as did Jack, Benjy and Fred. Alfie was just speechless, in complete disbelief at what he was witnessing.

"Now then, I want the Valenciennes gold, the Ducal fortune that I gather you now have, to make up for the monies I lost in Nice when you Interfered, and in Spain before that... and... The Shadow's hoard, and maybe some further payment to prevent making the demise of the woman who killed my father even more unpleasant than it's going to be. Retribution, finally, for his death and my lack of an anticipated inheritance. It completely changed the life I had expected to lead."

"You can have it all, every last penny I have. I'm one of the wealthiest men in England, but you have to let her go first," Francis grated instantly. Not giving in when his life was at stake was one thing, losing any of his family was another matter.

"I think we need a bit of entertainment, before we proceed any further with our negotiations, but this is all going to be so much easier than I anticipated." Bernheim was ecstatic at how the two men appeared to have capitulated so easily, but he wanted to watch them all squirm, wanted to see the fear on their proud, disdainful faces. "Gentlemen..."

Jack and Alfie, like Ashcroft and Ricky, were peering in through gaps in the wood. Alfie hadn't uttered a word and Jack, too, was almost speechless with anger and fear at the horror he was watching. Neither he nor Alfie had ever seen a lion in real life, and Alfie had only once seen a picture of one, and the sight of six, prowling around in the cage, had terrified the life out of both of them. Jack was worried he wasn't going to be able to rely on his friend at all. "Get a grip, Alf," he whispered, shaking the other youth hard. They'd been friends since Jack had originally gone to work in the Duke's stables at Firle and Alfie had befriended him there, the pair being of a similar age; but whereas Jack had come from the noxious alleyways of Seven Dials, Alfie had been found in an orphanage that the Duchess visited periodically, being one of its main patrons and source of financial support. She'd been taken with the young boy who seemed to have such a way with the animals he was tasked with caring for there, even if they were mainly farm ones or the two ponies that drew the farm wagon, and the trap in which the head of the charitable institution used to go to church or out and about. She fancied he'd be better off being trained up in gainful employment in Francis's stables as a groom, and as a new tiger for her husband on the occasion he took one with him in his curricle, so that was where Alfie had found himself at the age of ten, another of her fortunate waifs and strays. "We've got to get them out, double-quick, or they're going to be cat meat. I hope to God Ashcroft knows what he's doing," muttered Jack as he watched Alfie swallow hard and try to pull himself together.

Fred and Benjy were grey-faced. "You're going to need more than a pair of scissors," Fred was shaking with the terrifying sight of the lions which had him transfixed. He'd never seen any big, wild animals in real life, he'd rarely even seen a fox.

"Pull yourself together, Fred, and stop shaking. We need your help. I've faced a lot of wicked people with His Grace, and fought by his side on land and sea, you've no idea, and I'm buggered if I'm going to lose him now. I've got a lot of faith in Lord Ashcroft, more than most, and the Earl is no popinjay, believe you me. He's not quite the Duke, but near as dammit; you'll see..." Benjy didn't know who he was trying to convince, Fred or himself, and thought that not even in The Shadow's pirating days had he seen anything so frightening as those six hungry, snarling lions, and he'd seen a lot of bad things.

"Oh-oh, what now?" Jack took a deep breath as he watched one guard pull off the sacks and the other rip off the blindfolds from the captives and he watched their faces as they shook their heads, blinked and were instantly confronted with the lions in the big cage in front of them. Their faces were white, but impassive, every single one, and Jack was so proud of them all, knowing they had to be terrified.

"What? No fear? No horror?" Bernheim was disappointed as he lisped angrily, "And I've gone to all this trouble to find such an APPROPRIATE entertainment for you all, isn't that so, Your Grace, *notre LION de Valenciennes*" Bernheim sneered at Nicky.

"You're INSANE! I should have killed you when I had the chance in Nice. I'll never forgive myself that I didn't!" Beside herself, Bella screeched at Bernheim.

"So passionate. I'm quite looking forward to the pleasure of taming you, eh, *LIONESSE*? You remember Nice, what I particularly enjoyed? I can hardly wait to have at you, you screamed so loudly, and here was I thinking how much you enjoyed it."

"DON'T TOUCH HER!" Nicky yelled angrily. "Do what you like to me, but don't touch her again, You Vicious Pervert!"

"NOOOO!" shrieked Bella again. "I'll do whatever you want, go with you willingly, and he'll give you everything, we don't want it, but let them all go, don't hurt them, they've done nothing to you."

"So touching, so caring..." tutted Bernheim, "but the entertainment now, Abdul, if you please," and he clicked his fingers in the air towards the Arab.

The six people on the chairs and the six people outside couldn't believe what they were watching. One man cut then tore Daisy's dress down the front while the other released her hands. They rapidly stripped her naked and then pulled off the sack and removed her gag and blindfold. The poor girl wet herself, and screamed and screamed in abject terror as she was picked up and thrown through a gate Abdul had opened in the caging, and he shut it quickly after her.

It took the first lion mere seconds to pounce on his victim and drag her to the centre of the arena. He cut off her screams as he tore out a large lump of flesh from her throat, and then the other five snarled and fought to get a piece of her. Elise was sick at the gruesome, bloody spectacle and vomited, part on the floor and part over herself as she couldn't move. Bella shut her eyes and so did Eddie, but then the meaning of the daggers held by the men behind their chairs became clear. They were watching them and the thug behind Bella viciously tugged back on her hair and put his knife to her throat. "Watch," he ordered, "open yer peepers or else."

The same happened to Eddie and then Elise. Cat's eyes were glazed with tears; she appeared to be watching but her eyes weren't taking it in, and Francis and Nicky simply grimaced with sheer revulsion. Outside, Alfie retched into the dirt and so did Fred. He'd seen men blown apart on the battlefield, but somehow, that didn't compare to this grisly display. Jack closed his eyes and so did Benjy. Ashcroft and Ricky went white. It was beyond anything even Ashcroft had seen or experienced. Ricky thought of ancient Rome and the Christians who had been thrown to the lions in the Coliseum. How the crowds could go and watch and call it sport was totally beyond him. As his stomach roiled and bile rose in his throat he told himself the Empire had deserved to fall if that was what they did for entertainment.

"We can't wait any longer," Ricky shook Ashcroft's arm urgently. "Christ, who's going to be next? I can't believe what I've just seen..."

his stomach was still churning from the sight of a lion tossing what looked like the remnants of a bloodied arm in the air as he played with it and chewed what remained of the limp fingers. Ricky was glad he hadn't eaten anything back in Berkeley Square or he was sure he would have been sick.

"Believe it. I told you he was unhinged and unstable. That poor girl, at least it was quick. I'm going in, watch my back..." Ashcroft started to rise from his crouching position, gripping his pistol with determination, "...wait, what's he saying now?" he was white as chalk but on his feet and about to head in through the door of the barn when he paused to listen.

"*Alors, Mesdames et Messieurs,* wasn't that entertaining? Now then, that was the *hors d'oeuvres,* who will be the *entrée*? I want The Shadow's fortune. Where is it, please?" he looked at the six faces, degrees of shock now on all of them despite their best efforts.

"Let them go. I'll take you there, it's hidden on my Sussex Estate." Francis tried to pull himself together, tried to stop visions of Cat following the nursemaid. He could barely think straight. Nothing, not even the sight of men being blown to bits on his ship in the midst of a bloody sea battle had prepared him for what he'd just watched, nor the horrors of what he and Jack had witnessed on the smoking fields of Waterloo after the battle... at least most of those poor fellows had been dead.

"Don't listen to him, he's lying." Five pairs of eyes suddenly turned towards Eddie.

"I beg your pardon?" Bernheim looked at Eddie in surprise. "YOU know where The Shadow's fortune is?"

"Of course I do, and it's not where he says it is."

"Excuse me if I'm a trifle confused. Why would you know, Baron?" he looked at the quiet, scarred man.

"Because... I am The Shadow."

Chapter Six

F rancis nearly laughed, the whole situation was too surreal and he felt himself getting hysterical. "Eddie, what the HELL are you playing at?"

"Be QUIET, Francis, for once in your life." Eddie's voice was hard. "Look at me, Bernheim, look at my face. You know I limp, why do you think The Shadow suddenly disappeared at the height of his success? THIS is what your father did to me before he was killed by my sister, that's why she did it." Eddie was banking that Bernheim had no way of knowing Dupont had been responsible for his injuries, years previously, no one did except Francis, Cat, Bella and Nicky. He hadn't even told Elise, but he was desperate, he had to play for time; anything to stop a repeat of what he'd just witnessed.

"Well, this is very interesting. Two people claiming to be The Shadow?"

"Of course I'm The Shadow, *L'Ombre*, I'm French. Why do you think I rescued my parents from Rouen Fortress?"

Bernheim was confused. Had he got it wrong? He looked between the two men, "I want the truth, who is it?"

"ME!" Francis and Eddie spoke at the same time.

"Hood the others, I need to get to the bottom of this," snarled Bernheim and his men did as they were told, ignoring the objections of their captives and a further stream of abuse from Cat, and a torrent of vile language from Bella. Elise sat as still as a statue.

"Ajeet, knife please." Bernheim held out his hand to the Sikh standing behind him who placed his kirpan, the large, curved dagger he withdrew from his sash, into his master's hand. Bernheim walked around the semicircle of chairs until he stood behind Cat. "So, this is YOUR wife, and YOUR sister, very convenient." Through the sacking, he pulled back viciously on Cat's hair and yanked on the coarse cloth, raising the bottom of it and she gasped in pain; this action exposed the long line of Cat's throat and Bernheim ran the tip of the dagger around the base of it. A thin line of red appeared. Francis was beside himself. "EDDIE, for the love of God, tell him it's me," he cried hoarsely.

"Let them go and I'll take you to it, or leave them here, unharmed, and I'll still take you to it," Eddie said impassively, "but you won't find it without me there, and it's no good hurting or killing m'sister. I never told your father and look what he did to me."

The dagger drew another line, deeper, vertical this time, from Cat's throat to the top of her cleavage. "Eddie, pleeeease..." Francis begged the terror in his eyes obvious. The man who had previously laughed at death for himself couldn't stand to watch his beloved wife's life teeter in the balance.

"You don't expect The Shadow to be so feeble, surely?" asked Eddie, struggling to contain himself and look ruthless. "Remember my reputation, the men I've killed, ships I've sunk. Think how much gold I've amassed, all hidden away..." his words tempted.

Bernheim was torn, it made a lot of sense. "So, where is the treasure then?"

"On my estate, Arlington. It's not far from Firle, or the coast. Very quiet. Middle of nowhere. No neighbours to speak of, no 'nosey parkers' as they say in English, perfect."

"Tell me where it is?"

"Hidden underground."

"Where underground."

"I'll have to show you."

"Draw me a map."

"You'll still never find it, it would take you weeks of digging. I can only recognise the spot myself when I'm there, it's so well hidden under all the wild flowering plants and shrubs."

A second deep line went around Cat's throat and blood started to drip from it down her chest, merging with the blood seeping out of the vertical line, but she'd not uttered a word. Outside, Ricky and Benjy were staggered, but not surprised, they knew what she was like. Jack was aghast and more impressed than any of them watching.

Unable to see, Nicky was beside himself with anger and frustration, not knowing what was happening but he'd heard Francis's loud, terrified gasp and knew something shocking was going on and he prayed like he'd never done before for Ashcroft to arrive, praying to the Dowager and his step-mother that if they were watching this travesty from heaven, they could do something. He pulled and yanked on the ropes on his wrists, shooting pain going up his weak arm, but the ropes were tied firm and he couldn't move. He couldn't even get up off his chair. He got walloped around the head for his efforts by one of his guards. It caught the old scar from Waterloo and his eyes watered as he saw stars for several moments and shooting pains lanced along the side of his head.

"Well, it seems as if I have been misinformed. How very fascinating. However, you don't fit the description I had of The Shadow."

"That was twenty-five years ago and I wasn't grey then. I'm still quite tall but my injuries and limp make me seem slightly shorter," Eddie managed a small shrug.

"You're not that grey now," Bernheim peered at Eddie's fair hair.

"I used to wear a lot of disguises, especially a wig. I'm an aristocrat, no one really knew who I was, that's how I got away with it. Why do you think I called myself The Shadow and not my name?"

It all sounded so plausible and Francis couldn't believe it. What the hell was Eddie playing at?

"I fooled everyone, even you. Francis was just my cover. I knew him from visits to England to see my English godmother, and he had an aunt and uncle nearby in Normandy who he used to visit periodically, long before the Revolution, and then he became my brother-in-law. It was so simple, so clever, so perfect."

Outside, Ashcroft was staggered and Ricky was confused. "What the hell is going on? I don't understand…"

"No idea. What on earth is Eddie trying to do? Francis looks like death, he loves that woman ," muttered Ashcroft.

"Do you think this might be a good time to interrupt? They're all looking a bit distracted in there, and I really don't want to see another woman thrown in that cage."

"Ready yourself, I'm just about to put the cat among the pigeons," and Ashcroft headed for the barn door, a resolute look on his face, not daring to wait another second while the macabre events unfolded. "I'll take the two behind Nicky, you deal with the two behind Francis, if we can get them loose, we might have a chance; other than Jack, I'm not sure how well the other three will stand up to Bernheim's thugs, they're not fighters."

"I want to know where the treasure is. You CAN draw a map. You CAN give me directions. I'll send some men."

"That will take days. Let me go with you. You can have the Valenciennes gold as well, I also know where that is."

"You do?" Bernheim's eyebrows raised as his sibilant voice expressed his surprise.

"Of course, I'm The Shadow. I got de Bresancourt out of the Fortress when he was a child, remember?"

"This is quite amazing. It seems I've been wasting my time in the wrong direction, Baron."

"Noooo, Papa, what are you doing?" Nicky pleaded.

"Papa? I don't understand…?"

"I rescued him. He was an orphan. I adopted him formally," Eddie gave another of his slight shrugs, "you know he lived with me and my first wife." Eddie assumed Bernheim had done his homework and it was no secret that Nicky was his adopted son, not just his ward.

"I see. So, perhaps you are The Shadow after all? That imbecile from the forest said you were crazy, but he also said you were an exceptionally tall, well-built man with very dark hair. Are you The Shadow or not?" a third line crossed the base of Cat's throat from one side of her clavicle to the other. "Do you know what *Ling Chi* is, Baron?" and Bernheim watched Eddie's face go even whiter as the dagger point finally dug into the base of Cat's throat and this time she did cry out.

Francis didn't know what it was but he realised Eddie did, and a red mist was descending over him as fury such as he'd never known overwhelmed him at the torture he was helplessly watching and couldn't seem to stop. He didn't think he could bear to watch Bernheim finally slit his beloved wife's throat in front of his eyes and knew he would never, ever, get over it.

"Another line here and there, what do you English call it? Noughts and crosses I seem to recall. I could cut the pieces off and throw them into the cage; *croutons* of delicate flesh," and his malevolent laughter filled the air as he carved a square on Cat's white throat. "For the elucidation of the rest of you, *Ling Chi* is what you English may have heard of as the practice in China of death by a thousand cuts; it's quite an art, I do assure you, and I find it quite fascinating. I am therefore going to ask one more time and then, perhaps her ear comes off first as a tasty morsel. I'll have to remove her earring, of course, can't have the lion getting indigestion… so, which of you is The Shadow?" he rasped in a now vicious snarl as he lifted more of the sacking to reveal Cat's ear and he took hold of a lobe and raised the razor-sharp blade. It hovered over Cat's skin and Francis braced himself, holding his breath.

"Neither, as a matter of fact. Put your knife down or you're a dead man in two seconds, for you see, you are mistaken in everything. I… am The Shadow," and Ashcroft strolled into the barn, looking as cool as a cucumber, Ricky at his heels holding up two pistols in his hands just as Ashcroft was. As a piece of high drama at the eleventh hour and fifty-ninth minute, it was unsurpassable.

Francis did laugh, he couldn't help it, he knew it was ridiculous and they were all about to be thrown to the lions, but he simply couldn't stop himself, he was beyond hysterical. "Miles? And RICKY? Good God, what are YOU doing here?"

"Missing my dinner for a start, jauntering across to this outpost of un-civilisation, not to mention getting my new evening jacket creased in the process, that's what. And I have a major bone to pick with you, Francis Granville, but I'll tell you later over some food and a snifter or two of brandy. Oh, and I still think your taste in pistols leaves a lot to be desired…" Ricky tutted facetiously.

Bernheim gaped for a moment at the droll Englishman who was standing deceptively casually, even if he was holding a brace of pistols in the air, but then he pulled himself together. "More guests? Another claimant to the title? This is all unsurpassing fascinating. Don't you think you're rather outnumbered?" he asked sarcastically and didn't move, his knife still hovering at Cat's ear.

"Not at all, My Dear Bernheim, or may I call you Frederick?" Ashcroft took another few steps forward. "Perhaps not," disdain dripping from his icy voice, "since you are a piece of vermin and no friend of mine, or England. We have reinforcements down the lane. You don't think we would let YOU, some inconspicuous piece of French horse-shit, make off with one of our most highly regarded and well-known aristocratic families? As the Baroness so rightly said, this is England, in case you hadn't noticed. We behave ourselves here," tutted Ashcroft, "we are civilised and try to refrain from cutting pieces off each other, unlike the Chinese, and my friend behind me, the Earl of Keswick, particularly dislikes ill-dressed riffraff, he's just been telling me, so all of you, gentlemen, and I use the word lightly," Ashcroft waved one pistol at the thugs standing behind the semicircle of chairs, "if you'd rather be transported than hung, I suggest you put down your knives and whatever weapons you have, right now, because otherwise, I might give in to the huge temptation to feed one or more of you to these lions instead."

Francis threw back his head and guffawed with hysterical laughter, it was simply too much for him. Eddie struggled not to smirk and, beneath his hood, Nicky sent up a prayer of thanks to his stepmother and the Dowager, swearing to go to church at the earliest opportunity to light a candle to the pair of them.

"Now look here, Miles, My Good Fellow, what the devil are you playing at? I've told you before not to pretend you're me. And you there, you disgrace to tailoring," Ricky had tutted at Ashcroft but now turned and addressed Bernheim, his eyes in slits as they glittered at the man in hatred, "I reeeally don't like your waistcoat, but that's execrable French taste for you, I suppose. As you can see, I fit the

ANTOINETTE GEORGE

description perfectly, and I'm your man. This imbecile next to me, I regret to say, is my second-in-command and always did have a hankering to take over. I've had to come out of retirement, yet AGAIN, to put an end to your games. One would have thought you'd have heard how I soon dismissed that riffraff in the forest at Valenciennes, isn't that right, Jack?" Jack and Alfie had taken the opportunity, when all eyes had turned to Ashcroft and Ricky, to clamber in through a rotting window frame, bereft of any glass. "Allow me to present my apprentice, Jack Vallance, Esquire, and his assistant, Alfred, and I wouldn't annoy them if I were you, they have talents that make even me raise my eyebrows."

Ashcroft didn't know whether to laugh or cry, but the man was good, he'd got Bernheim completely confused and the Earl of Keswick went up in his estimation tenfold; but then, of course, he was a close friend of Francis Granville, so he should have expected it; two deadly cuckoos, Ashcroft told himself. He felt like laughing as hysterically as Francis was, perhaps more, as he momentarily contemplated the thought of the pair of them smuggling: A Brace of Shadows. He decided His Majesty's Revenue and Excise wouldn't have known if they were coming or going if it had come to pass.

Ricky was continuing, praying young Alfie hadn't been bragging. "Er... Alfred, perhaps you'd care to give us a demonstration with your whip, if you would be so kind." He eyed the lad across the far side of the barn and then looked at the knife in Bernheim's hand, now hovering in the air. Alfie had followed his eyes. "That's a nasty-looking knife; foreign, I take it?"

It was his instruction and the long horsewhip cracked through the air and curled around Bernheim's wrist as the deadly kirpan clattered to the floor. Bernheim snarled in pain and anger as all hell suddenly broke loose.

48

Chapter Seven

"FALL TO THE FLOOR!" yelled Ashcroft desperately, as loud as he could, hoping the six captives would understand him as he took aim and fired at the two men behind Nicky. Ricky shot the two behind Francis and all four dropped like stones. At the same time, Benjy and Fred broke through the flimsy, rotting wood, burst in and shot the four men behind Eddie and Elise. Their aim also deadly and true at close quarters.

Eddie had yelled at Elise even before he'd heard Ashcroft shout, realising what was likely to happen, "Elise, topple over, quick," and he threw himself in her direction, trying desperately to fall on her and knock her over as the rapport of firing pistols filled the barn and Francis had done the same towards Nicky, toppling his chair in his direction. Bella had no idea what was going on but had heard Ashcroft's voice and then her father's and threw herself sideways in what she thought was the direction of Cat who was next to her and screamed as she hit her head on the floor and felt a body fall on top of her.

Jack had shot the two men behind Bella and grabbed Alfie's pistol from his hand, knowing he was a far better shot than the groom, and took out another of the thugs, looking around at the sudden confusion and a couple of the guards had tried to shoot at the intruders in return. The lions were running around roaring and pawing at the caging, confused and frightened by the gunfire, and their sound was deafening and terrifying.

As the pall of smoke lifted, Ashcroft peered above a rotting stack of hay he'd taken refuge behind and, pulling his knife from his coat, he surveyed the situation as he looked anxiously around for Bernheim and the Sikh, wishing he'd brought more ammunition. He had a bad feeling about the giant and just knew he'd be trouble. He'd had some experience of them when he'd been in India and he'd never forgotten. He looked sideways and spotted Ricky sheltering behind a large wooden crate. There were several abandoned around the barn walls, obviously used to transport the lions, Ashcroft surmised.

"Can you reach Francis or Nicky?" he signalled, mouthed and pointed towards the two men who had been wriggling around on the floor during the momentary chaos, trying uselessly to free themselves, but were now lying still. Ricky produced his stiletto, nodded at Ashcroft and signed to him where he would go. Ashcroft nodded back and tried to make out who was still at large. He thought for a moment, trying to recollect how many shots he'd heard and reckoned if his group had aimed true, eleven men were down. A fair number and he hoped they were dead and not merely injured. He prayed to God none of the captives or their group of six had been hit in the melee as Bernheim's men had shot back at them before taking cover, and he couldn't see clearly across the barn as the caged lions were in the way. But everyone appeared to have taken refuge somewhere, as he and Ricky had done.

Ashcroft shouted out into the sudden pall. "Give yourselves up. The cavalry are outside the farm, it's surrounded. You'll never escape. Give up and I'll see you won't hang; if not, you'll wish you'd never been born."

One man suddenly stood up, looking around in fright. He'd appeared from behind a crate near where Bella's chair had been, but before he'd taken a few steps forward a shot rang out and he toppled to the floor as Bernheim's cold, lisping voice crawled over Ashcroft's skin. "No one abandons me and lives..." and a deathly hush suddenly filled the air. So, that was at least twelve down, Ashcroft surmised. That means there were seven of them left, plus Bernheim, and Jack and Alfie had a shot each left between them he reckoned. The odds weren't good, bearing in mind the seven and Bernheim were still armed, but he'd no idea how many of Bernheim's men had pistols on them as well as the knives he'd seen. Ashcroft wondered where the coach was with Browning and Carstairs and the other two grooms, not to mention the unit of cavalry. He sent up a fervent prayer they weren't far away, the situation didn't look good, not as critical as it had been when he'd shown himself, but still extremely dangerous.

"Who ARE you?" Bernheim's voice suddenly rasped from somewhere near the back of the barn and Ashcroft wondered where he was.

"I told you, I'm The Shadow," Ashcroft replied slowly and menacingly, "except I changed sides a number of years ago. Poacher turned gamekeeper," his voice had never been more sarcastically frightening, "and I work for His Majesty's Government now, so I'm still in the shadows. That's why you don't know me, but I've been following you for years, Bernheim. I know the menace your father was, and the havoc you've created across Europe for your own venal benefit, not just in the service of Bonaparte. I'm going to have you now, you'll never get out of here alive, any more than your father got out of the Fortress at Rouen. De Bresancourt worked for me, he had his own axe to grind, very conveniently, and you can see how successful we were at putting a stop to your nefarious efforts in Spain and Nice."

There was deathly silence and a lion growled. "That woman killed my father, de Bresancourt admitted it. She will pay. We'll still feed her to the lions."

"One move and you're a dead man, very painfully, I'll see to it. You've seen what we've done so far and there really are cavalry outside."

"Where are they then? You're bluffing."

"Waiting on my signal. You don't believe me? You think I'd come here without support? Why on earth would I do that? But I want the pleasure of killing you myself; the rest of your motley band are disposable, half of them are dead already and I'll feed the rest to the cats, just like you did with that poor girl."

The minutes ticked by and all that could be heard were the prowling, snarling lions or gnawing sounds as a couple still chewed on some remaining bones. No one was moving and Ashcroft wondered if some of the captives had been shot. No one was sitting upright, they were all on the floor, but he couldn't see properly and just prayed they were all right and wouldn't move. His brain worked frantically, trying to decide what to do; it was an impasse, but at least it had bought them some much needed time for reinforcements to appear and saved Cat from either losing her ear or having her throat slit.

The blood was thrumming through Ricky's veins, he could literally feel it. He wondered if this was how Francis had felt, this high excitement and sheer fright. Was this why he'd periodically disappeared from London and their bored, sybaritic existence? To chase a thrill and dice with death or capture? The man could have been hung and Ricky still couldn't get his head around it. He had slowly crawled and slithered towards where Francis was now lying, like a statue on its side, and Ricky sent up a prayer he hadn't been wounded in the hail of gunfire as he'd stopped moving. He raised his head carefully as Bernheim and Ashcroft taunted each other, trying to make out where the man was... and his accomplices. Francis had managed to wriggle himself nearer to where he and Ashcroft had been standing and wasn't far from him, but Ricky didn't dare move, unsure if there was a pistol aimed in his direction and frustration burned through him.

As he lay, suddenly, there was a crack in the air, and then another, and another, as one, two and then a third of the lanterns that were hanging around the walls or from the ceiling suddenly fell to the floor. Alfie! Ricky raised his head, just as everyone else had to be doing and without thought, took his chance. He slithered forward out of his protection behind a crate and across the open floor until he managed to reach out and grab one of Francis's legs and pulled for all he was worth, trying to shove the crate in the way to give them both some cover. The lions were roaring again at the sudden noise and then another lantern fell, glass tinkling, and in moments, Francis was there, and they were both behind the crate and Ricky attacked the tight ropes, sawing frantically and digging at the knots with his stiletto. Francis raised his head and quirked a brow at Ricky as the latter shook with relief the man was still alive. "Took your time, Rosie," Francis whispered, "always late, as ever. Some second you are; what were you doing this time, buffing your nails or fiddling with your cravat?"

"So sorry, Granny, lost a button off my waistcoat, had to look for it." Ricky grinned at his friend as he hacked at the thick ropes, their schoolboy nicknames for each other coming naturally after so many years.

Finally, with a groan of relief, Francis wriggled his hands free and kneeled up next to Ricky, impulsively giving the man an emotional hug. "Christ, I've never been so glad to see your ugly face in my whole damned life," and he rubbed his sore, chafed wrists as the circulation returned to them.

"Why the HELL didn't you ever tell me, or take me with you? ME! I was your oldest and closest friend," Ricky's whisper burst out. "I'm not some faggot or wimp, for Christ's sake."

"You'd have got your breeches dirty." Francis winked at him.

"Damn you, Granny, I don't think I'll ever forgive you. We'd have made a serious double act; the Revenue men wouldn't have known what had hit them."

"You can never have two shadows," Francis whispered. "The master might have spotted us," he grinned.

"I KNEW it," Ricky's whispered laugh erupted for a second as he shook his head at the forty-year old schoolboy memory. "You Damn Bugger, you could have got yourself hanged. Was it really worth the thrill?"

"Every time, absolutely nothing like it."

"God almighty, I still can't believe it; a bloody smuggler, all those years? Have you really got some treasure? What the hell was that about? Don't tell me you were into piracy as well? Smugglers normally just run brandy and tobacco in my book."

"My lips are forever sealed, but yes, the remains truly are buried underground at Firle, contrary to what Eddie was wittering about. No idea what to do with it now, but it was never about that, of course, I was just bored. It was the ultimate challenge."

"You mad fool. Who else knows?"

"No one, only the close family, but NOT my boys. Benjy knows, of course, and Ashcroft. I suppose Alfie knows as well now," he sighed.

"So do most of your senior servants, at least some of the story, if you but knew it. My God, Granny, you've NO idea what the hell has been going on today."

"Never mind all that, what the hell is going on here? How many of you are there? Are the cavalry really outside?"

"They're on their way, oh, and reinforcements, if you count Browning and Carstairs and two of your grooms," grinned Ricky as Francis gaped at him. "They were behind us in a coach, wild horses wouldn't keep them in London. Four of us came on horseback across country where we could, and Alfie came in your racing curricle. What a bloody whip he is, but I don't know where the others are currently. Miles and I HAD to come in, couldn't wait a second longer, thought they were going to throw you to the lions; talk about ancient Rome and all that. Never seen anything like it, frightened the bloody living daylights out of me!" Ricky looked at his friend anxiously. "But this isn't good, Granny, there's at least six of them still out there, and Bernheim, and this giant Indian fellow, nearly foot he is, nasty looking bugger too."

Francis swore under his breath and peered around the crate, but it had gone eerily quiet again. "I need to go get Nicky and Cat. Christ, I thought Bernheim was going to cut her throat. I'll cut his when I get hold of him, very slowly, and that's too good for the bastard," the vengeful, cold whisper didn't surprise Ricky but he put a restraining hand on his friend's arm.

"Don't be an idiot, look about you; get your brain focussed, if you can find it. One thing at a time. I don't know where the bastards are or how many pistols they've got, and we'll be sitting ducks if we move. If Alfie puts more lights out, we could try and move forward behind this crate and try and grab Nicky like I did you. Is he all right? I couldn't see after all that shooting…"

"I think so, playing dead, like me. Seemed the best idea. Hope his arm's all right, he crashed over and it's still not totally recovered, all his weight would have gone on it; I could hear him groaning." Francis looked worried. "I'm not sure if it'll mend a second time. You should have seen the mess it was after we found him at Waterloo, like the rest of him. No idea how Benjy got it right again, the bloody butchers we found in Brussels wanted to hack it off, but Benjy sewed it all up. Never seen anything like it, talk about special tailoring and invisible mending, and it's healed well or was healing," he whispered softly, his concern obvious.

"Better his arm than a ball in his head," tutted Ricky practically. "But never mind, wait and see what Alfie does next. Him and Jack, they're over there somewhere," Ricky pointed to the other side of the barn, "and Benjy and some fellow called Fred, Ashcroft's man, are over there too, further round. That's how we found you all, he was watching you in the park and followed the carriage they carried you off in."

"Bloody hell! Thank God for Ashcroft," Francis sighed and then he remembered. "Poor Bubbles, they beat the shit out of him y'know; he tried to save me, never thought he had it in him."

"Neither did I, none of us did, thought his brain was full of white fluff and cream buns, but he's hanging on. Benjy sewed him up as well. He staggered back to Berkeley Square covered in blood, that's what raised the alarm so quickly and started the whole hullabaloo. Last I saw of him, Mrs Morris was on her hands and knees feeding him warm chicken, cheese and brandy. He's probably pissed out of his brain right this minute, not to mention pissing on one of your lovely Aubusson rugs. I'd no idea dogs could be so partial to a drop of the hard stuff..."

"My God, I'd no idea. This whole affair..." Francis shook his head in disbelief at what had happened, his extravagant carpeting the least of his worries. "But I must get to Cat..."

"Stop panicking, we'll get her. But Nicky first, and we'll work our way round if we can. She's right in the middle with Bella. Jack and Alfie are nearer them than us, and Bernheim's there with that giant. It's not good, Francis; you've got to be patient and pray she'll hang on."

"Pray? I'm not bloody praying," Francis rasped. "That woman is my life. She risked and nearly lost her own to save me once and I'm not sitting here and letting some bastard slit her throat, cut bits off of her or throw her into that cage."

"Calm down, calm down! And when we get out of here I want to hear the whole story from you. In detail. From what I've gathered already it sounds like one of Sophy's gothic novels, too ridiculous and unbelievable for words."

"Whatever you've heard already, it's all true, believe me, and I'm NOT leaving here without her; I'd give my life for hers."

"I know that," Ricky whispered softly as he gripped his friend's arm reassuringly. "I've always known how much you love her, and she you; never mind unusual courtship, strangest damn wedding I ever went to, but that's the pair of you all over; we'll get her, Granny, I promise, or die trying. I'm by your side, whatever it takes. Two shadows in one, just like we were before."

"I'm in your debt, Rosie. I don't know what to say."

"It's nothing. You'd do the same for me, wouldn't you?"

"Always, Rosie," whispered Francis and as they looked at each other for a moment it was as if they were both eleven or twelve again. Both boys had found themselves bundled off to school at the age of nine and had found a soulmate in each other. Francis had been virtually uncontrollable by any of his tutors, let alone his feeble mother or his drunken father, and his redoubtable grandmother, the only one he took occasional notice of when he felt like it, had taken matters into her own hands and packed him off to school for some proper discipline; to mix with other boys rather than a house full of wittering women, and to get an education beyond that of endless tutors who couldn't seem to engage the restlessly energetic boy. Ricky's morose and curmudgeonly father had done much the same, because he couldn't deal with his disobedient, wild and belligerent only child either, and thought he needed incarcerating in a strict educational institution that wouldn't tolerate his misbehaviour. They'd been Granny and Rosie to each other ever since, though they hadn't called each other that for years.

Ricky smiled at his friend and squeezed his arm again and they both peered around the crate, one either side, trying to make out what was going on then returned to whisper to each other again.

The minutes ticked past and suddenly shots rang out again, the whip cracked, and more lanterns fell, and one of the lions in the cage collapsed. The others pounced on it and started to tear it to pieces and the barn was now in semi-darkness, only the light from the wall lanterns illuminating the scene. Francis and Ricky hadn't paused in the fracas, they'd shoved the crate along nearer Nicky and hauled him back to where they were, the strength of two of them making short work of it. A pistol ball had whizzed past Nicky's head and buried itself in the crate but all three made it back to where the two men had been.

Francis ripped the sacking off Nicky's head while Ricky attacked the ropes again with his stiletto, Francis yanking and pulling at the same time. Nicky sat up, his face a mask of pain as he held his injured arm to his chest and he looked at the two other men. "Where've you been, practising your fencing or playing cards? Terrie and Lizzie would have been quicker," he tutted.

Francis cuffed him round the head gently. "That's what you get from associating with elderly men. Has your arm broken again?" he looked at it worriedly.

"Hello, Ricky; nice waistcoat. I'm not sure, but I'll manage. I've got to get Bella," he half turned to set off back the way he'd been dragged.

Francis grabbed him and yanked him back. "I know, I know, but she's on the other side of the barn and you're not going anywhere. She's nearer Jack and Alfie, and Benjy and one of Ashcroft's men. It's a mess and there's still plenty of them out there, as well as Bernheim and his Indian friend. Did you see him before they put your hood on again? Giant bastard with a turban and beard?" Francis tried to calm him down, not letting him go, as he could see he was as anxious about Bella as he was about Cat.

"I caught a glimpse. I swear to God, Bernheim is going to die very slowly."

"Not with that bad arm," tutted Ricky. "That vermin is mine; I've got your rapier, Granny."

"Granny?" Nicky looked between the two men.

"Long story. He's Rosie. Schoolboy nicknames, and if I EVER hear you call me that, I'll personally cut your bloody arm off myself."

"Yes, Granny," Nicky chuckled softly at Francis. "Granville, Ambrose, Granny and Rosie, you sound like a pair of flower sellers in Covent Garden. How much is it worth to keep that one quiet?" and he

57

winked at the two older men. "But there's nothing wrong with my sword arm, he's mine, it's been a long time coming."

"Keep him in order, can't you?" whispered Ricky at Francis then spoke softly to Nicky. "You can't fight him with a bad arm, You Fool. Ashcroft says he's a killer, well so am I, and he's interfered with what was originally a nice relaxing day, not to mention making me go without my dinner."

"That makes two of us," grated Nicky. "What's Ashcroft up to? Where's the cavalry? Or was that Ashcroft bluster?"

"Oh no, they really are on their way, but no doubt it takes time to organise themselves at the barracks as they'd no idea what was really going on here, just following orders to come and deal with an enemy threat and wild animals on the loose; we got here first, record run from Mayfair, no time to dawdle with lions strolling around wanting THEIR dinner. We've just got to hang on until the soldiers arrive. Carstairs and Browning should be here by now though."

"Carstairs?" Nicky gaped at Ricky. "But he's over seventy, are you mad? And Browning?"

"Quite possibly, given what I'm currently doing, but he really is on his way, with Browning, they wouldn't be denied, and they've got more pistols as well as muskets in their carriage and two more grooms. We rode hell for leather to get here quicker, didn't have time to faffle about looking for spare powder and balls."

"Dear God, wake me up, Granny, I'm definitely having another nightmare." Nicky rolled his eyes.

"Don't Granny me, You Facetious Puppy. I'm still old enough to be your father. I'll take a strap to you if you don't behave, I did when you were eleven and stole off in my new curricle and I'll do it again now."

"I'd like to see you try, You Decrepit Old Bugger," Nicky grinned at Francis. "I'll never forget that drive," he reminisced for a moment, "and I couldn't sit down for a week afterwards; you coloured my arse black and blue. Talk about mistreatment and abuse of helpless little children."

"Helpless little children? That'll be the day. Serves you right. I nearly had a fit when I found it gone from the carriage house and I still don't know how you managed those greys; you could have killed yourself, never mind them."

"You taught me," smirked Nicky, "plus my ineffable natural talent to charm four-legged creatures," he chuckled softly, "as well as two-legged ones with bountiful, luscious breasts and a firm but soft…"

"When you two have finished reminiscing," Ricky grinned at the pair of them, "I think Ashcroft wants a word…" he tilted his head behind him where Ashcroft was gesticulating at them. "I suggest we pull back, very slowly and quietly; it's quite dark over here now so hopefully no one can see us. Oh Christ, look what's going on in there," he tilted his head in the other direction at the cage, pulling a face in distaste at the sight of five lions feeding on the sixth.

"They're hungry. I swear after today I never want to see another lion as long as I live," whispered Nicky with a shudder, "nor smell one. My blood ran cold when I heard their growling. I couldn't believe it, thought I really was having a nightmare."

"Me too," muttered Francis, "frightened the wits out of me, but does that include your golden pair?" he grinned.

"Golden pair?" Ricky looked at Francis.

"By my compost heaps, where everyone keeps giant gold statues."

"Beg pardon?" Ricky looked bemused.

"The Valenciennes golden treasure, we found it last summer, in the de Bresancourt family graveyard, would you believe? Two giant statues; we, along with everyone else, assumed they were stone, on top of his grandparents' ruined mausoleum, but they're solid gold. They toppled down in a bad storm when the mausoleum finally collapsed. Worth an absolute fortune, and we smuggled them out and back to England. Didn't want the locals to get their nifty fingers on them. They're currently sitting at the bottom of my kitchen garden at Firle, we didn't know what else to do with them for the time being."

"Bloody hell, after all this time. So it did exist after all?" Ricky chuckled softly. "Would you believe it?" he shook his head.

"I don't care about the bloody gold, I just need to get Bella," grated Nicky. "Is she all right? I HAVE to get to her, she must be terrified."

"No more than the rest of us; let's go talk to Ashcroft, come on…" and slowly and quietly the three slithered backwards towards where

Ashcroft was still behind his mound of hay and Francis worriedly watched Nicky and his arm.

When they reached Ashcroft, he ripped off his cravat and without a word, tied it in a makeshift sling and hung it around Nicky's neck. "We'll save it again, don't worry," he whispered and gently hugged the younger man lovingly. "Just watch yourself and we'll get Bella for you. Nobody ever gets left behind on my watch, not if I can help it, even the dead. Never mind Ashcroft's gospel, that's The Shadow's. That's why no one ever caught any of his men or associates to question or torture... or hang... with the solitary exception of Bernheim. He, unfortunately, got me," and for a moment Nicky thought of what he'd done in the aftermath of Waterloo, searching for him until he literally dropped from sheer exhaustion, according to Jack, and then went haring off to get Benjy. Francis Granville never gave up on anyone he cared about.

Ashcroft looked at the three men, sighing in relief to see them safe. "About time," he tutted. "What have you been doing? You're worse than gossiping washerwomen."

"Flower sellers, actually," grinned Nicky, but Ashcroft simply ignored him.

"Catching up on events," sighed Francis. "I owe you my life, Miles. Thank you seems somewhat inadequate."

"We're not out of this mess yet," Ashcroft tutted again, "but I've been listening out. I'm not sure, but I may have heard the sound of another carriage. Oh, and the baby has obviously woken up. I swear I can hear it bawling, poor little mite, I hope to God he's all right. I had a frightful suspicion they might have fed him to the lions already, but I didn't like to mention it earlier. I don't know why they didn't actually, why just that poor nursemaid?"

"Dear God, don't say that," gasped Francis, horrified at the thought. "It would destroy Elise and Eddie. Who could ever recover from watching their child being eaten alive? Watching Daisy turned my stomach as it was," he rasped. "I hate to say it, but maybe he was just too small to make an exhibition of, or maybe Bernheim was going to do it in a while to make us talk, except we told him what he wanted to know straight away. He could have every penny as far as I'm concerned, not that I trusted him not to kill us anyway, but you're here now, thank the Lord."

"Mmmm, you're probably right. It's all the most terrible business I've ever come across. But we have to resolve this and I'm still not sure how. I don't know what Jack and Alfie are up to, other than creating a diversion so you could get to these two," Ashcroft looked at Ricky. "Clever boys, those. Jack's idea, I dare say, and to get rid of some of the light, but Bernheim has to make a move and I don't like it. However, he doesn't know we're out of ammunition so he's pinned down for the moment and we've thwarted his plans. Can one of you creep out and go back and see if it was the carriage, or maybe head for the farmhouse and see if there are any weapons there? But be careful, for God's sake, I've no idea who has got out and might be prowling around or if there are any more still in the farmhouse. Mind you, any of those thugs with any sense, if they could get outside, would have made off."

"I'll go," whispered Nicky, "give me your knife, someone. I might not be able to take one of them on, but they'll be dead before they come at me. It only takes one hand to throw a knife."

"No, I'll go. We've no idea who's out there," whispered Francis, "and I'm a better man with a knife than you, believe me."

"Another skill I didn't know about, throwing knives around?" Ricky asked facetiously. "Quite the ducal pirate, Granny."

"Be quiet, You Facetious Arse. Right, I'm off. Er, Miles, where exactly are we?" Francis suddenly realised he had no idea.

"West of Richmond, over the river and then slightly north, on a deserted, semi-derelict farm in the middle of nowhere. We're in a large old barn building, rather strange, much bigger than usual, can't make out what the hell it was used for unless he's extended a bit of it. Can't really tell in the darkness, but it suits Bernheim's purpose, obviously. The farmhouse is to the left as you come up the drive, the entry lane is through the rotten gates across the yard. I should imagine they'll leave the coach down the lane and creep up here if they've any sense…"

"Richmond?" Nicky gaped. "Bloody hell, I thought we were in London."

"Well, there you go. Broke the record getting here across country, told you we rode hell for leather."

"Well, bugger me!"

"You've been associating with Mr Flowers too much," smirked Ricky. "Go on, Granny, hurry up, I'm not happy with all this delay. Something is going to happen shortly, I'm sure of it, and we've only got one rapier, one stiletto and Miles' dagger between us. That's not good odds whichever way you look at it."

"Keep your dagger, Miles, I can manage without it. I'll be back as quick as I can, I do my best work in the shadows, as my name suggests," and with those whispered words and a wink, Francis crouched as low as he could and backed slowly out of the barn.

Chapter Eight

Francis crept out the barn and stood up, flush to the wall and looked around, getting his bearings. The moon was drifting in and out behind clouds and it was eerily still, apart from the snuffling and growling of the lions inside as they feasted on one of their former number. He stared at the farm buildings and fields in the distance; like Nicky, he was amazed to find himself out in the countryside.

To his right, there was a soft glow from one of the downstairs windows of the farmhouse but no sound of movement within. Ahead of him, across the farmyard, he could see the entrance with the old broken gates hanging open and dilapidated.

He peered to his left but all he could make out were a cluster of ramshackle, ruined buildings. He listened hard and he, too, thought he could make out the whimpering of a baby somewhere, far over to the back of the farm sheds and barns. Tempted to go and see to the child, he realised he could do nothing for it, so prayed it was all right and would cry itself to sleep again.

He stood for a while but could hear nothing, so he decided to take a chance. He waited for a cloud to scud across the moon then, crouching low, every sense on the alert and feeling naked without a weapon, he ran as fast as he could over to the gates and called out softly, "Browning? Carstairs?"

He listened, but there was no reply. Nothing moved. He called out again, rustling the bush he was sheltering behind, but still nothing. He decided to investigate further down the lane but there was no sign of anyone. In despair, he turned around and started to make his way back to the farm buildings, wondering what it was that Ashcroft had heard.

Back inside the broken farm gates, Francis paused two things on his mind. One was their lack of weapons inside the barn, and the second was the noise that Ashcroft had heard. He didn't dismiss it as fancy at all, he knew Ashcroft better, and he believed the answer to both his queries lay in the farmhouse. As yet another cloud passed over the moon, Francis crouched down and made his silent way over towards his target.

It was a medium-size, dark building, looking like a typical farmhouse, and from the front, the solitary light shone through a downstairs window. He approached the property from the side and peered in through more dirty windows but all seemed still inside. He crept around the house towards the rear and his intuition was rewarded. Ashcroft had been right, a wagon and a pair of horses stood under the spreading branches of a large tree and a soft light could be seen shining through a window on the ground floor at the back of the house. A grim expression on his face, Francis crouched low and stealthily made his way towards the window and stood upright, tight to the wall when he reached it, trying to see in without being seen from the interior. He could make out the sound of voices but from his position could only see part of the room; it looked like some sort of kitchen. He ducked under the window and peered in from the other side, his ears straining to hear what the men inside were discussing.

They were having something to eat and drink and he could see a couple of pistols lying on the table next to some tankards, and platters with the remains of some bread and cheese. As he listened to their voices, his expression went dark. The four men had been tasked with taking Terrie and Lizzie, but from what he could make out, their plans had been thwarted by too many old biddies unexpectedly accompanying his mother-in-law in her large comfortable carriage on her visit to Cat's godmother, with a coachman and accompanying footmen up top to help the elderly ladies in and out and mind the little girls. The same thing had happened on their return, and apparently, his house in Berkeley Square had been surrounded by soldiers. All the old ladies had disappeared inside with the little girls and not reappeared thereafter. The four men had hung around but had given up and returned to Richmond, dreading having to tell their employer they'd failed in their mission and dismayed and concerned by the unexpected presence of the military. For a long, agonising moment, terrible images of the two little girls being thrown into the lions' cage after the maid filled Francis's mind; yet again he gave thanks to fate and Ashcroft's efficiency.

Francis was a brave man, but he wasn't a foolish one, nor the risk-taker he'd been in his nefarious youth. At his time of life, there was no way he was going to take on four armed and frustrated, villainous-looking men, unarmed as he was, but he knew he had to deal with them and get their much-needed weapons. His adventure in the forest outside Valenciennes was still vivid in his mind, a reminder of his age, capability and vulnerability. As he stood and thought for a while, rubbing the scar on his upper arm, his eyes turned to the tree and he looked upwards. The spreading branches reached near some of the upper storey windows and he wondered if any of them would take his weight.

Francis hadn't climbed a tree since his youth and as he stood at the bottom and contemplated it, for a moment his mind rolled back. He'd climbed masts and rigging countless times in his smuggling and pirate days, with plenty of footholds, but not trees, and he vaguely thought the last time was when he'd climbed up after Cat when they'd broken into the old de Mornay mansion to retrieve Cat's family treasures, what was left of them, before they'd rescued the family from Rouen Fortress. A brief grin lit his handsome face as he recalled the slender figure in the skin-tight boy's breeches she'd been wearing as she shimmied up the tree above him, her pert buttocks inches from his face. He still found her as enticing now as he had then, and as he thought of Bernheim cutting into her lovely creamy neck a while before, determination stole over his features and he focussed his mind.

He could see no way to reach the lowest branches but then he looked at the wagon and with a satisfied gleam in his eyes he carefully climbed onto the back and launched himself upward. He didn't make it the first time but with an enormous effort, cursing himself under his breath, he did on the third attempt and hauled himself up into the branches, panting and peering downward, hoping desperately he hadn't been heard by the men inside. For a worrying moment he saw one come to peer out the window, but obviously assuming it was one of the horses shifting about, the man turned back to the inside with a shrug.

Upward Francis clambered until he could see a bedroom window at the end of what he hoped was a long, and strong, leafy branch. He sprawled out and slithered along it, praying it would take his weight. For a terrifying handful of seconds it creaked and bent, but held, just as he held his breath, and he reached out to the rotting window frame. The window was slightly ajar to let in the spring air and it didn't take much effort to haul it open. With a wriggle, Francis slipped through and quietly dropped into the room, panting further with the effort of his climb. With a wry smile he told himself he needed to lose some weight and stop nibbling on the creamy buns, biscuits and treats the cook was so fond of leaving on his tea tray for Bubbles; less of that and more of the frequent energetic fencing practice with Captain Carnie in his studio. The man was several years older than him but still slim as a rake.

The moon had come out again and Francis looked around the room he found himself in, sniffing for a few seconds. The remnants of an exotic, cloying gentleman's cologne hung on the air and there were travelling trunks and bags against one wall and he realised this was probably Bernheim's bedroom. Wondering if he'd find a weapon there, he went over to the dresser and lit a candle and hurriedly opened the armoire and the dresser drawers, tossing expensive clothes and accessories aside in his search. Out of luck, he turned to the cases and bags. They also proved fruitless and then he turned to a large trunk, hoping it might contain at least a rapier, but unlike the others, this one was locked.

Francis went and rummaged amongst Bernheim's toiletries and found a small pair of nail scissors and a file and after some fiddling, the lock clicked open. As he raised the lid he gasped softly. The trunk contained a selection of shackles and light chains, ropes, whips and various other implements of extreme perverted, sadistic torture and pleasure. Francis knew what he was looking at, not unfamiliar with the depravity that occupied a select few members of polite society, even if he personally found it not to his taste. He and Cat had played their own amusing little games over the years from time to time, but never ever anything that caused pain or was remotely near the level he was looking at. He and Cat laughed while they pleasured each other, shackles and whips were another game entirely and he grimaced in disgust. He picked up a thick, multi-thonged whip, examining the narrow ends and thong tips which would cut through skin like butter when used by an expert, and briefly he remembered Nicky telling him how he'd been brutally whipped by Bernheim while he was held in Nice and how the man had done the same to a couple of young prostitutes he'd killed in Spain in the throes of his perverted lust. He shuddered and wondered if the man wanted to use any of the items in the chest on Bella? He'd heard the cruel threat in his voice as he'd spoken to her in the barn, and knew she'd already had a terrible time with him in her efforts to find out where Nicky was, so she and Jack could rescue him. No wonder the latter was so obsessed with killing him. Well, there were now two of them, and Francis knew that either he or Nicky would finally do away with the man before the night was out, or he wasn't The Shadow, and a vengeful gleam filled his narrowed, glittering blue eyes. Thirty years previously it had made other pirates quail as they'd faced him. He threw the sadistic whip back in the case but picked up a single, long, snake-like smaller one, one like he'd used on his ship on occasion to maintain order amongst his one-time pirate crew, the only discipline some of them understood. He knew how to utilise it to best effect. His family and friends would have been appalled if they'd seen him wield it, but they would never, ever, know about that short time in his life. It was a closed book, a temporary aberration around the time his father had died and he'd inherited the title and everything that went with it. Along with the whip, he took a small, sharp dagger and a razor-sharp rapier, all he could find in the trunk by way of practical weaponry, then he stole out the room, intended murder on his face. The nefarious, ruthless and deadly Shadow was on his game once more.

It was an enormous risk, the risk outweighing his sense again, but excitement pounded through Francis's veins, just as it had the previous summer when he'd faced down the soldiers in the forest, and he exploded into the little kitchen and cracked the whip, scattering the four men sitting at the table at the same time as the small knife embedded itself into the chest of one, and he dropped like a stone. The long whip snaked around the neck of a second and he gurgled as he tugged uselessly at its strangling grip. The surprise stunned the men and gave Francis a chance to grab one of the pistols off the table and cock it, pointing it at the other two. He didn't want to shoot either, needing to keep the weapons for use in the barn, as well as not alerting the occupants of it. The less Bernheim knew about what was going on outside, the better, Francis had decided. He pulled hard on the whip and the strangled man went blue, then limp and finally collapsed on the floor.

"Good evening, Gentlemen," he snarled. "You'd have been better served never to come back here, You Miserable Scum. If you'd laid a single hand on my little daughter or her cousin, I'd have strung you up from the nearest tree myself, alive, by the balls, and let you dangle, and don't think I wouldn't have enjoyed watching you scream. Now, put down your weapons, here, on the table where I can see them."

"Who're you?" gasped one of the men, a vicious-looking thug who stunk of the gutters, and he held up a pair of shaking hands.

"Me? I'm you're worst nightmare, but allow me to introduce myself. I am The Shadow, the man your master has been endeavouring to capture for his own venal and malicious ends, but he made a mistake in thinking he could ever better me and mine, and it was a gross mistake on your part to ever be inveigled to work for him."

"You're The Shadder? But 'e took yous in th' park...?" the man looked astonished. "Wot yer doin' 'ere?"

"Do I look like I've been taken? Now, I won't tell you again, your weapons, on the table." Francis nodded towards the table. "Very slowly. I won't miss from here, as I'm sure you can believe. Not that I miss from anywhere."

The two thugs looked at each other and then back at Francis. "There's two o'us, an' one o' yous. Yer'll be a dead man one way or t'other."

So, they didn't frighten easily. He was losing his touch, thought Francis. "So will one of you be. Are you going to risk it?"

"'Oo's Th' Shadder anyways, neva 'eard of yer afore nah?"

"You wouldn't want to know the details, but, to give you a general idea, amongst other things, for a time back in the eighties, The Shadow was one of the most ruthless pirates and smugglers who operated along the Channel, down through the Bay of Biscay and here and there further afield. Actually, for a very short while, I had a bit of a, let's call it a 'turn', and I'd rather like to think until I got over it, I was THE most ruthless. I actually frightened myself sometimes," Francis said facetiously.

"Yer crazy, but yer don't frighten us," and as one, the duo pulled out their pistols and raised them in the air, except they never got their arms to shoulder height or extension. The whip cracked again and a pistol shot rang out. Francis dived for the second pistol on the table and shot the second thug as he went for the knife in his belt. He fell to the floor, stone dead.

It wasn't what he wanted, but there'd been no other way. Having searched the bodies of the four dead men, Francis went on a hurried search of the rest of the farmhouse for more weapons or ammunition, all the time keeping his eyes and ears open, hoping more of Bernheim's men wouldn't come back to see what had caused the disturbance, but he now knew time was of the essence as he wasn't sure what the people in the barn would do. In the distance, he heard the sounds of more shots and abandoning his search, he raced back to the barn.

Chapter Nine

I nside the barn, the distant sounds of shooting hadn't been missed by those inside. Ashcroft had no idea who had caused it or where Francis was, but he didn't care, he needed to bluff to keep Bernheim away from the four remaining captives as the impasse couldn't continue. "You heard that, Bernheim?" his cold voice rasped across the silent interior of the barn, the lions now sitting quietly on the floor of their cage, still chewing through the remains of the dead one and a couple of poor Daisy's bones. "I told you the farm was surrounded and there were reinforcements outside; and the rest of you rats, are you going to wait around for your leader to kill you or give yourselves up and know you'll merely be transported and not hanged; for if you're taken with him, you will hang for certain, I can promise you that."

Silence hung over the barn and Ashcroft looked at Ricky, the hairs on his neck quivering, he just knew something was about to happen.

"I don't like this, Miles," whispered Ricky. "Where the hell is Francis or the cavalry? And what were those shots all about?"

"How the hell do I damn know," muttered Ashcroft in obvious frustration. "Those poor women out there, they must be terrified, not knowing what the hell is going on."

"They're strong-willed and strong-minded, they'll manage. I've known Marie-Catherine Granville since Francis married her," for a moment Ricky recalled the one time he'd seriously kissed the tantalising Frenchwoman and she'd airily informed him he wasn't a patch on her husband, not that she realised how close a friend he was of Francis. Talk about deflated ego, and he momentarily smiled at the memory before the smile turned to a hard look at Ashcroft. "I was his Best Man y'know, then the first time I went to dinner with them after she'd had their first set of twins and she was back to her normal size, she challenged me to a duel in their bloody garden; put on a pair of tight men's breeches and damn near perforated my testicles; never experienced anything like it. No man is going to get the better of that woman, take it from me," Ricky rasped. "I've also watched Bella grow up, and although she isn't up there with her aunt on the fighting front, even if she is a dead shot, she's no delicate flower to keep a handful like Nicky in order, and she's got a brain on her, so hopefully she'll engage it and won't panic; she'll know we'll come to get her as soon as we can."

"Damn right we will," Ashcroft rasped. "Do you think the other two are all right?"

"I can't see over there but I'm sure Eddie will have spoken to Elise, he seemed to topple over her way in all the chaos, but Benjy and Fred are over there so they'll get to them as soon as they can. What worries me is I've no idea how many of Bernheim's men there are left."

Nicky had crept over to where Francis had disappeared through the barn door and was looking out for any sign of him, or anyone going after him, and he'd watched him return from the farm gate and creep over to the farmhouse and disappear round the back, and then he'd heard shots and he was waiting, on tenterhooks, to see him come out alive. He crept back to update Ricky and Ashcroft, intent on going to see if Francis was all right.

"He's fine, he's in the farmhouse, he must have found more men in th…"

Suddenly, a malicious cry rent the air as Bernheim screamed to his men, "Kill them! Kill them all!" and as a shot rent the air all hell broke loose as men's heads popped up from behind crates and straw bales and suddenly Jack and Alfie, then Benjy and Fred sprang to help the four people still lying on the ground, tied to their chairs.

Ricky tore across the barn, his rapier drawn and ready, yelling at Bernheim, "Come and face me, You Bastard; where are you, You Cowardly Piece of French Horseshit?" completely oblivious as more pistols fired, the lions starting roaring, someone screamed and there was the sound of a whip cracking as yet another of the wall lanterns shattered and the candle went out.

Nicky was behind him, heading towards Bella when suddenly the giant Sikh appeared, apparently heading in the same direction, brandishing a large, curved sword. Nicky didn't stop to think, he threw Miles' dagger at Ajeet and watched as it buried itself in the man's shoulder. The Sikh had moved surprisingly swiftly for such a big man or it would have been in his chest… but to Nicky's horrified disbelief, the man simply stared down at it as if it was an annoying wasp sting and merely pulled the knife out, dripping with blood, and turned on Nicky with a feral snarl.

Fortunately for him, Francis had arrived. He thrust a brace of loaded pistols at Ashcroft, "These are all I had time to find, so they need to count. Are you a good enough shot, Miles?" he panted.

"Are you The Shadow?" Ascroft replied sarcastically. "We HAVE to prevail. No reinforcements as yet I take it?"

"No. Nothing that I… oh FUCKKKK," Francis quickly took in the scene of Ricky taunting Bernheim to appear and then the Sikh avoiding Nicky's dagger. He turned and headed to his rescue, yelling at Ashcroft to go get his wife and Bella.

"Leave him to me," Francis yelled at Nicky as he thrust one of the daggers he'd brought with him into Nicky's hand and he pushed him out the way of the Sikh's big, curved sword and parried it with his rapier, "go help Miles and the others…and mind your arm!"

Nicky would have made a facetious reply but didn't want to distract Francis as he faced the Sikh who was slashing at him with his big sword and brandishing the dripping dagger he'd just pulled out of his shoulder. The man looked mean and even towered over Francis, which was something few people did, tall as he was. Only Nicky came near him and even Francis' four sons didn't match their father in height and physique. Momentarily, Nicky thought of the picture of Francis's mysterious grandfather, the imposing Scottish aristocrat who'd loved and left the Dowager, and he reflected on how similar the pair of them looked and he wondered what had happened to the man, if he had a family in America, and if his heirs looked like Francis. He sighed to himself for a brief second, wondering at how strange it was in such fraught moments, odd reflections popped into one's brain. But the thought came and went in seconds as Nicky focussed himself on the matter in hand and looked over to where Cat and Bella were lying on the floor.

Cat was nearer to him and Nicky watched as Bernheim finally appeared out of the darkness at the back of the barn, rapier in hand, and, with a malevolent taunt at Ricky, finally engaged with him and started to fight. Nicky had known Richard Ambrose since he'd been a child, knew he and Francis were always trying to get one over each other and Ricky was a feared and fearless swordsman, easily Francis's equal, and better than Nicky, and he had killed plenty of men in duels over the years. But one look at Bernheim and Nicky knew Richard Ambrose had met his match. Apart from being younger than Ricky, Bernheim was extremely agile and his skill with a rapier was obvious. Nicky could see it immediately and he feared for Ricky, knowing how ruthless and underhand the Frenchman was.

Back and forth Francis and Ricky slashed against their opponents, ducked, thrust and parried, fighting for their lives and those of their loved ones, and every time Nicky was going to creep out across the floor towards Cat, one or other of the men got in his way and he feared to distract either Francis or Ricky from their concentration.

On the other side of the barn, more desperate fighting was going on, and the situation was fraught. Ashcroft had been right in his assessment of the numbers still alive to be dealt with. Jack was trying to fight two men with his dagger, snarling and slashing at them. He'd already killed one and was fighting like a man possessed. Fred had taken a ball near his shoulder, one eye was half closed and his face was bruised and swollen, as was the rest of his battered body, but he was still trying desperately to finally release Eddie and Elise, something he and Benjy had been endeavouring to do but kept having to retreat and take cover for fear of being shot at.

Alfie was grappling with the Arab with a small truncheon and a knife he'd picked up from a dead body on the floor, but he was no fighter like Jack and was barely able to defend himself. Benjy had stabbed one man with his scissors and was now wrestling with another who'd been shot in the leg, the vicious, sharp scissors now open wide and menacing, as lethal as any narrow dagger. Benjy had a long cut down his cheek and several on his arms and chest, but he was fighting with a wiry strength and determination he never knew he possessed, the long years at sea watching other men fight had taught him a lot.

Finally, Eddie felt his wrists come free as Fred fell back on the floor, gasping with the effort. "Good God, Man, you're done in," panted Eddie. "Quick, give me your knife and I'll help Elise; you take cover back behind those crates and take care of yourself," and without a word, he grabbed Fred's dagger and turned to help his wife. He made short work of the ropes and Elise fell into his arms with a sobbing cry.

"Oh God, Elise," gasped Eddie as he hugged her tightly to his chest and kissed her frantically, the pain of being on his knees forgotten in his desperation to release her. "I don't know what I would have done if they'd harmed you, I couldn't have borne it."

"Oh Eddie, you're so brave, saying you were The Shadow," sobbed Elise. "Daisy, that poor girl, and what have they done with my baby? I HAVE to find him, my precious little Harry," she wept forlornly.

"We'll find him, My Love. I'm sure I heard some crying a while back, somewhere outside. It had to be him... but I was damned if I was going to sit here and let them kill Francis and m'sister and Nicky. I just KNEW help had to be on the way, it was simply a case of buying time."

"You're still so brave; oh Eddie, I was SO frightened."

"You didn't sound it, My Love. You were very brave too, I'm beyond proud of you. Oh God, Elise, I love you so much, I couldn't have coped with it if they'd thrown you in that cage as well. I swear it would have destroyed me," he gripped her arms tightly and looked down into her eyes.

"Eddie?" Elise stared at her husband, stunned at his words. "You love me? Do you really? I... I... I thought you'd never love any woman after Carlotta... I... I..."

"I do love you, Elise; I care more than you could possibly know, but now isn't the time. Come, we need to get you out of here and find our son," and without any further ado, Eddie awkwardly hauled himself to his feet, hanging on to Elise for support until he was upright, and they hurried over to the gap in the rotten timber walls through which Benjy and Fred had got into the barn. He turned to Fred, now sitting behind a crate, "Will you be all right for a few moments? I'll help my wife out as we have to find our baby son, but I'll pick up a weapon somewhere and come back for you as quickly as I can. Can you hang on?"

Fred just nodded mutely and indicated with a limp hand for them to go. Eddie pushed another nearby crate in front of him in an effort to give him more protection and then awkwardly forced his way out into the night air, following Elise, stunned to discover they appeared to be in the countryside on what looked like an old farm. "We must find Harry and I need to find a weapon. It's critical in there, and there's no cavalry here from the looks of it. They need help back there, I can't abandon them," Eddie muttered, half to himself as he and Elise started to frantically hurry around in the dark, trying to follow the soft whimpering sounds both had heard.

Over the other side, the two duels ebbed and flowed and finally, an opening presented itself so Nicky half slithered, half crawled across the floor until he got to Cat and he blanched at the blood seeping down her throat and chest from under the sack.

He tugged it off and looked down into the big, tawny green cat's eyes, momentarily full of fear until they recognised the man above her and the years rolled back. "Hello, Auntie, my turn this time except I'm not a nun," and he bent and kissed her cheek briefly, stroking her hair back off her face lovingly. He'd never forget how she'd nearly lost her life in her efforts to save his in Rouen Fortress; he owed her his life and so much more. "Don't move when I get you free, it's too dangerous. Just wait, then I'll help you over to safety... there's a lot of them."

"*Mon Dieu*, Nicky," Cat spoke in French automatically, "I thought someone would never come. But where's Francis, is he all right?" it was her first thought and her voice was fraught with fear for him.

"He's fine, Ricky got to us first." He explained briefly in whispers what he knew of their situation as he tackled the ropes binding her with the knife Francis had hastily given him. As she struggled free, Nicky tore his cravat off and wrapped it around Cat's neck to stop the bleeding, not sure if she realised what Bernheim had actually done to her, and the pair of them momentarily sat, Cat cuddled protectively in Nicky's good arm, looking around at what was going on.

Not far behind him, Nicky could see Ashcroft, who had been on his way over to follow him to get to the two women, but he was also watching the two epic duels with deep concern, pistol cocked at the ready. Over the other side of the barn, a battle was raging between Bernheim's men and Jack, Alfie, Fred and Benjy... and by the look of things they'd released Eddie and he was endeavouring to do the same to Elise. In the midst of it all lay Bella, inert, and Nicky's heart thudded as he looked across at her, not knowing if she was dead or alive. Cat followed his eyes as she shovelled up her petticoats in a very unlady-like manner to grope around and find her knife. "Aha! They didn't find this!" She crowed as she brandished her stiletto, "We must try and help Bella, Nicky. That bastard, *Mon Dieu*, I thought he was going to slit my throat."

"I couldn't see what he was doing but I could hear Francis. I've never known such fear in his voice; so help me God, I'm going to kill Bernheim if Ricky doesn't do the job for me." Nicky snarled.

"He's a very good swordsman," Cat knew what she was talking about as they watched the desperate fight. "Oh God, Nicky, I hope Ricky can deal with him."

"Ashcroft is behind me, he's watching Bernheim like a hawk, he knows he's not to be trusted. You wait here, I'm going for Bella. Try and get back to Miles, he'll look after you... and DON'T do anything stupid, Cat," he admonished with a knowing look, waggling a finger at her.

"Don't you start telling me what to do, You Useless Oaf, or I'll box your ears," tutted Cat, "just like my other sons."

"At the risk of being exceptionally ungentlemanly, you can spank my bare arse if we get out of here, not that that would be the first time," he winked at Cat, "but you're fifty, not twenty-five any more, so for once in your life, do what I tell you, and BE CAREFUL!"

"You Disgraceful Brat, I'll do more than that. Are you inferring I'm old and past it? I've never, ever, done what anyone tells me, and that includes Francis. ESPECIALLY my dear husband, so I'm certainly not going to take any notice of YOU! So you go off and get Bella and leave me to look after myself," Cat huffed and tutted, waving her stiletto at him, "and MIND YOUR ARM!" The loud whisper burned his ear. She'd noticed how he was holding it to his chest, despite the sling, recognising Francis's monogram at the end of the length of material, and she surmised he'd hurt it though she knew he'd never admit it in their current circumstances.

"Oh Lord, now I know where Bella gets it from; heaven preserve Francis and I from the pair of you." Nicky rolled his eyes knowing Cat would take no notice of him whatsoever, and he simply prayed she didn't do anything rash. "Look, Cat, whatever you do, either carefully creep back to Miles and safety, or just keep still; whatever you do, DON'T distract Francis or Ricky, they're up against it and no mistake; not that you can't see that for yourself… but think before you do anything, least of all move, and watch MY back if you want to be useful. I've no idea who's over in the middle…" and with that, he planted another quick kiss on Cat's cheek and turned to survey the distance between where he was and his wife.

Chapter Ten

Back on the other side of the vast barn, several life or death struggles were going on. Jack had killed his second man and the third was fighting for his life against the crazed young aristocrat he thought he was battling, not knowing he was engaging with one of his own and stunned the youth could fight with a knife as he was doing. Benjy had done for the man with the wounded leg having slashed his jugular vein with the razor scissors. As he sank to the ground with blood spurting from his throat, Benjy turned to the first man he'd felled who was trying to get up, knife in hand, and ruthlessly thrust the long scissors into the man's heart. The servants at the Firle residences would never have believed it if they'd seen it, nor would his customers. The only man who wouldn't have been surprised was Francis, and as Benjy reeled back against the barn wall, gasping for breath and looking down at his blood-spattered clothes and hands, his grim expression was a million miles from that of the camp valet and tailor everyone was familiar with. As he wiped his hands and scissors on his shirt, he turned quickly as he heard moans coming from behind a couple of large crates and hurried over to where Fred was coughing up blood. He sank to his knees to do what he could for the man who was obviously in a bad way.

Alfie was struggling. He was now backed up against the wall facing what he thought was a crazed heathen. He crossed himself and that was like waving a red rag at a bull. The Arab, Abdul, took on a satanic gleam in his eyes and moved in for the kill, wailing in Arabic, *"In'a'al mayteen ehlak"*…"damn your dead, death to all infidels", as he screeched out a stream of profanities Alfie had no understanding of and he raised his curved dagger in the air. Jack saw him out the corner of his eye, but he wasn't quick enough. With an almighty effort, he plunged his dagger into the neck of his opponent and tore over to try and save his friend. But he was too late. The long, sharp khanjar slashed through the air and despite trying to throw himself out the way, it tore across Alfie's abdomen and he sank to the floor, horror and fright on his face, his hands trying to stop the blood pouring out his stomach.

"Nooooooo… BENJYYYYY!" Jack screamed as he turned on Abdul. "Elp 'im, fer th' luv o'God!" he yelled as Benjy's head appeared over the crate where he was tending Fred, and as Benjy sidled round the wall towards Alfie, keeping his distance from the now manic looking Arab, Jack turned to face the man, a frightening expression on his face. "Yer a dead man," he grated. "Yer won't cut ME open, but I's gonna split yer wide, an' pull out yer black 'eart an' vitals, or me name's not Jack Vallance."

Abdul thought he was fighting another worthless English Christian pig, as he taunted Jack in his own language, brandishing his bloodied weapon, but he soon realised Jack was no pushover and the pair circled each other warily.

Benjy bent down over the young groom, like Jack, his cultivated vowels temporarily on the missing list. "'Ang in there, Alf," he crooned as he rapidly cut Alfie's shirt off him and into pieces and stuffed them in the youth's hands, "Keep this over th' wound, press 'ard an' bend over, try an' stop th' blood. Jes' 'ang on; I'm goin' fer me bag," and as if the devil was at his heels, he shot to his feet and tore out through the barn wall, running to where he'd left his saddlebag in the bushes by the gate, praying he could save both men's lives but in despair at their injuries. Eddie and Elise had located the baby in the carriage round the back of the farm buildings and Eddie had found a brace of pistols on the driver's seat. Abandoning Elise to do what she could for the squalling baby, relieved beyond measure they'd found him relatively unharmed, if distressed and hungry, he half limped, half ran back towards the barn, bumping into Benjy as he reached the entry he'd squeezed out through.

"No time fer that, Eddie," Benjy rasped, "you gotta 'elp me. Fred an' Alf's 'urt bad, I can't tend 'em bowf."

"Whaaaat?" Eddie gasped. "I'm no surgeon, for God's sake," and his eyes widened apprehensively.

"Well, yous gotta be. Yous seen me deal wiv Francis an' Nicky, yer more cap'ble than most men so git to it. Yous deal wiv Fred an' I'll do me best wiv young Alf; 'is guts is spillin' all ovah th' barn floor an' e's bleedin' like a stuck pig; where's Elise, cud do wiv 'er an' all?"

"God almighty! But... but I've only watched, I don't know if I can..." Eddie looked shocked, "and Elise is back in the coach with Harry..."

Benjy swore uncouthly. "No time ter go git 'er then, an' she'll be frettin' wiv th' babe anyways. 'Sides, I didn't know nuffin' when I first started, so jes' git on wiv it. Use yer 'ead, no time fer th' collywobbles. Fred'll be dead wivin th' 'our if yer don't, 'e might die anyways, but yous gotta try an' save 'im. E's gotta ball in 'is chest so yer gotta git it out damn quick, an' e's been beaten bad; e's bleedin' like a stuck pig too, jes' like young Alfie. That fuckin' 'eathen 'as split 'im open from 'ere ter 'ere," Benjy drew his finger laterally across his stomach, "an' if it weren't fer Fred, we'd neva 'ave found all of yous, so git on wiv it, sharpish!"

"Oh, *Mon Dieu*," Eddie went grey then pulled himself together, bracing his shoulders and taking a deep breath. "Right, I'm with you. I'll do my best, Benjy; after you," and with a determined expression on his face he followed Benjy back into the barn, grimacing in apprehension as he saw the blood now trickling out of Fred's mouth and from the wound in his upper chest, near his shoulder.

With a painful groan, Eddie awkwardly sank to his knees again, and held out his hands as Benjy virtually threw some brandy over them. Then, with some instruments Benjy hurriedly handed to him, pointing out what he needed to do, he set to with a will, praying to God he didn't kill the man in the process.

Benjy returned to a semi-conscious Alfie and put a finger to his neck as he rummaged in his bag for what he needed. The pulse was faint but still there. "'Ang on, Lad, I's gonna try an' sew yer back up..." and he held a small bottle of laudanum to his lips, knowing he'd have to start before it took effect. "This is gonna 'urt but bear wivs me, 'cos if I don't do this, yer a gonner..." and he doused his hands in brandy as well, picked up his needle and thread and set to, muttering a prayer to God to kill all heathens, trying not to watch what was going on with Jack and the Arab, and the life-or-death battles raging on the other side of the barn.

As he tended the young groom, surrounded by fighting, not to mention the occasional growls from the lions, a part of Benjy's mind went back to when he'd been forced to help out on the navy ship he'd been press-ganged onto. He'd learned surgery from the doctor he'd been made to assist onboard, as fierce sea battles raged over their heads and men needed shrapnel and shards of timber pulled out of grisly wounds, terrible burns cleaned, and shattered and severed limbs dealt with. It had been a baptism of fire, but he'd learned his lessons well... until he'd been taken prisoner by a pirate ship that was running as a slaver and it had overrun and sunk his navy vessel, which was limping towards a safe harbour having been crippled in another battle. The Shadow, having engaged with and run alongside the pirate ship, thinking to trade brandy and other goods, had discovered its wretched, half-starved human cargo, chained up and crammed worse than rats below decks with little air or water. Having no truck with that trade, The Shadow had summarily sunk it with its barbaric captain and brutal crew, releasing and taking the desperate and sick captives from the hold onto his own ship first, as well as its booty. Having rescued him from the even worse hell he'd found himself in on the slaver than on the navy ship, Benjy had been devoted to Francis ever since. He'd added to his surgical knowledge by treating those of The Shadow's crew who'd got injured, including their captain now and again, and picking up tips and tricks at first hand from all sorts of disparate sources in the course of their adventures. His naval experience in particular, meant Benjy knew how to close his mind to what was going on around him and focus on trying to save Alfie's life, even if this was a totally different situation since most involved were close friends – a very different set of circumstances to life on a British Navy battleship.

Over the other side, Francis was in trouble. His slender rapier was meant for duelling or fencing, not dealing with the heavy curved sword the Sikh was wielding, and he'd had his work cut out defending himself and trying to get past the Sikh's guard. His body and head ached from the beating he'd taken in the park, but it was like time rolling back to the sea battles he'd fought, and those with Revenue men and other pirates and smugglers decades previously, and his tremendous willpower, determination and no little skill forced him on. The willpower and strength of mind neither Edgar Bernheim nor the vicious Pierre Dupont had managed to break, and the skill that had made him one of the best swordsmen and duellists in London in his youth. However, the giant man was also a skilled fighter and light on his feet, in spite of his height and build, and Francis had taken several deep slashes to his arms and torso. Despite piercing Ajeet's body a couple of times, the man seemed completely unstoppable and Francis knew he was struggling.

He'd realised as he fought him that under the bushy beard, the man was in fact quite young, in his late twenties or early thirties, Francis decided, and his youth and strength were beginning to tell. As Cat watched her husband with her heart in her mouth, with an almighty downward slash, Ajeet broke Francis's rapier in two and he was left facing the giant with just a dagger and the Sikh advanced on him, a nasty smile on his face as he threw away the small knife he'd pulled from his shoulder. In its place, he tugged his kirpan from his belt that he'd retrieved from the floor as he and Bernheim had taken refuge at the back of the barn. It was too much for Cat and, just as Nicky feared she would, she threw caution to the wind. Brandishing her jewelled stiletto, the very weapon Francis had given her so many years before when she'd first escaped from France, and the one she'd loaned to Nicky when he was in the army, and had then ended up in Bernheim's back courtesy of Jack, she launched herself in front of Francis and snarled at the Sikh.

"You piece of Indian cow dung," she screeched at the astonished man as she crouched and glared at him, panting, green eyes on fire, tossing the wicked knife back and forth between her hands, Nicky's bloodstained cravat still wound around her throat, "I told someone a long time ago, this man is MY property and no one touches him, except ME! He's got that inscribed on his bracelet, in case he forgets as well. That someone was your master's father, and I, Marie-Catherine Granville, killed him, that's why he wants to feed me to the lions. But he's as misguided as his father was. No one is feeding ME to any furry beast... and another thing... I would give them terrible indigestion..." she sounded just like Francis, or Ricky, or even Nicky - three deadly jokers she cared for deeply and passionately.

"Get out of the way, Cat," Francis ordered, beyond angry at her intervention, terrified the Sikh would kill her and loving her for her bravery, "what the HELL are you playing at, You Idiot Woman?"

"Coming to your rescue, AGAIN, My Love. I seem to make a habit of it, and remind me to have words with you later, Francis Granville. How dare you call me an idiot woman?"

"Oh for God's sake... GET OUT OF THE DAMN WAY!"

"The HELL I will! I've just told Nicky, I don't take orders from him, or you, EVER!" and she briefly turned her head and poked her tongue out at him saucily, as if she was a girl of thirteen again and not a mature woman of fifty and a Duchess. "After all, aren't I The Shadow's wife? And what's more, your grandmother told me a long time ago not to take any nonsense from anyone, and I've followed her words of wisdom ever since, and that applies just as much to you as it does to these bastards... and if you don't apologise, I'll paddle your bare backside like I've just threatened to do to Nicky."

The Sikh looked between the man and woman he thought he now had at his mercy, slightly bemused at their conversation and *sang froid*, but totally dismissive of it, so then raised his sword and dagger, poised to strike. "I kill you first, you are nothing, just a woman," he spat condescendingly at Cat, "and then I will cut YOUR head off." His narrowed, black eyes moving to glitter at Francis.

Behind Francis and Cat, Ashcroft raised his pistol, as bemused as the Sikh, slightly aghast at her inappropriate conversation with her husband, but not totally surprised given the madness of the Granville family. The Duchess's prowess with a sword was legend amongst them, even if Ashcroft had never witnessed it personally, and he now knew the story of what had happened between her and Bernheim Senior was no fairy tale.

"Heaven help us," muttered Francis to himself, "here we go again." He looked at the Sikh, "You've just signed your death warrant..."

"What is that?" Ajeet slashed the air with his sword and kirpan and advanced on Cat, and most women would have run screaming from the terrifying sight of him bearing down on them. But not the redoubtable Duchess of Firle. With her own shriek, sounding like a demented Harpie, Cat crouched low, suddenly ducked to one side of and under the blade of the slashing sword and thrust her knife in the Indian's gut, tearing downward towards his genitals through his baggy trousers. The Sikh reared back in pain and shock as blood poured out of him and at the same time, Francis's knife sailed through the air and thudded into the centre of the Sikh's forehead. The man looked at the pair in astonishment for a couple of seconds as he tottered and then slowly sank to the floor, dead before he got there. Miles Ashcroft simply gaped at what he'd just watched and lowered his pistol.

Cat threw herself into Francis's arms and he hugged her tightly, more precious to him than his own life. She sobbed into his chest, "Oh God, Francis, not again, I can't bear it," she wept, distraught as the trauma of the day and night finally caught up with her and for a moment her head swam and she fought the urge to just give in and let blackness claim her. But she was made of stronger stuff and pulled herself together with an enormous effort, as she breathed in the essence that was her husband, her lover, and her whole life. Francis knew all her bravado hid a lot of deep emotions and slowly he backed away to safety to where Ashcroft was crouching, but at the same time, he finally took in the epic battle that was now going on between Bernheim and Ricky and his and then Cat's eyes followed where Ashcroft was watching…

Back over the other side of the barn, the drama was continuing. As Eddie and Benjy battled to save Alfie's and Fred's lives, Jack was battling for his. He'd not fought anyone like the Arab and it was taking all his skill to match the man as they tussled, wrestled and each tried to gain the upper hand. Jack had already fought and killed three men and he was exhausted, but his life was now dependent on him prevailing against Abdul and the zealous, maniacal expression of hatred on the man's face.

Ricky and Bernheim were battling to and fro near to where Bella lay and Jack and the Arab were on her other side, in their own monumental tussle. Nicky had watched Francis and Cat deal with the Sikh and he was now totally focussed on reaching Bella before something happened to her. That his bad arm felt like it was on fire was for nothing as he painstakingly crawled and slithered across the floor towards her. Finally, he reached where she was lying, pushed off the dead body that was half on top of her, and snatched off the sack. He looked down on her terrified face, covered in tears as she looked up at him with such love and relief, his heart nearly burst with emotion.

"Sooty… oh God, My Sooty…" he bent, hugged and kissed her frantically, overwhelmed with relief she was still alive. "When you weren't moving… I thought… I thought…" he could hardly string two words together.

"Nicky, oh Nicky, I knew you'd come, or Uncle Francis or Ashcroft. I just knew it, I had such faith in you all," she sobbed. "Set me free, hurry, pleeease, get me away from here."

Nicky frantically cut and sawed at the thick ropes, cursing the pain in his injured arm that left it with no strength, until he had Bella curled against him, shivering with relief, and he briefly explained what had been going on. "I've got to help Jack, that Arab is a deadly piece of work with a knife," he muttered. "Francis and Ashcroft have their eye on Bernheim and Ricky. I wish to God Miles would just shoot the bastard, I don't know why he's hesitating, Christ, I would if I had a pistol," his venomous words were full of hatred.

"It looks to me like Uncle Ricky wants to kill Bernheim himself, but one or other of them will do for him, I'm sure of it," Bella whispered.

"This is no time for the niceties," muttered Nicky in frustration and, as they watched, suddenly the tide of the two epic duels turned and everything seemed to happen at once.

Something Bernheim said to Ricky seemed to galvanise him, or he suddenly found the strength for a final monumental push against the man who wanted to kill his oldest friend and his family. He surged forward and had Bernheim on the back foot and Bernheim stumbled backwards over the body of one of his dead henchmen. Without thought, his free hand went to the inside of his jacket and came out with a small pistol and, just as Jack had unwittingly foretold, with a vicious smile he shot Ricky in the chest at close quarters. He didn't even stop to take in Ricky's shocked expression as he sank to the floor but leapt across to where Abdul and Jack were still fighting, clubbed Jack around the head and yelled at Abdul, "Leave him, he's not impor-tant, get that woman in the cage for the lions," and then he turned to lunge at Nicky with his rapier flashing towards his heart. Nicky threw himself out the way as Abdul tore a screaming Bella from the shelter of his one good arm and hauled her over to the cage door where five lions were now prowling around again. In all the chaos, instead of finishing Nicky off, Bernheim suddenly turned tail and disappeared.

As Ricky fell, Francis howled with distraught anguish; Cat screamed as the pair of them ran to Ricky's prostrate form. Of every-one, the cool and collected Ashcroft kept focussed and his eyes on Bernheim, and as the man disappeared into the gloom at the back of the barn, Ashcroft followed, pistol cocked. He had actually been about to take aim and shoot Bernheim, consigning ethical behaviour to the devil, when the man had tripped and everything had descended to chaos.

Bella was no match for the wiry strength of Abdul and despite kicking and screaming, he hauled her towards the cage, opened the door and thrust her inside as Nicky struggled to his feet, blood dripping down his good arm from where Bernheim's rapier had cut him deeply, staring in terror and disbelief as he turned towards the cage.

In the midst of all the drama, as Benjy and Eddie turned from their desperate efforts to save Alfie and Fred and watched in frozen dread as five lions eyed up a terrified Bella... Browning, Carstairs and the two grooms burst into the barn, brandishing their pistols.

Chapter Eleven

They didn't need Francis to yell, "KILL THE LIONS!" at them as he launched himself over towards where Cat had dropped her stiletto, picked it up and threw it with deadly accuracy at the Arab. It buried itself up to the hilt in his chest at the same time as the rapport of several pistols went off. Two more balls thudded into Abdul and the rest tore into the roaring and snarling lions.

Nicky didn't even stop to think, he ran over, pulled open the cage door and almost fell inside in his rush, intent on sacrificing himself if necessary to save Bella. She had crawled away from the cage door and was completely petrified, backed up against the wire walls, shaking with fright. "DON'T MOVE, DON'T EVEN TWITCH... KEEP COMPLETELY STILL," Nicky ordered, trying to speak calmly although his heart was in his mouth. "For once in your life, Sooty, do as I say, pleeease," he begged. "Keep your eyes on them, stare into THEIR eyes. Whatever you do, don't shut yours or look away..."

Long ago childhood conversations with the keepers at the Tower Menagerie, accompanied by the indulgent Dowager on one of their many visits, percolated back into his mind. "Nobody out there move," he called out as slowly, he crept around to where Bella was, putting himself between her and the confused beasts. There had been five left, three were obviously dead, one was down, injured and growling, but one remained on its feet, blood oozing from a wound in its side. He was a huge and otherwise magnificent specimen, bigger than the rest, with an enormous, thick, tawny mane and as he opened his mouth to throw back his head and roar at the intruders, everyone could see his large, sharp teeth, still with remnants of blood on them and round his massive jaws. The spectators in the barn watched in frozen, petrified silence. Cat had Ricky's head in her lap as she held a pad from her torn petticoats to his bloody chest, but she put a hand to her mouth to stop herself from screaming. Francis was crouching over Ricky, his hands in fists, for a rare moment in his life not knowing what to do. Jack was half lying on the floor, trying to get up, woozy-headed from the blow from the stock of Bernheim's pistol and beside himself at what he was watching; both Eddie and Benjy were white with fright, unable to tend their patients or do anything. Carstairs, Browning and the two grooms were riveted to where they stood, unsure what to do but completely horror-struck at the scene they were confronted with. Real lions were outside their comprehension. Francis looked around frantically for Ashcroft as he was the only one left with a primed pistol, but he seemed to have disappeared, obviously in search of Bernheim, and he swore under his breath.

No one spoke or moved an inch as, step by step, Nicky inched closer to Bella. "Nicky... oh Nicky..." she whimpered. "What are you doing... save yourself, get out of here."

"Not without you, My Precious. Be brave, just do what I tell you," he whispered as he himself now stared deep into the black and golden eyes of the big, ferocious beast and started to croon to it.

"Wot th' 'ell is 'e doin'?" Benjy had crawled over to Eddie for a moment, in an effort to support the man as he watched his daughter and stepson face almost certain death.

"I think he's trying to be Androcles, would you believe," Eddie could hardly breathe as he watched, his heart thumping in fright.

"'Oo th' 'ell is that?" Benjy whispered.

"Long story. Long ago, Aesop's fables. Greek fellow in Roman times, escaped slave. Took a thorn out of a lion's paw in a forest and a while after, when he'd been recaptured and thrown to the lions in the arena as punishment, the lion who was supposed to eat him turned out to be the lion from the forest who he'd helped. The lion approached, then merely sat at his feet and refused to attack Androcles. The crowd and Emperor were so taken with what happened, Androcles got freed and the lion was sent back to the forest."

"Bleedin' 'ell, that's a bit far-fetched."

"Nothing ceases to amaze me since we brought Nicky back to life," muttered Eddie, now gripping Benjy's hand, needing to feel someone's comfort as he watched the surreal tableau in the cage unravel.

"Yer right in that, strangest fing I ever saw," muttered Benjy. "Good job that beast don't seem 'ungry anymore after eatin' poor Daisy, an' that t'other lion, but wild 'orses wouldn't drag me in there wiv it. I mean, jus' look at th' bugger... them teeth," he grimaced and shuddered theatrically.

"You're not in love with Bella," murmured Eddie. "Nicky would give his life for hers without a thought, and she for him... a bit like you and Francis..." Eddie looked tellingly at Benjy for an odd moment. "Oh, don't worry, I wouldn't say a word, but I do understand, My Friend," and he squeezed Benjy's hand.

Benjy didn't know what to say as he looked back at Eddie; his face had understanding and sympathy written all over it, the quiet man who always saw so much. "'E saved me life. 'E's everyfin' ter me, always 'as bin, everyfin'. I love 'im so much, deeply... I can never leave 'im... but yous mus' never tell, yer CAN'T tell..." he looked frightened and agonised at finally admitting his shocking secret to someone who obviously already knew or suspected... but understood.

"Of course not, what do you take me for? But that's how Nicky feels about my beloved girl," and without another word the two men sat side by side, holding hands, and prayed as they watched the inside of the cage where nothing was moving.

It was the most extraordinary thing, as everyone said afterwards. Nicky stood between the low-growling lion and Bella, forcing her behind him, and still crooning to it as if it was Duchess, his cat, and then slowly, imperceptibly, he finally moved, one step at a time, back the way he'd come, towards the gate in the cage. Everyone couldn't help it, they gasped in fright as the big beast, which had been sitting on its haunches, got to its feet, snarled and prowled forward, tossing the mighty mane as it moved.

"Oh God, Francis, DOOO something, I can't bear to watch," Cat now turned her head into Francis's chest where he'd come to kneel by her side, one arm around her and one hand gripping Ricky's even though his friend was drifting in and out of consciousness.

"What can I do? I haven't got a pistol and a little dagger is no use against that beast even if the cage walls weren't between us. Pray, Sweetheart, pray as hard as you can," he whispered. "Nicky seems to know what he's doing, it's uncanny. Oh fuckkk, where the hell is Ashcroft?" he finally muttered to himself.

The seconds and minutes ticked past as the pair in the cage confronted the wounded lion which was prowling back and forth in front of them, obviously confused and undecided what to do. Bella looked about to faint but Nicky had her hand in a tight grip, forcing her behind him as they started to move again, inch by slow inch, and blood from Nicky's wounded arm dripped unheedingly to the ground. "Go to the gate, Sooty, slowly," Nicky told Bella, not taking his eyes off the lion.

"N... n... no, not without y... you," Bella stuttered.

"DO AS YOU'RE TOLD, SOOTY," Nicky rasped softly. "NOW!" and gave her a little push but Bella refused to move.

Jack, completely gripped by the spectacle unfolding, had crawled forward and was at the gate; he heard Nicky's whispered instructions and opened it, beckoning Bella to him, but she seemed paralysed - unable or unwilling to move despite Nicky's orders. The lion prowled nearer and as Nicky pushed her, Jack darted into the cage himself, grabbed her hand and literally hauled her out, putting his hand over her mouth to stop the scream he could see rising to her lips. Jack shut the gate just as the lion prowled over to it and snarled, now putting itself between Nicky and safety, and Jack had to continue to keep his hand over Bella's mouth to prevent her shrieking in terror, convinced as she was the lion was about to pounce on Nicky and tear him to pieces, just like it had done to the nursemaid.

Nicky had never been so frightened in his life as he confronted the lion, and wondered idly why he was talking quiet nonsense to it in

Spanish, as he did to Duchess when she sat on his lap and he stroked her. But he persevered, having no idea what else to do, expecting it to leap on him at any moment. He could see where it was wounded: a long, deep furrow where the pistol ball had scored along its side, but not penetrated internally. In a strange way, he felt sorry for all of them, captured and dragged from their jungle homes far away, wherever that was, to be incarcerated in crates for weeks or months on end as they were shipped overseas to be brought to Europe or England. And for what? To be a public spectacle for the masses, permanently kept locked up in small cages and poked and prodded and gawped at, never again to be free to roam as they were born to be or, as in Bernheim's case, expected to eat some poor humans before no doubt being shot. They were stunning beasts, like giant versions of his own puss cat as they'd prowled around. And the one in front of him, it was almost as if its big eyes were sad... or was he being imaginative and hysterical. Probably, he told himself.

He continued to whisper softly to the lion, staring into its eyes, refusing to appear panicked even though he was terrified, and to his amazement, after a while, the lion padded off and sat down again with a soft growl. The second lion hadn't moved, its eyes were closed and Nicky hoped it was dead. He edged his way back, towards the gate, and as Jack opened it once again, finally tumbled out and into his arms, feeling as if he was going to faint for the first time in his life.

"Jesus Christ..." Jack gasped, "how the HELL did you do that?" and he slapped Nicky on the back as he went over and took Bella in his arms and held her tight, shaking with reaction, his breath coming in slow gasps as his heart rate finally slowed.

"I've no idea, Jack, but we're not going to kill that poor animal; he's as much a prisoner as we were. Someone, somewhere, was watching over us just now, maybe Madre up in heaven, or the Dowager. I prayed to them to keep us safe and for whatever reason, that lion wasn't going to kill me so I'm going to return the favour."

"Really?" Jack looked bemused. "I don't know what you're going to do with him, I mean what does one do with a spare lion? But that's your problem; in the meantime, Ashcroft and Bernheim have disappeared and the Earl is in a bad way over there. Benjy is looking after

Alfie, that Arab nearly split him in half and his gizzards are spewing out all over the place. There's nothing I can do, so I'm going to find Ashcroft and that bastard," and with that, Jack turned and hurried out the barn, picking up his dagger on the way and wiping it on his shirt.

Nicky and Bella hurried over to where Francis and Cat were kneeling over Ricky. "Is he going to make it? That evil bastard..." muttered Nicky as he sank to his knees next to Francis.

"Oh, Uncle Ricky," Bella wailed as she knelt next to Cat and picked up Ricky's limp hand and kissed it.

"Where's Benjy? We need him over here," muttered Francis, worry etched on his strained features.

"I gather he's trying to stuff Alfie's gizzard back inside him and sew him up," muttered Nicky.

"Oh Christ," breathed Francis, "not him, too. What do you think, Cat, will he make it?"

"Excuse me," a faint voice whispered out from Ricky's white lips, "don't I get consulted here?"

"Don't you give up on me, You Arrogant Fop," Francis bent over his friend and squeezed his hand, "You didn't survive all those damn duels to die on me now, you hear that, Rosie?"

"Take care of the family for me, Granny," Ricky whispered. "Look after Gus. Make him a man like you did Nicky... promise me?"

"You are NOT dying on me, Rosie, you're NOT!" Francis was beside himself. "BENJYYYYYY!" he yelled at the top of his voice, "Bella, go get him, NOW!"

"On my way, Uncle," and Bella shot to her feet, hoiked up her skirts and raced over to the other side of the barn where Benjy had suddenly appeared, glad to have something to do to stop herself going to pieces at the horror surrounding her.

"Now you listen to me, Rosie, we're going to have that ball out your chest and you're NOT going to give in. If you want to know what I got up to all those years ago, you're bloody well going to have to hang on or I won't tell you."

"Are you trying to order me about, Granny? Is that what you would have been like on your smuggling ship?"

"Too right. And if you didn't obey orders, you'd have got five or ten of the best."

"Oooooh, you know how I like to be whipped," Ricky cackled and a dribble of blood came out the corner of his mouth.

"Oh God, RICKY! Behave yourself!" tutted Cat, not knowing whether to laugh or cry she was so upset at the prospect of losing such a close and dear friend.

"Especially if it's by a creature as lovely as you, Cat, My Darling," and the ghost of a wink and a grin crossed his white face.

"You Disgraceful Man! What you get up to in your bedroom with Sophy is none of my business."

"You should see what I found in a chest in Bernheim's bedroom," tutted Francis, "it would have raised even your eyebrows, Granny."

"Reeeally?"

"But I'm not going to tell you that either, that's another story for later. Perhaps I'll make you a present of it, a souvenir of an unforgettable couple of days, and a second reason not to die on me," Francis grinned, desperate to take his friend's mind off the wound in his chest.

Benjy hurried over with his bag and lifted the pad of bloodstained petticoat Cat had been pressing down on Ricky's wound.

"Good girl," he winked at Cat. "We'll make a nurse of you yet."

"Glad I'm still a girl in someone's book," she smiled. "Look after him, Benjy, he's far too disreputable to lose; I've promised to whip him if he gets better," and she winked at a grimacing Ricky as Benjy poked around in the hole in his chest and she gripped Ricky's hand tight.

"Oh Gawd, are you misbehavin' again, Your Lordship?"

"'Fraid so, Benjy… aaaaaaargh…"

Ricky jerked and cried out as pain lanced through him when Benjy threw some brandy over his chest, and his hands, and some surgical instruments and then, with a deep breath, started to dig around. Benjy had himself in a firm grip now, having calmed down after the terrifying lion spectacle. He'd thought his nerves shredded and he couldn't take any more, dealing with so many serious injuries and now in someone who was close and dear to his master; someone he'd also known for decades and had never treated him like a servant or a lesser man, unlike many of his peers.

"Bella's stayed over the other side to help Eddie," Benjy finally spoke to Francis, Cat and a hovering Nicky as he worked. "He's watched me often enough now, and God knows he's read more on the subject than I'll ever know, so he's seeing to Fred and Alfie."

"Where's Elise?"

"Gone to look after little Harry, they found him in a carriage around the back."

"Thank God for that," sighed Cat in relief. "Now then, Benjy, what do you want me to do?"

"I'm out of here," Nicky interrupted. "Francis? Bernheim's still on the loose, Jack's gone out to look for Ashcroft, I think we need to go and find that bastard and deal with him once and for all."

Francis rose to his feet knowing there was nothing he could do other than pray for his friend, so he turned to Nicky. "After you, Lion Tamer. If Ricky dies," he whispered, "I'm going to pull that bastard apart one limb at a time, so help me…"

"You're in a queue behind me," grated Nicky, and the pair turned and headed for the door. They stopped there to finally speak to Carstairs and Browning who were supervising the two shocked grooms, inspecting the various bodies littered around the barn.

"I've never been so glad to see Your Graces in my life," a white-faced Carstairs bowed to the two men briefly. "Are you both all right? You look rather, er… bloodied, Sir." He looked askance at Francis's various cuts visible through his ripped shirt and then at Nicky's slashed and still bleeding arm, without thought taking off his cravat and tying it efficiently around the sleeve of Nicky's jacket like a makeshift bandage.

"I'm alive, Carstairs, thanks to you and Browning," sighed Francis. "You got here not a second too soon to shoot those lions."

"I owe you the Duchess's life." Nicky thumped the elderly butler on his back, "and you, Browning, it was a damn close call."

"I've never been so shocked at what we witnessed just now, Your Grace," muttered Browning. "What we did was nothing. To go into that cage, with that beast?" Browning shuddered. "Bravest thing I've ever seen."

"Nonsense," said Nicky dismissively, "but Francis and I are after

Lord Ashcroft and Jack, they've gone in search of Bernheim. You two stay here and help the Baron, Benjy and the ladies. Any sign of the cavalry?"

"They're waiting at the bottom of the lane, Sir, a small troop. It was all over by the time they arrived. The officer in charge was watching everything from outside, he could barely believe his eyes when he saw the cage and what was inside it, never mind when you went in. If Bernheim tries to escape down the drive, or on the nearby roads, they'll be waiting for him."

"Good Man. Tell them to wait there pending further instructions from Lord Ashcroft, but we seem to have done for most of Bernheim's thugs. There were a veritable army of them, no idea how we prevailed, but we seem to have managed it somehow. Come on, Francis, if I was Bernheim I'd be off across country knowing the military were on their way... but he's not getting away from me this time..." and with a grim look and a nod at the two elderly men, Francis and Nicky disappeared into the night.

Chapter Twelve

"Where to?" Nicky looked around him, just as Francis had done when he'd first exited the barn. "Christ, we really are in the middle of nowhere..."

"It's a derelict farm, and I've no idea. Where would you go if you were Bernheim?"

"Horse," said Nicky succinctly. "When he got away from me in Madrid, Reynard said he had an escape tunnel under the villa that came up a short distance away. Whatever else he is, he's a clever bastard, he'll have a way out ready, just in case, take my word for it. Well, wouldn't you?"

"I dare say, but he seemed so full of megalomania, having caught the lot of us, I wonder..."

"I still can't come to terms with it, I simply can't. It's like I'm acting out a terrible dream and I keep thinking I'm going to wake up in a minute and find myself in bed in Hertford Street with Bella sprawled out next to me and Duchess sleeping on the coverlet over my feet."

"Hah!" Francis chuckled for a moment, "You're bloody lucky you only have Duchess on your bed, I have Bubbles to cope with... God, I hope he's all right."

"Bubbles? What's he been up to? Eaten too much chicken again or another of Cat's bonnets?"

"Another long story. Tell you later; come on, it's far too quiet for my liking, given Ashcroft and Jack are also looking for him."

"Do you think Ricky will make it?" Nicky spoke softly as the pair of them crept quietly towards the farmhouse.

"He'd better, I couldn't live with myself to think he'd got drawn into this mess by accident and Bernheim had killed him; but you know he's no fool and the sarcasm is always just a front. If he was going to go, I think he'd be dead already, but it seems Bernheim's ball missed his heart, so who knows? He's a tough man, still strong under his waistcoats even if he doesn't look it, and if anyone can save him, Benjy can. He saved you and you were in a worse condition than Ricky is; he's GOT to hang on until we can get him home to some proper medical care."

"Well, Granny, you can always thump him on the chest as well," said Nicky facetiously, "then I can start calling you Jesus instead…"

"I warned you, enough of that Granny nonsense, Androcles, and don't be so unholy."

"Oh for God's sake, Francis, don't be ridiculous."

"Tit for tat. I'll start calling you Androcles in Brooks's and see how you get out of that."

"Grrrrrr… rawwwrrrrr…" Nicky growled softly, "card please… hmmm, I'll raise you a hundred guineas, rawrrrrrrr…"

"Idiot," Francis chortled quietly. "We're both quite mad, you know that?"

"Of course we are, the whole damn lot of us are, that's what makes us so wonderful. Come on, Granny, I want to see where they had us holed up, I swear to God I'm never going in another cellar as long as I live. Once was bad enough, twice is twice too much," and the pair quietly entered the farmhouse.

"If you see any weapons lying around, pick them up. I was in the middle of looking when I heard shots from the barn. I feel naked without one and there must be more here somewhere. I found the rapier and stiletto in Bernheim's bedroom, but I never got to check everywhere down here."

"Yes, Sir," Nicky saluted and Francis swatted his head.

"Good job you were never in my crew," he tutted. "You'd have been thrown overboard for insubordination in five minutes."

"No I wouldn't, I'd have organised a mutiny and MY crew would have made YOU walk the plank," Nicky swatted Francis back.

"How the hell did Ashcroft and Wellington put up with you?"

"They loved me, especially Uncle Arthur, I was his favourite spy."

"No wonder we beat Bonaparte, the French didn't stand a chance against you three."

"Oh, there were a few more apart from us, y'know... just a few, mind."

"Come along, You Silly Bugger, light that lantern and let's have a look downstairs."

The two went down a narrow wooden stairway and peered around at the dank and dirty cellar rooms they'd obviously been kept in. "Bloody rats," shuddered Nicky as they caught sight of the vermin scurrying about. "Can't stand them, they nibbled my toes in the cellar he kept me in, in Nice; at least I had my boots on this time."

"Lovely," muttered Francis. "I always wondered if you tasted nice, Darling. Marguerite's girls always said you did."

"Piss off, Granny... and what were you doing talking to Marguerite's girls, may I ask? I trust it was only talking?"

"Just passing the time of day. Do you think I want my liver cut out by an irrational Frenchwoman?" he grinned at Nicky. "I can't deal with HER, what the hell do I want more women for?" he chuckled.

"Chicken," Nicky clucked. "Completely henpecked, how are the mighty fallen."

"You can talk," Francis smirked. "You could apply to be the official midwife to the Ton now," and Nicky playfully grimaced and punched Francis in the shoulder, wincing as the action pained his slashed arm.

They hurriedly inspected every room as they bantered, until they were back at the stairway to the cellars. "Well, there's no way out of here that I can see," sighed Francis. "Solid walls and floors, and why would there be a passageway from an old farmhouse? Doesn't make any sense."

"I'm with you there. Anything worth looking at upstairs?"

"Only Bernheim's trunk full of personal torture equipment, as in for use with the ladies, at least I assume that's his inclination. Christ, he's a bloody pervert, I've not seen items like that for years, not since Ricky and I were in our early twenties and visited a very particular cathouse out of curiosity. De Sade would be well at home there. Nasty, painful stuff in it, don't want Cat or Bella to see, you know how nosey they are, but it'll give them nightmares, even if they did understand what it's all for. It needs disposing of quietly."

"So he wasn't kidding Cat then? Ricky? I never had him down as a serious pervert."

"He's not, don't be an idiot, no more than we are. He got involved with a woman who was, though. Christ, was she was strange. An Earl's daughter. Don't know if her husband knew or not, but don't actually think he did. He was older than her and spent most of his time in his club, gambling with his cronies, or at his hunting box in the season. She was a wealthy woman in her own right and had bought herself this little house south of the river and had it fitted out for the purpose. Far worse than Marguerite's dungeon, it was. Ricky was just curious, we'd seen the other cathouse and didn't really fancy getting involved, but you know Ricky, his curiosity was piqued. I went along to watch a couple of times, she liked that too... but it turned my stomach. He didn't stay with her long, extricated himself pretty damn quick, not his bag at all. But that was Ricky, he had to try everything out," Francis shrugged.

"Is there anything the pair of you haven't done?"

"Between us?" Francis smirked at Nicky, "I doubt it. I had my little... ah... sailing hobby... and he raked it around London. I'd bet there's absolutely NOTHING Ricky hasn't tried, in bed or out, even with men; every single entertainment or perversion you could think of, and some you haven't, including opium, hashish and all sorts of weird and strange habits."

"And I thought I'd done most things," Nicky chuckled. "I can't believe he outdid me in his youth."

"Don't think Ricky actually charged anyone for his services though, I have to say... unlike you..." Francis said facetiously.

"You knew?" Nicky's eyebrows raised.

"Of course I knew. Someone had to keep half an eye on you, You Randy Little Sod. Besides, you know what gossip is like, you were well recommended in certain discreet circles, very talented in some directions, I gather. As soon as I got wind of your nickname, I realised immediately. I was highly entertained," Francis drawled with a smirk, "considering I taught you a lot of it. I could have been your pimp; imagine that!" and he grinned wickedly as for a moment his eyes sparkled with humour.

"What? Give you some of my fee? Greedy bugger, as if you aren't rich enough. Oh God, does Cat know?"

"I don't think so. I'm sure she would have mentioned it if she did, she'd never be able to keep a little gem like that to herself, you know what she's like with salacious gossip. Not to mention bending YOUR ears about it, let alone mine. And Eddie doesn't know either, at least I hope not. That's one good thing about him not tattling with the ladies a lot."

"I'm glad about that. I'd rather Papa never knew."

"Well, it's all water under the bridge now, Androcles. Every lion has his day and then needs to retire. Come on, I don't like rats either, had my fill of them on my ships. I suggest we have a quick check around upstairs again for a couple of pistols, in case I missed something, and then inspect the other farm buildings. The other two must be somewhere."

The pair made quick work of searching the rest of the farmhouse, Nicky coming up short when he went in the kitchen and found the bodies of the four men Francis had killed. "They were waiting to take Lizzie and Terrie," Francis grated, "but fortunately, my dear mama-in-law was collecting that daft old bat, Emily Southwater, on the way to Harriet Aubrey's for tea, and another of her ancient cronies, and they'd taken some footmen with to help them in and out the carriage, they're so fat and doddery they can't manage by themselves, and obviously to keep half an eye on the girls, stop them wandering off or getting into mischief if they got bored waiting around, so they must have been forestalled. Then, when they all got back to Berkeley Square, Ashcroft had already got soldiers posted outside, and in Hertford Street by the way, so they abandoned their little kidnapping plan and came back here. I overheard them discussing it. They were shitting themselves at having to tell Bernheim, but imagine, Emily Southwater saved the day," and Francis chuckled.

"I'm glad you killed them," Nicky grated wrathfully. "What the hell have our little girls ever done to Bernheim? They're still babes... what the devil did he want them for anyway, when he had all of us?"

"Pressure," Francis rasped angrily. "He obviously presumed we wouldn't talk, not after his experience with you in Nice. He probably intended to throw them to the lions, after Daisy."

"I'll cut his bloody bollocks off when I find him," grated Nicky, incensed at the images suddenly filling his mind. "Come on, I'm not farting around here a minute longer. Let's go outside, I don't need a pistol, I've got a dagger now, he's mine, Francis!"

"All right, all right, calm down. I suggest we take this lantern, the moon seems permanently obscured now so we'll need some light to find our way around. I'll collect another from the kitchen then we can split up if necessary. I think you're right about getting a horse some-where, let's hope he hasn't yet or we'll never find him now... unless Ashcroft followed him. Christ, I can't deal with the thought of him still being on the loose. I'll not sleep a wink until I know he's six feet under."

"Me too, and Bella. It took her long enough to get over what happened in Nice, and I'm sure Cat will be the same. Do you think her throat will scar, Francis? That'll be a bugger to explain."

"I don't know until we look and see how deep she was cut, but quite possibly."

Nicky swore under his breath. "They looked deep when I got to her and wrapped my cravat around her neck. As if she wants a permanent reminder of all this. What a fucking nightmare," he swore again to himself.

"We're all alive, that's the main thing, and we've got to hope Ricky and Alfie hang on, and Ashcroft's man, Fred. He followed the men who took me, brave and clever to do that. I owe him, they would never have found us in time otherwise."

"It's fate, Francis, I tell you. It wasn't our time to go. I've had so many close shaves over the past few years, I really believe that now."

"I'm beginning to think you're right. Now then, let's go look over this way…" and the pair crept round the back of the farmhouse and set off to check out the various farm buildings.

"Do you think we should get some of the soldiers to help search?" Nicky suggested as they peered into what looked like an old stable, the roof of which was mostly missing.

"No disrespect to them, but he's far too clever. They've no idea who they're dealing with. If one did find him, he'd slit their throat before they could raise the alarm. Best leave them on guard spread out down the lane and towards to road to Richmond, all in a troop, as Carstairs said. At least Bernheim will know they're there and it might throw his plans to escape off course."

One by one, they inspected the ruined outbuildings until they discovered the little group of carriages and wagons that had been used to transport them all to the farm. Francis jumped up to the various driver's seats on the carriages and finally procured them both a pistol. "That's better, I feel a bit happier now I'm armed," he muttered, handing one over to Nicky.

"Where are Elise and Harry? I assumed she was out here looking after him and keeping her head down?" Nicky looked around, raising his lantern and wincing again as his wound pulled, so he nonchalantly put it on the ground for a moment to let his arm rest, hoping Francis wouldn't comment.

"Perhaps she went back into the barn while we were in the farm-house?" and the two men looked at each other.

"I don't like this. I didn't hear a baby, I'm sure we would have…" Nicky looked more than worried.

"You're right. I heard him whimpering when I came out the first time. Elise isn't feeding him anymore, as far as I know; not that I'm interested in all the women's baby gossip about feeding regimens, colic, wind, wet nurses, nannies, and all that… a bit beyond a mere man… so he must still be hungry, and therefore crying, poor little bugger. This is NOT good, Nicky. I'm getting a bad feeling again."

"Where the hell is Miles, and where's Jack?"

"I'm here," a quiet voice suddenly said behind them.

"JACK!" Francis and Nicky both spun round suddenly as they said his name in unison.

"You'd never make a burglar, either of you. What a pair of clodhoppers," he grinned momentarily, "not to mention, given the situation, I could have stuck my knife in both your backs. What the HELL are you both playing at?"

"You seriously need your ears boxed, Young Man," Francis tutted, "but you're right. I must be getting old," he sighed, "and you, Androcles," he poked Nicky in the ribs.

"Androcles? Hah! I know who he was, I was awake in that Classics lesson too. Love the new name, Nicky, should I call you Andro for short?" Jack smirked.

"Enough of that, thank you, You Saucy Sod," Nicky rasped as he playfully cuffed Jack round the head. "Where's Miles, and Elise? Have you seen her and the baby?"

Jack's face was instantly serious. "No, I haven't, I was wondering the same as you. And I haven't seen Lord Ashcroft either. I don't like it. I've searched all around here and was just going into the farmhouse when you came out. I followed you both all the way over here."

"You've been following us?" Nicky looked astounded.

"Not just a handsome face and wondrous fuck," Jack grinned at the pair of them. "I kept my head down in case Bernheim suddenly popped up and surprised the pair of you, but he didn't. I hope to God he hasn't found Lord Ashcroft and killed him," he added in a worried tone.

"So do I, Lad," muttered Francis, "and I have no wish to hear about your love life, thank you very much; riveting though it no doubt now is."

"You've no idea," smirked Jack. "Were those men in the farmhouse really going to take Lizzie and Terrie?"

"You heard us?"

"Of course I did. I was just casing the place outside when the pair of you went into the kitchen. The window was open," he shrugged.

"Well, now you know."

"I'm glad you killed them, or I would have. I killed three of them back in the barn, you know. I'd have taken down that Arab if Bernheim hadn't clouted me on the head," he gently touched the large, throbbing lump on his temple.

"He's dead. I never missed when I threw my knife, at least that's one skill that's not gone rusty," Francis sighed.

"Right, so what now? Any ideas?" he looked at the other two.

"For once, I wish Miles was here," sighed Nicky. "There's no one better for analysing the situation and strategising different scenarios. I always remember him saying that conceited megalomaniac, Bonaparte, should never have gone into Russia, it would be his downfall, and all the reasons why, and what would likely happen if he did. He was absolutely spot on. Uncanny. Good job he's on our side and not the French."

"And I'm an idiot?" Francis said sarcastically.

"Yes, Granny, actually. Miles has been on Bernheim's trail for years, if anyone knows how the man is likely to think, it would be him."

"I'm so redundant, I don't know why I'm bothering. I might as well go and sit in one of the carriages and wait for someone to drive me home so I can have a cup of cocoa and go to bed in my bedsocks, gown and nightcap."

"Shall I go and find your walking stick and bath chair as well?" Jack nudged Francis in the ribs.

"See what I mean? No one listens to me anymore, no one shows me any respect. I'm treated like a doddering fool. Oh, woe is me. I'm going to retire to Bath or Harrogate and take the waters."

"For God's sake, WILL you be serious," tutted Nicky.

"You sounded just like Lord Ashcroft," chuckled Jack. "He couldn't cope with Lord Ambrose when he was fooling around in the Hertford Street stables while we were sorting out the horses."

"Me? Like Miles? Perish the thought. But we can't just stand here farting about, we have to DO something and I'm like Francis, I've got a funny feeling too. In fact, I suggest Bernheim's gone to ground somewhere here… and you know what, I think he's taken Elise and Harry with him as an insurance policy."

Jack swore roundly. "I think you're probably right," muttered Francis, "the question is, where? And I wonder if Ashcroft followed him? If Bernheim had killed him, I think we would have found the body, he wouldn't have had time to hide it and I'm damn sure Miles wouldn't have gone down without a fight, we would have heard SOMETHING, surely?"

"You didn't hear me creeping around after you. I told you I could have knifed you in the back or slit your throat without warning, and you'd be dead on the floor before you could say 'where's my smelling salts?'"

"No, I wouldn't, M'Lad, and don't you EVER think you can get one over me. Big heads get chopped off extremely easily, you ask Robespierre," he admonished.

"How can I? He's dead."

"And that's why. He thought he was too clever by half, just you remember that. Anyway, enough of history." Francis began to muse thoughtfully, "So, if I was Bernheim, and as Nicky has already suggested, being him and based on what happened in Spain, he would probably have had a fall-back plan... just in case. Ergo, where would he vanish to around here, where he could get to quickly and disappear out of sight, and pick up onward transport?"

"Richmond?"

"Hmmm, probably, it's where transport is, and the river. Very convenient. Therefore, how would he get there? Suppose, just suppose, the authorities found him out, and he saw or heard them approaching, he would know he couldn't just ride down the lane, away from the farm, as that would be how THEY would arrive, so he would have to go across country, across all these fields."

"That makes sense. But it's so dark, the clouds have obscured the moonlight we had before. How the hell can we decide which direction he'd go in?" Jack sighed.

"Good point, and there's two options. The obvious one is direct, as the crow flies, straight towards Richmond village. The second is a roundabout route that would give him cover to hide in if necessary. I suggest the latter is what he would do. I would if I were him."

"You're obviously not just a pretty face and wondrous fuck either," drawled Nicky, nudging Francis, "even if you are old enough to be my father. Nice analysis, and I think you've got it spot on, especially if he's dragging poor Elise and the baby with him. My God, is this nightmare ever going to end?"

"Ah, so I'm rehabilitated in your esteem then, I'm soooo relieved," Francis said facetiously. "Now then, which way is Richmond from here?" he looked at Jack.

"Over there," he pointed.

"Good, and remember he's not going to be able to move quickly, I'm damn sure Elise won't be going quietly, or willingly, so we need to see if we can find any evidence of which way they set off. Now, if I was Miles, I'd know either we or the military would be following, so if I was him, I'd try and leave some sort of sign or trail. I suggest we split up and have a look around, pretty damn quick."

"Will I ever get to be an amazing man like you?" sighed Jack humbly, completely overwhelmed by Francis's grasp of the situation and forward strategy. "I'm no Shadow really, am I?" he looked downcast and suddenly dejected in the light of Francis's lantern.

"I was just like you are, once upon a time, Jack, heaven help me, my head full of willing women and big ideas. I thought I was untouchable, but I learned my lesson the hard way, and so will you one day, though I hope not as painfully. Just try and remember that and think before you do anything rash, it does help sometimes..." Francis grinned at the youth, "You'll be a second Shadow yet... just keep practising..." and both he and Nicky chuckled.

"Really? Do you think so?" Youth looked up at experience and grinned hopefully.

"Regrettably, yes, and I just hope you manage to keep your head on your shoulders in the process, and not stretched either, and your brain is up here," he tapped Jack's head, "not in your breeches, in case you forget," he tutted with a wink. "Now come along, Apprentice, we've only got two lanterns so you come with your Master. Nicky, you look around over there. Shout if you see or hear ANYTHING," Francis ordered.

Chapter Thirteen

They left the carriages and sleeping horses behind them and started scouring the ground at the entry to nearby fields. It wasn't long before Nicky gave a shout and Francis and Jack ran to where he was standing by a length of hedgerow that divided a couple of fields. "Look, I found it wound through the brambles," Nicky held up a gentleman's cravat with his wounded arm, his lantern raised in the other.

"Do you reckon that belongs to Miles?" Francis peered down at it. "It's just a plain cravat."

"Here, smell it, it still carries a very faint scent of cologne. This hasn't been here for days or weeks, it's been left today, tonight, I'd stake my life on it."

"Bloody hell!" Jack sniffed and looked between Francis and Nicky. "You're right, he's gone that way. What are you waiting for? Come on…" and without waiting for an answer, he grabbed Francis's lantern from his hand and set off at a lope to run along down the side of the field.

"Aah, the exuberance of youth," sighed Francis, "and the energy. Well spotted, Nick," Francis himself lifted the cravat to his nose. "Mmmmm, that does vaguely remind me of Miles. Well, that puts my mind at rest on one count, Bernheim hasn't done for him yet. Come on, Androcles, best foot forward, let's get after that jackanapes before gets himself, and us, into trouble," and the pair started to jog along behind in Jack's wake.

Bernheim was raging, he was incendiary, out of his mind with fury and frustration. Yet again, his perfect plan had been thwarted at the eleventh hour, just when it seemed not one, but two fortunes were within his grasp, finally there for the taking. Who were those men who claimed to be The Shadow? He was sure the fair man, the Baron de Mornay wasn't. He didn't have that hard look about him, or a commanding presence, which is surely what a leader of ruthless men such as a crew of smugglers and pirates would have. A man who had taken on six hardened and determined survivors of Bonaparte's decimated army from the Russian campaign, and who had also lived through the carnage at Waterloo; those venal men weren't to be trifled with in that forest glade on the outskirts of Valenciennes, with or without his young accomplice. But what about the grey-haired one, surely he couldn't be? He looked too aesthetic, too grey, but who knew? Was that why he called himself The Shadow, because that was where he resided? In the shadows, deadly, and out of the limelight? It was more like to be the elegant fop, he certainly fought skilfully enough and had the right colouring and bravado, and a deadly look in his eye as he fought… but it was the demeanour and look of the grey-haired man who had given Bernheim pause. And what of the Duke of Firle, Francis Granville, the man who he'd concluded was his father's nemesis? What of him? It had taken six of his best men to overcome him in the park, as he'd suspected, and the man had been unarmed. What a fool, a typical, arrogant English aristocrat, sauntering about in a deserted park with just a stupid dog for company.

Bernheim continued to rage as he was confronted with four men who all claimed to be The Shadow, the man who'd reportedly amassed an enormous fortune, not only money but also in gold, jewellery and precious stones. The man who'd been in his father's clutches only to be spirited away, leaving his father dead on the floor of his apartments in Rouen Fortress, alongside his pig of a second in command, Dupont; their corpses stinking by the time a couple of his father's former thugs had come back to see if there was any more work available and discovered half a dozen dead bodies, and no clue as to who had perpetrated the murders.

After he'd been informed about his father's unexpected and untimely death, he'd detoured to Normandy on his way from and back to school in Vienna, seeing the lawyer in between, but had found out little more than the shifty lawyer had told him, only rumours about the mysterious *L'Ombre*, infamous local smuggler and suspected pirate, but what he looked like, or what had become of him, no one knew, so which of the four men who'd just escaped his clutches was the real one, Bernheim wasn't sure. However, whichever one it was, the man and his fortune had eluded him yet again and his rage was all-consuming.

But more than that, he'd lost the *Duc de Valenciennes* again too, him and his famed gold; his nemesis, with the wife who'd made a fool of him... *La Lionesse*. That black-haired witch, an aristocratic Lady on the outside and a whore underneath, the woman who'd enticed him and betrayed him, and who he craved in his bed again to drive him to the brink of pleasure like he'd rarely known, her beautiful body his to torment and torture and do with as he pleased until he'd sated his craving and lust for her.

Over and over, Frederick Bernheim's mind seethed as he'd watched them all, assessing the situation, deciding what to do, his thirst for revenge and their gold at odds with the need to escape. His self-preservation won out, but not before he'd had to take on the fop and at least dispose of him. But he'd been unexpectedly difficult to overcome until a momentary distraction had presented his opportunity and he'd merely shot the fop and taken his chance in the melee to disappear out into the night. He'd always remembered his Latin classes at school in Vienna and had taken to heart Tacitus's words... 'he who fights and runs away may turn and fight another day'. That credo had served him well, more than once, over the years he'd served Bonaparte and personally profited in the process... until his nemesis, de Bresancourt, had put a curse on every lucrative opportunity he'd involved himself in since he'd gone to work in Spain. He dismissed the ill-gotten gains he'd accrued from the dead after Waterloo, they were but a pittance against the Rothschild gold or the money he'd been offered if Bonaparte could escape from Elba and be reinstated.

Bernheim ran silently round the back of the farmhouse and immediately spotted the wagon and nag standing by the kitchen entrance and he'd gone into the building, calling for his men, the missing band who'd been sent to take the little girls, his final threat to make the men hand over their secrets in return for not throwing them to the lions, which of course he intended to do anyway... but one look at the floor and he realised they'd been disposed of. Dismissing them as useless, he hurried into the small sitting room and over to the fireplace. He quickly pushed aside the threadbare rug, lifted the loosened floorboards and pulled out the large, heavy satchel which contained money, weapons, disguises and a change of clothes. He slung it across him, replaced the flooring and rug, and with a furtive look around, he hurried out and round the back of the outbuildings, intent on unhitching a horse from one of the carriages to make his escape.

However, as he'd crept along, he'd heard the unmistakeable sounds of hoofbeats and carriage wheels in the distance and he'd had to angrily reassess his plans, yet again. He would have to go across the fields to the small, ramshackle animal shelter where he'd stabled a horse at the ready... just in case of such an eventuality, and from there he could reach the nearby village of Richmond, and from there hit the road or go down the river, to either London, Bristol or the coast, and a boat to take him back to France.

He got to the small group of wagons and carriages and discovered one of the Granville women, the Baron's wife, trying to comfort the infant they'd left there as too small to be bothered with, it's constant squalling driving him insane. He wished he'd disposed of it earlier and simply fed it to the caged beasts, except he'd wanted them starving and still hungry, but the child would have done in the absence of the little girls who still had not appeared.

The Baroness fell into his hands like a ripe plum, the perfect hostage and guarantee of his safety until he could disappear into the English countryside and escape.

Bernheim tore the infant from her arms, bundled it up in its blanket to quieten its screams, and with a knife to its face and throat where he drew blood to illustrate his threat, the woman had been easy to persuade in front of him, carrying a small lantern from one of the carriages, as they hastily set off across the fields. Bernheim decided he'd kill and ditch the child at the shelter, and take the woman on his horse and then dispose of her when he got to Richmond, his insurance policy in the event he was chased.

But he hadn't reckoned on Miles Ashcroft. His fatal mistake in underestimating the quiet, grey man.

Chapter Fourteen

Ashcroft had seen enough. There was no way he was going to let Bernheim escape to continue to be a threat to everyone, no matter how much danger Francis and his family were in... he had to rely on them to prevail because the greater good, the safety of England, was also at stake.

Who knew what other mischief the man had planned? He'd caused enough death and destruction already. Bonaparte had been on St Helena, the remote island in the south Atlantic off the western side of Africa, since the previous October; however, he'd escaped from Elba and caused further mayhem and that was enough for Ashcroft. He knew Wellington couldn't stomach another epic battle like he'd had at Waterloo and Bernheim had been deeply involved in the plot to bring Bonaparte back to Paris, foiled only by chance by de Bresancourt's wife and young Jack. The remaining plotters had regrouped and continued their scheming without Bernheim, and had eventually prevailed, but Ashcroft wasn't going to risk another uprising. A third coming. Waterloo had been too close a call, he and Wellington agreed it could so easily have gone the other way if fate, luck and God hadn't been on their side. But, as Wellington had privately opined, that was what sometimes happened.

So, reluctantly, and no little torn, Ashcroft had watched Bernheim like a hawk and when he saw him disappear, he went after him.

As Ashcroft crept out of the barn he looked around, wondering where Bernheim had gone. He looked towards where he knew the coaches and horses were and he looked at the farmhouse. It was a gamble, but he set off in the direction of the farmhouse, a gut instinct telling him Bernheim would want to collect either money or more weapons before he made his escape and he followed his instincts. It was what he would have done if the situation had been reversed. Unless he had money stored somewhere else, Bernheim wouldn't be able to go anywhere without the means to pay. Had he got another bolthole in London? Ashcroft deliberated quickly but decided it was unlikely. This was the perfect place for Bernheim to hole up and oversee his plans. It was near enough to London to get there easily and quickly, but far enough away to keep a low profile and remain unnoticed. So he'd need to go to the farmhouse first.

Ashcroft stole up to the side of the house and peered in the windows but could see nothing. Then he heard a quiet curse from inside and hurried round to the rear and saw the wagon and horse there and realised there must be more of Bernheim's men inside. Men who had obviously arrived while they'd all been in the barn, distracted by the grisly spectacle of the lions and the maid. Just like Francis, Ashcroft wasn't afraid but he wasn't a fool either, he wasn't going to risk taking on a group of men, and Bernheim, with only a couple of pistols. He wasn't Francis, or Nicky, he knew his limitations, and he paused to think.

As he hesitated, Bernheim collected his bag and crept out the front as Ashcroft finally stole up to the rear window where a light was glowing and risked peering inside. He spotted a couple of bodies on the floor and hurried indoors. He looked at the bodies of four dead men and knew immediately Francis had been responsible as he recalled the two shots he'd heard which had set off the battle in the barn, and yet again Ashcroft marvelled at how an unarmed, middle-aged man had managed to take on and kill four thugs without so much as a scratch and calmly reappear back at the barn without mentioning a thing. Even now, nearly thirty years after his heyday, Francis Granville truly was still The Shadow and he had no peer.

Without looking at the dead men again, Ashcroft hurried through the ground floor of the farmhouse and realised Bernheim had exited via the front door which was still ajar. He stole out into the night and crept off in the direction of the carriages, wagons and horses, an expression of deadly intent on his face. His grey eyes glimmered in the dark; this was his moment, he decided; no longer the puppeteer, he had to be a man of action now. As he'd come out of the house, he'd heard distant noises of horses and, was that a coach? A grim smile of relief crossed Ashcroft's face; at last, reinforcements, and not a moment too soon. They would have Bernheim one way or another, and his menace would finally be stopped once and for all.

It was her short, sharp cry of fright that stopped Ashcroft in his tracks as he peered around the corner of the ruined pigsty. Bernheim had obviously discovered Elise and her baby, supposedly safely hidden out of the way of any further trouble, and he was holding the child in his arms, a knife to its muffled face as he forced Elise in front of him and towards a field that merged into the now black night. Ashcroft heard her pitiful pleas, "No… for the love of God, don't cut him… leave him alone, he's just a baby… leave him, I'll go with you, do whatever you want, just, please, don't harm him, I beg you…"

Ashcroft raised his pistol to fire at Bernheim's retreating back but he was fearful the shot might make him jerk and the knife at the child's throat might kill it. Boiling with frustration, he could do no more than follow, praying someone would come to look for him and follow him.

Bernheim had set off across a muddy field and Ashcroft looked around, his mind fizzing. How would anyone know to follow him? The fields surrounding the farm were vast. In desperation, he tore off his cravat and wound it into some hedging, spreading its length along the top of the thicket, the snowy whiteness stark even in the darkness. He hoped someone would notice and know it was a sign, that it was his. He could do no more than pray as he stealthily followed the man, woman and baby into the cover of night.

Before Bernheim had found and forced Elise to accompany him, she and Eddie had hurried out into the darkness from the barn, looking around them, trying to make out where they were. Eddie put his arm on Elise's and held her still, putting a finger to her lips, and for a few seconds they stood silent, listening... and there it was, a series of whimpers. Elise cried out softly and Eddie set off again, limping along hurriedly in the direction of the sound. They reached a small group of abandoned wagons and carriages and as Elise dived into one where her baby obviously was, Eddie surmised these were the vehicles that had brought them all to wherever they were, trying to piece together what had happened.

Elise cuddled the distressed child to her, crooning and whispering to it in an effort to stop its cries and comfort it, knowing the infant must be hungry. He was also wet and smelled and, practical as ever, she stripped off his soiled underpinnings and laying him on the carriage seat, she started to rip up her petticoats to use instead, as Eddie half watched and half looked around trying to make out some clue as to where they were. All was silent on the deserted farm, the only sounds that of fighting and growling coming from the barn. Deciding Elise was safer outside than back in the barn, and wanting to return to do what he could to help his family and friends, Eddie bent his head inside the carriage. "I have to go back, it sounds desperate in there, I can't just stand here and do nothing. You stay here and do what you can for Harry. Stay in the carriage, mind. If anyone comes along, try and keep Harry quiet and hide yourself, or run off into the fields as fast as you can. It's dark there so lie flat on the ground and stay hidden. Do you understand me, Elise?" he leaned close to her face so she could see how serious he was.

"Go, My Love, I'll be completely fine here, don't worry, but take care of yourself, please be careful... and... Eddie," she put a hand to his face, "tell me you love me, again..." she whispered.

Eddie took her face between both of his hands and leaned down to kiss her tenderly. "I love you, Elise de Mornay, very much," he whispered. "Look after yourself and our son. If it goes quiet in the barn again, come back and join us as I'm sure Francis, Miles and Ricky Ambrose will prevail; I don't know three more determined and capable men, and Nicky, when he gets free. I don't like leaving you out here by yourself, but on balance it's probably safer here than inside at the moment with all the shooting and fighting."

"Whatever you think best, Eddie, and you're right. Besides, Miles said some cavalry were on the way and I'm sure he wasn't bluffing. I'm quite certain he wouldn't have come alone without arranging for reinforcements before he left London. I'll listen and come back as soon as the fighting is over... besides, someone might be hurt and need care," she whispered, worry obvious in her voice.

"Don't even think that. We've survived so far, we HAVE to all come out of this alive, that's why I have to go back..." and with a final kiss and squeeze of her shoulders and a kiss for his little son, Eddie limped back towards the barn and bumped into Benjy as he approached.

That was how Elise was walking back and forth, rocking and shushing the baby, wondering where she could find some milk or even water for it when a large figure loomed up in front of her and before she could gather her wits, Bernheim had ruthlessly pulled the baby away from her and a long, thin, evil-looking dagger was mere inches from its face. Images of Eddie's terrible facial scar flashed through her mind and a horrible sense of *déjà vu* overtook her. Like father like son. Elise couldn't bear it; his scars had marked Eddie terribly, inside and out, it hadn't taken her long to realise that. It had never remotely bothered her, she'd always seen the man behind the terrible puckered scarring that ran across one side of his handsome face, but she'd seen other women flinch from it. They would either stare or give him pitying looks and she realised how he still preferred the company of men rather than freely mixing and socialising with the ladies on any social occasions, despite his charm and wit which all the family knew he had in spades, not to mention the seductive French accent which reduced her and other women to a pudding when he was in the mood to be playful. But normally, he always kept to the background, standing in corners, obviously self-conscious and aware of the stares his looks elicited from those who didn't know him, refusing to dance though Elise knew he could now waltz, slowly and not energetically and well, and had done so, but only in the bosom of his family at times such as Christmas. It had always made her angry how a twist of fate had impacted on his life, and she'd never asked for the details of how it had happened, only knowing he'd been attacked in his youth by highwaymen, but she'd never, ever, commented on his looks or his limp, deciding she would simply ignore it all and pretend he looked and walked as normally as every other man. It was easy for her, she loved him.

However, the thought of her precious little boy, the child she'd always longed for and never thought she'd have, growing up being marked or scarred like his father with all that would mean to him, was a complete nightmare and she was prepared to do anything, sacrifice herself willingly, if it would prevent that. She'd therefore gone with Bernheim, both frightened and angry and telling herself, yet again, to be strong and help would come. Eddie, or Ashcroft, or someone, she was sure, she had to believe and keep her head and not panic.

Eddie was so wrapped up in events in the barn, between the fright of watching Nicky and Bella face the lion in the cage, and then continuing to help Benjy with Fred, Alfie and then Ricky, that he realised Elise hadn't returned. He dismissed it for a while, completely absorbed in doing what he could to assist Benjy, but then he started to worry. First of all, he told himself she'd probably fallen asleep, after all, it was very late and it had been a terrible day... but then he reflected more attentively. Elise would never be able to sleep with a hungry, crying and restless babe to deal with and he was sure she wouldn't rest herself until they were all safely back home. The more he thought, the more he began to fret. Carstairs and Browning were now hovering, offering assistance where they could and the two grooms were standing on guard, having gone out to reload their pistols and have a cursory look around.

Browning had gone out to have further words with the officer from the cavalry, telling him to wait for further instructions as the man was concerned that Lord Ashcroft and both Dukes seemed to have temporarily disappeared and he wanted to institute a search. "His Grace said to wait, so that's what you have to do. The man you are after, the villain of the piece, might still try and escape from the front of the property, but I can assure you he will NOT get away from the men who have gone after him, probably at the rear, that I can promise you," he tutted disdainfully to the officer. "Besides, you are only a small troop, you can't search the whole countryside in the darkness. I suggest we all wait. Master Jack, the Duke of Valenciennes' ward, also appears to be missing and he will come back with a message if their Lordships need assistance." Browning was quite something when he got into his supervisory, officious mode. Years of working for the Duke of Firle had honed his skills in dealing with anyone and everyone who wanted to see him or have something from him, and the bemused cavalry officer was no match for him; the man reflected the superior butler had a point as he stared across the dark fields into the distance.

Eddie decided he needed to go and see what had happened to his wife, so leaving Cat and Bella to follow Benjy's instructions, along with Carstairs who seemed to be making an able surgical assistant as Benjy endeavoured to repair the hole in Ricky's chest, he took a pistol from one of the grooms and hurried outside and back towards the carriages where he'd left her.

He took one look at the empty carriage, the door hanging open and Elise's handkerchief on the ground and foreboding filled him. He looked around and peered into the distance across the fields. He squinted and thought he could make out a flickering light, but couldn't be sure, but it was enough to confirm his deepest concerns. The vision of Elise and their baby in Bernheim's hands again was a nightmare not to be contemplated and so, with a determined expression on his face, he set off in its direction, hoping what he'd seen had belonged to Francis and Nicky, Ashcroft or Jack, knowing all four wouldn't rest until they'd found Bernheim and make him pay for the dreadful day and night they'd all just been through, not to mention what the man had already done to his own daughter and step-son. If it wasn't their light, he had his pistol and Bernheim would pay. One shot was all it would take and he pictured Bernheim's malevolent face with a neat hole in his forehead, those black obsidian eyes glassy in death.

Chapter Fifteen

After hastening across the fields, hassling and shoving a deliberately dawdling Elise, Bernheim finally reached the small shelter where a horse was asleep amongst a supply of hay and a water trough, and a saddle was lying in a corner. He dropped the baby onto the pile of hay, uncaring of its wail, and turned to Elise, grabbing the small lamp from her hands. They could still barely see each other in the darkness; apart from the dim lamplight, the moon continued to be intermittently obscured.

"If you so much as twitch, I will kill the child in front of you," he snarled, his soft, sibilant voice sending shivers down Elise's spine.

"Then I'll never do what you want," she bit back, refusing to let him see how terrified she was.

"It makes no difference," Bernheim shrugged, "I'll kill you both."

"You'll have no hostage then."

"I'll be long gone and it will not matter."

"They'll find you, no matter where you go or where you try and hide; my husband's family will find you and then one of them will pull your black heart out of your chest, preferably while you're still alive!"

"So bloodthirsty for an insipid Englishwoman," Bernheim looked her up and down.

"You may think that, but I have my moments." Elise drew back her shoulders, tossing her head, "I may look insipid, but that is one thing I am NOT. I had a very good mentor and role model."

"Mentor?"

"The Dowager Duchess of Firle, Francis Granville's grandmother. The epitome of English womanhood and she was many things, but most definitely not insipid, either in looks or behaviour, right up until she died. She was a close friend of mine, and she wouldn't have tolerated you for one single moment. If I can be half the woman she was, you should be very afraid."

"I'm cowering in my boots," Bernheim's sarcastically chilling laugh floated on the air as he pulled off his cravat. "You're all mad, you English, mad. As if I would be afraid of a mere woman."

"Your father underestimated Francis's wife, and look where that got him," Elise said with asperity. "In his coffin."

"She will pay for that," Bernheim snarled again as he grabbed Elise's wrists and they tussled. "You will all pay. I will return, *je reviens vous chercher...*" he muttered in French. "I will come back, and I will find you all, and one by one I will kill you all. None of you will have a minute's peace, knowing I am out there, wondering when or where I will strike again."

"I told you, you ARE insane. We're not the mad ones, you are!"

Bernheim wrapped his cravat around her wrists and dragged her over to one of the wooden posts supporting the small shelter and fixed them to it. He then hurried to saddle up the horse, his mind going over where he would go once he'd got to Richmond village, whether to head to the south coast, to Portsmouth or Plymouth, or go west to Bristol and lose himself there. He had all sorts of disguises in his satchel, wigs and beards, spectacles and cosmetics, and he'd used them frequently as he'd sat and watched the various houses in London and down in Sussex, dressed as a beggar or vagrant, or a street vendor, even an old woman from time to time, noting the comings and goings, making conversation with the servants and grooms in the taverns, until he had a complete picture of the family and their habits and interests. When he'd matched that with the intelligence from his planted footman in the Baron's household, it had been simple to plan when and how to take them all, one by one.

The horse was saddled and he retrieved a pair of pistols from his satchel which he stuck in his belt along with his stiletto. The rapier was back in its scabbard at his waist. He was ready to go and he went over to the recalcitrant woman, dithering over whether he needed to take her or not. He briefly looked around but all was silent in the grassy field, just the odd night sounds of animals and birds. He decided to err on the side of caution, one could never be sure with this family, they'd already caused him more problems than he'd bargained for. He pulled out his knife, determined to put an end to the mewling infant now it had served his purpose, and as Elise screamed, he bent towards the child, stiletto raised in the air…

"Don't touch him," the soft voice came out of nowhere and he froze. Ashcroft crept out of the shelter of the hedging where he'd been hiding and watching, waiting for his opportunity to shoot Bernheim as soon as he came out of the little lean-to.

"YOU!" Bernhein snarled as he whirled around and went to stand behind Elise, his knife across her throat as his other hand went for his pistol.

"Yes, me, again," Ashcroft spoke slowly and coldly, "you didn't think you were going to escape, did you?" his pistol was aimed directly at Bernheim's forehead.

Bernheim knew there had been something about the grey man, his intuition hadn't been wrong. "So, you are The Shadow after all," he grated.

"Wrong again." Francis crept out of the darkness where he and Nicky and Jack had been watching. "I am The Shadow," and he raised his pistol in the air, "don't you EVER listen?"

"And me…" Jack went to stand beside the other two men, knife in hand, "the junior contingent, outstanding apprentice… *à votre service*…" his bow was so obviously insulting that for a moment Francis's lips twitched; the lad was coming on leaps and bounds, he thought.

"Well, what do you know, it appears to be a little *soirée*." Nicky joined them, pistol cocked and ready, four grim-faced men of various ages, all lined up to confront their enemy, looking at him in the light from their lanterns.

Bernheim looked at them all, his mind on fire, he'd never felt so frustrated or so angry. Was there no escape from these men? They confounded him at every turn and he felt like his head would explode with rage, but his fury was cold with malice dripping from every word. "If you shoot me, her throat will be cut as I fall," Bernheim threatened, and they watched as the deadly blade pressed into the white skin of Elise's neck and flecks of blood appeared.

"Let her go," Francis seethed and Bernheim merely stared back at him, black eyes glowing in his sallow-skinned features.

"Who are you?"

"WE, are The Shadow," Jack indicated the two men on his left. "We are a collective, a triumvirate... you see how learned I am?" and for a moment he smirked his best supercilious expression at Bernheim, which made Francis and Nicky want to chuckle. "This wondrous Gentleman, he is the past," Jack pointed to Francis. "This very estimable Gentleman is the present," a nod to Ashcroft, "and I, a hand-some face with a lot of other amazing talents which I won't go into here... I am the future."

"And him?" Bernheim nodded towards Nicky.

"Aah, this venerable gentleman," Jack turned to his right and indi-cated Nicky, "this is our Continental representative, *Le Lion de Valenci-ennes*. He periodically comes out of the shadows in Europe, to deal with vermin such as yourself; very apt, wouldn't you say? If you had stayed to watch, you would have seen him deal with your lions, unarmed and temporarily injured. A lion by name and a lion by nature." Jack was getting quite carried away and Ashcroft would have laughed at his nonsense had the situation not been so dangerous. "But put us all together, and, as you have discovered, we are invincible. *Invictus*, which you would understand, of course, had you been a serious Latin scholar like myself." Francis and Nicky, like Ashcroft, would have been entertained by that claim were they not so distracted.

"And the man I killed inside, who is he? Not so invincible, obviously."

"He's not dead. It takes more than a ball in the chest to kill the Earl of Keswick, and he is one of us too. Almost another one of me, in fact, we are so similar at times... and I don't kill easily as your father discovered. As I gather someone recently said, we come from the same nest," Francis elbowed Ashcroft in the side, he'd been amused when Jack had repeated Ashcroft's words to him as they'd been creeping down the field in his wake, Jack and Nicky doing their best to reassure a worried Francis that Ricky would pull through with Benjy's care, they had such utter faith in his surgical skills and Ricky's determination to fight for his life.

"It matters not how many of you there are, you will never take me. Better men than you have tried and failed. Now, if you don't want to watch me slice open this woman's throat, very slowly, so she drowns in her own blood, I suggest you disarm your weapons, carefully, all of them, and put them on the ground in front of me, including your knife," he nodded at Jack.

For a moment, no one moved, including Elise, unaware of what Bernheim had already done to taunt Francis with his knife at Cat's throat. Francis wondered how strong a woman Elise was, and how much belief she had in him. He took a chance she wouldn't go to pieces. He shrugged, "The greater good is at stake, isn't that right, Miles? One woman instead of how many others? But at least YOU will be dead." Elise didn't move or say a word.

"My pistols have hair triggers. I'll take one of you with me... now which one, I wonder?" and the pistol moved slightly as he took aim at all four of them, one by one, as it moved along their line. "You," he started with Francis, "you were responsible for the death of my father; or you," he paused at Ashcroft, "you've completely frustrated my plans today; the rest of you would be lion food if it wasn't for you." The pistol then hovered at Jack. "You. You nearly killed me in Nice, but I'm also difficult to kill as well, as you see... or finally, there's YOU!"

he snarled at Nicky. "YOU... you've been a thorn in my side for years."

"It was my complete pleasure," said Nicky sarcastically, "but as Francis said, whatever happens, you will be out of the way, once and for all."

Bernheim was thinking frantically as he surveyed the four men in front of him who wouldn't back down... or would they? Back in the barn he'd merely had to threaten the women and they'd capitulated, but maybe this one wasn't so important to them? He decided the woman wasn't worth troubling himself over. She couldn't do anything, tied up as she was, so he'd have to deal with the men, one of whom was injured. Three had pistols and one had a knife, and he knew how deadly HE was. Bernheim's back itched. For himself, he had his knife and two pistols, one in his hand. He weighed up the odds, deciding who to shoot and who to throw his knife at. His horse was saddled, ready to go, and he had the woman to hide behind as cover.

The five men stood watching each other, just as had happened in the barn. Impasse again.

Suddenly, Bernheim moved, striking like the snake he was. He kicked Elise viciously on her ankles making her jerk and cry out and at the same time his knife flew through the air and his pistol went off. Nicky dropped like a stone, despite throwing himself to the side as soon as he saw Bernheim twitch, his own pistol ball going wide of Bernheim's head. Francis staggered back and fell to knees, a knife in his upper chest, his ball searing a furrow across Bernheim's arm, a few inches wide of his chest. Francis had paused for an infinitesimal second too long, fearful of hitting Elise... and as Ashcroft paused to take aim, also fearful of hitting Elise, Bernheim whipped his second pistol from his belt, shot low as he raised it, and Ashcroft dropped to the ground, a ball in his leg, his ball also mere inches from Bernheim's head.

Jack had thrown himself to the ground, trying to watch Bernheim's eyes intently in the lantern-light, just as he'd been taught by Francis, with added facetious but useful commentary from Ricky, the ultimate duellist, when he'd come across the pair of them doing target practice down at Firle one day, as competitive with each other as ever. Jack rolled across the ground and to his feet, knife still in hand, as Bernheim scythed round, grabbed for his satchel and virtually threw himself at his startled horse which was skittering about, rolling its eyes as the guns had gone off around it. It would have bolted had it not been loosely tethered.

Bernheim was in the saddle, hauling on the reins, about to gallop off into the darkness when Jack launched himself at him. With every ounce of youthful, wiry strength he possessed, he flung himself at the man he feared had just killed one or both of the two men he idolised. Uncaring of himself, his impetus knocked Bernheim flying and the pair fell off the horse to the ground and started to wrestle.

Ashcroft's and Nicky's words raced round in Jack's head. "Don't trust anyone... expect the unexpected," he could hear their voices as clearly as if they were standing over him as Bernheim's hand went to his boot and a small, razor-sharp dagger suddenly glinted in his hand. They wrestled, both trying to get the upper hand, their deadly knives inches from each other's throats. Over and over they rolled in the muddy grass, stabbing and slashing where they could find purchase or an opening, death hanging in the balance for the pair of them. Bernheim was the bigger man, as tall as Nicky, but slender like Ricky, and it belied a lean strength that was far greater than Jack's; the youth from the gutters struggled desperately to put an end to the man who'd been a blight on the lives of his adopted family for as long as he'd known them.

Jack felt Bernheim's knife slash under his ribs; he gasped and rolled away and to his feet, breathing heavily, his hand to his side to stem the flow of blood. Bernheim leapt to his feet and faced the youth, an insane gleam in his eyes and then, taking Jack by surprise, he suddenly spun right around, kicked out with his foot, and the impetus sent Jack's knife flying out of his hand and away into the grass and he staggered. As a chopping hand then sent him to his knees, he knelt, defenceless and gasping, as Bernheim advanced on him with his dagger raised, moving in for the kill. "You see, I learned more from my late Chinese friend than how to wield the needles," he hissed. "Goodbye, Jack Vallance..." and the knife flashed.

Suddenly, like a wraith from the shadows, Eddie rose from the hedging where he'd been creeping up to the scene and raised his pistol. *"Je t'ai DIT que je suis L'Ombre...* I TOLD you I was The Shadow..." he spoke in French and as an astonished Bernheim froze and gaped at him, the pistol fired and Bernheim staggered and fell to the ground, a neat hole in the centre of his forehead.

"Eddie?" Jack struggled to his feet, wondering how he was still alive. "Oh fuck... Eddieeeee," Jack staggered over to him, sobbing with reaction, tears coursing down his face, lost for words, and he fell into the older man's arms.

Eddie hugged the youth hard and reassuringly, "He's dead, Jack. Dead. You hear me? Finally. It's over, finished... quickly, go to Francis and the others, I need to release Elise." and he shoved Jack over to where Francis and Ashcroft were kneeling over Nicky's prone body.

As Eddie hurriedly picked up Bernheim's dagger and cut Elise free, Jack sank to his knees beside Francis. "Oh God, nooo, not again... Nickyyy..." and his tears started once more as he bent over the still body and picked up Nicky's right hand.

"He's still alive, Jack... we're all alive, just..." Francis whispered, his eyes slightly glazed as he cradled Nicky's head on his lap. "Thank God Eddie got here in time to save you."

"I don't matter," sobbed Jack. "He does. Nicky... Nicky..." he frantically kissed the hand he was holding. "You can't die on us now, pleeeease..."

Nicky's eyes opened and flickered. "Franci'? he whispered faintly, looking up into Francis's despairing blue eyes, "look... aft'r... Bella... f'me. Is... is 'e dead?"

"Eddie killed him. Oh, Nicky, you can't die, you can't, not after everything at Waterloo... you just CAN'T..." Jack was completely distraught, interrupting Francis before he could speak.

"I thin'... m'... ni' lives... are fin'ly used up, Jack..." Nicky whispered.

"Get out of the way!" Elise fell to her knees amongst the men. "Get the light over here one of you, quickly..." and she bent over Nicky, "now you look here, Nicholas de Bresancourt, we're all alive and he's dead, on his deserving way to Hell no doubt, and I'm NOT going to go back and tell Bella we've lost you too." She stroked his forehead as she tutted at him, tearing up even more of her petticoats as she spoke, uncaring who saw her bare legs, and she ripped open his bloodied shirt and examined where he'd been shot. She pressed the pad of material to a gaping hole, "the ball has gone into your upper chest, near your shoulder, straight through by the looks of the blood on Francis's lap... so you're NOT going to die, you've just lost a lot of blood which is making you lightheaded. You haven't used up all your lives yet, You Big Pussy Cat, so pull yourself together and stop being so feeble. We're going to take you back to Benjy and he'll sort you out, AGAIN, and then I'm going to nurse you better, just like I did before, and no more of your nonsense; Bella's far too soft with you..."

"Oh G'd, not 'nother bossy w'man," Nicky whispered. "Franci'...?" he looked up into the big blue eyes, "'re y' all ri'?"

"I've got a hole in me too," Francis whispered, holding a hand to his shoulder where he'd pulled Bernheim's knife out and was trying to stop himself from passing out as waves of dizziness kept threatening to overwhelm him, "but he's gone, Nicky, it's over. At long last. Eddie saved the day... again. He always was a dead shot, another member of our little group of shadows, eh, Miles?"

Ashcroft had ripped off his cravat to tie round his leg where blood was oozing from a wound in his thigh. "I KNEW we'd get him in the end. I was absolutely determined, but thank God it's finished, finally..." he looked shellshocked, faint and greyer than ever.

"Francis?" Elise turned to look at Francis more closely, realising his wound was also serious. "Are you sure you're all right? Don't you pass out on me, your wife will run me through if I let anything happen to you."

"I'll survive, I need stitching up though. How the hell are we going to get back to the barn or the farmhouse? Talk about walking wounded."

"I'll go. I'll get a wagon and come back for you," Jack struggled to his feet and started to totter for a moment or two.

"Jack! Your side...you're covered in blood!" Ashcroft cried out, aghast to see what was obviously more than a minor cut.

"Oh hell... right. I'm going," announced Eddie who had joined them, cuddling his now wailing son while Elise did what she could to stem the flow of blood from Nicky's chest, half an eye on Francis and now Jack. "I'll bring the soldiers, they can come back and help you all."

"We all owe you, Eddie, thank you..." Francis looked up at his brother-in-law.

"None of that, I'm merely glad I wasn't too late this time, eh, Francis?"

"You weren't too late before. Dupont would have shot Cat if you hadn't shot him."

"There aren't any more of them, are there? No more Bernheims hiding in the woodwork that we don't know about?" Eddie asked, "I've just about had enough of that family."

"Not as far as I know," sighed Ashcroft. "This has to be the end of it. He was after your family for nigh on twenty-five years, not to mention the trouble he caused wherever he dabbled. You've no idea the number of men he killed, either himself or through his plotting, and that doesn't count the collateral damage, countless innocent people who died because he didn't care who died or got injured as a result of his activities. He was the very Devil."

"He nearly did for all of us. Look at the damage he's wrought today," murmured Francis.

"But we're ALIVE and that's all that matters" tutted Elise. "Now, go on, My Love, go and get help as quickly as you can. We need to get this ball out of Nicky's chest, and deal with the other injuries,"

"I'm off, I'll be as quick as I can. I'll take Harry with me, Bella can look after him, feed him or get him something to drink in the farm-house," and with that, Eddie turned and limped hurriedly back in the direction of the barn. The quiet, unobtrusive, disabled man who had finally saved the day.

Elise did what she could to patch up the men's wounds, tutting and fussing over them, and Francis whispered to her as she tore up his shirt to put into a pad to hold against his wounded shoulder, having run out of petticoats, "You're a very brave and strong woman, Elise.

Most women would have had hysterics after what I said to Bernheim."

"I'm not really," she whispered, "but I had faith you knew what you were doing," she said stoutly. "I had to believe, but, truth to tell, I was petrified out of my life. Sadly, I'm not Carlotta, she would have given Bernheim hell, I'm sure. I'm not strong like she was, you see. Eddie thought the world of her," she sighed forlornly, "she was everything I'm not..." she bent and shook her head and Francis heard the sadness in her voice. So that was the way of things, he thought, and instantly realised she was trying to live up to a constant shadow in her life, to compete with a ghost, because she loved Eddie and it was obviously eating at her. It was plain to Francis how much she cared for the man and he thought Eddie cared for her in return, but Carlotta had been the love of his life. Oh, what a damn mess it was; the poor woman, he thought. So, with a prayer of forgiveness to Carlotta, he partly lied as he responded.

"Carlotta wouldn't have done what you did today, and I knew her well. You do yourself down, Elise, quite unnecessarily. She would have been in pieces, especially if it had been her child involved... and to watch her maid being eaten?" he gripped Elise's hand to emphasise what he was quietly saying, "You're just as strong as she was, stronger even. You're a very different person in all respects, so never let me hear you say anything like that again. Don't even begin to compare yourself; I'm sure Eddie never does. He cares for you a great deal, My Dear, believe me. You've given him his life back again, we all know that, and are endlessly grateful he found you... and Carlotta has been gone for nigh on fifteen years. Eddie is a very quiet, deep man, but it doesn't mean he doesn't care. He does, believe me; so have faith, Elise, and, for what it's worth, I personally think you're a wonderful woman."

"You're such a good man, Francis, under that front you put on. Your grandmother always said how deep your rivers ran. I'd like to believe you, really I would, but I KNOW what happened in Rouen all those years ago, what Carlotta did, and she was carrying Bella at the time as well. I doubt I could ever have done that."

"You never know how you will react in times of crisis until you find yourself in one," said Francis knowingly, "and you surpassed yourself today; whatever you think or say about yourself, you're a strong woman. My dear grandmother would never have befriended you if you'd been a brainless ninny with no backbone, so you just remember that."

"I think about her a lot, you know," Elise sighed. "She was such a wonderful woman. I thought about her a lot today, wondering what she would have done if she'd been in my shoes. She gave me courage," she whispered.

"I miss her too, and think about her often, like you. She gave me courage as well, she wouldn't have tolerated me giving in to anyone. She would have thrashed me, I can assure you, no matter how old I was," Francis smiled.

"Hah! That would have been a sight to see," Elise smiled back as she tried to picture such a scene. "You were her whole life, her *raison d'etre*," Elise sighed. "She loved Nicky too, like another grandson, but it was always you. YOU were special to her in some extra way. I don't know what it was, but you were more than just a grandson."

Francis knew why, but it was his secret, and he was amazed Elise had realised there was something beyond the ties of ordinary filial affection and closeness between him and his grandmother. She was a very perceptive woman, he decided.

"Enough of all this," he smiled at her again and gave her hand another squeeze, "go and look after Nicky and the others, I'll be fine," he said softly.

"Stop pretending, Francis," Elise tutted. "You've had Bernheim's knife in your chest, not been playfighting soldiers with Lizzie and Terrie. Another few inches and you'd be lying next to that snake over there. I can see how much it hurts and how dizzy you keep getting, and that's not claret seeping out into that pad either. I'm going to have a few words with Cat when we get back to the barn. SHE won't tolerate any of your nonsense and will make sure you stay in bed and behave yourself until you're healed properly. The last thing you need is to get an infection in that wound," and she waggled her finger at him.

"I never behave myself in bed, Elise," Francis winked at her, wondering how she'd react. He'd never addressed her in such a suggestive manner before. Elise merely looked back at him completely impassively for a moment, "in fact," he continued mischievously, "I'd go as far as to say, the older I get, the more I misbehave…" and a brow quirked in her direction.

"Well, Francis Granville, I'm exceedingly pleased to hear it. Is it a case of an old dog learning new tricks to keep up with the younger generation in the family?" and Francis gasped in amusement as the teasing barb went home. "As someone told me a while ago, reading gets sooooo very tedious at your time of life, but then, I suppose it depends upon what one's reading matter is, and if it's of a particularly educational nature, and naturally, one is never too old to broaden one's education in the very widest sense, and I do mean wide…" and with a broad wink back at him, she got up and returned to fuss over Nicky and the other two men as Francis watched her with a chuckle, wondering what the hell Eddie had found in the quiet Widow of Hertford Street, and why she had such a complex about competing with Carlotta with a saucy wit like that, as prim she most definitely was not….

Chapter Sixteen

SUMMER 1816

I t had been inevitable that gossip would rage about what had happened to the extended Granville family. Between the military presence in Berkeley Square and Hertford Street, servants' tattle, and Cat and Eddie's mother and her cronies, the Ton had been agog. Although all the household staff and the old ladies had been told not to discuss the matter with ANYONE, inevitably that was a forlorn hope.

The old ladies had arrived back in Berkeley Square all together, to deliver their two little charges and inspect the latest addition to the Granville offspring before returning home, only to be told by an army officer and the housekeeper they were not allowed to leave until further notice; at which point they had all had a fit of the vapours and Cat's poor mother had taken to a spare bed in complete shock on learning the whole family had disappeared. The nightmare of what had happened to her and her husband and daughters a quarter of a century before looming large in her mind.

The two little girls had found Bubbles, injured and half-drunk, in the sitting room in front of the fire, with the cook still tending him lovingly. With all the chaos around them, they refused to go to bed or do anything until their parents had returned and they were belligerent and completely inconsolable, especially Lizzie, somehow sensing something was deeply wrong. The staff eventually gave up and let them sit by the big front windows of the mansion, maintaining a vigil until they fell asleep, whereupon they were put to bed together in Cat's suite with armed footmen guarding the doors inside and out and the faithful Clara asleep in an armchair, a loaded pistol on her lap as well. The fact she had no idea how to shoot it she deemed irrelevant, merely saying she would rise to such matters if the need demanded it, her mistress would expect nothing less of her!

Word was therefore put out that the family had been the subject of a dastardly kidnapping plot by would-be revolutionaries, but it had all been foiled and no harm had been done to anyone, and it was all a storm in a teacup. After a while, the gossips moved on to the next bit of scandal and the matter was forgotten. That was helped by Eddie putting in an appearance at Almack's, with Elise and Bella on either arm and all three had dismissed the gossip as embroidered nonsense. On enquiry, Bella said airily her husband was over at his Ducal estates in France, which he was endeavouring to put into order now Bonaparte was off the scene and the countries were no longer at war. However, she'd stayed at home in London as their baby had the sneezes and she didn't want to expose the new heir to a sea crossing, as he was far too little and precious. Eddie said his sister and brother-in-law had gone to the country for Easter with their little daughter and new infant son, and all three were so dismissive and vague, spending the evening chatting and dancing without a care in the world, no one was any the wiser. It was a masterly piece of acting by all three considering most of the family had been traumatised by what had happened to them all.

When everyone had arrived back at Berkeley Square the following morning, the military presence had mysteriously dispersed as fast as it had appeared, and stretchers bearing Ricky, Nicky, Fred and Alfie had been quietly carried in from covered wagons through the servants' entrance, away from curious eyes. Up in the bedrooms, a harassed Benjy flitted between the four, inspecting, fussing and tending his handiwork on their wounds. Alfie found himself in a proper, not to mention luxurious, bedroom for the first time in his life, much to his amazement, and Fred felt like he'd returned to his childhood, though nothing as comfortable as the bedroom he too found himself in. As well as the four seriously injured men, Benjy also tended the walking wounded: Francis, Ashcroft and Jack, all three refusing to be carried on a stretcher despite Benjy's remonstrations as Francis and Ashcroft staggered into the mansion, leaning heavily on Browning and Carstairs for support... and then there was the catastrophe that was Cat's throat wounds.

Ashcroft was the first to leave, his thigh injury merely a flesh wound, albeit a deep and nasty one, and with it stitched and bandaged up he resolutely hobbled off, with the aid of a stick and the support of the redoubtable Chalmers, who had mysteriously appeared with Nelson in tow not long after everyone had arrived and categorically refused to leave until his leader did. Ashcroft went back to his small Mayfair house where his housekeeper blanched when she saw his wounded leg. She shooed him off to bed where he stayed and fretted for several days, finally giving in to the pain and discomfort he'd striven to hide from everyone, trying to make light of his injury... with Nelson sitting on the covers, not wanting to leave his master's side. Chalmers pithily said they should change his name to Hardy, and ferried mounds of papers to and from the Department of Information as Ashcroft facetiously told him he needed the distraction of work to take his mind off his injury, and there wasn't room for two men with a warped sense of humour in their office!

Progressing to sit in his study, with his leg propped up on a thick cushion on top of a large stool, Ashcroft finally dictated a masterpiece of a report for his superiors. It related how a dangerous French agent, long sought after by the British and their Allies, had finally been run to earth just outside London where he had been in the process of carrying out a plot that had threatened the lives of various members of the

Establishment that would cause untold repercussions across London, the least of which was fermenting trouble among potential anarchist or even revolutionary factions. However, said agent had been dealt with and shot before any real harm had been done, along with his band of associates, his plot averted, and the man would finally be no further threat to His Majesty's Government, his subjects and the country's Allies. The report was circulated and explained the deployment of soldiers and cavalry, but since nothing particularly untoward appeared to have publicly happened, no one took much notice of it. A copy of the report went into the filing system and the masterpiece never saw the light of day again.

Ashcroft also had the contents of Bernheim's saddlebag on a table in his study and was busy investigating the small book he found in it together with notes of interesting names and addresses in Paris and further afield across Europe and even the Americas. Who these people were, he had no idea, but each and every one would be followed up and investigated. Ashcroft was nothing if not thorough and no stone would be left unturned to get to the bottom of Bernheim's perfidy and stop any further repercussions in England from his plotting, or indeed plots to destabilise governments or institutions across Europe. The Continent was only just recovering from the turmoil caused by Bonaparte with many countries still unstable. The last thing Europe needed was the rise of another individual with delusions of international power or indeed to succumb to widespread bloody revolution and the rule of anarchy like France had suffered. Ashcroft wasn't that concerned about the internal politics of other countries, other than he was a firm believer in democracy and the rule of law, but he suspected Britain might well get drawn into another conflict and that was something the country could do without. Ashcroft believed his native land needed a long period of peace and stability to rebuild her economy after more than twenty years of war on several fronts, and to focus on enterprise and trade, not the huge cost and upheaval that serious international conflict brought. So that was his mission, to help his beloved country become a great empire, not via war but through peace and trading around the globe, and to spread its influence benignly and he would do his bit to flush out and extinguish any troublemakers like Frederick Bernheim, who sought to cause mischief and havoc.

The grey spymaster sat for many hours in his study, dog on lap, staring out the window, going over the events of those traumatic twenty-four hours. If it wasn't for the wound on his leg, he felt as if he'd been in a bad dream as he'd never been so close to personal death, nor witnessed so much drama and horror in such a short space of time, if ever. He privately told Nelson he'd had his fill of excitement for a long, long time, even though for a few hours he'd felt more alive than he ever had in his entire life. He'd also been The Shadow for a very short while… and he finally understood what had motivated Francis Granville to become what he had

The clerk on the front desk at the Foreign Office disappeared without trace to the nether regions of endless paper pushers in a distant office.

Francis refused to stay in bed when they finally got him there. Elise nagged and Cat threatened and swore at him as the pair of them took him to task. Cat promised to tie him to the bedposts if he didn't do as he was told and rest and recover from his wound, and Elise didn't know where to look as he chuckled and smirked at his wife and said it had been a while since she'd done that to him but, as she was well aware, that would wear him out more than getting up and going down to his study. Cat told him in no uncertain terms to behave himself with visitors present, whereupon Francis simply replied with a dirty laugh that he'd told Elise not a few days before that he never behaved himself in bed and Cat had gone apoplectic and almost exploded with wrath at her husband. Elise didn't understand what Cat said back to Francis in a stream of voluble, irate French as she stood and ranted at him, making him chuckle all the more, but she got the general gist and beat a hasty, laughingly embarrassed retreat from the pair of them as sparks flew, remembering her promise to herself back in her cellar prison. She was so jealous and desperately wanted that rapport and a loving, laughter-filled, passionate relationship with Eddie.

So Francis sat and recovered in his study and he, too, spent hours gazing out the window to the garden reflecting on what had happened. He hated getting old and finally admitted to himself he wasn't the man he was. He wasn't the deadly Shadow anymore. He'd always been a crack shot and couldn't believe he'd missed Bernheim, even if he had been wary of hitting Elise, and tried to come to terms with the fact his reflexes and stamina weren't what they were. It had nearly cost Jack and Nicky their lives and he could barely live with himself. As he'd climbed the tree he'd already decided to stop nibbling on Bubbles' treats, stop smoking so many cheroots and cigars and promised himself he'd go to Captain Carnie's several times a week in a concerted effort to lose some weight and regain some semblance of his former fitness. He gazed across at the big, lazy dog, lolling on a rug in front of the open French windows, miraculously and mostly recovered from his injuries, apart from bald patches on his fur where Benjy had shaved it off to stitch him up. Francis told him in no uncertain terms his days of wandering around the park at a snail's pace were now over, and he wasn't going to turn into a drunken sot either, the dog having taken quite a fancy to a small drop of sweet port every time he heard a decanter clink and he would sit and pant at the feet of whoever was having a drink, his tongue hanging out, a pathetic expression on his face which few could resist.

Francis was also worried about Cat.

Cat refused to go out at night. She fussed and fretted over Francis until he was almost demented, and went about her charitable works as before, shopped in Bond Street and greeted friends and acquaintances so no one realised there was a problem, but now she wore a high-collared jacket with a blouse with a high ruffled neck and a silken scarf carefully wound around it to boot, and she never took them off when she was out. But she resolutely wouldn't go to any social event where evening dress was required, not knowing how to explain the livid red scars around her neck and throat. As she shouted at Francis when he remonstrated with her - what was she supposed to do? Tell the Ton she and the entire family had been held hostage by a deranged Frenchman who knew her husband had been a renowned smuggler and pirate who'd made a fortune he coveted, and he'd half cut her throat in an effort to get Francis to reveal where his illicit fortune was concealed?

Francis said they could think of some excuse, but she said she simply couldn't face the questions and gossip her appearance and the scars would create, and it was far too risky, so she refused to budge and they argued and argued, round in circles, and got nowhere. Francis was at his wits' end as he grappled with coming to terms with getting old and Cat withdrew from him, and Society, more and more.

Chapter Seventeen

Marie-Catherine Granville, the Duchess of Firle, stared at her reflection in the mirror, looking at her figure. But, as always now, she was also focussed on the lurid red lines across her neck. It had been more than six months since Marcus had been born and she was still struggling to get back into her dresses, no matter how tight Clara pulled her corsets, for stays weren't enough… and, of course, she didn't wear a corset to go to bed at night… and Francis was usually waiting for her there.

Francis Granville, the Duke of Firle, the man half the women in London still lusted after, even at his age. But his age made no difference; he still looked as suave, elegant and handsome as he had over twenty-five years before. The elusive and reclusive Duke of Firle, now just more distinguished, with the thread of silver in his dark hair and at his temples, more noticeable since the affair of the lions. He was also Alex, HER swashbuckler, HER Shadow, and always would be. As far as she knew, he'd never strayed, but if she didn't get a hold of herself, he might… and that would destroy her, not that she wouldn't kill any woman she found chasing after him. Nevertheless, she was desperate to get her figure back and she wasn't going to let Francis see her still fat; she wanted to be able to walk across his bedroom in some of the underclothes she'd bought in Paris and have him look at her again with that curling smile on his face and with lust in his eyes, not make excuses then creep into bed with the candles out as she'd been doing until now.

Cat had never been vain, but she loved the fact Francis lusted after her, in bed and out, and she enjoyed dressing to please and tantalise him. He told her frequently as he made love to her, how much she still excited him, and how beautiful she still was, and she loved it. She ate hardly anything now, fenced at Captain Carnie's frenetically, rode daily and had walked miles and miles at Firle. She was getting there, but it was all taking so long, and she wasn't in her twenties any longer, and then Bernheim had happened and now she had the scars to deal with as well. She was marked, just like her brother, and she empathised with him all the more now. She had horrible, ugly red lines around her neck and a long red line down to her cleavage. How could any man gaze at her and want her, looking like that? She'd seen pity in Francis's eyes and it had devastated her, made her cringe, and cry and cry in the privacy of her room with only the understanding Clara to console her. She didn't want his pity, she wanted his desire again.

She couldn't bear to go out to any parties or dinners where evening dress was required, she couldn't cover the disfiguring scars, they were too big, too wide, too long. And how could she explain them? She was terrified someone would ask too many questions, poke their nose into the affair they all wanted desperately to forget, and find out about Bernheim… and that would lead to Francis and his deadly secret. It was a risk she wasn't prepared to take, she loved him far, far too much. So, not knowing what to do, she was going to do nothing. Live a quiet life, possibly retire down to Firle and look after her young children and leave London behind. Besides, her mother was still traumatised by what had happened and was only just getting over it, and she was busy caring for her too. But then, what would Francis do? He had to stay in London most of the time to oversee his affairs and if she wasn't there, would he stray? But if she stayed in London, they'd continue to argue about her not going out with him or being a hostess at dinners and soirees they would normally hold in Berkeley Square.

Round and round it all went in her head until it ached, as she stared at herself in the mirror. Despair filled her big green eyes as tears rolled down her face and she turned away from the long looking glass, threw herself on her bed and sobbed herself to sleep.

Francis had quietly bought Fred Dyer a little country cottage, and he went home there to recuperate in his small garden, still amazed at the Duke's generosity but now safe in the knowledge he had somewhere to retire to when he'd finished in Ashcroft's service. And Ashcroft had looked after him as well - a promotion and more money and even a small pension… courtesy of Francis if he but knew it, but he didn't… and all because of that one fateful afternoon.

Richard Ambrose had had a lucky escape. The bullet had gone into his chest, glanced off a rib and so avoided doing as much damage as it could have to his lungs… and it had been mere inches from his heart. He'd lain in bed convalescing in Berkeley Square, having sent a message to his wife that he'd gone off to view a possible business venture with his old friend Francis, so she shouldn't worry over his non-appearance down at Foxmoor. With Benjy and Cat fussing over him, he'd avoided any infection and was making a slow but steady recovery. As he lay in bed and gazed out the windows of his room, Ricky decided that perhaps he was glad after all he hadn't been a smuggler with Francis. One afternoon and evening of pretending to be The Shadow had been enough and had nearly got him killed. He was still in disbelief at Francis's secret life for years and the pair had spent hours reminiscing and talking as Francis had regaled him with tales of what he'd got up to, and Ricky had been alternately amused, amazed and even shocked, and was still deciding if he was jealous or not.

Eventually, sheer determination and boredom had driven Ricky out of bed and downstairs to convalesce in the garden on sunny days, but once he was back on his feet he returned to Surrey, to Foxmoor, where his wife had shrieked blue murder at him when she'd found out what had happened. Both extremely short-tempered, they'd had a blazing row, as usual, and she'd slapped his face she was so angry at how he'd risked his life, and he'd slapped her back, telling her to contain herself, but then also, as usual, she'd ended up kissing him passionately, and they'd retired to their bedroom much to the titters of the household staff, well used to the inappropriate behaviour of the eccentric couple... the foppish, laconic man who was no such thing and secretly ran a growing publishing empire, and the beautiful socialite who was, in reality, something of an academic and a closet writer of torrid romance novels and acerbic newspaper articles. Their gaggle of children were none the wiser about anything, except their young son, Augustus, who'd watched, goggle-eyed, through the bannisters, and then peered through the keyhole of their bedroom door until hauled off by his tutor who threatened to cane him, again, for misbehaving, not that it ever did any good, and even if he didn't understand all he saw and heard, Gus Ambrose knew far more than anyone about his parents' activities!

The various residents of Hertford Street were dealing with their own issues. As soon as Benjy deemed it safe to move Alfie and Nicky, the de Bresancourt family had returned back to their house after dark one night, and Elise spent most of her days there, nursing the pair of them and demonstrating to Bella how to change bandages and tend wounds, and Benjy regularly called in to supervise and check no infection was lurking.

Bella had consigned everything about the terrible day to yet another box in her attic, but it still didn't stop her from having terrifying nightmares about Daisy and herself being eaten by lions, and she frequently woke in the night, screaming with fright and drenched in sweat. She was so traumatised by all the events of that dreadful day and night that she couldn't even bring herself to write about them in her diary. She decided the horror was beyond anything she could write that would describe it. The entry for that day was therefore inane and simple:

"It wasn't a very good day today, to put it mildly, and we had some Trouble with a group Feral Cats, but at least there was one bit of Good News. HE is finally Dead and will be consigned to an Unmarked Grave, with his Associates, according to MA. Good Riddance. That is all I have to write on the matter."

And so the dreadful events were consigned to the darkness of history. A permanent and unrecorded Sooty Secret and never spoken of again in the de Bresancourt and de Mornay household except occasionally in private.

Jack had been stitched up by Benjy but was too restless to stay in bed. Instead, he spent some time every day sitting with Alfie, who was recuperating slowly and, in between, he spent hours down the street with Eddie, preparing himself for his last term at school and his end-of-year exams. Conversations had also started about what he would do with himself when he left Eton, and everyone agreed Oxford or Cambridge was not an option, being far too academic, despite how well his education had gone. Jack was adamant he had to make his own way in the world and, sympathetic to his feelings as he had been there himself, Nicky had suggested he go to work for Francis. Eddie thought that an excellent idea and suggested perhaps he could travel overseas and see a bit of the world and educate himself further that way, and Francis had agreed, telling Jack that his haggling skills when he used to fence his stolen goods would no doubt prove useful!

In the meantime, Eddie insisted on coaching Jack for his exams and told him that, even if he was going to work for Francis, he should still spend time in between his trips continuing his studies with him, and he would ensure they covered all sorts of interesting areas that he hadn't explored at school. English and foreign politics and current affairs, new developments in science and medicine, principles of business, and anything else Eddie could teach him about the Gentlemen's world he now inhabited.

At the end of the holidays, he went back to Eton, escorted by Eddie and Francis, who told him pointedly not to get into any fights and risk his wound, and a story was concocted for the Headmaster that the family had been waylaid by highwaymen over the Easter weekend and Jack had sustained a minor injury in the fracas so was to be excused doing anything energetic. That Francis also had his arm in a sling supported the story and the Headmaster tutted about the dangers of travel these days and promised faithfully to keep an eye on Jack and ensure he kept out of mischief.

Alfie was making slow progress. Benjy had stitched him up, inside and out, but had warned it would be months until he healed properly inside and on NO account was he to strain himself or stretch his abdomen. So he lay in bed, bored and frustrated, his days broken only by visits from Jack and some of the household staff who would sit and read to him to relieve his boredom. When she realised Alfie couldn't read or write properly, it gave Bella something to do and she set to, to teach him, aided and abetted by Jack, and suddenly Alfie's days became filled with lessons and books and little Terrie would sit and go through her own simple alphabet books with him, innocently reciting her letters and looking at pictures, and the pair became fast friends, much to everyone's amusement.

Chapter Eighteen

Nicky was another matter, but his personal hell was buried deep and went back to his childhood. His bad arm had sustained several knocks and strains during that fateful day and Benjy was reluctant to open it up and investigate exactly what was wrong. Doctors and specialists were called in to consult, but they hummed and hawed and, like Benjy, were none the wiser. Some thought the fragile bones had fractured or broken again and would mend, others thought it was the delicate muscles and tendons that might have been sprained or torn again, which explained the weakness, inability to move, and the agonising and continuous ache. One even suggested cutting it off to save any further problems and he'd been seen off by an irate Bella with short shrift. Whatever the cause, Nicky was in constant pain every time he tried to move his arm and the only relief he got was from taking some laudanum for the interminable ache. But Eddie, well familiar with the problem from his own experiences, counselled him not to resort to that if he could help it, and said he should just strap it up and let it heal itself gradually, and to do what he had before - keep the arm moving and stretched to ensure the muscles and tendons remained flexible. However, one thing every single expert and doctor had agreed on, including Benjy, was he had to be careful not to do anything that would risk further damage.

Apart from that burden, which left him incapacitated and one-handed, there was no strength to do anything with his other hand. Apart from the slash of Bernheim's rapier in his right bicep, which was nasty and deep, Bernheim's pistol ball had percolated right through his upper chest and out his back. Benjy said he was lucky that it hadn't hit anything critical and he should eventually heal with no repercussions, but Nicky's right arm was now also in a sling as his shoulder and upper arm healed and he felt like a cripple and raged privately, feeling worse than a disabled soldier from Waterloo, and half a man. It was all he could do to drink from a glass and feed himself, with an effort, and he refused to let anyone, especially Bella, help him.

As soon as everyone had healed enough to safely manage the journey, Eddie decreed, in a rare moment of forcefulness that brooked no denial, that the whole family should decamp down to Arlington and stay there for the duration of their convalescence, so Elise could nurse everyone and the quiet, fresh and balmy country air would do them all good and they could be a family again like they used to be. So they all set off and Bella and Nicky returned to their childhood home where they'd grown up and been idyllically happy until Carlotta had died, Eddie had withdrawn into himself in grief, and the pair had gone to spend most of their time with Francis and Cat. A bereft Bella had needed a mother to care for her and a teenage, headstrong and wilful Nicky, also grieving in his own way, needed a strong, loving hand like that of Francis to mentor, guide and steer him as both a young man and also as befitted his status of a Duke, albeit a penniless one. Wallowing in his sorrow and heartache, and feeling completely lost, Eddie had been unable to do either and had buried himself in the country with his books and his precious little son, the unwitting cause of his mother's death... until fate and the Dowager had interfered, and Cat had engineered a meeting between her reclusive brother and Elise.

The summer days grew long and Alfie progressed to sitting out in the sunshine, Terrie never far away with her dolls and books of letters and numbers and pictures, and the education of both continued, supervised by Bella, amidst much laughter. Nicky was quiet and would sit in the sun too, Duchess on his lap purring blissfully, and he'd smile at them all and joke appropriately and play chess or cards with Charlie, or would sit and pose while the boy tried to sketch or paint him and the cat, and Elise watched him with concern as he would withdraw into himself as soon as he was left alone.

One afternoon, in the privacy of his room, while she was changing the dressings on his wounds, Elise decided to grapple with whatever was bothering Nicky.

"Look, Nicky, I know I'm not your step-mother, not quite old enough to be, and I'm no relation... although I suppose officially I am your new sort-of, adopted step-mother... but I care for you and I can see something is bothering you, no matter how much you try and hide it. Would you like to talk to me? Sometimes it's easier to talk to someone outside of your close family; I... I'm part of you all, yet I'm not. I'm new to you all, but I know everything and understand... so perhaps you'd like to share your thoughts with me like you used to do with the Dowager? She used to talk to me, you know, in her last years; she worried about you a lot, bless her..."

Nicky looked at the quiet woman sitting on his bed and sighed. "You're very kind and caring, Elise, and you are one of us now, don't ever think you're not, but I'm fine, really I am. I just need time to recover from all this again." His right hand waved in the direction of his body and his left arm. "After Waterloo, I thought I'd never be injured again, and I was so thankful to be alive, still with four limbs, two eyes and no terrible burns or scars, some things didn't matter... but, here I am again, and I'm not a very patient patient, am I?" he smiled at her.

"No, you're not, but it's more than that. I'm not a fool, I can see something isn't right. Are you worried you won't heal? Is that it? Because you are healing, you can see it. Your right arm and shoulder are getting better, you'll be right as rain and wielding a sword before you can say Duke of Wellington."

"I doubt that, Elise, and you well know it. Save your fairy tales for Terrie."

"I KNEW it," cried Elise softly. "You're worried you won't get better, aren't you? But you will, you are. You're a strong man, Nicky, and it was only a wound in the upper chest and a slash on the arm. Oh, I know the ball did some damage to your shoulder and you lost a lot of blood, but, my God, if you'd seen yourself after we found you at Waterloo, then you would have reason to worry. This is nothing after all that, believe me."

"But I died... I still can't believe I did and came back to life, it's all too unreal... but I still died and I'm obviously not the man I was. I let those bastards take me at *Le Lion d'Or* with no problem on their side at all, so how do you think that makes me feel? And I couldn't escape, I couldn't free myself. Dear God, Elise, I didn't even have the strength to push Bella out of that lion's cage, Jack had to drag her, and then, in that field, I couldn't shoot straight enough to take Bernheim down. Eddie had to do it. I'm not a man anymore!" he finally burst out and Elise could hear the anguish in his voice and was filled with concern.

"Now you look here, Nicholas de Bresancourt. You're more man than most men I know, I can assure you," Elise tutted and poked him in the chest where she'd been bandaging him, "and if you pardon me for being a trifle indelicate, this is the second time I've nursed you, although last year you were well out for the count so didn't know. I've therefore tended wounds all over your naked body, washed you, shaved you and cleaned you up... and the reason I'm telling you this is that when I washed you... er... all over..." she gazed knowingly towards his pantaloons, "once you'd done your Lazarus bit but were still asleep, sometimes you, how can I put it politely... reacted; your subconscious must have known it was a woman tending you, so don't tell me you're not a man anymore, because that's utter nonsense. If you could manage that in your sleep, after what hit you at Waterloo, and dying and coming back to life on top of it, I refuse to listen to any twaddle about you not being a man anymore."

Nicky stared at Elise for a moment then threw back his head and guffawed with laughter for the first time in weeks. "You Wicked Baggage, Elise. I always knew there was more to you than the quiet woman everyone sees. Wash me, did you? That must have been quite some bed bath if that's what you want to call it. Did you enjoy yourself, for I obviously did; exactly how much did I react? You evidently gave me an extremely thorough wash..." his golden eyes sparkled at her, alive with amusement.

"Oh, be quiet, You Disgraceful Wretch," Elise went bright pink. "Stop teasing me, I did nothing of the sort. I was just sponging you down and keeping you clean," she was suddenly all flustered and Nicky chuckled at her discomfort. "Heaven knows who or what you were thinking about in your dreams, Bella, I trust... but of course NOTHING surprises me where you're concerned, absolutely NOTH-ING, You Shockingly Wicked Casanova," and she suddenly gave him a knowing look, but then remembered herself and sat up straight. "Anyway, I was just trying to prove a point..." she huffed.

"Where I'm concerned? I'm shockingly wicked?" Nicky quirked a brow. "Really? And why is that, pray? I'm a respectable ex-army officer, a married man and father... and how do you know who Casanova is, or was? A nice refined, genteel lady like yourself?"

"Oh, nothing," Elise muttered, "nothing at all. As I said, I was just trying to prove my point that there's nothing the matter with you now, it's all in your mind. You simply need to be patient, and if those bastards could take Francis, what with him being The Shadow and everything, why the hell are you berating yourself?" she tutted.

"Never mind Francis, but he IS old enough to be my father and not the man he was twenty-five, or even twenty years ago, Shadow or not, so that's different. However, that's beside the point and don't you DARE tell him I said that," he muttered, "because he'll be mortified and no doubt strangle me once and for all; but tell me, why does NOTHING surprise you about me, Elise?" Nicky wheedled, knowing she'd inadvertently said something she hadn't meant to.

"Never mind, it really was nothing. As I said, you're disgraceful, inferring I'd do anything... er... anything... well, you know... er, inappropriate," she blushed again.

"No, I don't know. Tell me... and it's obviously not 'nothing,'" Nicky grinned at her, his voice teasing and cajoling.

"Oooh, you're impossible! How did I get into this conversation? I was just changing your dressing. Behave yourself and let me finish with this and then we can go back downstairs and you can try and have another go at beating Charlie at chess."

"That boy is fifteen, half my bloody age, never mind half my size, and I've beaten him ONCE since we've been here, once; and that was only because he was half asleep; and one draw because he felt sorry for me the first time we played as he thought I wasn't up to it! How many times has he beaten me? He's just like his father and sister, I don't know why I bother. It gives me a headache every time I play him, he's completely impossible!" Nicky huffed with a resigned smile. "However, I'm not interested in chess with Charlie, I want to know what you were referring to, and we're not going downstairs until you tell me..." he had a grip of Elise's hand now and his golden eyes looked deep into her hazel ones.

"No... no, I couldn't possibly," Elise muttered and cringed. "It was nothing... years ago."

"Tell me, Elise," Nicky chivvied her. "I promise, I'll drive you completely mad until you tell me. I'll nag and nag and nag," he grinned, "and I want to know how you know about Casanova as well."

"Oh, all right," Elise gave in and sighed, "but don't be cross with me, because it's not my fault I know... about you... and Casanova."

"But he was Venetian, although he spent time in many parts of Europe, and I wasn't aware his reputation was that common knowledge among nice ladies here in London."

"I do read news and gossip sheets, you know, and other news items from abroad. I always liked to keep myself informed about continental affairs," Elise huffed, "even if my language skills aren't a touch on yours."

"'Affaires' being the precise point," Nicky smirked, "but enough of him, what else were you referring to? Come along, out with it... or I might tell Papa about your washing proclivities," a teasing threat he would never dream of carrying out but Elise blanched for a moment as he grinned wickedly at her.

"Ooooh noooo, Nicky, you wouldn't... You Villain," she gasped. "Oh, all right, I give in," and she took a deep breath. "I know what you used to get up to…" Elise finally burst out, "with certain ladies of the Ton."

"Whaaaat?" Nicky looked at her, somewhat disconcerted.

"And I don't mean just *affaires*… I mean," she whispered, "what you were paid to do."

"Good God!" Nicky's mouth dropped open. "How the HELL do you know about that?"

"You… er… you… one of my friends… one of my friends paid you for your services, and she nagged me to do the same as I was in a similar situation to her and had been terribly lonely for years… and curious I have to say, and I had finally persuaded myself to actually do it and make an… er… appointment, when I found out who you were and your relationship with the Dowager," Elise gabbled it all out. "There; now you know," and she sat back as Nicky simply gaped at her.

"OH. MY. GOD!" he was almost speechless as he stared at the woman opposite him.

"Oh Nicky, I'm so sorry, I would never have said anything if you hadn't nagged, and I'll NEVER breathe a word of it, I swear. My friend doesn't even know I know you, she doesn't know who you were… are… your relationship with Eddie. Thank God you used a different name; imagine if it ever got out now?"

"I don't believe it," Nicky was still stunned. "Who was she? You have to trust me, Elise, there weren't that many. I… I was just short of money for a while and I refused to take it from Papa or Francis."

"I'm not telling you, it's best that way, and I know now how proud you were, like Jack is, but that was a terrible risk, Nicky. Are you sure no one knows?"

"I don't mix in those circles anymore, thank God, but Francis found out; I didn't know he knew until recently, but he's the very devil with what he picks up, and of course he'd never say a word either. He thought it was rather amusing, but you have to understand, Elise, I didn't deliberately set out to do it, it sort of just happened as these things sometimes do. And I was going to join the army anyway, and it was around that time and just after, either before while I was racketing around Town, or after when I was in London on leave and temporarily short of funds... and then when I got drafted down to the Peninsula, I started to work as a liaison with the Spanish guerillas because of my language skills and was away for months on end, years even eventually, and it didn't happen again as I'd got involved with Bella and the whole *Lionesse* thing... and, well, you know what happened after that..." Nicky tried to explain in a garbled fashion.

"Oh, Nicky, or should I call you Leo?" Elise grinned naughtily. "You Bad Man, can you imagine if I... you... we... had done it... and then I'd met Eddie and seen you again? It's too surreal..." she giggled.

"Fuuuuuckkk..." Nicky gasped and swore slowly and wiped a hand over his face, aghast at what had nearly happened, "oh, beg pardon.... but it doesn't bear thinking about. How much did your friend tell you, Elise?" he hoped it wasn't much, and of course it depended on who she was.

Elise looked at him. "EVERYTHING," she said the word slowly and looked him in the eye. "What you charged, what you'd do, my friend was very explicit. She was a widow too, but far more knowledgeable and experienced than me in bedroom matters; my hair nearly went curly at some of the things she said you did with her."

"Oh, Christ!" Nicky rolled his eyes, "Promise me, Elise, you'll never breathe a word of this to Papa, or Cat, or certainly never to Bella. I'm not even sure how much Francis knows. If he knew as much as you obviously do, I'm sure he'd bend my ears something rotten and wind me up a treat; I'd never hear the end of it "

"My lips are forever sealed," Elise patted his hand. "Now then, having got that over with, are you going to tell me what is really bothering you? I take it it's all to do with you being injured?" Elise deftly moved the conversation back on to her original query.

"Of course it bloody is!" It was Nicky's turn to burst out. "Can you imagine how I feel after what we've just discussed? I can't even make love to Bella now, it's too awkward. It takes me half an hour to get into my breeches or pantaloons, let alone do them up properly by myself. My left arm is useless and hurts like damnation when I even try to flex it, and I've still no strength in my right arm... between that slash from Bernheim and the hole in my shoulder."

"I wasn't aware one needed arms to make love," Elise said sardonically.

"Don't get flippant, Elise. You're not naïve, you're married to Papa for God's sake," Nicky rasped angrily. "I can't do what I used to, of course I need my arms and hands, and I refuse to be serviced by Bella like I was a damn limbless cripple and she was a cheap whore doing her sympathetic bit for charity to give me a release."

"NICKY!" Elise was shocked and went bright red.

"Oh God, Elise, I'm so sorry, I forgot myself…" Nicky put a hand to his face again, horrified at his explicit outburst.

Elise put her hand on his. "No, don't mind me, I'm just not used to men being so forthcoming; but I understand your frustration, Nicky, and don't be so hard on yourself. Bella loves you, I'd want to be the same with Eddie if the situation happened to us. And you ARE getting better, the slash is healing quickly and your right arm and shoulder will be strong again in a week or two, just be patient."

"What about my left arm, Elise? Is that ever going to get better? I don't think so, not again," he said bitterly.

"I don't want to hear that sort of talk. It got better before when everyone else had given up on it and at least you still have an arm, unlike a lot of those poor men who were at Waterloo who I see begging on the streets, or even Lord Uxbridge, imagine losing your leg," Elise admonished tartly. "It's going to take time, but you have to persevere. Take it slowly, one day at a time. Do the exercises you did before, slowly and gently. There's no infection in it and you still have feeling in it as a normal arm, so there's no reason why it won't recover. Eddie said you were wrestling with Jack at Christmas so it was like a normal arm then and I don't see why it can't be again."

"Jack went easy on me," Nicky grated, "and I was bloody careful."

"Of course he did, and of course you were, but you were still fighting around the garden, throwing punches I gather, so that is exactly what you're going to do again, I promise you. Nurse's promise," Elise smiled and leaned forward and rubbed Nicky's injured left arm. "Personally, for what it's worth and I'm no doctor, I don't think you broke it again. Maybe cracked a bone when your chair toppled over, but I think you strained or tore some of the muscles, the tendons and ligaments and connective tissue. One or two of the doctors you saw did suggest that, and I've thought about it a lot and, you see, if you were tied up like I was, and I'm sure you were, far tighter than me actually because I was just a woman, and you were you and they didn't want to risk you getting free, it would have really pulled and strained the muscles, and torn them if your bad arm was pulled back really hard and tethered there, like this," Elise put her arms behind her and pulled her shoulders back to demonstrate, "and I'm sure you yanked and strained to try and loosen them and that increased the damage. Your arm WAS healing and I saw it when Benjy cut it open to remove some of the thread he bound the bones with; the muscles and other connective tissue had been terribly damaged, Eddie and I looked in anatomy books with Benjy to study it all. Did you know the pair of them even went off in the middle of one night to open up and inspect the arm on an unclaimed, just dead cadaver, in a mortuary, in exchange for paying for its burial and a 'consideration' for the assistant? They refused to take me with as thought it too disturbing and gruesome, but they said it was really helpful for Benjy in understanding the reality of how everything was connected in an arm that wasn't injured, before it decomposed too much. And you were gradually stretching the tissues again as your arm healed last summer and autumn, you and your wine flagons," she grinned as Nicky's eyes widened and then he pulled a face at what Eddie and Benjy had obviously got up to.

"However," Elise continued her little lecture, "if you tore the muscles again because they weren't fully healed and capable of stretching properly, then you're back to square one and have to start again from scratch, and it will all take time, months and months and months, and torn muscles are terribly painful. I know, I pulled enough in my back looking after my late father and husband." She sat back and took a deep breath, "So you look here, Casanova, Leo, Androcles, Lazarus, or whatever I should call you, seeing as you're a man of so many parts, never mind being far too handsome for your own good, quite the most handsome devil I think I have EVER seen, and you haven't been facially scarred at all from your adventures, only that scar in your hairline which no one can really see under your thick hair, and the women still swoon over you… and, you also are one of the strongest, most determined men I've ever met. You have never given in to adversity and, as your nurse, I absolutely refuse to let you wallow in your own self-pity. There are a lot of men I know who would give their left arm to lie back and think of England if Bella was... er... servicing them," Elise tutted, "so stop whingeing and complaining," she finished angrily and poked him hard in the belly.

"Where the hell did Eddie find you?" Nicky lay back on the bed as Elise returned to her ministrations and bandaging. "No wonder Bernheim didn't frighten you, you bloody frighten ME."

"Don't be ridiculous, I was a nervous wreck. I just gave in to whatever he wanted because I was frightened for Harry. As I told Francis, I'm not your stepmother. Carlotta was an amazing woman, I'm nothing like her, unfortunately."

"Now who's being ridiculous? No, you aren't anything like my Madre, but she was a completely different woman. She was born a Spanish aristocrat and circumstances made her a tempestuous, passionate and streetwise woman. You are everything the opposite: a cool and calm, well-born English Lady, supremely intelligent and informed for a woman. Whether you are also passionate inside, that's between you and my step-father, but I suspect your rivers run deep, Elise. As you so rightly pointed out, I know women well, and I always wondered what he saw in you. I've watched you ever since he introduced you to us and I thought more about it last summer at Valenciennes, and now I'm beginning to think I was right. Look at your rant just now. You're passionate in your belief I'm going to get better, so if you're like that in the bedroom, Papa must have his hands full," he smirked.

"Really, Nicky, don't be silly," Elise tutted, slightly embarrassed. "Our relationship isn't like that at all. Your father was lonely and he wanted a companion. We got on well, we like the same things, enjoy the same interests, we certainly don't have all the passion and fireworks that Francis and Cat have, or even you and Bella. We never argue, we just care for each other deeply, that's all." Elise shrugged. "He says he loves me and that is all I care about and he's very gentle and restrained and caring of me in return."

"No, that's not all," Nicky said forcefully. "Harry didn't arrive in

Hertford Street via a stork, and if all Papa wanted was a companion he cared for, or just loved a bit, he could hire someone to be that, or even take a mistress. And it obviously bothers you if that's what you think your relationship is like and you're so defensive about it, you should have just heard yourself. Just because he's scarred and limps, doesn't mean he's not a passionate man inside, just like Cat is. She drives Francis insane, but she loves him to death and he's as entranced with her now as he was when they met in Normandy, when they dragged me out the Fortress in Rouen. Papa is her brother and although quieter and studious, he has his moments too. I should know, I grew up with him. I personally think he's only quiet and studious partly because of what happened to him when he got injured as a youth, and maybe he has some of his father in him, he was also a quiet and thoughtful man, but of course we'll never know. However, when he lets loose, he's something to behold, believe me. Just as crazy as Cat is, ranting and raving in French; I mean, just look at him when he ordered us all down here a few weeks ago. I thought he was going to put Bella over his knee at one point," he chuckled, "and I know he would NEVER marry someone just because he wanted a companion or someone simply to make do and to say things to for the sake of it, or to keep them quiet. I think your problem is you love him a great deal, don't you, Elise? And I mean physically, not like your first husband."

"I... ah..." Elise's cheeks went pink, "yes... well, yes, I do, but what's wrong with that?" she whispered.

"Aaah, but I also think you've got a complex about my Madre and yourself... and my dear Papa, Gentleman that he always is, wouldn't dream of doing anything to offend or upset you. Don't do yourself down or think my step-father doesn't love you deeply, because I'm damn sure he does, even if he's had a problem coming to terms with it after mourning Madre for so long. He wouldn't have married you otherwise... and by the way, you haven't gone to pieces over what happened with Bernheim. A weaker woman would have been wailing in her bed, just like I gather Cat and Papa's mother has been doing, and she wasn't even there. So there you are. How's that for a theory from Casanova, Leo, Androcles and Lazarus?"

"You're a fine one to lecture me, Nicholas de Bresancourt; how did we ever get on to this topic of conversation? You're the one with troubles, not me... that's what we were discussing so don't try and change the subject."

"I think we both have our own little problems," Nicky mused knowingly. "Tell me, Elise, why do you blush so much when we mention sex in our conversation? After all, you're married to Papa so you can't be a shrinking violet... or are you? Is that what YOUR real problem is?" Nicky mused. "Worrying about his love life with my Madre because she was all Spanish fire and passion and you've got some maggot in your lovely head that you can't compete with a ghost? And what's more, don't know how to," and he knew he'd hit the nail on the head with his random guess when Elise paled, "and my dear, sweet Papa obviously doesn't want to offend or shock you. Oh, what a mess," Nicky whispered with a knowing smile, "after all, you said your hair nearly went curly when your friend told you what we'd been up to, but since I know EXACTLY what I did with all the women who bought my services, and know most of them would never be friends with you in a million years, not because you're not lovely, quite the other way round in fact, and they were the ones I - how can I put it to spare your blushes? - misbehaved somewhat inappropriately with - so that leaves a scant few, some of whom were very nice and were just lonely and needed a man in their life to make them happy for a while, just like your widowed friend obviously did. But I know I didn't do anything outrageous with any of those, so whatever this one told you, I hardly think it would make any woman's hair curl, other than someone rather shy and inexperienced in bed and lacking the self-confidence to express herself there and say what she likes and enjoys... and thereby get all the passion she feels inside, out on to the surface... hmmm?" he quirked his brow at Elise knowingly.

Elise sat, still as stone, an impassive expression on her face. "I should never have told you. You see far too much," she said quietly. "Can we leave this now, please? I've nearly finished with the bandage and then we can go back down."

"Talk to me, Elise. I'm no more your step-son than you are my step-mother. You know what I did; hell, if it wasn't for a twist of fate you would have been in your friend's shoes and you WOULD have talked to me then, I promise you. Tell me, did your friend enjoy what we did? Did she say we got on well?"

"Yes," Elise whispered. "Apart from being outrageously good looking and charming, she thought you were wonderful. Her husband had been a lot older than her, just as mine was, and it was all a revelation for her."

"Really..." Nicky's mind rolled back as he tried to remember the women, and one who was a widow with an elderly husband. There hadn't been that many although most had been bored, titled ladies in arranged marriages with husbands who'd got mistresses to keep them occupied and their wives were simply lonely and frustrated, or they had an open marriage and each had their own affairs. A couple had private idiosyncrasies they wanted indulged, but that had been a different kettle of fish entirely, a very lucrative kettle of fish as he'd charged a lot more to indulge them. A picture of a blonde woman came to mind. She'd been a widow, her husband an army officer killed in India, and she'd been left comfortably off as he came from a wealthy family. The man had been away for most of their married life and he'd found her an amusing and witty woman, once he'd got her to relax, if a bit plain-looking, but Nicky could imagine her just the type to be friends with Elise. "So, what happened to her, after I went to the Peninsula and abandoned my lucrative sideline," he grinned.

"She got introduced to a colleague of her late husband's, another military man though a bit younger, and they married. They were very happy for a short while, and then he got killed at Waterloo... it was tragic," Elise said softly.

"So many died there, and during the various battles down in Spain. I lost a lot of friends," Nicky sighed sadly, "so young and full of life, it was SUCH a waste, all because of that megalomaniac," he said bitterly.

"All war is a waste, whichever side you're on," Elise sighed too as both sat for a minute or two and reflected on those they'd known who had died or lost someone dear.

"I know who she was, Elise." Nicky then spoke quietly, "There weren't that many women, and most were married. I'm so sorry about her husband, she was a sweet woman. We laughed a lot. Do you still see her?"

Elise looked worried for a moment but then sighed again. "Yes, but it tends to be very occasionally now, only when she comes to Town. She went to live with her second husband's family in Berkshire, they had a child, you see... she wanted to bring him up in the country with his relations."

"She always wanted a child, I remember. I'm glad for her, even though it's all so sad." He didn't tell Elise the woman wanted HIS child, never believing she'd find another husband, and decided to get one by her own devices, then move away from London and start afresh with the baby and no one would be any the wiser as she was a genuine widow. But he wasn't going to play her game so had quietly left her, saying he'd been called back on duty urgently, not that he wasn't always as careful as he could be about inadvertently getting a woman with child... until he'd got entangled in *Lionesse*'s claws.

"He didn't come back, you did. Her child has no father to grow up with. Be glad you're alive, Nicky," her tart words brought his mind abruptly back to the present.

"I am, believe me. I thank the heavens every day when I wake up after what I saw at Waterloo. The carnage and death were terrible, but that's why I'm so frustrated. I want to make the most of every moment of my life now, not live a half-life like this."

Elise squeezed his hand. "Be patient, Nicky, just be patient and it will all come back. You've got Terrie and little Herring to enjoy now, and perhaps more children in the future. I'm sure you'll be wrestling with Terrie and Lizzie soon, just like Jack does with them, just like you did at Valenciennes last summer. I remember you rolling around in the mud with them in the pigsty, as if you were three as well. Have faith, Nicky... please."

"I'll try, Elise, I promise, and what about you? Are you going to tell me your problems, or have I got to carry on guessing?"

"I can't," she whispered, "I couldn't possibly," and Elise went bright red.

"Oh Lord," Nicky sighed. "I think your problems are much more easily solved than mine, but you would need to talk to me, and I don't think you could bring yourself to do that, could you?"

Elise just shook her head, went an even deeper red and took a sudden interest in the pattern on the bed cover, not even able to look Nicky in the eye. "Mary was just like you," Nicky sighed, "but you're far cleverer than she is. You need to find yourself some reading matter, My Girl, and I don't mean gothic romance novels from the circulating library, nor some rather untoward Greek or Latin poetry, nor some scientific treatise to discuss with Papa, or a diagram of arm muscles. I mean what they refer to as erotica. What goes on in the here and now, mostly in whorehouses but, believe me, plenty of the Ton and everyone else, high and low born, have their little idiosyncrasies. Have you ever even seen a pamphlet or book like that?"

"Of course not," Elise looked up, slightly shocked, then blushed again and giggled. "Well, perhaps in one or two very untoward shops in Paris when I visited there with Cat and Bella last summer, but I certainly never bought one, I was far too embarrassed. Aren't they all in French anyway? So I'd never understand them; the illustrations and diagrams I happened to glance at were quite enough as it was."

"Mostly, but they are translated, you know." Nicky grinned wickedly, thinking of some of the tomes and pamphlets he and Francis privately knew Richard Ambrose published, or imported, from all sorts of eastern countries. Available under the counter if you knew where to ask. "However, I've got a much better idea. I think you should have tea with a friend of mine one afternoon. She's a woman, so perhaps you might talk to her. She's a complete airhead, I'm afraid, can't add up to save her life and only reads the gossip sheets, but she can inveigle a diamond bracelet out of the tightest old fart and already has a nice little jewellery collection put away for when she retires."

"She's a courtesan? A common harlot?" Elise goggled at Nicky.

"Of course she is," Nicky chuckled. "I met her years ago, long before I joined the army, so I must have been nineteen or twenty, and she was a dancer then, about seventeen as I recall. Wonderful... er... legs," he smirked, "very talented, and I'm NOT talking about her stage performances. We had a little dalliance. I didn't have much money, as you know, and certainly couldn't afford to keep a mistress, so we did a deal. In return for her favours, and I learned quite a bit from her little tricks, I taught her to speak properly, nice manners, dress tastefully, generally how to be a refined lady capable of mixing with aristocratic gentlemen, and then when we parted, on good terms I hasten to add, as I was going travelling, before I left I introduced her to some friends of mine who did have money… and she went from there."

"Good God, how on earth did you find the time for all those women, those liaisons? Didn't you EVER sleep?"

"Who wants to sleep when the world is full of lovely ladies crooking their fingers at you? You just sleep afterwards, and much more deeply." Nicky grinned then burst out laughing at Elise's expression. "Anyway, Isabelle is still in London and owes me several favours, so if you can get over your prejudice, meet her one afternoon; I'm sure you'll find her fascinating and extremely informative and educational."

"I can't go out for tea with a well-known courtesan; suppose someone sees me? Suppose Eddie found out?" Elise looked shocked.

"Don't be ridiculous, I credited you with more sense, You Silly Woman. You're not a snob, Elise, far from it, and it would certainly have never stopped the Dowager if it was in her interests, and you well know it. What on earth will she do to you? She won't give you the plague, and since I assume this is all for my step-father's benefit, if he knew, I daresay he'd find it vastly entertaining."

"Weeeel, even if I did agree to see her, it will have to wait until we all go back to Town," sighed Elise. "Eddie wants to stay here all summer, he's absolutely adamant."

"No problem. I'll write her a note and invite her down here. She might fancy a day out in the countryside, away from the crush of London… depends on who her current keeper is, of course, but she'll soon sort him out, don't you worry."

"Down HERE? Are you mad, Nicky?"

"I don't mean here, here; she can come to Lewes, perhaps, and you can meet her there, or Eastbourne. Say you need to do some shopping or something. Medical supplies, I don't know. Make it sound boring or Bella will want to accompany you, you know what she's like when you mention shops. I'll write a letter to Isabelle, suggest she comes to Brighton for a few days to take the sea air, and then you can go from there. How's that for a plan?"

Elise looked overwhelmed. "How did this all come about? An hour ago I was just changing your dressings and now here I am, consorting with a common prostitute. I must be out of my mind."

"There's nothing common about Isabelle, I promise you," grinned Nicky, "and if you didn't know who she was, you'd think her a titled Lady. I'm a VERY good teacher," he chuckled, "of all sorts of things. You know, Elise, you've made my day. I was bored out of my mind a few hours ago and now I've got something to do and something to look forward to. I can't wait to hear how your meeting goes," he winked at her. "If you want to spice up your love life and seduce my Papa and get over your maggot about my late stepmother, this is the way to do it."

"You Disgraceful Man. I haven't said I'll go anywhere yet," tutted Elise, "and who said I want to seduce your Papa? Since when does he need seducing?"

"Every man wants to be seduced now and again, especially by a beautiful woman, even if it's his wife. There's a lesson for you for a start; it boosts his ego, makes him feel like a king, or the most desirable man in town," Nicky's smile would have made a lot of women swoon and Elise blushed. "I could elaborate, but I'll leave that to Isabelle," he grinned. "You love Papa and want to get over your inhibitions, don't you?"

"Yes," the blush returned as she whispered, "I don't want to be treated like a nice delicate china teacup or someone who would keel over in shock at something wicked in the bedroom, although you obviously think I would."

"Well, there you go. It's Leo or Isabelle, take your pick?"

Elise threw a rolled-up bandage at him and smiled as he ducked. "I don't know how Bella puts up with you, You Scoundrel, but now I know why you were such a successful agent for Ashcroft, you could get elephants to fly."

"I doubt that," Nicky grinned. "Talking of elephants and Leo, I wonder how the real Leo is getting on?"

"He should be halfway back to Africa by now," sighed Elise. "Are you sure you didn't get a knock on the head as well as a ball in your chest? Chartering a ship just to send a lion back to the jungle... you're completely mad as well as extravagant."

"He didn't eat me," chuckled Nicky. "I owed him, besides, he had such a sad look in his eyes. Tell me, Elise, how would you like to be shut in a cage for the rest of your life with people goggling at you all day and poking sticks through the bars to make you growl or roar. Never seeing the sunshine again that you grew up in, or roaming free, never getting to mate with a lioness and fathering cubs."

"Oh Lord, don't start all that AGAIN," Elise laughed. "I know, I know, it's all true when you look at it like that, but I still can't get the image of poor Daisy out of my mind. I'll never forget that terrible sight as long as I live," she shuddered. "I swear it was your Leo that attacked her first, he was such a big beast, he looked to be the leader of them."

"It gives Bella nightmares," Nicky sighed. "She won't sleep with me because she thrashes around and we're frightened she'll hit my arm or hurt my chest."

"You mean YOU'RE frightened," tutted Elise. "I'm sure if you slept together all night she wouldn't have such bad nightmares. Come along, Nicky, you've got to get over all this nonsense about your arm. You slept together when we were all at Valenciennes last summer. You're not one of these couples who sleep in separate rooms all the time, not YOU."

"How do you know?"

"What, the Duke of Lovely Ladies with Crooked Fingers?" she smirked. "Actually, Terrie told me," Elise giggled. "She wanted to know why you and Bella didn't wear nightgowns in bed when SHE had to, and why couldn't she get into bed with you for a cuddle as well, in the mornings when she comes to see if you're awake?"

"Oh Lord," Nicky rolled his eyes in amused embarrassment.

"Yes, it was highly diverting. You should have seen Miles Ashcroft's face, it was a complete picture. Eddie had mild hysterics; I was just relieved Charlie had disappeared off somewhere to sketch that afternoon."

"She asked you that in front of Miles, and Papa?"

"I'm afraid so, hasn't Miles ever mentioned it?" Elise said airily. "You do surprise me."

"No wonder Miles thinks I'm beyond redemption, not to mention our entire family," sighed Nicky. "Look, Elise, how come you can laugh and joke about me, but clam up like an oyster when we discuss you?"

"I don't know," Elise sighed. "I still can't believe I've discussed my very personal and private life with you."

"Well, we haven't actually discussed it, but it's been an interesting afternoon, that's for sure. Now then, why don't you go down and order some tea, and I'll write a note for Isabelle and come and join you shortly?"

Elise got up from the bed. "Oh Nicky, I'm not sure..."

"Eliiise..." he waggled a finger at her.

"Oh, all right," she gave in with a sigh, "whatever have I let myself in for?"

"Endless nights of extreme pleasure with my dear Papa, hopefully, getting up to all sorts of things that will make your hair curl," grinned Nicky and he laughed as Elise went bright red again and shot out of his room.

Chapter Nineteen

As he heard Elise hurry off down the corridor, Nicky sat for a moment and smiled to himself. Elise was so sweet, and it never ceased to amaze him how everyone seemed to have their own private little problems and angst that no one knew about, and he got off the bed and wandered over to the little desk in his room and slowly wrote a letter to Isabelle, explaining as briefly as he could to her about the favour he wanted, knowing she would appear as soon as she was able. The minx had always had a soft spot for him, he knew, and he was glad she'd made a success of her life from her hard beginnings in the workhouse, as she was as kind-hearted as she was silly and streetwise, a soft touch for any beggar, so easy to tease, but hard-hearted when it came to her protectors and the monies and jewels they gave her.

The effort of writing his missive made his arm ache, and he sealed it and put it by his sling to give to a footman when he went downstairs again to send off to London as quickly as possible. He went back to his bed and lay down as the black cloud he constantly fought to keep at bay descended on him again.

He lay against the pillows and looked at his useless left hand. He could waggle the fingers and hold a cup or knife, but he couldn't cut up his dinner with it, or fill the cup, not unless he wanted to spill the contents. If he tried to lift his arm and flex it or do anything, the pain was intense no matter how gently Elise encouraged him to move it carefully every day, and she'd massage and rub it with arnica and other oils from the apothecary to help ease the interminable ache... but it was still the same. Useless.

He waggled the fingers of his right hand and flexed the arm. It ached and the newly healed, deep slash on his bicep pulled and twinged. His shoulder ached and he tried to lift his right arm. He got as far as halfway and stopped. He couldn't even raise it above shoulder level, never mind so much as get it that far. His mind reeled back and he remembered trying to shoot Bernheim as Bernheim's pistol ball had torn into his chest... too slow, he berated himself, and off-target. The fact his arm had been dripping blood didn't come into Nicky's equation. As far as he was concerned, his poor reflexes and poor aim had nearly cost them all their lives, especially Jack, who'd flown at Bernheim with everything he possessed to try and kill the man. He definitely wasn't the man he was, there was no escaping it, no matter what Elise said. And he was even less of a man now... an aching arm from merely writing a letter, and it was all he could do to hold a hand of cards without dropping them.

Elise had called him a Casanova, but some lothario he was now. He couldn't even caress Bella properly, what a joke of a man he'd become, and the effort of rolling around in bed for a simple act of love was almost too much, making him feel ungainly and awkward, unable to support himself on one arm, the other hanging useless and in the way. It was too much for him and in frustrated anger at the loving pity he'd seen in Bella's eyes, no matter how much she'd denied it, he'd sent her to sleep in her own bedroom and now slept alone, apart from Duchess for company, lying awake long into the night, listening to Bella's night-mares as she thrashed around and cried out in her sleep about lions. And she wasn't the only one. He heard lions roaring in his head some-times, he dreamed about them, imagining them eating Bella as they had the nursemaid, or Terrie, or him.... and he dreaded falling asleep much as he wanted to escape everything.

He couldn't sleep because he wasn't tired, apart from the constant ache in his arm which didn't ease no matter what position he put it in. He sat around all day, apart from going on long solitary walks over the nearby fields and hills, but he hated walking; wandering along gave him time to think and he didn't want to think, because all he thought about was why he was walking and not on a horse. What he wanted to do was go for a long gallop on Shadow, or race his curricle down to the sea. His curricle? Hah! He needed two strong arms to handle his lively horses and that wasn't going to happen now, so he might as well sell the damn thing or give it to Francis or Jack. And as for riding Shadow, he admitted it to himself, he was afraid. Afraid, him, Nicholas de Bresancourt? Some lion he was.

Until he'd found himself at the mercy of Frederick Bernheim in Nice, he'd never been afraid of anything in his life... not since he was four and in the Fortress at Rouen and found himself and his parents at the mercy of the man's father, Edgar Bernheim, and the foul Pierre Dupont... but that man had merely disgusted and hurt him more than he'd really terrified the life out of him. Even when he'd watched his mother being raped; it was like a dream, something he hadn't really understood as he'd stood in silence, just like his frigid father had, as he'd watched his wife being beaten and abused, and then when they'd turned to him and done the same thing; that had bewildered and hurt him the first time. He hadn't really been terrified of throwing himself out the window there, to put an end to his miserable existence, well maybe afraid just for a few moments as he'd braced himself to jump, except Dupont had caught him teetering on the sill, looking down at the drop, and hauled him back in and beaten him black and blue before having his way with him and leaving him bleeding and hurt and barely able to walk. He'd been kept in a cage after that. As for witnessing what Edgar Bernheim had done to his father... seeing him that last time, the man with a face battered and bruised almost beyond recognition, covered in blood and abrasions everywhere, with teeth, fingernails and actual fingers missing, and heaven knew what else... but still disdainful of his tormentors to the last; it had all given him horrendous nightmares, and he'd not been able to conceive of that being done to him; he'd been four and such acts were beyond his comprehension... but every time he'd looked at his own hands, that HAD terrified him.

But now he was an adult, with an adult's understanding of the world, he was afraid again. Afraid he couldn't mount Shadow without a high block and some help, or hold the reins firmly enough with one hand, and he'd fall off and damage his arm properly and then they WOULD cut it off, and he couldn't bear that. The prospect of being armless did terrify him. He knew he was too vain, but he couldn't help it; and also, he could easily break his neck, it wasn't that uncommon an occurrence for men who went hunting. Riding spirited horses over the hedges and fields and losing control of them, and he didn't want to die, he wanted to live and watch his children grow up. Except he was living a half existence, unable to pick up his daughter and laugh and tickle her, or roll around on the lawn with her and play silly games, like they had in Francis's muddy piggery at Valenciennes the previous summer, or take her swimming. All he could do was sit with his son in his arms, no better than Eddie's elderly mother as she cuddled her little great-grandson before handing him back to Bella with a silly smile, still bemused he would grow up to be a wealthy duke one day.

He'd wanted to breed horses, train them to race and win. But he would never be able to ride one, school one, even hold the leading reins of one if it pulled hard - so what was the point of that ambition? It would frustrate the hell out of him; he'd always been a doer, not a watcher.

What could he do with himself? The empty years stretched before him: interminable estate paperwork, or involvement in business like Francis or his Papa. Except he wasn't Francis or Eddie, he enjoyed the negotiating, but that was it, he hated the detail and paperwork.

And his final, personal, nightmare and terrible fear... the dark. They had come back again, the nightmares about Nice, now made even worse by his experience in the cellar of the Richmond farmhouse. And he'd experienced that horror before, way back in his childhood. Locked in a stygian black cell with the dead and decaying body of his mother, and scrabbling rats. Only the distant crying and wailing of other prisoners to break the silence. Alone. Bewildered. Always shivering and cold. Hungry and thirsty. He'd no idea what would become of him, and then he'd seen his father, and then Dupont and some of the brutal guards had started to use him for amusement, as if he were a toy, and he'd come to dread Bernheim and Dupont to the depths of his soul... enclosed in the stygian darkness with nothing but rats and his imagination and sheer fright to keep him company. If he didn't do what Dupont wanted, would he end up looking like his father... missing fingers, nails and teeth?

The darkness. It was always the same, fearing the unknown. What was going to happen to him as he'd sat in the cellar in Richmond, not knowing where he was again, hearing the rats squeak and scrabble in the dirt, knowing he wouldn't be able to withstand Bernheim's torture again for very long, wondering if the bastard had found another Chinaman with needles, or had some other unknown torment in store for him. So now he slept with the curtains open, always with a candle burning, and if he woke up and it had gone out, and it was moonless or cloudy outside, he'd shiver with fear and have to get up and get another candle, frightened to go to sleep because of the terrible nightmares... and that was a another pathetic struggle, trying to light a candle with one hand. Everything was an effort. What sort of a man was he now, barely able to light a candle to keep the dark at bay?

For a moment he thought back to his playful and erotic games with *Lionesse*, and Nicky couldn't bear it; never mind not being able to make love to Bella like that again, he'd be too scared to be blindfolded now, he'd even be too scared to play children's parlour games with Terrie and Lizzie. It was all too much for him and with a soft howl, he turned and buried his face in the pillow and wept hot tears of frustration and anger at himself for his irrational weakness and fear, compounding his depression that he was also now so unmanly as to be crying over it.

He didn't go down to dinner that night, merely sent a message he had a bad head and his shoulder ached. He pretended to be asleep when Bella crept into his room, stood watching him and then quietly crept out with a little sob, and he felt like a worm... but he knew when Elise was standing over him, could feel her intimidating presence. He rolled over and opened an eye; she was standing by the side of the bed, her arms crossed.

"You don't fool me, Nicky; you're just running away again."

"Go away, Elise," he muttered, turning over, "and for your information, I've never run from anything in my life."

"Probably not, until now, but I won't let you give in to this depression that's got a hold of you. Sit up and give me your arm, let me massage it. I've got the therapeutic oil here, you know it eases it."

"It won't make it better, Elise. Christ, it aches like the Devil sometimes."

"YES, it WILL, and I know it aches, but this helps, you know it does. Now do as you're told. I swear you're worse than Charlie when he has one of his strops."

"Charlie doesn't get strops, he's like Eddie. Always well behaved, the perfect child," Nicky sounded sarcastic and belligerent.

"And you weren't, of course. Well for your information, neither is he. That child spends far too much time with his head in a book and not enough grappling with the real world. He doesn't like it when I send him outdoors to run about in the fresh air; in fact, I've got Eddie to agree to send him over to his sister's for a few weeks until the end of the summer and they go back to school. Severine's children are more of an age with him, and they go out and about on picnics and outings and behave like normal children and get muddy feet and dirty hands. It'll do him good to mix with them and socialise a bit more."

"And you know all about muddy feet and dirty hands?"

"I'll hit you over the head with this bottle of oil if you don't behave yourself, You Sarcastic Oaf. Now, do as you're told and sit up, no more of this malingering."

You are SUCH a pain, Elise," Nicky grumbled, as he heaved himself back up against the pillows with a groan, "and I'll have you know I was a cherub when I was small. I had golden curly ringlets, butter wouldn't melt in my mouth. Everyone thought I was a little angel."

"Everyone obviously needed spectacles." Elise poured some aromatic oil on Nicky's arm and started to rub, massaging deeply, making him wince and moan.

"I had a sailor suit," he started to reminisce as Elise rubbed, "and a matching hat. The Dowager got Benjy to design it for me, she said I looked like a miniature midshipman when she took me for a boat trip down the Thames one day," he grinned, his humour temporarily lifting under Elise's withering comments, "and I used to wear it when Francis took me to the park when he walked Fluffy, Cat's original giant specimen of a dog. I had a little ship he got me which I used to sail on the pond there, with one he had, pretending they were the Navy versus pirates or smugglers. I never realised how apt it all was, of course, no wonder he thought it all too funny for words."

"I take it you were the Navy?"

"Of course, I was a bit confused though. I was only about six or seven and hadn't been in London for more than a couple of years, so I thought I should've been the French Navy at first. I hadn't quite got my head around being English at that point, but when the Dowager got to hear about that, she soon put me right. Said she'd have me keel-hauled for consorting with *sans-culottes* and revolutionaries or get Francis to make me walk the plank off his yacht!"

"And did he? Make you walk the plank off his yacht, I mean," Elise laughed at Nicky's memories, visions of him in a little sailor suit with golden curls jumping around with Francis or the Dowager, created all sorts of entertaining pictures in her mind.

"Frequently," Nicky chuckled. "He always had this thing about everyone who went on it being able to swim, and I mean seriously swim quite a way. Talk about paranoid," he chuckled. "We often used to sail along the coast in the summer if there were some nice warm sunny days, and we'd stop and have picnics on a beach and Francis would build sandcastles with me, and if Papa was there too, he'd be full of complicated plans for moats and rivers and bridges."

"And what was Carlotta doing?" Elise couldn't help but ask.

"Gossiping with Cat usually, no idea what they talked about, but they nattered away constantly, nineteen to the dozen. Depends if we had Alex and Rennie with us when they got a bit older, or Bella was there. If we had Fluffy with us as well, it took everyone to stop him destroying our sandcastles... or else the ladies would walk down along the beach, paddling in the shallows and throwing sticks in the water for him. It was all very informal and casual, just like last summer when Cat and Francis disappeared off with Terrie and Lizzie and Bubbles down to the beaches on the coast of Normandy. It's funny to think of Francis doing the same things twenty-five years on that he did with me."

"You're very close to him, aren't you?"

"Mmmm, he's been like a part older brother, and a sort of not quite father, nor an uncle either. Not like Papa though, he was a proper father and I love him dearly, unlike my blood father. It's a strange relationship really, what I have with Francis, and it's evolved and changed over the years as I've grown up. He's been my mentor, my guide, a teacher… someone to share my problems and worries with, he's more like a very close best friend now, I suppose."

"Why don't you talk to him about your worries, Nicky?"

"All the family always go to him with their problems, as if he can wave a magic wand and deal with them, but for once, he can't help me. None of you can," and he stared out the window into the darkening skies as Elise rubbed and massaged on in silence.

"Well, if not Francis, you must talk to Bella, Nicky. I can see she's upset, just as I can see you're fretting. She was in tears tonight when she left your room; please don't shut her out, she loves you so much and she doesn't understand or know what to do." Elise finally spoke again as she finished her self-allotted task.

"It's funny how you can solve other people's problems, but not your own, isn't it?" Nicky sighed. "Thank you, Elise, that has eased it a bit. By the way, the letter to Isabelle is over there on the table, by my sling. I'll leave it to you to give to a footman to send off to London first thing in the morning; you will do it, won't you?"

"I'll do it if you promise me you won't hide away up here any longer, hmmm? Go for a drive with Bella tomorrow, if it's fine. Go in the little gig I use with my pony. He just ambles along or trots, easy to handle if you're worried about pulling on the reins. What about it, Nicky?"

"It's not my curricle."

"Remember what I said before, one step at a time. You'll drive your curricle again, I promise you, but you're just like Charlie, you need to get out and about. Why not go down to the river and have a picnic, or perhaps go down to Alfriston and have a spot of lunch there?"

"I'll think about it. All right?"

"Well, then, I'll think about sending off your letter to Isabelle."

"It's not the same, Elise. You really should meet her."

"Yes, Nicky, it is the same."

"I said, I'll think about it,"

Elise gave up. She didn't want to argue with him but she didn't know how to get through to him. So she smiled, "I suppose that will have to do for now. Can I get you anything before you go to sleep? Aren't you hungry? You didn't have any dinner."

"Not really, I've no appetite, but thank you, Elise. I know I'm being a pig, but just leave me be, hmmm?"

"You're not a pigglywiggly, you're a lion... rawwrrrrrr..." Elise teased him. "See, I can deal with it now, we all have to come to terms with these things. Besides, I haven't heard you oink all day. Go on now, get some sleep and I'll see you in the morning for more massage; and think about what I said, Nicky, please?"

"Goodnight, Elise."

"Goodnight, Leo, I know you'll roar again," and with that Elise slipped from his room, the letter to Isabelle in her pocket.

She went back downstairs slowly, pulling the letter out and turning it over and over in her hands, trying to decide what to do with it, wishing Nicky had done it himself then she wouldn't have been faced with this decision. Her mind went back to the cellar and her thoughts. She looked up at the big painting of Carlotta on the wall over the fire-place in the large drawing room. She paced to and fro, and then, finally, a determined look on her face she went out into the hallway, handed the missive over to a sleepy footman and told him to send it to London by courier the following morning as it was an urgent dispatch from His Grace. Having done that, she headed up to bed.

Eddie made love to her, as always; tenderly, gently and lovingly, making her writhe and cry out quietly as her climax overwhelmed her in the darkness of the big four-poster bed in his room. Even that made her paranoid, imagining him doing the same thing, in the same bed, with Carlotta... except she imagined it being wild and passionate, not the quiet, intense act they invariably shared. Folded in his arms afterwards, Eddie spoke softly to her, "What's the matter, *Chérie*? You've been quite distracted all day."

Elise pulled at the sheet, not quite knowing what to say, how much Eddie noticed, not wanting to break any confidences Nicky had shared with her. "It's Nicky, I'm worried about him. He's so depressed, I don't know where our laughing charmer has disappeared to. Oh Eddie," Elise turned in his arms, "he's not himself anymore and I don't know what to do; I can't seem to get through to him. He's convinced himself he's never going to get better and is nothing more than a helpless cripple. It's not like last summer, he's different this time, and I can't understand why."

"I know, *Chérie*, I can see it too, and I've tried broaching the subject with him, but he just clammed up and said nothing was the matter, it was just his arm hurting. Something is bothering him, but he was never the most patient of people at the best of times, so we must just bear with him and hope his arm heals quickly."

"That's not going to happen. I'm sure it will heal, but it will take months again. It's as if he's frightened to do anything; it's very strange, not like him at all. I mean, he hasn't even been out on Shadow and you know how he idolises that horse. He always used to ride him every day, but he hasn't even been near the stables. One of the grooms was telling me it's as if the horse was pining for him, off his food and everything, especially with Jack being away at school as well, and there's no Francis to ride him out either. The sooner Jack comes back and livens everything up, the better, in my opinion. And impatient doesn't begin to describe Nicky. I don't know, I can't get to the bottom of it at all."

"Don't fret, *Chérie*, I'm sure it will all come right soon. As you say, Jack will be back in no time and I'll have a quiet word with him and between us, I'm sure we can chivvy Nicky back to his usual sunny self. I can see Bella is unhappy, so the sooner we all do something, the better. I tell you what, I'll tackle Nicky again tomorrow and have a few choice words with him and see where that gets us, how about that?"

"Go easy on him, Eddie. I tried that, and a bit of cajoling, but if you push him hard, he just withdraws all the more. Do you think Francis might help?"

"I don't know, he's always our last resort. Let's just leave it be for the moment, hmmm? He's got his hands full dealing with Cat. She's not herself either. I'm sure it's those scars on her throat and chest. I swear to God," he thumped the bed, "that bastard is still haunting us, except now from the grave. I've never known the family so at odds with itself. We were all so happy at last at Valenciennes last summer, and at Christmas, and now look at us all. At least we're happy, aren't we, My Love? We haven't got any problems," he leaned down and kissed Elise tenderly. "Sweet dreams, *Chérie*," and he sighed as he sank back on the pillows and closed his eyes.

"Yes, Eddie, everything is just fine, goodnight, My Love," and she kissed him back, snuggling down into his arms, wishing she'd told him the truth.

Chapter Twenty

They didn't go for a drive. Nicky didn't even emerge from his room until noon and then he looked drawn and haggard and was in a foul mood. He went and sat by himself, sullen and silent in the library, a book on his lap but he didn't take in a word he read. He pushed his dinner around his plate and spoke in monosyllables when anyone tried to talk to him, even Terrie couldn't bring him out of his bad temper and he sent her off in tears when she clambered onto his lap and teased him about wanting a lollipop, and could he take her to the village to buy some, as she kissed his face and twirled his hair in her chubby little fingers… something that normally got round him in two minutes flat.

Bella had had enough and that was the final straw. She waited until everyone had gone to bed and she strode determinedly into his room. She found him sitting in the candlelight, in an armchair, staring morosely out the window, pulling at the chain around his neck. An empty bottle of brandy was lying on the floor.

"What the hell are you playing at, Nicky?" she burst out without any preamble. "I don't know what the matter is, but since you won't talk to me anymore, I'm sure I don't know. I know your shoulder and arm hurt, and you're frustrated about your left arm, which also aches, but the right one is getting better by the day; Elise says so, and your left one will just take time. So what IS it?" she ranted. "And don't you dare shout at Terrie again like you did this afternoon, what was all that about? All she wanted was a sweetie or at least some attention from her father. You've hardly spent any time with her lately and she's confused. In fact, we all are. We're all doing our best to help you and what are you doing? Ignoring us or yelling at us. Well, I for one have had enough!"

"Go away, Bella. I don't want to listen to your tantrums now."

"MY tantrums? You're a fine one to talk, skulking away up here, day after day, or disappearing off to sulk all by yourself. Are you drunk?" she spotted the empty bottle on the floor.

"I said, go away," he pulled at the chain around his neck, tugging almost absently.

"No, I will not 'go away', not until you tell me what the matter is."

"Nothing is the matter, except you're annoying me," he said icily. "Just go to bed and leave me alone, unless you want to go and get me another bottle of brandy?"

"Go to bed? Leave you alone? That's all I ever do these days." Bella's temper escalated, "And forget the brandy. What happened to the man I knew, the father of my children? The man who normally can't keep his hands off me? Actually, the man who couldn't keep his hands off half of London before that!"

"I'm not that man anymore, and I said, GO AWAY!" he bit out, now yanking at the chain angrily. "Go and see to the baby or something; pick flowers, teach Alfie some algebra... just leave me the fuck ALONE!"

Bella had expected some reaction from that taunt, but couldn't believe the icy, venomous reply and she watched him pull uselessly on the chain around his neck, almost as if he was trying to break it.

"I will NOT go away. Stop giving me orders and how DARE you talk to me like that?" she yelled back at him, storming over to his chair to stand in front of him. "Stop ignoring me, I've had enough of it."

"Well, I've had enough of you. GET OUT!" and he yanked hard on the chain.

"What the hell are you doing? You'll break your chain," she put a hand out to stop the pulling but he shoved her away from him.

"Get off of me, get out, leave me alone," and he swore under his breath as he tried once more to pull on the little lion charm around his neck.

"Nicky, you'll break it, STOP IT! Whatever is the matter?"

"I WANT to break it," he swore again. "I want to take it off, but I can't even do that, see how useless I am?" he sneered at her. "Go away, Arabella, I won't tell you again," and he surged to his feet, pushed past her and stormed across the room to stare down into the empty fireplace, flags of red on his cheekbones, chest heaving.

Bella went after him and pulled him round to face her, uncaring of his sore arm. "I'm not going anywhere until I get an answer from you. Why are you trying to break your chain? It's your most precious possession, what IS the matter with you?"

"I don't need it anymore, I'm not *Le Lion de Valenciennes*. I've had enough of that title, and the rest of them. I'm not a Duke, I'm not Leo, or Androcles or Lazarus, nor León or Nico. I'm just a plain, useless man: crippled, good for nothing. See... I can't even break this," and he tugged at the chain again and swore.

"I know about your León and Nico aliases, but who's Leo?"

"The man who couldn't keep his hands off half of London," he sneered again. "I can't even undo my breeches now without a struggle. What a joke that is."

"That's enough, you're either drunk or maybe something the apothecary sent has done this to you, but STOP IT!" Bella stamped her foot, "You ARE *Le Lion de Valenciennes*, don't be ridiculous."

"No, not any longer, even Bubbles is more lion than I am. Now get out, Arabella, before I lose my temper and throw you out. Hah, I doubt I could even do that." So he bowed facetiously, "Please be so kind as to remove your unwanted and distasteful presence from my sight, if it is not too much trouble, Your Grace." His hand fluttered in the air disparagingly, as if he was shooing off an annoying fly, "I find it offends me greatly," the icily dripped words and action could have been his father speaking if he'd but known it.

That was it, Bella slapped him, hard, round the face, "How DARE you," she breathed.

Quick as a flash he slapped her back. "I've warned you before about hitting me, Arabella," but it was a feeble slap and that seemed to anger him all the more and his face went redder as he swore roundly at her and started to yell, "GET OUT! GET OUT! I DON'T' WANT YOU HERE! GET OUT OF MY SIGHT! I'm going home to Litlington tomorrow and then I think I might go to Valenciennes. I want to be by myself, away from all your pity and promises and fussing... and you're NOT to come after me, DO YOU HEAR ME, ARABELLA?! I don't want to see you, or my children. Is that understood?" he marched over to the communicating door to her rooms and held it open.

Bella gaped at him, her hand to her cheek. She'd seen him angry before, they'd had their moments in their stormy relationship until they'd made it up before he'd gone off to serve Wellington before Waterloo, but she'd thought he loved her now and they'd got over all their issues. She'd never seen him like this, so full of self-loathing, and no matter how he felt about her, whatever maggot was driving him now, he was devoted to his children, she knew that. They were his life, his pride and joy, she simply couldn't understand him.

"I'm waiting." He looked at her and the open door.

Bella stormed past him. "Do what you like," and she turned again and slapped him for the second time, watching his head rock back. "Don't you EVER speak to me like that again, and I'm not letting my children near you until you apologise. You DISGUST me," and with her head held high she strode through into her own suite, hearing the door slam and lock behind her, and she promptly threw herself across her bed and broke down in floods of tears.

By the time she emerged the following morning, hollow-eyed from crying all night, he'd disappeared. A footman told a bewildered Eddie he'd been up before dawn, ordered his bags packed, summoned his carriage and been driven off without a word as the sun rose. Enquiries in the stables revealed he'd ordered the coach to head to his Litlington estate.

Eddie and Elise tried to console Bella but they were all confused. Elise finally told them both she believed Nicky was depressed because he didn't believe his left arm would ever recover, his right arm would never get its strength back and he felt half a man; at least that's what he'd told her. But she was sure there was something else eating at him and none of them knew what to do. Eddie suggested they leave him alone for a week or two, see if he would calm down and come back, otherwise then go and confront him.

Bella was worried he'd go off to Valenciennes, but Eddie simply said it didn't matter where he went, they'd just follow him and have it out with him there. Elise sensibly pointed out that the longer it all went on, his arm would still be healing, and when he realised that, he'd probably come to his senses. So they decided to let him sulk, sit and stew for a while and let time heal his wounds.

Nicky went back to Litlington and buried himself there, cut off from everyone and everything. He hated himself and he hated the world and what the Fates had done to him. He started to drink, the only way he knew to escape his conscience about how he'd treated Bella and the fears that beset him, and occasionally took a dose of laudanum when the brandy didn't make him sleep and the ache in his arm got too much. He'd always sworn never to take the evil stuff, knowing how addictive it was, but some nights he was so desperate for oblivion, he couldn't help himself. He spent most of his days staggering around the empty house, half-drunk, muttering and berating himself, becoming totally inebriated by nightfall when a couple of footmen would invariably put him to bed.

Hoping to help alleviate matters, Elise had sent Shadow over to Litlington. However, instead of ignoring the horse as he had before, Nicky would now spend hours sitting in the animal's stable, talking to it, interspersed with swigs from a brandy bottle, telling the horse he couldn't ride it anymore, before going back to the house and finally drinking himself into a stupor.

The confused household staff didn't know what to do with the withdrawn, drunken man and sent a message to Carstairs who had remained in London. He took it upon himself to go down to Litlington, especially if the Duke was now in residence there, and was completely shocked at what he found. One day, when Nicky was particularly bad and ranting at himself and the world in general, Carstairs, for the first time in his illustrious career, turned on his employer and very politely read him the Riot Act. He'd known Nicky since he'd been five and couldn't believe the man he'd watched grow up and had survived the Peninsular War, nefarious activities for Lord Ashcroft that were shrouded in mystery, then the carnage of Waterloo, and had since faced down a snarling lion, was currently going to hell in a handcart, as he told him plainly. Nicky just sat and looked at him with glassy, dead eyes, politely thanked him very much for his concern, told him to go back to London and then went to bed with another bottle of brandy.

Carstairs went back to London and consulted Browning about whether to tell the Duke. Browning knew the Duke had his own problems, servants seeing so much from the sidelines as they do, but they were about to go down to Firle and join the Duchess who'd been holed up there for weeks, so he took it upon himself to tell the Duke what Carstairs had told him and suggested diplomatically that the Duke might like to call in at Litlington on the way to Firle.

Francis was alarmed at what Browning told him of Carstairs' tale, and secretly glad to have something to distract him from his own problems, he did just that and when Francis jumped down from his curricle and strolled into Litlington and finally ran Nicky to earth, drunk as a skunk in Shadow's stall in the stables, dirty, smelly, unshaven and talking to the horse and virtually unable to stand up, he went berserk. He sent for Carstairs to return immediately and ordered every bottle of alcohol to be cleared from the house. He found Nicky's laudanum and threw that out as well; then, irrespective of his injuries, he punched the living daylights out of him. That Nicky merely stood, and let Francis hit him without so much as raising his fist in defence, spoke volumes, and it infuriated Francis even more.

When Nicky had sobered up in his room and looked at his black eyes, bruised face and cut lips, even that didn't seem to reach the remote place his mind had retreated to and he'd staggered downstairs to come across Francis, seething and waiting for him in the library. He ranted at Nicky like he'd never done before, even when he'd been a rebellious teenager. On and on he went like an erupting volcano, trying to get beyond the vacant look in Nicky's eyes, shaking him and yelling at him until finally, and feeling sorrier for himself than he'd ever been in his life, Nicky broke down in sobbing tears and told Francis he wasn't a man anymore and wanted to die because he was afraid of the dark... except he wasn't even capable of loading a pistol by himself, never mind have the strength to pull the trigger.

Francis was completely dumbstruck, stunned to his core, and not knowing what else to do, pulled the shaking, weeping, distraught man into his arms; hugging and comforting him as if he'd been a small, frightened child. Bit by bit, the fears for the future, the nightmares of the past, the angst and trauma finally all came out; years of it, long and deeply buried. The shock and unmitigated terror, followed by the perversion and brutal depravity he'd experienced in Rouen Fortress when he and his parents had been taken there and tortured; so far back in his childhood, and in far more graphic detail than he'd told Francis in the cemetery at Valenciennes the previous year; and then his years of racketing around London and the shame of selling himself, no better than a street whore, because of his stupid pride; and the endless stream of faceless women he'd bedded when he knew he had Bella sitting at home waiting for him, loving him, a wife he didn't think he wanted, deserved or could provide for... and finally, the horror of what he'd experienced in Spain, latterly with Bernheim, but prior to that, with the Spanish guerrillas, something no one, not even Ashcroft apparently, knew about. Francis had heard about what some of the Spanish rebel guerrillas had done to any poor French soldier they happened to capture and some of the stories had turned his stomach; the barbaric butchery, torture and mutilation being beyond belief, but he'd never dreamed Nicky had been involved in anything like it, even if he hadn't been responsible or done any of it himself, and Francis simply didn't know what to either say or do.

He sat for days with him, and sometimes deep into the night, listening as Nicky finally poured his heart out, like a burst dam, wishing he hadn't ordered all the brandy thrown out as he desperately needed some for himself.

Then, after all that, late one night when Francis had gone into his room to wake Nicky from some disturbing nightmare, all the trauma of his fear of the dark had come out, way back to the stifling, stygian black cell in Rouen Fortress together, inevitably, with further details of what had been done to him in Nice and how the farmhouse cellar in Richmond had brought all that back. Francis reeled, there seemed no end to it all and for once he actually thought his own few bad years, his deepest secret when he'd gone pirating, were nothing in comparison with what the young man lying exhausted and traumatised against the pillows had gone through in his life, and he'd bottled it all up inside him until he simply couldn't deal with it any longer, and one final incident had obviously tipped him over the edge and it had all, finally, overwhelmed him. Francis privately thought any lesser man would probably have been in an asylum long before now with the horror of it all. But Nicholas de Bresancourt wasn't a lesser man, Francis believed; he wasn't half a man as Nicky claimed to be, and Francis was certain the strong-willed, brave and deeply caring man Francis knew that he was, also buried deep inside him, would resurrect itself again at some point. He prayed it would.

That Nicky was having, or had had, some sort of breakdown was obvious, but now he'd got it out of his system, it seemed like some sort of catharsis, and gradually, the shaking and tears stopped and he started to get a grip of himself.

Carstairs had reappeared, hugely relieved to find Francis in residence, and between them, they watched Nicky like a hawk; he seemed to have overcome his urge to drink and just sat still and silent for hours, gazing out the window, fiddling with the chain around his neck.

He was still too frightened to go for a ride on Shadow, even with Francis to accompany him, but they did go out in his curricle, even if Francis did most of the driving, watching Nicky squeeze his eyes shut periodically as he'd deliberately raced along and careered around corners. Francis felt it was a major achievement when Nicky ranted at him on their return that they could have been killed with his reckless driving. At least he was showing some emotion now, and even better, he'd got him in the curricle in the first place. That Nicky used to drive far faster and more dangerously than that, Francis declined to remind him.

Francis had quietly written to Eddie to tell him what had happened and counselled him to keep Bella away until Nicky got stronger, mentally as well as physically, fearful the loving but volatile Bella might inadvertently say something to cause a row and Nicky would do or say something else back that he regretted, or Bella would fuss over him and compound the lack of self-esteem that currently seemed to beset him. He'd told Francis how worthless he felt as he couldn't be a proper husband or lover to Bella, and Francis had spent hours pithily telling him it was poppycock, appalled at what he'd heard Nicky say, in complete disbelief the former rake and consummate lover and charmer he knew the man to be, had lost so much confidence in himself.

Finally, having done his best to get his head straight, Francis inspected Nicky's arms. To his mind, his right arm seemed right as rain and the wound in his shoulder looked to have healed well. The housekeeper had fearfully peered under his bandages and changed the dressings when she could, when he'd been out for the count. until they seemed to be redundant and healed up on the surface, if not inside, but that would gradually happen, everyone knew. That Nicky's left arm was improving was also obvious, but Nicky was still in complete denial about it and fearful of hurting it again, and nothing Francis could say or do seemed to make any difference. He decided Nicky would finally come to realise it himself and eventually, counselling Carstairs to keep a very close eye on him, he took his leave and headed across to Firle, completely exhausted and overwhelmed by the previous unexpectedly traumatic fortnight, deciding when he'd recovered, he'd ride over to Arlington one morning and sit down and tell Eddie, Elise and Bella what had happened and let them take over as he had his own issues to deal with.

He hadn't realised it, but The Shadow had had his final, if different hurrah. It had always been his mantra never to abandon any of his men or leave anyone behind, even a body, if he could help it, and he'd felt the same about Nicky - determined to drag him back from the deep, black hell of his trauma and depression. A mental captivity by different demons, but a captivity nonetheless.

Chapter Twenty-One

While Nicky had been having his crisis and thinking him merely sulking at Litlington, Bella had thrown herself into the care of her children and Alfie, who had become her little project and a welcome distraction from Nicky's problems, and took no particular notice when Elise disappeared one day to go to Lewes to replenish some medicines and herbal massage oils, she said, just in case they might be needed by Nicky.

Eddie had gone off to deliver Charlie to his youngest sister's home in Hertfordshire, spend some time with her and her family, and settle Charlie in. Knowing Elise would probably spend hours with the apothecary, in deep discussion over possible useful medicines, salves or muscle rubs, Bella just waved her off. For once she was in no mood for shopping. She didn't take much notice when Elise had sent a message back saying she'd bumped into an old friend and would be spending the night in Lewes and nor did she see her when she arrived back late in the evening the following day, which was just as well as Elise looked completely shellshocked.

Isabelle Cartwright was formerly plain Isabel Carr, but she changed her name to make it sound more interesting and upmarket, and preferred the French spelling of her Christian name, as suggested by

Nicky. She was also just as Nicky had described her and it was obvious to Elise she was still half in love with the man, continually rambling on about how handsome he was, what an amazing lover, and enthusing about his beautiful body and charm, much to Elise's amusement. When she started to reminisce about their affair and what they'd done together, that was when Elise's blushes started and an extremely forthright Isabelle had told Elise that Nicky had asked her to explain what was what in the bedroom and how she could seduce her own husband and drive him mad with lust for her, and thereby turn their apparently placid love life into something more passionate and erotic, for both their benefits. At least that was what Nicky had written to her, and she found it all extremely funny and she'd be delighted to do ANYTHING, if it would please Nicky!

Elise, sitting in a quiet little coffee shop, had gone from pink to red, not knowing whether to laugh or run away as she listened to that announcement, but Isabelle was so matter-of-fact about the subject matter of their discussions, Elise finally relaxed, and the two women had adjourned to a local hostelry where Elise had requested a private dining room and sat and listened throughout a small luncheon and the whole afternoon as Isabelle prattled on, with much demonstrating, drawing and giggles. Elise had just sat with her mouth dropping open, which had made Isabelle laugh all the more.

Time flew by and it was far too late to journey back to either Arlington or Brighton by the time they realised the hour, so the two women had dined late and stayed overnight, and their conversations had continued well into the small hours, helped by copious amounts of wine, until Elise tottered off to bed, completely bemused and fascinated, and fell asleep to dream of all sorts of things that had her sitting up, wide awake just before dawn; hot, flustered and feeling quite strange… not that she was now unfamiliar with that feeling, but she'd assumed only Eddie could make her feel like that and that it didn't happen by itself.

Further conversation with Isabelle over breakfast soon put her straight about that, and the two women continued their discussions for the rest of the day, just as the previous one, with more amusing demonstrations from Isabelle which now made Elise laugh. They finally parted, late in the afternoon; Isabelle to return to Brighton where she said, with a wink, she'd met a very interesting and rich Gentleman who was staying at her hotel, and Elise to return back to Arlington, her head bursting with instructions and as she'd sat and gone over the past two days on the boring carriage drive in the dark, she'd been shocked and amazed at what she'd done, never mind discussed.

Now all she had to do was somehow put some of her new-found knowledge into action.

Chapter Twenty-Two

Francis hadn't seen Cat for weeks. Their rows had got progressively worse and more frequent as she refused to go out or act as hostess when he'd entertained, hiding away in her room, pleading a headache or some other spurious excuse, and she'd avoided his bed unless he crept into her room late at night to get under the covers and take her in his arms to try and make up their argument, whereupon she often burst into tears and kissed him passionately. However, the following morning the status quo was back to normal. Inevitably, he got fed up with that and after an especially noisy and vicious row with lots of ornaments, flower vases and cups and saucers being thrown and smashed, not an uncommon occurrence in the Firle household in the early days of their marriage when the pair of them had been at loggerheads, which was thankfully less frequent these days, Cat had flounced off with Lizzie, Marcus and Bubbles and said she intended to spend the rest of the summer and thereafter down at Firle.

Seething with anger and at his wits' end, Francis had let her go, thinking she'd soon be back, assuming the boredom of Firle by herself except for two young children would drive her mad. But he was wrong. Days turned into weeks and he hated the big empty house he now occupied, silent without the noise of children or barking dogs or shouting wives that he always jokingly complained about. He didn't know what the matter was with Cat but suspected it all had to do with the affair at Richmond, as the family now referred to it, mention of lions banned by unspoken agreement. He knew she barely ate, her neck scars bothered her and she had the occasional nightmare, but there was more to it than that, he was sure.

All the rest of the family were down at Arlington and eventually, missing Cat and his young children like the devil, even Bubbles, and worried more than he cared to admit about Cat, Francis decided to go down to Firle and try and talk to her and get to the bottom of what was the matter. And then, just a couple of days later, as he'd been sitting in his study, lonely and frustrated with only a bottle of port and a cigar for company, having decided to leave for the country at the weekend, Browning had ventured in and hesitantly told him the story he'd recently got from Carstairs.

Galvanised to action and glad to have something else to occupy him, Francis had set off immediately and the next two weeks were taken up with dealing with Nicky. As Francis finally drove himself over to Firle, he wondered why he always ended up solving everyone else's problems but struggled with his own.

When he finally arrived at Firle, Cat seemed delighted to see him, much to his relief, but he was shocked at her appearance. She'd lost a lot of weight and he immediately worried she was ill. When they went to bed that night, he realised just how slender she'd become as he looked briefly at her body before she doused the faint candlelight and, not wanting to say anything that would cause another row, he merely told her, as he always did when he made love to her, how beautiful and desirable she was and made up his mind to broach the subject as soon as an opportunity presented itself as he could feel her thinness as his hands roamed over her body under the bedcovers.

Francis watched Cat closely for a few days, noting how little she still ate even though he could have sworn she looked longingly at the pastries and puddings the cook prepared for them every day... and they invariably ended up being eaten by Bubbles as Francis was mindful of the promise he'd made to himself after his adventures tree climbing, sword fighting and running down through muddy fields in Richmond.

He took himself off early one morning to drive over to Arlington, saying there was a business matter he needed to talk to Eddie about, and disappeared off for the day. He hadn't told Cat about Nicky, fearful she would worry and lose even more weight, but he knew he'd have to talk to her about that as well, sooner rather than later, and it all went round and round in his head as his curricle bowled along.

Jack had returned from school, having passed his final exams with flying colours, much to everyone's amazement and no little pride and pleasure, and he was currently staying in Hertford Street, racketing around London, and no doubt misbehaving himself, as Bella pithily told Francis who merely grinned at her, knowing exactly where Jack was, his treat to the lad for passing his exams. However, when he sat down and told Eddie, Elise and Bella what had happened with Nicky, they were distraught, even though Eddie and Elise already knew some of it. Francis didn't go into details but merely gave them an outline of the terrible outpouring of bottled-up memories, horror, angst and trauma that had poured out of him and, as he'd expected, it took all three of him, Eddie and Elise to stop Bella jumping up and setting off for Litlington straight away.

He told them all he thought Nicky was pulling himself together and his arms were much better, but he was his own worst enemy and he said, jokingly, he might well have to engineer another fight with him, or create some other drama to make him realise he was only frightened of himself as, in his opinion, there was nothing the matter with Nicky now, that time, peace, quiet and rest wouldn't cure.

After much discussion, they all agreed to leave Nicky to rest and recover at Litlington, as Francis said he doubted Nicky intended to go to France any time soon, and if he hadn't pulled himself together and reappeared at Arlington within a month, then perhaps everyone should get together and decamp to Firle for the rest of the summer and take Nicky with them, whether he liked it or not. In the meantime,

Carstairs was keeping a close eye on him and keeping Francis informed of what was going on, and he would let them know if there was any news or change.

After spending half an hour with a now virtually recovered Alfie, who proudly demonstrated his newly-acquired reading and writing skills, and who begged to return to work before Bella turned him into a bookworm, and little Terrie who clambered on his lap and artfully demanded a lollipop or treat, a laughing Francis finally climbed into his curricle to set off back to Firle and his worry about Cat, leaving three concerned people behind but who'd given their word to an adamant Francis to leave Nicky alone for a while yet.

Bella stood by the horses as Francis made ready to set off and climbed up to his seat. "Are you SURE he's all right? I can't bear to think of him being by himself at Litlington, you know he doesn't like his own company, surely I ought to go to him? I'm his wife, I love him so much, Uncle," and tears started to run down her face. "I'm sure it was my fault he ran off. We had such a row, and I hit him, twice," she started to sob. "I got so cross and frustrated with him, I didn't know what I was doing."

"Ah, Bella, My Poppet, don't cry," Francis leaned down and offered her his handkerchief with a gentle smile. "I think this was an overdue explosion waiting to happen and something would have set it off sooner or later. I don't think it was you, even if you did hit him twice, You Bad Girl," he tutted humorously, lying through his teeth. "I dare say he deserved it if he was in the mood I found him in. No, it was the whole affair at Richmond, it was the final straw for him I think, the trauma with the lions and our confrontation with Bernheim. It's affected all of us, not just him," Francis sighed, "but somehow, now he's unloaded to me, got it all off his chest, I think he'll soon get better. We all need time to ourselves at some point, Bella, take it from me, I've been there. You'll understand as you get older, I'm afraid. Peace, quiet, time to reflect and think… I used to go deep-sea fishing, that was my escape. Hauling nets, fresh salty air, nothing like it. Time is a great healer and I think Nicky needs to come to terms with everything, put it in the past once and for all, and then move on with his life with you and your children. He's been through more trauma in his short existence than most people see in a lifetime, but he'll come through it, mark my words, the Nicky I know won't be able to keep away from you for much longer." He leaned over and patted her on the head, "He loves you a lot, Bella, you were his rock, he told me, a constant, always there in the background of his life amid all the storms and tossing seas around him, and he's beside himself about you, so I know he'll come back to you soon."

"Do you really think so, Uncle?" Bella looked completely bereft.

"I know so, Sweetheart; trust me. If not, you have my permission to go and hit him again, harder," and with a chuckle, Francis flicked his whip and the curricle swept off down the drive leaving Bella staring sadly after him, wanting to believe her Uncle's words but guilt still riding her hard.

Francis had thought long and hard about Cat on the drive over to Arlington and on the way back to Firle. He toyed with calling into Litlington on the way, but decided against it. Bella was right, Nicky didn't like his own company much, but Francis wanted him to return to his wife and the bosom of his family of his own accord, when he was ready, and so he decided to leave him alone. Carstairs' last missive said he still hadn't drunk anything other than the odd glass of ale or wine with his dinner, although he wasn't eating much, and sat around a lot all day, staring out the windows or, if it was fine, outside in the sunny gardens, always deep in thought, forever fiddling with his necklace. He still hadn't ridden Shadow or driven his curricle, but visited the stables regularly and continued to talk to the horse or the cat, Duchess having mysteriously appeared one day. Like Shadow, Elise's doing yet again. Carstairs still thought it very odd a Duke should sit in the hay in a stable stall and talk to a horse in French, and a cat in Spanish, and that made Francis laugh.

Remembering back to when Nicky had been very small and he was recovering from his incarceration by Bernheim and Dupont, and Nicky had adopted one he'd found in the garden and brought it indoors, a momentarily droll Francis toyed with sending a rabbit over to Litlington with instructions to speak to it in English as it was a British bunny... but he wasn't sure Nicky was ready for his jokey humour yet, so decided to leave it a week or two... and then his mind inevitably returned yet again to Cat.

Chapter Twenty-Three

A couple of days later, it dawned clear and sunny. Francis told Cat he wanted to take her for a ride to show her something and they would take a picnic with and make a day of it, just the two of them. Lady Elizabeth Granville was not impressed to be left behind by herself, and Francis knew she ran rings around her new governess, Marcus's nanny and the nurserymaid, and all the household staff, and they would no doubt return to some calamity, probably involving Bubbles, who watched them leave mournfully despite the tasty marrow bone firmly grasped between his teeth.

With the picnic in their saddlebags, they set off late morning and the horses ambled along and across fields until they reached the far side of the Firle Estate on some farmland, and they arrived at Francis's Folly, as he'd called it. A small, open-sided Greek temple affair on the top of a grassy knoll. It was small, plain and had just a stone bench inside a handful of columns. The view from the folly was quite picturesque with the sea in the distance, if one craned one's neck, but otherwise, it was indeed a folly: an out of place, otherwise useless edifice in a remote, slightly inaccessible location unless one was on horseback, in the middle of fields of grazing sheep and cattle.

"Is this what you wanted to show me?" Cat smiled at Francis as he pulled up and slipped down off his horse, going round to help her down off hers. "I have seen it before, you know, not that I didn't always wonder what on earth you were doing putting a Greek temple in the middle of some fields in the middle of nowhere?"

"That's why it's Francis's Folly," he grinned at her. "But the view is nice, can't you see the sea?"

"There are better places on the Estate where you could have built something if you wanted to see the sea," Cat responded tartly. "I suppose it's another demonstration of the vagaries of men."

"Absolutely, My Sweet," Francis merely smiled at her and set about tethering the horses and carrying the saddlebags with their picnic up inside the little building. He spread a small rug and a couple of cushions on the floor and bowed to her, "Your table awaits, Your Grace," and his eyes twinkled.

"Well, that was a short ride. What are you up to, Francis? You've got that funny expression on your face." Cat strolled up after him and sat down and watched as he poured them both a glass of wine from what appeared to be bottomless bags.

"Nothing at all, My Love. I just thought it was a perfect day for a picnic and some time together, away from the horrible hordes; you know, screaming infants, anarchic daughters, drooling dogs…"

"But you told me you missed the horrible hordes terribly while we were away," Cat laughed. "Make up your mind."

"I missed YOU," Francis said softly.

"I missed you, too," Cat toasted him with her glass.

"Did you, Cat? Did you really? You've been so distant lately, I did wonder."

"Of course I missed you, I always miss you when I'm not with you, surely you know THAT after all this time?"

"Then why did you run away down here? There was no word, no funny little amorous notes… you used to send them to me all the time when we were apart for even a week or two. Don't you remember THAT?"

"Is that what all this is about?" Cat spread her hand to indicate the picnic, "Recriminations?" her face turned mulish.

"Not at all, calm down, it's just a picnic. Here, have some food. I got the cook to make all your favourites…" he opened a small box and Cat looked inside at the delicate little concoctions of strawberries, cream and meringue and sighed.

"What else is there?"

"How about some of these…?" another box was produced full of her favourite pastries, and another with little tartlets. Everything Francis produced was something she craved but had avoided for months. She knew one mouthful and she'd be back on the slippery slope to plumpness again. She had a perpetual vision of her elderly mother, her godmother and their bosom friend, Lady Emily Southwater, in her head. The Three Puddings, Francis had nicknamed them, because they were all so plump they waddled. There was no way on earth she was ever going to let herself get like them, she'd sworn to herself, and pastries and delicious food had been their downfall; too much mid-morning chocolate, afternoon tea and gossip, followed by rich dinners.

"I'm not really very hungry at the moment, we haven't come far and I've not got an appetite. I thought we'd be going further, for a long gallop?"

"We can later, if that's what you want. I just thought it would be nice to sit and relax in a bit of peace and quiet."

"Mmmm, it is nice and quiet here, I give you that; even the cows and sheep haven't got a lot to say for themselves." Cat sighed and lolled back on a cushion, trying not to think about the contents of the little boxes and her stomach rumbled noisily.

"I thought you weren't hungry?" Francis's brow quirked. "Had a large breakfast did you?" he'd seen her eat half a dry roll with her coffee as he'd peered round the door of the breakfast room.

"Oh, yes I did," Cat said airily. "I decided I ought to set myself up for the day, I THOUGHT we were going for a long ride; it's just indigestion."

There was definitely something wrong and Francis was getting more worried now he knew she was lying, but before he had a chance to broach the matter, Cat sat up and changed the subject. "So, what did you bring me over here to see, then? Come on, Francis, I know you well enough; we aren't here to look at sheep, eat pastries and squint at the sea view."

"You're not eating any pastries."

"Neither are you," she bantered back.

"All right, all right, but I do want to show you something. It's something I probably should have shown you, told you about, a long time ago." Francis got to his feet and offered Cat his hand to pull her up. He took her in his arms and looked down into the face he loved, and gently pushed a stray lock of hair off her forehead, his own expression now serious. "This is all about The Shadow, my life before I met you, and it's somehow coloured my entire life since. Well, perhaps with a gap when the boys were growing up, but I had no idea the repercussions it would have, even up to just a few months ago, even now in fact, and I need to tell you about Nicky, later."

Cat looked at him in slight alarm as he continued, "Everything in Richmond led back to me, even Frederick Bernheim's obsession with Nicky was connected, because I, we, stole Nicky out from under his father's nose and Frederick wanted his treasure as well as mine. Everyone suffered that dreadful day and night, and it's mostly my fault. And you, My Love, look what he did to you." Very slowly, Francis peeled away the thin silk scarf Cat had wrapped around her throat and undid the high ruffled neck of the blouse she had on under her riding habit. As she gasped and tried to stop him, he lowered his head and kissed her tenderly along the scars on her neck, noting they'd faded, but were still visible, although not nearly as bad as the last time he'd seen them in London. Even when they'd gone to bed when he got to Firle, she'd blown out the candles when he'd started to make love to her, her long hair artfully draped around her neck, so he hadn't really had a chance to look at them properly as she always kept them hidden under a scarf and high-necked blouses or day dresses.

"No, Francis please, don't look at them, they're ugly," she tried to push him away and do up her blouse.

"Nothing about you is ugly, My Beautiful Cat, nothing, not even a few scratch marks. Have you any idea how I felt when I watched him do this to you, knowing it was all my fault?" he muttered angrily. "But you've got to stop running away from the world because of them.

You're such a beautiful woman, no one will care, and since when have you EVER worried about what people said about you? You've gone out and about in Society in the most outrageous clothes, don't you remember when we were first married? The Ton was agog at your outfits; my dear grandmama nearly had apoplexy at some of them, but you didn't give a jot, did you? Just because you wanted to get back at me. So why worry now? I don't give a fig and I refuse to let you hide yourself away and cower from the gossips. I love you so much, Cat, I always have and I always will; you could NEVER be ugly in my eyes, even if your face was marked like Eddie's; don't you realise that?"

It was the same conversation, the same argument, except he was so passionate, so obviously upset by it all, tears filled her eyes. "No, Francis, I'm marked now, just like Eddie, and people WILL notice. Not that I care about that, I don't care about what they think of me, that at least is right... but if it got out about YOU, I couldn't bear it. Too many people know what happened, I'm amazed the real story hasn't leaked out by now. The servants, the soldiers, and my mother's gossipy friends... they couldn't keep their tongues still if their lives depended on it and sooner or later someone will say something about a man named Bernheim, or I'm frightened I'll let something slip. I can't take that risk, Francis, I simply can't. I couldn't live with myself if anyone found out about you because of me."

"Cat, I've got to the point where I simply don't care anymore. If someone finds out, so be it, but they'll have the devil of a job proving it was me, that I was The Shadow. I was so very careful, that's one of the reasons I never told Ricky. I never told anyone, not even Grandmother, and you don't get more secretive than her, as we now well know. Benjy was the only soul in England who knew anything. Reynard and Uncle Gerard were in France and Gerard certainly wasn't going to say anything when he came over to visit, as he was as involved in it all as I was, albeit only from his chateau. To this day your dear mama and sisters still don't know me and Alex are one and the same, because they only saw Alex once and they were overwrought and distracted because of what they'd been through. People see what they want to see, and they saw a long-haired, bearded man," he shrugged. "I was so careful about everything, I never even got rid of my treasure because I never wanted anyone to ask any questions, and unlike Nicky's father, who we think probably killed the men who melted down and cast the Valenciennes gold to hide in those statues, I couldn't do that; so I just left it be. It was never about the money anyway, you do realise that?"

"No, of course not, I realised that a long time ago, once I knew what you were like. But the risk, Francis, it's enormous. You could hang. You're a wonderful man but you have enemies, people are always jealous of those with more than themselves. If Bernheim found out all about us, don't you think someone else could? Bonaparte is gone now and France is not at war, other people could go digging."

"I refuse to cower away and live in fear. I've been living in fear for the past couple of years since Bernheim surfaced and tortured Nicky in Nice, and I've had ENOUGH of it. I'm not doing it any longer," he rasped. "If someone wants to dig, let them dig. Who was The Shadow anyway? Not many had heard of him over here, unless you were a Revenue man or in the trade, as I tried even more on this side of the Channel to keep a low profile; *L'Ombre* was more well-known in Normandy, and I doubt they'd find anything now, the world has moved on, between the Revolution and Bonaparte's doings, and it was all thirty years ago. A generation, a lifetime even. For a variety of reasons I was winding it all down when I met you, and Rouen Fortress is gone, both Bernheims are gone, so are Dupont and his soldiers. There simply can't be that many left from the old Normandy militia. A lot of them were grizzled veterans in the 1780's as it was. Bernheim and Dupont never could be doing with soft young soldiers, wet behind the ears; like always attracts like, and you remember some of them, don't you? You know, the ones on duty in the Fortress the weekend when your family escaped, or the ones you killed when you came to rescue me?"

"Oh Francis," Cat didn't know what to say, "it's so dangerous, it only takes one. Even over here, a Revenue man with a long memory, or whoever you traded your illicit cargoes with... or wh..."

"Cat, stop being irrational. You're thinking like a woman, much as it pains me to say it, and that's not like you. The Cat I know and love has never run from anything, so why are you running now? God help me, I am, was, The Shadow, and like it or not, you are The Shadow's wife, my woman, my everything, and that's what I want to show you. You're entitled to see what it was all about, why you nearly had your beautiful throat cut."

"Francis?" she looked confused but with a quick, hard kiss Francis turned from her and knelt down and fiddled at the base of one of the columns. Cat heard a slow grinding sound and to her astonishment she saw one of the big marble paving slabs gradually slide down and backwards, leaving a gaping black hole in the ground.

"Francis? What the hell is that?"

"Aha!" Francis's blue eyes suddenly sparkled. "Come with me to my lair, Oh Beautiful Damsel," he put on a clowning piratical accent and Cat's eyes widened as he tugged her hand and went down some steps into the black void, pulling her gently behind him. As he reached the bottom, Cat heard him strike a flare on the stone behind him and from it, Francis lit a series of oil lamps hanging along the wall of what appeared to be a large chamber excavated out of the rock, just like the stairs they'd come down. She stood and gaped as she looked around. There were a large number of enormous chests ranged along the walls, many with Francis's insignia on the top, just like his ring, and on the far side of the chamber, in the gloom, she could just make out what looked like a pair of big, wooden doors, capable of allowing a wagon to pass through.

As Cat watched, stunned into silence, Francis went over to a large chest, released the clasps and threw back the lid and she gasped, putting a hand over her mouth in astonishment at its contents. Francis went to the next and did the same, and then another and another. Finally, he stood back and looked at her, a strange smile on his face. "Welcome to The Shadow's secret hideaway, Your Grace... *et voilà, Madame*," he spread his hands, "this is it, the treasure everyone has been after for the past twenty-five years and more."

Cat looked around her, at the contents of the open chests as Francis went and sat on the edge of one. He picked up a handful of gleaming golden coins and let them trickle and fall back into the chest through his fingers as he watched Cat's face. There were piles of gold ornaments in one enormous trunk, old fashioned but beautiful jewellery in another, crowns and regalia in another and all manner of strange, obviously foreign artefacts in another... but they were all gold or silver. Paintings and furs and rolls of somewhat musty but still beautiful materials were in another couple of huge crates. Golden plates and platters were in another and one chest was full of shimmering, sparkling jewels, all manner of precious or semi-precious stones... rubies, emeralds, sapphires; opals, topazes and amethysts, and pearls... and they glowed in the light of the lamps. Several were simply full of gold coins and the last chest, smaller than all the rest, sitting on the floor next to where Francis was perching, still had its lid closed. She still hadn't spoken a word as Francis leaned over and slowly lifted it and Cat's eyes nearly came out on stalks as she gasped again... it was almost full to the brim with diamonds.

"Francis! My God, Francis..." she was virtually speechless as she whispered and staggered over to sit next to him.

"And this isn't all of it," he chuckled at the expression on her face.

"Not ALL of it?" she spoke slowly, in disbelief. "There's MORE?"

"There was. I gave a load to Reynard and bought him a beautiful new caravan with easy access because of his leg; lord knows what he did with it all, though. Nicky said there was still some plate and gold items under the bed in the self-same caravan. He showed it to Nicky when he stayed with him when he went to recuperate in his camp after Bernheim shot him in Madrid. I gave another pile to Benjy, that's how come his shops and design studio are so beautifully fitted out and spacious... and I've no idea what he did with the rest. Fenced it very carefully, I hope, and invested it in a proper bank for his retirement."

"Why on earth is he still valeting for you, then?"

"I haven't the remotest idea. He says he gets bored dealing with idiot or fat gentlemen and ladies with no taste and no figures," Francis shrugged and rolled his eyes. "Mind you, after our adventures in Richmond, once he knew everyone was going to be all right, he said he needed a holiday and disappeared off to Paris to look at the fashions, and lie down in a dark room to recover!" Francis laughed and did a quick camp imitation of his overcome valet with a hand to his forehead. "So that's why he hasn't been around lately. I just let him come and go as he likes, he orders Bannister about and keeps an eye on my clothes, and he tells me when I need something new... and I just let him get on with it if it keeps him happy," he chuckled.

"Anyway, back to all this. Uncle Gerard kept it all originally, under a similar little building on his estate, that's where I got the idea from. When I disappeared, after that little interlude you engineered in my study with my drugged brandy," he winked at her, "which I NEVER recovered from, I met up with Reynard and Benjy and it was us who blew up the remainder of the Fortress ruins," and Cat gasped. She'd suspected, but never known for sure, that he or Reynard had been at the bottom of the destruction of the hated building. "And while I was over there, Benjy and I quietly moved a load to my yacht and shipped it back over. A lot was Uncle Gerard's retirement fund, that's how he quietly bought and retired to that nice little estate down in Hampshire. It's such a shame he never got to see the end of the War and go back to Normandy again," Francis sighed. "But we gradually moved and shipped over the rest, bit by bit, very carefully, as I was damned if some head-chopping *sans-culottes* were going to get their nifty fingers on it, and we had to be damned cautious about it. Anyway, that's why I had this built, in the most obscure place I could think of, and those doors lead to a tunnel that goes all the way down to the sea. It comes out in some cliffs you can only access at high tide from a boat, no beach to speak of, you just sail in. Clever, eh?" he grinned like a mischievous schoolboy. "As you can see, the tunnel is big enough for a wagon to go through as it's quite a way on foot to carry anything heavy. We had thought to put Nicky's stone lions in the tunnel but they were just too big, way too cumbersome to shift without attracting attention, even if we could have got them to the cave entrance by sea, which Eddie doubted; hence their appearance near our compost heap."

"But, those jewels, and those diamonds, Francis. Where did they come from? I've never seen the like... so many ..."

"Ah, the jewels and the diamonds," Francis grinned as he picked up a handful of diamonds and let them slip carelessly back into the small chest, like a twinkling, sparkling waterfall. "Behold the cream of the treasure of the late and much-missed, Marcus Bonaire. I believe he acquired them, along with a hoard of gold and more precious stones, during the last century, from ships on their way back to Spain and

Portugal mainly. They originally came from the mines in Brazil or some of the other South American territories, and some stones came from a couple of ships all the way from India, headed to England I would think, from some eastern nabob or Indian Maharajah, and over several years, but where some of them were cut, I've no idea. I presume they were ultimately meant for some royals here or in Spain or Portugal, maybe France or elsewhere in Europe like Austria or Russia, but who knows? Marcus was a good friend of mine, something of a mentor, and he left his treasure to me when he died as he had no other family. I did him a favour once and he never forgot it. Now you know why I wanted to call our little boy, Marcus, after my old friend," Francis paused for a moment then added very softly and slightly bitterly, "you avenged him, My Darling, for you see, he was killed by Edgar Bernheim…"

"Nooooo, oh Francis. The evil of that family just goes on and on."

"I know. Bernheim caught up with him in St Malo, he'd somehow heard about his famed diamond treasure and other jewelled hoard, but Marcus thought he was safe. I have to say, I don't know how or where Bernheim got his intelligence, but he certainly knew and picked his targets, and not just among the aristocratic community, as you can see. Marcus had retired and was living quietly on a nice little estate he'd bought in Brittany, somewhere between Rennes and the coast; thought he could grow apples there and make cider, a bit different from pirating. However, Bernheim wanted the stones so he enticed him to St Malo on some clever pretext. Marcus was no one's fool, believe me, he was always very wary… but Bernheim got him even so, then he and Dupont cut all his fingers and toes off, once they'd pulled his nails and teeth out, along with some other unpleasantries I won't go into, then he cut his throat. He didn't get his diamonds and other jewels, I got them instead, and his gold, but Bernheim didn't know that when he had me in his clutches; surreal isn't it? I vaguely remembered afterwards, a snatch of conversation between Bernheim and Dupont came back to me, while I was dangling in that chamber, half out of it. Dupont was commenting that Nicky's father, Marcus, and I, were the only ones to resist their torture… not that they'd finished with me at that point and it was just before Dupont set to with his flat irons. They were an evil, barbaric pair of bastards to be sure."

"*Mon Dieu*," Cat muttered, completely horrified. "They could have done that to you after Dupont burned your back. Oh God, Francissss," and for a moment she buried her face in his chest as the imagined images poured into her mind

"Hush now, it didn't happen, so don't think about it. You came and you stopped them." Francis soothed and moved on to a lighter anecdote. "I had so many precious stones, even before Marcus's demise, I never knew what to do with them. It was a joke when Benjy said I should use them as buttons, so I did... and that's how it all started. The Ton knew I was rich anyway, so just assumed I was being eccentric and my usual self, and starting a new fashion, except few could compete or follow me. My dear grandmama said it was tasteless and vulgar, so of course that encouraged me all the more, and that from a woman who covered herself in jewellery ever. to have breakfast. Ricky told me I'd run through the Firle fortune and be a beggar on the streets I was being such a lunatic, but he'd no idea what I'd been up to or just how many 'buttons' I had..." and Francis grinned to himself at the memories. "Anyway, as you can see, I wasn't short of jewels, so that's where they all came from... not to mention Fluffy's collar, Nelson's collar, that first diamond necklet I gave you before we were married... and a lot of your other jewellery, oh, and Carlotta's rubies and mantilla comb, but you can't tell Bella, you know that?"

"N... no, of course," Cat was still staggered at what she was staring at and she gazed around her, completely overwhelmed with it all.

Francis turned, took her hand and looked at her. "This is what the Bernheims wanted, both of them. I actually don't know if they really knew how much is here; I mean, how could they? I kept it all as quiet as I could, but inevitably word gets out when a pirate sinks and steals treasure from a New World treasure ship or another pirate vessel."

"I always knew you were more than a mere smuggler, once I got to know what you were like... being you. you would never have settled for just fiddling about back and forth along the coast," Cat sighed.

"Fiddling about?" he chuckled. "Smuggling isn't exactly a picnic, I'm telling you," Francis tutted with a smile, "not if you take it seri-

—

ously and have a lot of ships plying up and down and to and fro across the Channel, coming ashore all along the south coast; it took a lot of co-ordination, bribes, decoys… you've no idea."

"You had a FLEET of ships?" Cat looked at him in amazement.

"Let's just say, quite a few," he grinned, "more than people realised."

"Dear God…" she whispered, "and I thought there was just a handful, maybe half a dozen at most."

"No point in doing things small time; maximise the profit potential, that was my motto. Gospel according to the first Elizabeth Granville," he laughed at her, vastly entertained at her bemused expression.

"But the piracy, Francis, that was bad; why?" Cat finally got around to what she'd always wondered about, what had always bothered her and was a subject she'd never broached. "You said yourself, you were a rich man, why wasn't the smuggling enough?"

"I don't know, a chance to go further afield, an added thrill, a challenge?" Francis sighed. "Once you master one thing, you inevitably want to move up a notch… and my father was not a well man, he drank too much, his escape from my domineering grandmother, I'm positive, as he wasn't her tartan adventurer, Alexander Kinross, replicated in his son; he was HER father, unfortunately. It's all so clear now," he sighed. "Anyway, at the time I could see my future responsibilities mapped out for me, getting nearer and nearer, and I hated the prospect of so much, so soon: the title and responsibilities, my life not my own anymore. So I started to dabble, then dabble deeper and further afield, and then he died and I inherited, and I just went a bit insane for a while. I had an enormous row with Grandmother and just ran away; I was gone for well over a year, nearly two, without any serious contact, just a couple of short messages to reassure her I was indeed still alive and 'busy', as she'd no idea where I was or what I was doing, and you should have heard her when I finally reappeared. I nearly turned tail and ran away again!"

He gazed deep into Cat's eyes then, looking suddenly serious. "I've never told a living soul about what I did, not even Benjy was with me on every trip, only some, and of course that was how I originally found him in the first place… captive on another pirate vessel I thought to trade with. When I found they were a slaver with British souls on board amongst many others, including women and children, all chained up below decks and half-starved, including Benjy, who'd been pressganged on to a naval ship which had been sunk by this pirate, I saw red and sunk the ship with the bastard captain and bosun, and most of the rest of their brutal crew still on board. So now you know what I was like... and you deserve to know, now you've seen all this, after what you've been through. So ask and I'll tell you whatever you like, unpleasant though it is, and I don't think you'll like me very much afterwards," he said, shamefaced, his voice husky, "but it's about time you know it all, who I was, what I was..."

She was overwhelmed and wanted to know, but didn't, was almost frightened to ask, but she had to. "Did you kill a lot of men? Apart from that crew of the slaver," Cat almost whispered. "Benjy actually did tell Carlotta and I a bit about himself, when we came chasing after you when Bernheim got your Uncle Gerard and his family; well, we didn't know much about him then... but not any specifics... like that..."

"Yes, I did." He just looked at her and she knew somehow, he was now baring his soul and what it was costing him to reveal everything to her and she was both humbled and frightened at what she was about to hear.

"Sink ships? More than that one... with people on board?"

"Yes."

"Oh God. Did you kill innocent people... women? Children?" they were almost whispering now, at least Cat was, Francis could barely hear her final words.

"Not if I could help it. But it happened. Some drowned, it was inevitable in a sea battle if their ship was damaged, and I didn't like it... but I never let my crew at any of the women and children we took on board if we had to sink their ship, I give you my word. They knew what would happen to them if they disobeyed me, I ruled them with a rod of iron."

"Nooo... were your crew that bad? Were you that bad?"

"They weren't like my smuggling crews, even if they weren't exactly civilised or gentlemen; this crew were true pirates, the dregs of society, the lowest of the low mostly. Think Bernheim's militia, they were a similar breed. If I wasn't stronger than them, tougher and a more capable fighter than them, and generally more ruthless than them, I didn't stand a chance if they had no respect or fear of me. That was the reality, not some romantic fantasy in a novel from the circulating library."

"What... what did you do to them, Francis?"

"You really want to know?"

"Yes," she whispered, "I have to..."

"I thrashed or beat them, personally, or had them whipped, and if they disobeyed me twice, I threw them overboard."

Cat blanched. "Overboard?" her hand covered her mouth in horror.

"Yes."

Cat looked at the man she loved. "Into the sea? *Mon Dieu... non,* Francis, that's not you... you're not like that."

Yes, I was. I told you, you wouldn't like me." His face was completely expressionless as he admitted what he'd done, what he'd been like... and his heart thudded as he watched her face go white. "The only thing I will say in my defence is that if I hadn't kept control of them, they would have raped every woman who came on board, and they would possibly have turned on me one day if they weren't happy, and thrown ME to feed the fish. Now you know why I have this thing about swimming, I actually learned that from Marcus. His crew mutinied once as they weren't happy with their share of some booty they'd taken. They threw him overboard but because he was such a strong swimmer and kept his head, he made it to the coast. It was miles, I still don't know how he survived, but he did; unfortunately for them."

"Unfortunately for them? What did he do?" Cat's eyes were round, she could hardly believe what she was hearing, his tale like something from a nightmare.

"He tracked down his ship where it had put into port, and shot or cut the throats of the ringleaders in a tavern on the docks; then he got a new crew together, stormed the ship and took it back, and then hung most of the rest of the mutineers from the yardarm. He sailed off with the dead bodies swinging from the masts as a warning to his men never to dare turn on him. He left them there until they rotted and fell down, but the nooses stayed as a reminder. No one ever disagreed or complained to him again."

"Dear God, it's all unreal, I can hardly believe it; and my son is named after this man?"

"It was kill or be killed, it was a brutal, ruthless, sometimes barbaric world where life was cheap. I probably would have done the same... and now you know."

Cat sat for a while, absorbing what she'd heard, her whole body frozen with shock. She had never expected anything like it, her romantic ideas of what a pirate was, nothing like the reality of what Francis had just told her.

"There's a lot more, Francis, isn't there?" she whispered eventually.

"Yes," he held his breath, wondering what other questions she might want to ask.

"I don't want to know any more." Cat just sat and looked at him. "I've always known deep down you were a ruthless man, I've seen the way you run your estates and holdings, and the business enterprises you try so carefully to keep quiet about, hard but fair... but I've also seen the good side of you, the charity no one knows about and all the people you've helped. Dare I hope a lot of this has gone to good causes?" her hand swept around the chamber.

"Yes, more than you know, but I have to be careful. The gold coinage is foreign and old, a lot if not most of it. I can't just hand out strange coins in the street or to committees of do-gooders. Nor do orphanages want golden platters, crowns or ruby necklaces... and I can't simply walk into a bank in the City of London with a chest of coins and say, 'hello, here you are, invest this for me, if you would be so kind,' without someone asking a little bit about where it came from. And walls have ears and people see things." Francis sighed, "If I tried to get a lot of this melted down in a refinery, the risk would be too great as far as I was concerned. I'm sure if I shipped it overseas I could find somewhere quiet and get it done, but what if pirates overran my ship and stole it all on the way back?" and Francis suddenly burst out laughing. "Talk about ironic," he guffawed into the quiet chamber, the whole conversation more than surreal.

"You're completely mad, you know that?" Cat simply looked at her husband, wondering how much she really knew him.

"I know, Sweetheart. So, are you going to make ME walk the plank when we next go sailing? Can you still love a ruthless pirate, despite what I did? I know I was bad, but I've tried to make up for it since, truly, as much as I could, and, I give you my word, I have never, ever, killed someone just for the sake of it, or for pleasure. Nor have I ever tortured anyone in some barbaric fashion like both Bernheims enjoyed doing. Do you believe me? I promise all those stories you first heard about me, or rather The Shadow, cutting off people's noses and ears, and all the rest, they WERE stories. Other pirates did that, and far worse, that's where I got the idea from, but I give you my word, I never did. I or Reynard spread the tales around to enhance my reputation, put the fear of God into people, on both sides of the law and it worked."

Cat looked at her husband for a long time. He'd bared his soul to her, she realised that, after twenty-five years, she'd finally got the truth; but was he all bad? It seemed to her he'd spent the past twenty-five years repenting for the pirating aberration. He'd given huge amounts of money away, she knew that, and she still had no idea how rich he really was, with or without the treasure that surrounded her, and although the mansion in Berkeley Square was large and luxurious, and he owned far bigger houses and estates all over the country, Francis was happiest in the inconspicuous, rambling country house at Firle, sitting on only a small bit of land, saying he disliked his other holdings up north and had no wish for a vast, ostentatious, palatial estate somewhere, as so many other Dukes and high-ranking peers had.

He enjoyed keeping a low profile and out of the limelight. Now she understood why. So, in many ways, wasn't he also therefore a very good man? He was a conundrum, an enigma, a reformed villain, a fallen angel... but not a villain like either Bernheim, surely? Men who did kill and torture for pleasure or the sake of it. So how bad was bad? And she knew how good and kind he was, and he'd risked his life for her and her family so long ago, without thought or asking any payment, she'd never forgotten that... and she knew he'd give his life for her now, because he loved her… just as she loved him and would do the same. She'd never, ever, considered him a bad man in all the time she'd known him, indeed thought him quite the reverse, therefore in her mind, there was no case to answer. Did that make her as bad as him? Cat could go no further or answer herself.

"Yes, actually, I do believe you. Francis. You're the most complicated, unbelievable man I've ever met, and I don't want to know any more about your past. I love you as the man you are now and the man I've always known, and if you love me, that's all that's important to me," then her lips curled in a saucy smile as she consigned his revelations to the back of her mind, deciding she wasn't going to dwell on them anymore or let them worry her, it was all so very long ago and it was like some third rate, gothic novel one read and then simply dismissed and forgot about. "But I'll still make you walk the plank next time we go sailing. However, I'll have to tie you up first, seeing as how well you can swim… er… just how far can you swim, Francis?"

Francis looked at the love of his life, he'd been holding his breath, wondering what her reaction to his revelations would be, deciding, praying, that if she really loved him, she would hopefully understand and forgive him, and he finally exhaled, hugely relieved. "If I love you? What sort of a question is that, You Gallic Baggage? And I used to be able to swim for miles, but I've no idea how far I'd get now. Does that mean you'll come back to London with me and stop hiding yourself away, and we'll face the world together, and they can go hang with their questions and tattle?"

"Yes, I'll come, but I'll have to get Benjy to design me some evening gowns with high necks and ruffles. I simply CAN'T go out in Society marked like this, Francis, it's too much. I mean, what on earth do I say to the Prince Regent or the Prime Minister? I'll just have to start a new trend, like you and your buttons."

"You are NOT going anywhere with a high neck and a ruffle, Madam. What, hide those beautiful breasts of yours, that's sacrilege. Ricky would no doubt agree and we'd both be distraught," he chuckled and winked at her, "he always did have a fascination for that little freckle you've got just above your areo…"

"Really, Francis, you're too much," she giggled, "and what would

Sophy say if she heard that? She'd be devastated… and then hit him on the head with a very heavy book, knowing her!"

"Which brings me to another point, where have they gone?"

"Where have what gone?" Cat looked nonplussed for a moment.

"Your voluptuous breasts, and I'm being serious, Cat. You're not ill or anything and not telling me? I KNOW you're not eating, deliberately it seems to me. I know you didn't have a big breakfast, a mouse would have eaten more than you. I'm so worried, Sweetheart, you've got to tell me what's the matter." His whole manner had changed and he squeezed her hand, "That's why we came here, well apart from this," and another handful of coins was picked up to trickle back onto the pile in the chest he was perched on. "I needed to talk to you. I've been out of my mind and seeing you when I got to Firle, too thin and without that lovely bloom you always have about you, what's happened to you?"

"You think I'm too thin?" she whispered in alarm, her eyes widening.

"Of course you're too damn thin!" Francis didn't mince his words at her shocked expression, his worry overshadowing any plans he had to be diplomatic. "Your cheeks are hollow, your whole face gaunt, and never mind your bloody scars, your chest and collar bones are sticking out and your beautiful breasts have shrunk. There's nothing of you, so tell me before I go mad, what's the matter with you? Do you need a doctor? If it's something serious, I'd rather know than you keep me in the dark."

"I am NOT gaunt. I've always had high cheekbones, my grandmother had them and so has Eddie."

"I'm not interested in your grandmother, or bloody Eddie's cheekbones, I'm interested in yours; and if I say you look gaunt, you look gaunt," Francis rasped angrily.

"I can get into that black dress you always liked, you know, the one I wore that evening to the Birthday Ball at the Palace, the night you ran off to France. I know it's old fashioned now, but I might get Benjy to alter it a bit…"

"Whaaat? What the hell do I care what dress you can or can't get into? Why are you so damn thin and why aren't you eating?"

"I am NOT thin, I'm just thin-ner. I'm slender again, like I was when I met you. It was bad enough after I had Lizzie, but I was even fatter after Marcus was born and nothing fitted me, and I couldn't seem to lose weight this time as I did before after the twins, so I just cut back on what I ate. What's the matter with that?"

"You IDIOT woman!" Francis exploded. "Are you telling me you tried to look like this deliberately? You're starving yourself to get into a dress you wore twenty-five years ago? You're deranged! You've got fewer brains than Bubbles!"

"How dare you! I am NOT deranged, nor an idiot. I refuse to allow myself to get like Aunt Harriet or Mama or Emily Southwater, sitting and stuffing themselves with pastries day in, day out. They look like a trio of elderly, grey-haired, overstuffed, gossiping monkeys when they're together. You were spot on when you called them The Three Puddings because they don't walk, they waddle."

"I don't believe this," Francis was almost speechless.

"You wouldn't like me if I got fat, would you? You're always harping on about how tubby all those turbanned matrons are who line the walls at Society parties and balls, and years ago when I met you, I distinctly remember you saying how much you loved my slender figure and all the round and fat girls at Almack's were definitely not to your taste."

"Oh, for heaven's sake, you remember a throwaway comment from twenty-five years ago? You're mad; no one was to my taste after I'd met you, I was so infatuated and besotted and in love. I thought no one could possibly compare. As for now, I don't like you looking like a scarecrow, that's for sure, and you were NOT fat after Lizzie or Marcus was born. You've never been fat as long as I've known you, right back to your father's orchard. Good God, Cat, you're fifty, not twenty-five again, you can't possibly expect to look like you were then, and I don't want to go to bed with a broomstick. I want a woman next to me, soft and warm, with curves and breasts, not branches and twigs digging into me."

"Ooooh, are you telling me I look like a broomstick or a scarecrow?" Cat yelled at him. "Typical man, you don't like me fat, you don't like me slim, there's no pleasing you."

"Are you seriously trying to tell me you've been starving yourself because of ME? That this is MY fault? When the hell have I ever told you you're fat?"

"Well, never actually, but I KNOW you, you wouldn't tell me, you always say how lovely I am, even if I look like I've just fallen off a manure cart, even when I looked like an elephant when I was *enceinte* with Lizzie and Marcus... and then you'd just go off and bed another woman, someone younger and slimmer, like I USED to be, especially now I'm all scarred and ugly as well," the final, truthful worries finally burst out of her.

"Whaaat? Whatever gave you that mad idea? You're not deranged, you're completely insane!" Francis threw his hands up in the air in despair, then, as the ridiculousness of the whole situation struck him, he simply threw back his head and burst out laughing.

"Are you laughing at me, Francis Granville? How dare you laugh at me; of course this is all for YOUR benefit. Do you think I enjoy living without a single pastry in my life? Or a potato, or food without delicious sauces, or some creamy gateau, or a croissant in the morning covered in fresh jam or honey?"

"I've no idea," he guffawed. "Dear God, and I thought you had some terrible wasting disease and were fading away. No wonder you've been so grumpy for months, denying yourself anything pleasurable to eat. What have you been living on, cabbage and water?"

"Now who's being ridiculous?" Cat tutted crossly.

"And as for your neck, I'll show you what scarred and ugly does for me," and he pulled Cat onto his lap and kissed her hungrily, falling back into the chest of gold coins as she started to object, but then simply gave in as the pleasure of kissing him overwhelmed her, as it always had done and still did.

"You must be the only woman in England to be made love to on a pile of gold," he chuckled as he came up for air and stared into her green, cat's eyes, now alive with passion.

"Does that make me a pirate's moll?" Cat grinned at him.

"I don't know, I need to investigate further," and his hand roved up under the petticoats of her riding habit.

Cat writhed and squirmed under his knowing hand and fingers, one of her own deep in the pile of gold coins beneath her as she then moaned with pleasure.

"Definitely a moll, so wet, so easy to please," Francis teased.

"And you would know?" she gasped as a knowing finger started to agitate deep inside her.

"Well, us pirates with black beards have to stick together," and with a bit of wriggling he undid his britches, tossed up Cat's skirts and impaled her down on top of him.

"This is what scarred and ugly does to me, and you're not lovely, you're stunning, still more beautiful than any woman in London… even if you are a bit of a broomstick," he teased. "Oh God, My Pussy-cat, My Mad Frenchwoman, I've missed you so much," he groaned as she moved on him, lost with pleasure.

"Remind me to hit you with one when we get back to Firle," Cat gasped as he thrust upwards.

"Is that before or after you tie me up and make me walk the plank?"

"I'm still deciding, it's been a while since I did that," she stilled in his lap and just looked at him with a saucy smile on her face.

"We're not on my little boat; oh dear, so much for your evil plan."

"Who needs a boat, we could adjourn to our cottage for our picnic; it's been a while since we were there too. I've … um… had some reno-vations done."

"Renovations?"

"My surprise, I was thinking of moving in there actually, retiring from London life; you could say I wasn't well and had become an invalid. I didn't want to live in that big old house all by myself with just the children while you were in London."

"Whaaaat? You? Retire from life? An invalid? Another harebrained French idea. Where do you get them from, You Silly Woman? What the hell have you been up to since you've been down here?"

"Oh, I started it last year, as I said it was meant to be a surprise for you. I thought about it after our last little, ah, adventure there… but then Waterloo happened and then we spent the summer at Valenci-ennes and, what with one thing and another with the baby, it all got delayed, but I got it finished, finally, you'll see. It's got an upstairs now with a proper bedroom, and more rooms downstairs, and a pretty garden at the back... and some proper stables."

"Aren't you being a bit presumptuous? I need a proper invitation to this cottage, as befits my status, then I might consider a visit to inspect; but I might be too busy. Who owns this amazing dwelling, anyway?" He gave her a curling, wicked grin, "Proper bedroom, eh?"

"The Duchess of Firle, and nobody ever refuses her, not even villainous pirates or idiot Dukes."

"Idiot Dukes?" he grinned. "Is that so? But I thought you were a pirate's moll?"

"I can be a Duchess AND a pirate's moll, I know people who have two personas, or personae, as Eddie would say" she winked and then looked him up and down, "mind you, I obviously charge a fee for my services, being so special, and SLIM."

"You do? How much? Can I afford it? I've been away at sea for weeks, I'm desperate, even for a broomstick or scarecrow. Any port in a storm, you know the saying."

"Weeks? What about last night and the ones before that? Broomsticks charge double, by the way, and scarecrows treble, and I am a very special and secluded port."

"That doesn't make up for weeks of celibacy, not to mention stress and worry. I was just practising and remembering how to do it, that's why they were so quick, not up to my usual pirate standard. How much is double?"

"How much have you got? I only take gold, you know."

"I might have a few coins."

"I suppose that'll have to do; but of course, I'll need to check they're real."

"I can promise you they come from a reputable source."

"Reputable? Aaaaaaargh," she groaned as he moved and thrust, holding her down hard on him and she writhed around, her head thrown back as the sensations built and built and she gave up trying to talk.

"Word of a pirate... that's it... ah... ah... ahhhhhhhhhhhhhh....." and the pair of them toppled over into the chest as their climax overwhelmed them, laughing as they fell into the piles of gold.

"Oh God, that's disgraceful, what WERE we doing?" Cat tottered to her feet and straightened her habit.

"I told you, practising. You realise, if we go back to the cottage, all hell will break loose back at Firle in our absence, especially if we stay there overnight."

"What can she do? She's four, and there's a whole houseful of servants to keep an eye on her."

"Burn the house down? Shoot someone? Run through the new governess? The list is endless," Francis grinned as he stood up, straightened his own clothes and started to close the lids on the chests, but gave a thoughtful look at the diamonds before closing that box as well.

"Oh, let her get on with it, it's your fault, she's your daughter, you have no control over her whatsoever. You spoil her terribly."

"Pardon me? And she doesn't have a deranged Frenchwoman for a mother? Someone who wants to go and retire and live in a remote gamekeeper's cottage with two uncontrollable children and a giant daft dog?"

"There's a lot to be said for being remote, no one can hear you or find you, and there are daisies in the lawn in the garden so Lizzie can make bracelets; there's a pond with frogs, and roses in the beds and there is even a bathing room upstairs now. I got Eddie to design it, the workmen thought he and I were quite mad with all the pipes everywhere and equipment to heat the water and complicated diagrams; I don't think they'd ever heard of the Romans," she laughed.

"Romans?" Francis chuckled. "But where are the slaves to heat the water? Not that that is as important as making a daisy chain, or having frogs in my pond. Why would I be bothered about a bath when I can contemplate frogspawn," he chuckled again.

"You can't exist without a bath, the amount of time you loll around in yours."

"I do some of my best thinking in my bath."

"Is that what you call it?"

"There's nothing else to do, no one is ever around to scrub my back these days, or wash my hair or my feet."

"Wash your feet?" Cat burst out laughing as the pair mounted the stone steps and returned to daylight, blinking in the sunshine.

"There are other parts of me that would require particular attention but they get ignored as well," he sat down on the rug and helped himself to an apple and a wedge of cheese.

"Such as?"

"Have a pastry and I'll tell you," he waved a box under her nose.

"I'll get fat."

"I'll spank you, I'm warning you. EAT!" his expression was full of playful threat.

"You wouldn't dare, we're in the middle of a field, a shepherd might come along to see to the sheep or a farmhand to take the cows in for milking."

"You don't milk cows in the middle of the day, Your Grace, and the sheep are quite happy grazing where they are. Now EAT... or else."

Cat poked her tongue out at him but sighed with pleasure as she popped the flakey pastry into her mouth.

"There, isn't that better, or perhaps you would rather be spanked? It can be arranged, knowing the effect it has on you..." his big blue eyes sparkled at her and then he winked.

"You know, you get worse as you get older," she tutted.

"Well, that makes two of us. Now, are we going to this spectacular cottage with frogs or not? Or are we going to eat all this food here?"

"Of course we are, I suggested it. Come along, You Villain, I need to find my indoor plank and you can think of a way to send a message back to the house explaining why we're not going back there tonight, when there's no one around here for miles, shepherds or farmhands would have their uses you know."

"I'll think of something, I simply can't wait to find out what an indoor plank is!" And with a ribald chuckle, Francis packed up the picnic again and returned everything to the horses who'd been grazing quietly in the shade.

"Oh, you'll see," Cat giggled, having no idea and setting her mind to work on some wicked games to occupy them for the rest of the afternoon and evening, revelling in the prospect of having Francis to herself for even a short while, before life and their children intruded once more, and they set off for their little cottage hideaway; back once again to their closely devoted, loving, playful selves, their worries and traumas now settled and resolved, and the little folly simply sat in the afternoon sun with sheep grazing around it... on top of the biggest hidden fortune in England.

Chapter Twenty-Four

E ddie had returned from his sister's home and Bella, unable to settle and trying to control the urge to go over to Litlington and see how a still silent Nicky was doing, had taken herself up to London to check on her gambling saloons and to see what Jack was up to. He'd apparently been racketing around London, doing she knew not what, but a recent message said he was shortly to go off and spend a couple of weeks at the country home of a schoolfriend, somewhere up north.

Elise, therefore, had the house to herself and also Eddie… and ever since her meeting with Isabelle, that woman's laughing instructions had been burning a hole in her mind. With all their worry over Nicky wearing them down, Elise decided now was the perfect time to put her plan into action.

She'd spent the past fortnight wondering how to go about it, how to manoeuvre her husband to the situation the amused Isabelle had suggested… but Eddie wasn't any ordinary man to manoeuvre and Elise had been at her wits' end until a chance conversation over dinner about Nicky's arm gave her an idea. The pair of them had talked round in circles about his injury and Eddie, as ever and always interested in new scientific developments, had researched all manner of medical literary matter and written numerous letters to learned doctors abroad, as well as discussing how best to treat torn muscles and bone fractures with all sorts of so-called experts in London. Given his own ongoing problems with his shattered pelvis, he was extremely well informed on medical matters in that department and the studious Charlie, extremely close to his father, had lately declared that he was considering becoming a doctor when he grew up.

She dismissed her maid, got herself ready, then walked back and forth in her bedroom for a short while, bracing herself until, with a deep breath she made her way back downstairs, told a hovering footman he wouldn't be needed for the rest of the night, and then made her way to her husband's study, knocked and sauntered in, looking completely casual.

"Ah, I thought I would find you here," she smiled as Eddie looked up from a letter he was busy penning. "Are you very busy?"

"Never too busy to talk to you, My Love," Eddie smiled up at her and leaned back in his chair. "Is there something you want? Is Harry all right?"

"He's fast asleep, my little angel, smiling away, obviously dreaming of something nice… but I was wondering if you could spare me a few minutes? I was reading something and was thinking about Nicky's arm. I'm so concerned no one at Litlington will be massaging it properly and stretching those muscles. Francis or no Francis, I'll be glad when the end of the month comes and we can all go there and see what he's up to, and I can get back to making sure it heals properly."

"I know," Eddie sighed, "and you're so conscientious, but we promised and Francis is rarely wrong. I know Bella has the impatience of youth and love, but you and I are older and wiser, and I have to agree with him, sometimes we all need a bit of time and space to come to terms with things."

"Time and space is all very well, and I don't disagree with you, considering everything that has happened to him, but if his arm doesn't mend properly, he might well inadvertently tear the muscles again. Actually, that's what I was after, if you're not too busy, I just want to try a little experiment; do you want to finish whatever you're writing first?"

"No, of course not, it can wait until tomorrow." Eddie put his arms back and stretched them with a sigh, "What sort of experiment?"

"Oh, nothing very much. Could you spare me a moment upstairs?"

Eddie shrugged. "Upstairs?"

"Yes, it will be easier up there, you'll see, it really won't take more than a few minutes, I promise,"

"Very well," he picked up a book from a pile on his chaotic desk, "I might as well call it a day and catch up on my reading before I go to sleep," and he stretched again, rose from his chair and limped over to the door to follow his wife down the quiet hallway and slowly make his way up the stairs after her. "What maggot have you got in your brain now, *Chérie*? I didn't think there was any avenue we haven't explored about Nicky's arm?"

As they walked slowly down the corridor, Elise held open the door to her bedroom, "Just come in here and I'll explain, it's nothing new really, just something I wanted to clarify."

Eddie made his way into his wife's bedroom, inhaling the light floral scent she always used which permeated the air in there, and turned to her with a smile and a quirked brow. "Well?" he shrugged.

"Just take your jacket off, could you?" Elise went to stand behind him and helped him remove the jacket he'd put back on as he'd left his study, and hung it over the back of a chair. "Now then, I want you to cast your mind back to when Bernheim's thugs overcame you. When you came to, in the cellars, how were your arms tied?"

Eddie looked at his wife, slightly bemused. "What has that to do with anything? Behind my back, like everyone. Why?"

"Yes, I know THAT," sighed Elise, "but you men were bound much more securely than us ladies, for obvious reasons."

"Not if they knew m'sister," chuckled Eddie with a roll of his eyes, "but I fail to get your drift, M'Dear?"

"Well, I want to see how you were bound. I need to understand how they pulled Nicky's arms behind him, then I might understand better just which muscles he might have pulled."

"Oh... right. I SEE..." Eddie sighed. "Well, at least I think I do. Do you really think that will help? We all think he cracked a bone as well, when his chair toppled over."

"Very possibly, but cracked bones heal. If his muscles tore and don't stretch as they heal, then they'll still hurt and restrict movement, isn't that what we've discovered?"

"Yeeees, but I still don't think having your hands bound would tear a muscle," mused Eddie.

"Probably not, unless the muscle was still healing, or wasn't stretched back to what it was previously, as in Nicky's case; and also, I'm sure he wrenched and pulled while trying to loosen his bonds. Didn't you?"

"Yes, of course, it's an automatic reaction, surely; but I was bound so tightly, there was no give at all, no matter how I tried," sighed Eddie. "I'd thought, since they knew I was a cripple, they might not have bothered so much with me; but obviously not," he muttered.

"You're NOT a cripple," tutted Elise.

"Of course I am. I limp, I can't ride, I can't run or jump, I can't crouch, I can't kneel and bend easily, stairs take me forever to go up and down... I can't even dance," Eddie muttered bitterly, reciting the familiar litany almost under his breath.

"You CAN dance; you dance with me at Firle at Christmas."

"Not really, that doesn't count."

"Of course it does. Now everyone waltzes, I don't know why you don't. We managed perfectly well, albeit more sedately than the others, and you said waltzing was easier than other dances as holding me makes you feel more stable... and it was divine," she said dreamily as she started to sway and hum to herself for a moment. "I loved waltzing with you."

"No, it WASN'T 'divine', don't be ridiculous," Eddie seethed softly and she immediately stopped.

"Look, we're not here to discuss your dancing," Elise said dismissively, wanting to get away from the sensitive subject of her husband's disability, knowing what a delicate and sore subject that was for him. "Back to the matter in hand. I want you to show me how they bound you, how your arms were pulled, and then, when you pull to demonstrate, I can see and feel which muscles YOU are straining. Can we do that?"

Eddie shrugged. "If you really think it will help?"

"I don't know if it will, but it will be useful to see. I don't know why I didn't try this before, but do you mind?"

He shrugged again. "No of course not."

"Wonderful. Er... may I borrow your cravat?"

Eddie chuckled. "Not quite the same, but I suppose it will do for demonstration purposes. They bound my wrists and my upper arms, one won't be enough, do you want another? Go help yourself from my armoire, Roberts won't mind, there's plenty in there," and he started to casually undo and unwind his artfully tied cravat, his fussy valet's pride and joy.

"Ah... of course. Just a moment," and Elise strolled through the connecting door into Eddie's bedroom to retrieve another couple of cravats, delighted her little stratagem had worked. She wandered back to find him sauntering around her room, admiring the soft furnishings.

"You know, I really like the way you've redecorated in here; it's so serene and tasteful, just like you, and light and airy... it goes with your scent," he sighed, staring around at the creams and pale greys of the furnishings and carpets.

"You're sure you didn't mind?"

"Mind? Why should I mind? This is your suite of rooms, you can do what you like with them. If you wanted them purple, yellow and pea green, it's your choice," he laughed, pulling a comical face as if he was about to retch.

"Well, I wasn't sure; you know, it was Carlotta's..." Elise said quietly.

"They're YOUR rooms, I told you. You're the *chatelaine* of the house now, the furnishings are down to you. If you want to redecorate the whole place, go ahead."

"What? Even your study?" Elise laughed.

"NO! Definitely NOT my study; that's my sanctuary, my refuge from the mad world out there, and maybe not the library. After all, bookshelves are bookshelves and if you took the books out, it would be a devil of a job to put them all back in the right places again; they're catalogued just the way I like them."

"Well, seeing as they are all your books and mine are in London, I'll leave well alone; but are you serious about the house, Eddie? I have to say, I would like to makeover some of the rooms," and get rid of the countless pictures of her predecessor hanging everywhere that gave her such a complex, Elise thought; but one step at a time.

"My Love, you can do whatever you like. The décor in Hertford Street is delightful and you have perfect taste as far as I'm concerned, so feel free to do what you will. As long as the painters don't try and paint or wallpaper me, you have *carte blanche*," he chuckled, "and when I finally sort out the de Mornay estate over in Normandy, you can do the same there."

"You're so generous, Eddie, are you sure?"

"Of course."

"Are you STILL battling with the new administration in Paris over the de Mornay estate? You haven't mentioned it much lately."

"It's never-ending," Eddie sighed. "There's no problem with the old mansion, as you know, and the gardens and parkland around it, but all the fields and villages became state property and were taken over by the local people and I doubt I'll ever get that land back. It's the same problem Nicky has got, except he hasn't got the papers to prove all the land belonged to the Valenciennes Estate in the first place, only hearsay."

"Well, in my opinion, it doesn't matter. You have the family home back again, with all its history and memories, that's the most important thing, and your income source has long changed now, so I don't think worrying about crop failures and harvests is any loss. The same goes for Nicky."

"I suppose," sighed Eddie. "Bonaparte changed so much and the world is a different place now, well, France certainly is with everything so centralised, but it would have been nice to hand it all down to Charlie with the title, like I thought I would inherit everything from my father once upon a time."

"If he does become a doctor he wouldn't want the responsibility of running a large estate over there anyway, but I understand how you feel about your lineage and title."

"If he becomes a doctor, I'm not sure who will oversee all the investments and business matters," sighed Eddie, "and sometimes, after everything that's happened in my life over the years, since the

Revolution and I came to England, having a title seems so unimportant compared to having one's life."

"That's rather a profound statement, Eddie, and you never know, mayhap little Harry will inherit your head for business; but time enough to worry about that. Now then, where were we?" she brought their chatter back to the subject in hand.

"Nicky's arm?"

"Oh yes; come and sit down on the bed and let me experiment."

"Oh, very well," and with a good-natured sigh Eddie made his way over to Elise's bed, perched on the edge and put his arms behind him.

Elise almost crowed with delight as she scrambled onto her luxurious four-poster and secured Eddie's wrists. Then she picked up the second and third cravats and secured them around his well-developed biceps as well. They had a short conversation as Eddie twisted his arms as best he could and told Elise which muscles pulled as he did so, but then, that was it. For Elise, however, it was now her moment.

"Well, does that answer your questions?" Eddie tried looking over his shoulder at his wife.

"Mmmm, it's interesting, but it's obvious it depends on what positions they tied his wrists."

"All I know is I couldn't bloody move, much like now, in fact; oh, come along, Elise, undo me, I don't think we can achieve anything else from all this."

"Just a moment, there IS something else." Elise got off the bed and headed towards her dressing room. "I'll be back in a moment; just bear with me and be patient."

"Elise? *Chérie*? For God's sake, where are you going now?" Eddie called after her.

"You'll see," her laughing tones wafted out of her dressing room.

Feeling a bit of a fool, Eddie sat patiently and waited for her to reappear and when she did, he goggled at her.

"Elise? Eliiise..? What the..?" Elise's face had undergone something of a transformation as she stood and looked at Eddie from the end of the bed with a saucy stare, and she started to slowly unpin her long, thick, blonde hair which fell, like a straight river, right down her back to her bottom. Normally clear of any cosmetics, except when they went out in the evening to balls or parties, when she now applied a little soot to her lashes, a hint of kohl to enhance her clear hazel eyes, a hint of rouge to give her cheeks a glow and a touch of gloss to her lips, and she'd considered even that quite daring compared to how she used to be before, and how fashion for genteel Ladies decreed… now she had gone the whole hog. Her much-enhanced eyes looked large in her face and she'd rouged her cheeks more than normal and her lips were reddened and glistening with salve as she licked them suggestively. Eddie watched in stunned silence as her hair cascaded downwards and she started to slowly unbutton the front of her simple, indoor day dress as they didn't bother to dress for dinner when they were at home in the country and dined by themselves. One by one the buttons on the high bodice came apart and she let the garment fall to the floor unheedingly as she wriggled out of it. A couple of petticoats drifted to the floor next, until she stood before him in merely her stays over what appeared to be a red silk chemise.

Slowly, almost teasingly, she undid the cords of the stays and they dropped to the floor and she was left looking at him in nothing but a wisp of red silk that clung to her breasts, held up by nothing more than a red ribbon over either shoulder and finished at her thighs. She was wearing crimson silk stockings that were held up over her knees by a froth of red lace and beribboned garters, and instead of her usual flat slippers, she had on some little red, heeled shoes. She struck a saucy pose with hands on her hips and smirked at him. For a middle-aged woman, she looked youthful and quite stunning.

"Well? What do you see before you, Baron?"

"You… good God, Elise? What the hell are you doing? You look like a harlot!" Eddie gaped at his wife, staring at her long, shapely legs.

"Do I? How fascinating. Don't I also still look like the Baroness de Mornay?"

"Yes… NO! Of course you bloody don't; not like THAT."

"Oh, but I am the Baroness, just a different version." Her hands stroked suggestively up and down her torso over the clinging red silk and she watched as Eddie's eyes followed them. "The question is, do you like what you see?"

"I..." Eddie was lost for words. "I... what on earth are you playing at?"

"Who me? Ah, now, that is the precise point," Elise purred. "I've decided we need a little more... ah... excitement, shall we say, in our bedroom life, so I'm going to entertain you tonight, *Mon Chèr.*"

"Excitement? Entertain me?" Eddie could barely take his eyes off her, off the full breasts thrusting against the tight, thin silk which looked suspiciously damp, the nipples turgid from where she was stroking them almost absently. She moved slowly and prowled over to the side of the bed where he was sitting.

"Shift up against the pillows and put your feet on the bed."

"I can't. Undo me," he ordered.

"Oh no, I couldn't possibly do that, that would spoil the fun," she purred again and leaned down over him and he was overwhelmed with the light, flowery scent, and she started to kiss his face. Light feathery kisses and suddenly, she kissed his mouth; except this wasn't her usual tender offering, this was hungry and demanding as her hands grasped his head and held it still for her predation. At first, he was stunned, but not for long, and he responded as her tongue roved around his mouth and toyed with his. Eventually, she lifted her face away from his and looked downwards and the evidence of his response was obvious. "Move up the bed, Eddie."

As if mesmerised, he did as he was told and she lifted his legs onto the covers as he lolled back against the mound of cream satin and lace pillows. "What do you want, Elise?"

"In a word, you." She followed him on to the bed and straddled his lap, looking down into his bemused eyes, wriggling against the hardness in the front of his pantaloons, and she kissed him again, now running her hands over his chest and abdomen and then up into his slightly wavy, blond hair.

"What on earth has got into you? Let me go, I can't move."

"I know," Elise smirked. "I have you now. I can do what I like with you, finally."

A bonfire burst into flame in Eddie's head. "Is that what all the experiment was about earlier, so you could make me your prisoner?"

"Mostly, but not totally. It was interesting, but nothing I hadn't already considered and investigated before. I tried it on Jack, you see, before he went back to Eton."

"You Conniving Baggage!" Eddie swore at her. "Why, Elise? You only had to ask if you wanted to play games."

"Really? This from a man who doesn't make love to me with the candles or a lamp lit, even one, and won't let me see him naked?" her voice was slightly sarcastic.

"I thought you were relatively innocent, I didn't want to shock you." It sounded an inane excuse and his voice trailed off, not wanting to admit to his fear of her reaction on seeing the terrible scars on his lower body.

"I WAS relatively innocent, well compared to you, but I wasn't a virgin. I was actually waiting for you to progress matters and since you haven't, I got tired of waiting, so I decided to take said matters into my own hands," she shrugged.

Eddie swore again. "*Mon Dieu*, Elise," and he rattled off a stream of voluble French, a sure sign, Nicky could have told her, of his growing anger as he tugged on the bonds restraining his arms.

"You know, between you, Cat and Nicky, not to mention my summer at Valenciennes last year, my French vocabulary is coming on leaps and bounds; not that I QUITE grasped everything you just said, perhaps you might care to translate later, I'm sure what you just told me must be riveting; now then," she turned to survey Eddie's legs. "I really don't think I want your shoes on my lovely new cream coverlet," and as instructed by Isabelle, Elise shifted herself back from Eddie's lap, turned herself around and crawled down the bed on her hands and knees, knowing perfectly well she was offering her husband an outrageous view of her bottom and nether regions, completely naked under the short red shift. Telling herself it was nothing he hadn't already kissed and investigated intimately, even in dim moonlight, she wriggled her bottom suggestively before kneeling up to tug off his shoes, one by one, smirking to herself at the continuation of his muttered stream of obscene Gallic epithets. With another theatrical wriggle, the shoes were tossed to the floor and she turned around again and crawled back towards him. She slithered up his body, pleased to feel the telling bulge in his clothes which she paused to

229

caress, resulting in a strangled groan, before she reached up to kiss him again, extremely carnally, revelling in his response.

"Now, what shall I remove next?" she finally purred against his lips, before starting on the buttons of his waistcoat. They took but a minute to undo and she was left with his shirt. She reached across to the nightstand where she had deliberately left a small pair of sharp embroidery scissors. The effort of stretching out her arm caused a breast to pop out of the confines of the red silk and Eddie's language got even more venomous as he took in the sight of her rouged nipple. Elise completely ignored him as she grasped the scissors, sat back up and, before he realised what she was at, she cut the top of the beautiful lawn shirt, tossed the scissors on the floor and with an almighty rip, tore the rest of the garment apart from neck to hem, dragging it out of the waistband of his pantaloons in the process.

As he swore and shifted beneath her, Elise's eyes lit with pleasure and she bent to savour the hitherto rare pleasure of kissing and licking down his exposed torso.

Edouard de Mornay was a similar age to Francis Granville, and the effect of what had happened to him during that long ago ambush and hold up when Dupont and his men had murdered his and Cat's grandmother and maids, and beaten Eddie half to death, had been profound and life-changing, just as it had affected his impressionable eight-year-old-sister. While she had cowered in fright in the carriage under the seat, covered by her grandmother's voluminous skirts, and avoided being raped and probably murdered like the innocent maids, the barely adolescent Eddie, slightly built, all gangling limbs and full of youthful and naïve bravado, had tried to fight the men who had attacked their coach and laid out their parents. He'd been kicked, clubbed, and beaten viciously for his efforts, which had crushed his pelvis and broken ribs, his femur and many other bones, not to mention Dupont laying open the side of his face with his big knife for good measure.

Surgeons had sewn up his face as best they could, but the scar from temple to chin it had left down one side, although the wound had thankfully avoided his eyes and mouth, was ugly and puckered. He had lain for months, incapacitated, as his bones had healed. Unfortunately, however, his pelvis had been crushed beyond repair, which had affected his femur, even if the break in that had healed, with the result he'd become a limping cripple. He'd spent long months in bed, and then more months in a chair with wheels, hauling himself around or being pushed and carried everywhere, and then more time on crutches, and the former laughing, charming, intelligent and energetic young boy had become morose, withdrawn, bitter and studious with no other means to occupy or entertain himself.

By sheer dint of a strong will neither he nor his concerned family ever knew he possessed, he'd forced himself to walk again without the aid of crutches and then a stick, and tried to socialise, but, young girls had turned from his former blond good looks with cringing distaste and he'd withdrawn even more from Society, his self-confidence and esteem permanently affected. As he'd grown into an otherwise handsome and tall young man, depending on which side of his face one looked at, he'd immersed himself in academic and mental exercise rather than physical ones. He couldn't dance and found it difficult and painful to ride, never mind getting on a horse in the first place, and the jolting of a curricle or phaeton was impossible to deal with, even coach journeys were a nightmare for the same reason, roads being what they were, especially going over cobbled streets.

So, his mind developed and Eddie spent his days studying and reading, anything he and his despairing parents and sister could lay their hands on, whether it was academic and scientific or medical books and papers, especially if they related to his injuries or disability, or current affairs, or latterly, as he got older, commercial matters. He was blessed with a clever brain anyway, and developed an almost reproductive and pictorial memory, and when he did venture out with his solely male friends who merely accepted his scar, looking on it as a badge of bravery rather than something to run from in fright like the naïve girls in their social circles, he played cards and gambled as did all young aristocratic men in Paris.

He became an extremely competent gambler and won often, though he was careful to not draw attention to his capabilities and patronised a wide variety of gambling dens and clubs because of that. Since nicely brought up young girls shied away from him, even older

Society Ladies, he tended to avoid them all, and he paid for his carnal favours and interaction with women; they didn't care what he looked like as long as he had money. As he progressed into his twenties, and unknown to his family, he gambled more, won more money, and kept mistresses; his bedroom prowess grew as he learned and was entertained by a stream of beautiful courtesans and *demi-mondaines*.

Vowing never again to be at the mercy of highwaymen or brigands, he became a dead shot, and although the lower half of his body was weak, especially one leg, his upper body was strong. Months and years of hobbling around on crutches or hauling himself around in wheeled chairs and in and out of furniture or beds had given him strong, well-developed arms and biceps and a tautly muscled upper torso and abdomen. His pelvis and thigh on one side of his body were terribly scarred from where an endless stream of doctors and surgeons had painfully tried and failed to mend his shattered bones and muscles, but it hadn't affected his ability to enjoy sex, and his mistresses just ignored it, as they were paid to do.

He made a point of keeping his upper body as trim and strong as he could, never being sure if his pelvis or crippled leg would give out one day, and he'd be forced back to crutches or a chair, and he had his own private set of weights and exercises he went through daily to maintain his strength and fitness and that had continued all his life. As a result, Eddie's upper body was leanly muscled and far fitter than that of most men his age, even if his lifestyle was so sedentary.

Elise revelled in the body of her husband, having been married to a man old enough to be her father, almost her grandfather, and the still firmly-muscled torso was a pleasure to caress, look at and explore; Eddie couldn't stop her and she made the most of it. She'd done it before, infrequently, and it had always been in the dimness of shaded moonlight in the bedroom or in the dark, and she'd never had the time, space and illumination to inspect and tease. Now, however, her room was deliberately lit by the soft light of a myriad of candles and glowing oil lamps. She nibbled and licked, she bit his nipples and sucked them, and she gradually kissed her way down from his neck to his belly. And then she stopped.

From a miasma of groaning pleasure, Eddie opened his eyes as

Elise sat up and her hands went to the fastenings of his pantaloons. "NO!" the tormented order was gasped. "Elise, pleeease, don't do this," and suddenly his eyes looked apprehensive and haunted.

"Why ever not? You've just enjoyed what I was doing, and don't try and deny it, the evidence is obvious," and she slowly caressed the obvious, restricted bulge.

"NO! Put the candles out and douse the lamps."

"I most certainly will not; anyone would think I'd never seen a naked man before," she laughed softly. "It's about time I saw you, you are my husband, for heaven's sake, Eddie."

"NO!" The apprehension turned to anger as he rasped his order.

Elise completed ignored him, quite unfazed. "Give me one good reason why. Good heavens, Eddie, I've touched and caressed you enough."

"No, I'd rather you didn't," he tried pleading again.

Elise simply looked at him and knew why. She'd felt the terrible scarred and puckered skin and lack of muscle, compared to his other leg and had sensed that was why he always crept out of bed in the darkness and put on some soft, silken, loose trousers before they went to sleep, if he'd taken them off to make love to her as he always went to bed with them on. But she didn't say a word, she merely ignored his plea and undid the fastenings. Slowly, she peeled the garment down, knowing his eyes were closed and he was holding his breath, waiting for a shudder or expression of revulsion but she acted as if he looked just like a normal man. She caressed him lightly and bent to kiss the naked flesh she'd revealed, now suddenly gone limp and shrunken, and wriggled backwards to tug the tailored pantaloons off entirely.

"Well, now you know," his quiet voice was low and bitter.

"Know what? That this is the source of so much pleasure for me?" she said, smiling as she caressed him. "Of course I know you're scarred, so why you bother with your silken trousers is beyond me," Elise shrugged nonchalantly. "Why should I worry? It doesn't affect you, so why would I take any notice? You are such a beautiful man otherwise, you love me so wonderfully, that's all that matters," and she bent to kiss up and down his hard thighs, ignoring the ugly, puckered scars that covered one; teasing, licking slowly upward as Eddie held his breath until her lips were on him, nibbling, little butterfly kisses tantalising up and down his length as it grew and hardened again.

Elise gazed up at his face, it was a mask of torment and his eyes were closed. "Look at me, Eddie," she ordered softly. "Look at what I'm doing. This is me, Elise, look how much pleasure this gives me. I've been your wife for a year and a half, it's about time you let me do this. Heaven knows you've done the same to me often enough."

"That's different, but I can't stop you, captive like this," the bitterness was still there.

"But why should you?" Then, she had to ask, "Did Carlotta do this to you?" she whispered.

The silence hung in the air. "Yes," he said softly.

"Well then, why not me? Am I not your wife now?"

"Yes… but… you're different. You're a Lady, not all women want to do this, especially not inexperienced ones like yourself. You…" he paused, hesitating, "you're not Carlotta."

"No, I'm not Carlotta. I'm Elise. And I couldn't give a fig about what other women do, inexperienced or not. I want to do this. I love you, Eddie, and I want to give you as much pleasure as you give me. It excites me," she whispered as she caressed him, moving her hand slowly up and down in a way she knew he liked and had taught her, twisting it occasionally and moving her fingers teasingly which made him groan with pleasure. "I want to excite you; don't you want to watch me pleasuring you? For that's what I'm going to do. I thought men liked to watch…" and with a deep breath, she took him in her mouth, endeavouring to remember what Isabelle had told her to do, what apparently Nicky had liked, not that she wanted to know that information and had squirmed in embarrassment when Isabelle had waxed lyrical, and in great detail, about how she'd pleasured him, and the tethered man under her gasped and swore, jerking on the bed as his eyes blazed open.

"ELISE!"

She lifted her head and a satisfied smile, like a Cheshire cat, curled on her lips. "Are you watching me now? Does it excite you?" she licked the tip and savoured the glistening moisture that oozed from him. "I wondered what you would taste like," she mused wickedly.

"God almighty," Eddie breathed as he watched her, completely overwhelmed. "Where the HELL did you learn to do this? You knew nothing when I first took you to bed."

She knew he'd ask and she had her answer ready. "I CAN read, you know. Or had you forgotten? And books do have illustrations, even when one can't understand strange foreign languages. What one can acquire in certain shops never ceases to amaze me, never mind what's contained in certain classical texts!"

"*Mon Dieu*! Let me go, *Chérie*, let me love you, we can do this properly. Untie me, please," he cajoled.

"Oh no," she smirked up at him. "I told you, you're my prisoner tonight. You're therefore going to lie there and although I know I'm obviously not very expert, you can either give me instructions of what you like, and direct me, so I can practise, or just lie back and think of England, or France, though I'd rather you did neither as that is extremely boring, and I will endeavour to give you as much pleasure as you give me."

Eddie gave up. He knew Elise well enough by now to know how determined she was when she put her mind to something, and he was reeling from what she was doing, never having expected anything like it from the refined, reserved, ladylike and quiet woman he'd married. He'd been shocked enough to see her tarted up like a harlot, the seductive, thin redshift sending the blood pounding through his veins, and when she'd wriggled down the bed with her bottom so tantalisingly in the air, all sorts of lascivious visions had poured into his mind as he wondered if she'd realised what she was doing; now he was certain she had.

She was younger than him, by nearly ten years, still in her early forties, and she was always busy and energetic: gardening, which she loved; riding or pottering around the countryside, visiting tenants and local neighbours in a little gig, even walking to the village shop if it was a nice day, striding out and enjoying the fresh air like the country girl she'd originally been. Otherwise, she was always busy in the house when she wasn't sitting quietly reading and so, despite her pregnancy, she was now slim again with full breasts and rounded hips and a narrow waist, and he lusted after her, always trying to restrain himself and conscious of his disability and how awkward he was in bed sometimes, never wanting to shock her or put her off. But the more he made love to her and she responded to him, the more he wanted her, in all manner of ways that he'd never, ever, consider doing. And now, here she was, fulfilling a fantasy he'd privately harboured since he'd first made love to her.

Eddie lay and watched; closed his eyes and felt; groaned and jerked, instructed and encouraged her, until he sensed his climax approach. "Elise, *Chérie*. That's enough, stop; untie me… I can't take much more."

"Really?" she crooned, obviously pleased with herself, licking her lips. "Good. I didn't know how long it would take. I've nearly finished then?"

"No… you don't understand…"

"Oh, but I do." She licked lasciviously up and down his length, causing another groan. "Let go, My Love. I want to feel you climax, watch it, I want to taste it all," and he was deep in her mouth again, the hard sucking sending his brain into orbit.

That was it. Captive, and overwhelmed with what she was doing, Eddie couldn't stop her, or himself, and he exploded with a cry as his body jerked and he erupted down her throat.

Elise sat back, coughed slightly and wiped her mouth with the back of her hand, immensely pleased with herself and then, overwhelmed with the need to be close to him, she slithered back up his body and kissed him hungrily, her own body so on fire, she barely knew what to do with herself.

"I rather think I'd like to do that again," she whispered seductively against his lips. "Can you taste yourself in my mouth?"

"Yes, You Tease." Eddie opened his eyes and gazed at her, "What HAVE you been reading and wherever did you find it? And you didn't learn all THAT from any classic texts I know!"

"Oh, I couldn't possibly tell you," she whispered saucily back, "as long as you enjoyed it?"

"Enjoy it? Elise, what sort of inane question is that? Let me loose now and let me return the favour. I want to taste those rouged breasts of yours, I want to…"

"Oh no, I haven't nearly finished with you yet," she purred.

"Whaaaat?" he tugged uselessly on the cravat around his wrists.

"There's no use you wriggling, I tied the knots tight. I'll let you go when I've finished with you, and only then," she laughed, sitting up and looking at his smiling but shocked face.

"But... but you can't."

"Oh yes, I can."

"But I'm uncomfortable, dammit. Pleeeeease, Elise, be reasonable."

"Too bad and don't wriggle. I couldn't deal with one man with pulled muscles in this house, I don't want another," she chuckled.

"Oh God, what on earth have I done to deserve this?"

"It serves you right for withholding yourself and your delicious body from me."

"But... but I thought it would shock you, not just the act, my scars."

"You know, for a clever man, you are completely brainless sometimes. What does Cat call Francis? A bumpkin? Well, that makes two of you."

"A bumpkin? To hell with that."

"What's a bumpkin, or a numpty, in French?"

"A numpty?" Eddie laughed. "I am NOT a numpty, whatever that is."

"Yes, you are, but at least you won't go skulking around in those silk trousers anymore," she smirked.

"They're very comfortable to sleep in, and to wear," he huffed. "The Turks and Arabs have some sense, y'know."

"If you want to sleep in my bed, or want me to sleep in your bed again, they're banned. I want to feel your skin against mine now."

"Who said anything about sleeping? Oh, come on, *Chérie*, let me go," he grinned at her playfully.

"No. Now then, would you like a drink? How about a nice chilled glass of wine?"

"I'm a trifle incapacitated for refreshments," he quirked a brow at her, "and my hands have gone to sleep."

"I don't believe you, You Villain," she laughed. "I'll be back in a moment." Elise crawled off the bed and padded through to her dressing room and returned with an ice bucket and two glasses. Quite efficiently, she drew the cork on the bottle of chilled white wine and poured out two glasses and held one to his lips and he drank thirstily, leaned back and sighed.

"I'll pay you back for this, I promise," he threatened with a smile.

"Is that so, Baron?" Elise laughed as she tossed back her own glass. "Well, I haven't finished with you yet, maybe another time?"

"What are you going to do to me now, You English Witch?"

"Aha! Wait and see!" and she put the two glasses down next to the ice bucket on the nightstand and returned to straddle his lap. "Why do I like kissing you so much?" she mused as she started to kiss him again.

"I don't know, you tell me."

"I suppose because you're so good at it. You must have had so many ladies in your life," Elise sighed.

"Not really," Eddie said quietly, certainly not the ladies she obviously meant.

"That is a complete tarradiddle; your French accent makes me weak at the knees, don't you try telling me it doesn't have that effect on the rest of my sex. You're such a charmer when you want to be, just like Nicky and Francis."

"No, truthfully, Elise," she'd no idea, he thought.

"I don't believe you. I'M definitely not a numpty," she laughed. "I think I was smitten from the moment I was introduced to you and you opened your mouth and said, *'Bonjour, Chère Madame'*, although I didn't realise it at the time. No woman on earth could resist you when you whisper in their ear all that amorous nonsense you speak to me in French, or English when you ham it up with your accent; you're completely irresistible when you lay it on thick."

Why did she make him feel so good? Eddie wondered as he gazed at her as she started to kiss his chest again. He felt completely normal with her, and she compared him to Francis and Nicky. She was so wonderful and he loved her so much, and now tonight; he'd never dreamed he could find such happiness. She was everything he'd ever fantasised about in a woman: beautiful, passionate in bed, a Lady out of it, and she had a brain.

Up and down his body Elise teased him. From the bottom of his bare feet to his temples; with her hands and her mouth, until he was swearing and sweating, alternately pleading with her then berating her angrily in French as she brought him to near climax and then pulled away. She did it again and again, until he was mindless with frustration and yelling at her, and she couldn't do it any longer.

She sat back then, straddling his thighs and she started to caress herself. "I want you sooo much, Eddie," she whispered. "Look what pleasuring you does to me," and she peeled down the straps of her shift, running her hands over her exposed breasts and nipples, teasing herself, and throwing her head back with a moan, her long blonde hair, now tousled and tangled, swinging against her back. Her hands roved down her body as her eyes half closed and one went between her legs. Eddie almost gaped at the wanton sight of his previously sedate wife. "I'm so wet, so hungry to feel you inside me..." on and on she went, repeating what Isabelle had written down for her to memorise, but now totally carried away on her own tide of lust and desire, her body on fire again as she writhed on his legs, knowing he could feel her swollen sex and the wetness there.

"Ride me, Elise. Hell, I can't take any more of this," Eddie gasped hoarsely in French, head thrown back, eyes closed, perspiration running down his temples, "or let me go. I want to fuck you so much, I'll go crazy if you torture me anymore. You want this as much as I do."

"This time, it's for me," Elise opened her eyes, glazed with passion and desire, realising she'd finally got to him, he was as lost as she was as he shifted restlessly on the bed beneath her, swearing and muttering, whatever control he maintained over himself long gone, and she'd never seen him like this. "...with my perfect man," she whispered and rose up to impale herself down on him hard, with a soft cry of pleasure, her nails digging into his shoulders as she rocked on him, feeling the maelstrom start, she was so wound up and lost to pleasure, she'd never known anything like it.

"MOVE!" Eddie yelled at her, overwhelmed with frustration. "MOVE, DAMMIT!" he ordered as she bent to kiss him, starting to rise and fall, as his mouth fastened over hers and he almost ate her alive, so wound up and out of his mind with lust and desire, he couldn't think straight.

As he burst inside her like an erupting volcano she screamed wildly, "EDDIEEEEEEEE," and contorted on top of him as wave after wave of contractions overwhelmed her and she eventually collapsed in a heap on his chest, her brain elsewhere, heart hammering, barely able to breathe.

"Oh, dear God," she finally opened her eyes to peer up into bemused green ones, feeling his own heart thudding erratically under her palm. "I thought I was dying," she whispered.

"*La petite mort*; that's what they call it in France," he whispered. "That was quite something, *Chérie*. Are you going to let me go now? Or I suspect I really will die next time."

"I'm never letting you go, Edouard de Mornay. I love you so much, you're my whole world."

"You called me your perfect man before you screamed your head off," he smiled crookedly at her. "Am I, *Chérie*?"

"More than perfect," and she kissed him. "Oh dear, was I very noisy? I don't remember."

"Slightly," his lips twitched. "I hope the servants are partly deaf, and my hands really have gone to sleep. Pleeeease, Elise?"

"Oh no, really? Oh, I'm so sorry, I thought you were teasing," and she pulled herself off him with a soft groan as he rolled over onto his stomach and she grappled with the knots she'd industriously tied in his cravats. Giving up, she slipped to the floor, hunting for her scissors, and cut the material and he sighed with relief as he rolled back, rubbing his reddened wrists and he pulled her down into his arms.

"Come here, You Dreadful Woman, are you all right?"

"Am I all right? Look at your wrists," she pulled them to her lips and kissed them. "I'm so sorry," she whispered again.

"I'll live, I think, but I swear that's the last time I ever let you 'experiment' on me," he chuckled. "I think I'll need to supervise your reading matter in future!"

"Don't pretend you didn't enjoy that as well, You Wretch," Elise laughed softly, "both times."

"I might have, but don't let that give you any more ideas or I'll run away, back to Normandy."

"I'd just come after you, you'll never escape me now."

"Are we sleeping here tonight?" he yawned.

"I'm not moving; can you blow the candles and lamps out?"

"Ah, now she wants the darkness," he chuckled.

"Don't you tease me, You French Numpty," she giggled as she watched him get out of bed, strip off the remains of his shirt and waistcoat and limp around the room with nothing on, the first time he'd ever done that in her presence, snuffing out the candles and lamps and drawing the curtains. He got back into bed and extinguished the last oil lamp on the nightstand.

He pulled her into his warm arms again and she nestled up against him with a satisfied sigh. *"Je t'aime, Chérie, je t'aime plus que tout,"* he whispered as he kissed her tenderly on the forehead, "and you made your point, I won't hide myself from you anymore." He pulled off her shift, "Fair's fair, Sweet Harlot," and she heard the amused smile in his voice.

"You've forgotten my stockings," she giggled.

"I most certainly have not forgotten your stockings, or those interesting garters. I think that's all you should wear next time. Nothing else."

"Ah, so now you're a licentious French numpty," she laughed softly.

"What am I reduced to?" he chuckled back and settled down with a sigh.

"Just you wait," she whispered back as she lay staring into the darkness, listening to his steady breathing. "I still haven't finished with you, Edouard de Mornay," and she rolled into his embrace and fell fast asleep.

Some time just before dawn, Eddie woke and made love to her once more. Gently and tenderly this time, as he always did, and as she hovered on the brink of sleep again, Elise told herself her suspicions might still be right and she was even more determined to carry out the second part of her little seduction plan.

Chapter Twenty-Five

The bed was empty on his side when she woke again and, as Elise stirred herself and sat up, memories of the previous night filling her head, she looked around and noticed the evidence of their interlude had vanished. His torn clothes and cut cravats had disappeared, as had the red shift, and the half-finished bottle of wine in the ice bucket was now sitting innocuously, next to the glasses on a table in front of the empty fireplace and her clothes were neatly hanging over the back of a chair. She doubted her maid was responsible or the wine would have been cleared away; it must have been him and she smiled to herself, wondering what he'd done with her shift.

They sat, as usual, across from each other at the breakfast table, discussing mundane domestic matters and what they were each going to do that day. Elise was privately wondering what her husband was thinking and how she was going to get through the long hours until the evening.

Immaculately dressed as he normally was, Eddie sat desultorily looking through the previous day's newspapers that came down from London each morning by courier, his personal indulgence which he couldn't do without, and knowing that his wife pounced on them as soon as he'd finished, as addicted to politics, news and gossip as he was, not to mention anything that interested him from a business perspective. It gave them topics they frequently discussed over their meals, arguing back and forth if their opinions differed. It was stimulating and a distraction away from the usual more mundane domestic matters which were mostly the same from one day to the next.

However, that morning, Eddie was trying to concentrate on what he was reading but getting nowhere, his head full of images of the previous night. He drank his coffee and thought about the slip of red silk, now locked in a private drawer in his bedroom, and what had come over his wife. He decided he needed the peace and quiet of his study to mull it all over and he rose with a benign smile, "I have so much paperwork to catch up on, Chérie, and some contracts to read over for Nicky; he hasn't done a stroke of paperwork for months and his secretary is in despair; so if you will excuse me, My Love, I will leave you in peace." He rose, nodded his head at her and the butler, then limped towards the door of the sunny breakfast room.

"Oh, of course, and I must get on with supervising the jam-making; the strawberries will rot if we leave them; I must go and talk to the gardener and the cook," Elise mused half to herself, "and it's such a lovely day. Come and find Harry and I in the garden later when you take a break from your paper mountain; you can help me stop him trying to eat the daisies and dandelions," she laughed.

Mention of strawberries caused visions of reddened nipples to fill Eddie's head for a moment and the blood thrummed around his body. "I'll come and have some coffee with you both outside and play with him later. That child has no taste whatsoever; daisies indeed, he needs a botany lesson, he could at least try and eat a rosebud," and with a chuckle at his own joke, he limped out somewhat hurriedly.

It was an unremarkable, peaceful day, like most others, and they sat again at dinner, discussing the news and politics from London, now Elise had caught up with the newsheets as well, and other current topics of interest and gossip. Her stomach was now in knots as Elise contemplated the night ahead. She had gone only so far with Isabelle, and what she now had planned was something of a whole other matter, even if they'd touched upon it briefly.

She'd not been lying when she'd told Eddie her reading had been extensive, especially some of the salacious and erotic books and pamphlets Isabelle had sent her after their meeting, on top of one or two exceedingly obscene books she'd come upon by accident when she'd gone shopping with Cat in Paris the previous summer, not that she could understand all the text but they were full of mind-boggling illustrations, and what she had planned for that night shocked even herself; however, it was a means to an end and she knew it was something she had to do, to prove a point.

Dinner was always earlier when they were in the country and kept country hours, and when it was just the two of them, they never bothered with dressing formally, even the dapper Eddie. As the meal ended, Elise yawned and rose. "If you don't mind, I think I'll leave you to a glass of port or brandy. I want to look in on Harry, he was a bit fretful earlier, too many daisies for tea no doubt, either that or your botany lesson got too much for him," she chuckled, "and then there are a couple of overdue letters I must write to go off in the morning. I meant to do them this afternoon but the jam-making took longer than I expected; you don't mind?" she smiled innocently at Eddie.

"Of course not," he waved a dismissive hand in her direction and nodded at the hovering butler who brought some decanters to the table as Elise disappeared out the dining room.

She hurried up to her suite, via a quick glance into her little son's nursery where he was sleeping peacefully, as she well knew, and ordered her bath made ready. Her maid had already been forewarned her mistress would want one straight after dinner, so it didn't take long to prepare. Once she was out and sitting in front of a low fire, drying her hair, Elise dismissed the maid, saying she wanted an early night, then as soon as the woman had bobbed a curtsey and gone off, Elise set to, her body trembling in anticipation with what was ahead as she looked at her naked self in the mirror.

Eddie couldn't settle. He abandoned his solitary contemplation of the port decanter and retreated to his study, but he couldn't work either, just as he hadn't been able to all day. He gave up eventually and made his way to his own bedroom suite where his valet helped him disrobe and he put on his usual silken trousers and an ornate dressing robe. But he was restless, so changed his mind and ordered the man to fill his bath then dismissed him after he'd been helped into it. A snifter of brandy in hand, Eddie lazed in the hot water until it cooled, the warmth always easing his aching joints which is why he sometimes bathed twice or three times a day, especially in winter when the cold and damp got to them. Then he hauled himself out, re-dressed as before, then went to stand and stare out of his window across the now moonlit gardens, smoking a cheroot and nursing another snifter, trying to decide what to do. He looked intermittently at the communicating door that led through to his wife's rooms, feeling unusually uncertain of himself, knowing the whole tenet of his relationship with his wife had subtly changed. On a whim, he went and fished the redshift out from the locked drawer and gazed at it as he ran it through his hands, his mind full of memories of his life before he'd met Carlotta, and then after he'd married her. He had baggage his current wife knew nothing about, nor even his first one.

He turned as there was a quiet knock on his door and Elise opened it and sauntered through, and for the second time in so many nights, he gasped softly.

She was wearing black.

As she strolled across the room towards him, Eddie could see the black stockings with the saucy frothing black lace and ribbon garters around her knees through the gap in her peignoir, just like the red ones that had so entranced him the night before, and her heeled slippers were black to match. The peignoir was fashionably Empire line and gossamer-thin black voile, tied with a matching long wide sash under her breasts, and through the material, he could easily see the black corset she wore underneath. It pushed her luscious breasts up and outward, enhanced by the tight sash of the robe, and left them bare; no shift; and the corset ended on her hips, leaving the rest of her body uncovered. Her face was painted again, eyes enhanced by kohl with sooted lashes, reddened lips glistening and her hair was half up and half down and curled down her back this time. Her only decoration was a thin black lace ribbon tied around her neck. She looked alluring, slightly French in some way, and resembled an extremely high class, more mature and experienced courtesan. He went as hard as a rock, instantly.

"Hello, Eddie," she purred and went to stand in front of him and kissed his cheek and the scent of her perfume surrounded his senses.

"Elise..." he whispered, and without conscious thought, he pulled her into his arms and kissed her hard and hungrily; the kiss deepened and she writhed in his arms as she felt the stunning arousal against her belly.

"Do you prefer the red look or the black?" she asked archly.

He was incapable of making a decision, never mind an intelligent thought. "*Mon Dieu*, what are you doing now?"

"Well, I did tell you last night, but I think you fell asleep," she purred. "I haven't quite finished with you."

His mind reeled. "You haven't?"

"Not quite."

"I thought you had letters to write?"

"Like you had contracts to read, business to attend to?"

"I couldn't concentrate."

"Neither could I, this is unfinished business too."

"Unfinished business? Is that what you call this?" His eyes blazed up and down her body through the enticing gossamer-thin voile.

For a moment, Elise thought of Isabelle and wondered what Eddie would say if she asked him for a diamond bracelet. Given the look on his face, she decided he'd give her two, and she finally understood what Isabelle was talking about and how easy some men were to manipulate, their brains in their britches, and almost laughed out loud.

"Would you like some champagne? There's some cooling in a bucket on the table in my room in front of the fireplace, if you'd like to get it?"

He came back with the now opened bottle and two glasses and poured them both a drink. "What now, Elise?" he toasted her and looked at her expectantly.

"Well, you see," she began, as she started to prowl around the room, knowing he was looking at her. "Do you remember what you said to me last night?"

"I said a lot last night; about what precisely?"

"About what we did, what I did, to be specific."

"Remind me."

"Eddie, do we have an equal relationship? Oh, I know it's rather bizarre in Society, but you are one of the few men I know who don't look down on women as an inferior species; it's one of the things that attracted me to you."

"Of course I don't look down on you. You've got more of a brain in your beautiful head than a lot of men I know; what sort of a question is that? The Dowager was one hell of a woman, and m'sister and Bella are no fools either, especially my lovely Bella. Just don't get me started on m'sister, mad woman that she is with her stiletto and rapier."

"Good. So, all's fair in love and war then, as far as you're concerned?"

"What on earth are you driving at?" he poured himself another glass, having no idea where she was going with her conversation and trying to concentrate and not be distracted by the view he had as she sashayed around his bedroom.

"Well, last night, if you remember, you said you would pay me back for what I did to you."

"Did I?"

"Yes, you did, but that isn't totally what this is all about."

"Elise, you're not being very clear, or am I missing something here? I know I'm only a mere man, but I don't follow you at all," he grinned, teasing her as he often did about her liberated ideas.

Elise stopped her prowling around and went to stand in front of him and held out her glass for a refill. He topped it up and looked at her expectantly again.

Why had she thought this would be simple, she sighed to herself. She took a deep breath and burst out, "I'm fed up with being treated like a cross between a piece of Sèvres porcelain, an unworldly academic and a naïve *ingénue* at Almack's!"

"Beg pardon?" Eddie raised his brows.

"I am NOT an innocent, not a bird-brain nor someone who faints if someone goes 'boo' at me, I'm simply a well-read, intelligent, grown woman, but with needs and desires you've liberated, and I won't break or faint if YOU say boo to me in the bedroom; nor do I want to be cared for as if I was little Terrie or Harry!"

"BOO!" Eddie laughed as he shouted at her suddenly and she jumped in surprise.

"I'm serious, Eddie, don't tease me," she couldn't help her lips twitching.

"What on earth are you rambling on about? Of course I'm caring of you, you're very precious to me, and you're the most capable woman I know. Nothing fazes you and your intelligence even frightens me sometimes, but what on earth is wrong with that? Oh, come on, *Chérie*, can't we just go to bed, as that's obviously what you want."

"Ooooh, typical man, that's beside the point," she stamped her foot. "Don't you see, You Idiotic French Numpty, sometimes I don't want to be treated like a capable, intelligent woman, or a Baroness, or like one of Cook's meringues."

"You don't? I rather like our cook's meringues, especially with strawberries and cream," Eddie mused, deliberately being obtuse. "Those ones we had tonight were delicious."

"WILL you be serious!" grated Elise.

"So, how do you want to be treated?" Eddie was getting quite amused by all her outpourings.

"I want to be treated like a woman, an ordinary woman, or a common harlot even. Last night you ranted and raved at me, you were so carried away; if your hands hadn't been tied, I'm sure you would have forgotten yourself and turned quite wild, rough even, and it would have been an even more amazing experience than it was."

"Wild? Rough? Good God, you want me to treat you like a prostitute?" Eddie's eyes widened in incredulity, thinking he hadn't heard her right.

"If that's what it takes for you to let go with me, then yes," and she grabbed the champagne bottle and filled up her own glass and tossed it back like lemonade.

"Is that why you dressed like you did last night, and what this is all about?" his hand indicated her outfit.

"Yes... NO! Well, partly. I just want you to look at me in a different light sometimes."

"I HAVE opened Pandora's Box, haven't I?" he quietly spoke the thoughtful words slowly as he looked at her, sounding slightly sarcastic.

"Don't patronise me!" she stamped her foot again.

"I'm not, *Chérie*, believe me. I'm completely fascinated. Why don't you just tell me what you want, very simply, before you put your lovely shoe through the floorboards."

"Oooooooh, I just warned you!" Elise stamped her foot for the third time then took a deep breath and looked her bemused husband straight in the eye. "I want you to do to me what I did to you last night. There. That's it!" the words burst out of her.

"WHAAAT?" he gaped.

"You said you'd pay me back. Therefore, I want you to do it to me. I want to see what it's like. I want you to wind me up like a clock, make me desperate, and beg and plead, just like I did to you. I want to FEEL like you did, out of my head with desire until I can't think of anything else, and then experience an earth-shattering release, more than I felt last night. I've read about it, I endeavoured to do it to you, and now I want to experience that for myself. It gave me an enormous amount of pleasure doing it to you, I think you saw that, so I assume it will be the same if the situation is reversed? At least I hope so, if you love and desire me and want to please me; is that right?" Elise simply stared at him as she asked, the words having poured out of her like water through a breached dam.

Eddie merely stared at her in utter astonishment.

"Would it please you to master me, get the better of me? Just for fun and pleasure? Like my game last night to get the better of you?"

He nodded slightly, not sure what to say.

"I haven't shocked you, have I?" his face was a complete picture.

Eddie shook his head, gathering his scattered wits. He wasn't shocked, just completely taken aback and slightly speechless.

"I take it you have done this before, then? To other women? Er... Carlotta?" and the words hung in the air.

"This has nothing to do with Carlotta, but yes, *Chérie*, I have," he said quietly.

"So, it is a commonplace act then? And did you enjoy doing it? Did they?"

"I believe so, and as for commonplace… I dare say plenty of people play all sorts of games in the bedroom, but it's not exactly an acceptable topic of conversation in any social circles I've ever mixed in…" and he simply stared at her, then suddenly, as the air fizzed around them, he threw back his head and burst out laughing. "You extraordinary woman. I don't believe I'm hearing this, it's too funny for words."

"What's so funny?" she huffed.

"You are, *Chérie*, you never cease to amaze me." He was laughing so much he had to sit down on the side of the bed. "So that's why you look like some high-class courtesan. Are you trying to seduce me, You Blonde Baggage?"

"Yes, if you must know."

He seemed to find that even funnier and howled with laughter. "Oh, come and sit down next to me, stop standing there like some tantalising statue, we have to talk about this."

Elise perched herself on the bed next to Eddie in high dudgeon. "I don't know what you find so funny, and what is there to talk about? It's not very complicated, surely?"

"No, *Chérie*, it's not, but I just need to make sure you understand what you're asking of me."

"Of course I understand, didn't I just explain? As I said, I am NOT some naïve *ingénue*."

"No, Elise," an amused Eddie got himself in hand and finally stopped chuckling, "but I want to know how far you want me to go?"

"OH!"

"Precisely 'oh', My Love. At least that tells me you do understand what we are discussing."

"Look, Eddie, I've read everything from Ovid to a translated de Sade, and I certainly don't want anything to do with the latter; I want pleasure, not pain, even though I gather the two are somewhat connected so there has to be a middle way with that. 'Teasing torment that heightens and extends the pleasure' as one rather torrid and erotic pamphlet described it. But I will leave it all up to you. You, apparently, are the expert."

"Really?" his lips curled in a wicked smile as his brow quirked. "My, my, Elise, your latest literature acquisition sounds fascinating."

"Well, you just admitted you have indulged in this type of activity before, so you're the expert while I'm a mere novice, and needed to gain some pertinent information. Oh Eddie," she turned to him, "don't you see? I just want to be more than an efficient wife, someone who runs your household and mothers your children and acts as your hostess… or discusses more highbrow matters sometimes. I want you to do with me whatever you did with the other women in your life."

"They were my mistresses," he said softly.

"Well, then, can't I be your wife AND your mistress? Er, you don't keep one now, do you?"

"What sort of a question is that? Refined Ladies don't enquire about their husband's private love lives," he tutted in huge amusement.

"This one does, and she would be extremely displeased if her husband kept a mistress, even though it's not uncommon in our world," Elise huffed.

"Chérie, I give you my word I haven't had a mistress since I met Carlotta."

"Good God!" she gaped. "But you were a widower for years."

"I know," Eddie said softly, taking her hand, "but when Carlotta died, something in me died with her and I had no interest in women for a long time. I became a celibate recluse, and simply buried myself away down here with Charlie; until I met you, and you enticed me back to reality and into the world of the living."

"Really? Oh, Eddie, I'd no idea, that's very sad in a way."

"It was a long time ago, it doesn't matter now."

"This is a very strange conversation, isn't it?"

"It is rather. Mama would be shocked," he grinned.

"I know, wives don't discuss their husband's mistresses, they just pretend they don't exist. They certainly don't discuss what they do with them."

"They certainly don't."

"What did you do with yours, Eddie?" she gave him a saucy look.

"That, Madam, is absolutely none of your business," he chuckled.

"Why? Can we do what you used to do?"

Eddie dissolved into laughter again. "You Saucy Madam, is there no end to your curiosity?"

"No, actually, and now I know about them, I'm determined to worm it all out of you eventually. Oh, Eddie, we've always been friends, long before we became lovers, and we've always talked about and discussed everything, all sorts of topics... everything from slavery to more rights for women, monarchies versus republics, to how to treat the insane and feeding regimens for babies... and..."

"Oh God give me strength," Eddie sighed in more amusement as he interrupted her. "Look, *Chérie*, can we leave all this for another time, surely we have other, more interesting matters to deal with tonight?"

"I won't forget," Elise leaned over and kissed his scarred cheek.

"I know," he sighed manfully, "now, are you sure you want to do this?"

"Yes."

"And you trust me?"

"Now who's asking inane questions? You wouldn't hurt a fly, except vile insects like THAT MAN," she tutted. She never mentioned Bernheim's name if she could help it.

"I have had my moments, believe me, Elise."

"Not with those you love or care about," she huffed. "And really, Eddie, you're the gentlest man I know," she laughed for a moment. "You don't even like setting mousetraps," and Eddie rolled his eyes at her complete faith in him, uncaring of anything he'd might have done in his past, and that was only his memories to know about.

"Do you really understand what you're asking me to do? Tell me the truth, Elise, this is serious; reading about something is completely different from experiencing the real thing."

"That, Edouard de Mornay, is precisely the point. Stop prevaricating and get on with it. You have a willing captive here; unless you don't want to, that is?"

"*Chérie*, the prospect of playing games and having you at my mercy is a temptation I couldn't possibly refuse. I'm going to make you feel things you never believed possible. Whatever you've read, the written word is simply incapable of describing some sensations and feelings, believe me. So are you absolutely sure that is what you want?"

"Yes," she whispered and went bright pink.

"You look so delightful when you blush, y'know, even though it's beyond ridiculous given the conversation we're having, not to mention what you're wearing. Have you rouged your nipples again, by the way? They were a devilish temptation last night."

"Yes," she giggled, "did you like it?"

"Shocking behaviour for a respectable matron," he chuckled. "I can't wait to inspect them close to," and he smiled as she blushed again.

"Oh stop teasing me, You Wretch."

"I'm going to do more than tease you shortly."

"I think I need another glass of champagne."

"NO! If you need alcohol to give you courage, we won't do this."

"I don't need courage from a bottle, thank you; I just need to get my head around all this, what we're going to do."

"For the last time, are you sure, Elise?"

"If you ask me once again if I'm sure, I'll hit you over the head with that bottle," she tutted, then laughed. "Final drink for the condemned prisoner?" she held out her glass.

"I think I need one as well. All this has come as a bit of a shock to me, shrinking violet that I am," and as they both laughed he got up and retrieved their glasses and poured the remainder of the champagne into them and he toasted her with a grin. "To Pandora's Box. I had NO idea it had such interesting contents!"

"Harlots, courtesans and mistresses," Elise clinked his glass. "I'm about to join their number," and with a grin, she pulled another of his cravats from a pocket of her robe where it had been sitting, tightly rolled up, and let it unravel to dangle in front of him as she emptied her glass.

"Shocking, absolutely shocking," he chuckled as he tossed off his champagne and took it from her. "I hope the Dowager is asleep up in heaven and not watching us tonight."

"That woman would be vastly entertained, I'm absolutely certain," she smirked, "she had a wicked and quite inappropriate sense of humour at times. So, come along, Baron, do your worst." She stood up and watched him watch her as she started to undo the bow on the front of her robe and then let it slip off her shoulders and she tossed it onto the bed.

"Glorious," Eddie murmured as his hot eyes roved over her corseted torso, fascinated with the rouged nipples.

"You like? Better than the redshift?"

"Each has their merits," he mused. "Are there more where these came from?"

"There could be," she tossed her head saucily, a hand on her hip.

"Paris? I assume? Last summer?"

"Can you tell?"

"Intelligent guess. There's something about that corset, a bit of *je ne sais quoi*."

"You should have seen what else they had in that particular shop. It was quite shocking, even Cat raised her eyebrows."

"Did you buy any of it?" he looked at her hopefully, quietly wondering what it was and whether the shop only sold clothes or any other items. All sorts of licentious visions went around his head.

"That, Baron, is for me to know and you to find out; if I enjoy myself tonight."

"Well, I'd better make sure you do, Baroness," and with a dangerous smile, he crooked a finger at her and twirled it around, indicating she should turn her back on him.

He tied her wrists firmly, but not uncomfortably, and then, unable to resist the temptation, pulled her back against his chest and let his arms come around her and his hands roamed over her breasts, toying with her nipples, making her sigh and then squirm, feeling her bottom rub against him. He already knew how sensitive her nipples were and knew exactly how to tease them and her sighs gradually turned to moans. Slowly, one hand roamed lower and teased down between her legs, feeling the dampness, reassuring him she was being truthful and was happy with what they were doing, and he pulled aside her hair and kissed the nape of her neck.

"You're wet already, You Tempting Baggage," he whispered in her ear. "This is going to be such pleasure, for both of us."

He turned her around and gazed at her engorged nipples and bent, slowly, to lick one and then the other. "*Fraises*," he whispered, "you taste of strawberries." He looked bemused as he licked his lips in pleasure.

"That's what happens when you make jam and have the remainder for dinner with meringue and cream. I mixed a squashed one with the rouge," she giggled. "Do I taste nice?"

He burst out laughing. "Whatever next! How very creative and delicious, but then you always do taste delicious, and I'm going to taste you all over, just like you did me last night. Hmmm, but something is missing..." and as she stood and watched, he limped quickly into his dressing room and returned with a couple more cravats. "Roberts is going to wonder what on earth is going on with my disappearing wardrobe," he chuckled. "Come here, *Chérie*," he crooked his finger as he stood and admired the view. With a smile on her face, she danced backwards. "Oho, it's like that is it? I SAID, come here." He crooked his finger again.

She shook her head. "Make me," she whispered and poked her tongue out at him.

With a laugh, he caught up with her and despite her struggles, he wrapped another cravat around her upper arms, pulling them back tautly. "There you are, just as you did to me, don't pull YOUR muscles now, or I'll have to refer you to the house nurse," he joked. "Now turn around," and he spun her around. Her breasts, supported cleverly on top of the saucy French corset, jutted out and his eyes sparkled with pleasure as he bent to kiss them and lick more of the flavoured rouge off her nipples, nibbling and then sucking hard, making her mewl with pleasure as he suddenly bit them, all sorts of visions and ideas going round and round in his brain; but he told himself to hold back; one step at a time, he decided. That was another game, for another night. He still could barely come to terms with what was happening in his formerly sedate and conservative life.

Eddie stood back and looked Elise up and down, seeing her eyes already slightly glazed with her arousal, as she fidgeted in front of him, and with a gleam in his eye, he pushed her gently over to the corner of his enormous four-poster bed and tethered her to the post with another cravat. Pinioned, she couldn't escape his hands as they roved over her breasts and down her body, scything between her legs as she closed her eyes and mewled again in frustration, writhing on the fingers that crept inside her for a short moment.

He knew what he wanted to do, but once again the shadow of his disability and awkwardness crept over Eddie and the lack of self-assurance with the beautiful woman in front of him filled him with angst, as it had so often in his distant past. As he hesitated, his eyes passed over the abandoned peignoir on the coverlet and he picked it up and pulled off the long voile sash and he went to stand in front of her. "Now then, *Chérie*, you will truly be at my mercy," he whispered softly as he wrapped it around and around her eyes, blinding her completely, and tied it tightly, watching her suddenly go rigid. "Without sight, your other senses will be heightened. You'll feel more vulnerable yet everything I do to you, every sensation, will feel more intense with nothing else to focus on except me; you'll savour more of what you taste, be less inhibited and your pleasure will be unbeliev-able, I promise." Eddie paused for a moment, holding his breath, "Are you all right, Elise? Tell me if you want me to take it off, you have to talk to me if we're to play this sort of game. This isn't chess or picquet."

She nodded, shook her head and shivered. "I trust you completely," she whispered, and he kissed her.

It was deeply carnal and erotic, and nothing like she'd experienced before with him as he took her head in his hands, except very briefly the previous night when he'd been so aroused. His tongue licked her lips and he bit them gently, making them swell, and then he attacked her mouth. His tongue roved deep to explore and tantalise and while he did that his fingers played with her nipples, and they went hard and taut, and her belly spasmed and contracted at the sensations she was experiencing. She felt like she was being eaten alive as the carnal, predatory kiss went on and on, more licking, more biting, lascivious and completely different from the way he'd kissed her any other time, even the previous evening, and when he finally lifted his head away she couldn't speak. "Did you enjoy that, *Chérie?*" he whispered, and she was so overcome, she simply nodded, wondering what on earth she'd let herself in for. He'd felt like a different man. His mouth continued to kiss and lick and roved down her neck. He nibbled and sucked, and she jolted as he reached the joint with her shoulder and she moaned. Downward he continued with his carnal path, pinching and biting her nipples, making her cry out, watching her reactions carefully to ensure he didn't go too far, but it was far further than he'd been before. "I will have this off, later," he whispered as she felt his hands roam over her tight corset and then she heard a rustle as he took off his dressing robe and he kissed her deeply again, now feeling his hard body against hers, his arousal obvious through the silk of his loose trousers as his hands grasped her buttocks and he pulled her tight against him, rubbing against her, but not giving her what she wanted, the feel of his skin and the silk against hers and his hardness between her legs.

Knowing she couldn't see him, Eddie sank slowly and inelegantly to his knees, holding on to the side of the bed for support, fine as long as he didn't have to bend or crouch. His hands went to her buttocks again. "Spread your legs for me, *Chérie*; do you taste of strawberries here too?" His tantalising words crawled over her and she felt his mouth and tongue lick and nibble in her soft curls.

It was almost too much as Elise felt his hot mouth on her, writhing against him, not getting the satisfaction she wanted as his tongue tasted and licked and delved, but never far enough and then she felt him tweak her nipples and she jerked and cried out as spasms roiled in her belly again. "Oh God, Eddie..." she moaned, "please..."

"Please what, *Chérie*? I've only just started. You have hours of this torment to endure; think about it." His soft voice teased her senses, "This is what you wanted, Elise, this is what you asked for, and I will give you hours of it. You won't know yourself, this is nothing; you'll be screaming and begging me by the time I've finished with you. You won't be the Baroness, you won't be a mother, or a hostess or a chatelaine; you won't be an articulate, highly intelligent woman even; your brain will disintegrate and you won't even know your own name... and then, finally, when I think you can't take any more, I'll give you what you crave and you'll scream so loudly, they'll probably hear you in Firle. And then, maybe I'll do it again, as you'll be so wound up, once won't be enough. Think about that in your darkness, *Chérie*."

Elise listened to the voice and soft words, shivered and went hot and cold. Was this what she thought was going to happen? It was nothing like it. Why had she thought it would be a playful game like the previous night? Because despite her bragging, she was inexperienced and out of her depth. It was already a torment and they'd barely started though, she'd no idea how long it had been; she was totally lost in her own frustrated world; and he said they would be at this for hours! What had she let herself in for?

"Oh God," she moaned again, pulling uselessly on her bonds, unable to get her head around what he was saying, promising, threatening. Who was this man who was setting her body on fire? Did she know him? Was this her husband? Was this Baron Edouard de Mornay? Reserved, gentle, amusing, witty, kind Eddie? The easy-going and amiable man who rarely raised his voice, let alone lost his temper; the scarred, crippled, self-conscious yet handsome man who was so full of angst and embarrassment about his disability, but who in reality was obviously a deeply passionate, sensuous, and an expert and experienced lover of women. What a revelation he was turning out to be: a man of many mistresses as well as Carlotta's husband; but he was hers now and she had to, wanted to do this.

Elise shuddered again, knowing this was finally going to change her relationship with her husband forever, now she'd finally broken through the wall he'd erected around himself. She loved him more than life itself and gave herself up to the intense pleasure she was sure he was about to give her. Despite what he'd unexpectedly done to her, she trusted him implicitly.

She could barely stand up by the time Eddie levered himself to his feet, easier to kneel down than to get up again, as he knew. He carefully placed the wide stool from her dressing table between her legs to keep them far apart and she swore at him in frustration, making him smile; he'd never heard her use language like that, ever, and wondered where on earth she'd got it from. He sank to the bed, heart racing, his body on fire with lust, wanting her so badly he could barely deal with it, this mixture of love and erotic lechery simply blowing him away; he'd known nothing like it, even when he'd been married to Carlotta, his relationship with her so different. He'd no idea how he would manage to keep going and give Elise the torment and pleasure he'd promised, and knew what the solution was, but wasn't sure she would do it. This was all so new, this little game she'd been so determined to play. When he'd done this previously, so many years before in his youth with his particular ladybirds in Paris, they all knew what the game was and did it with alacrity, all part of the pleasure and erotic excitement and what they were paid for; but this was Elise. Not a paid harlot or courtesan, no matter what she said; but just who DID live under that ladylike veneer? She'd done it the previous night, but this was a different situation and there was only one way to find out. In for a guinea... Eddie was the ultimate gambler and invariably won; this time he had to believe the odds were in his favour.

"So, *Chérie*, how are we feeling? Frustrated? Hmmm? Well, I did warn you," he laughed as he whispered to her.

"You Evil Bastard, I never expected this, I never did this to you," she ranted at him, beside herself with frustration, feeling slightly humiliated and inhibited, desperate to put her legs together, wondering if she could bring herself to release to spite him and put herself out of her misery.

"But I'm not evil, *Chérie*, nor a bastard; my poor mama would be grossly offended to hear you speak of me like that." He bent and suckled an engorged nipple and she groaned. "Ah, no more strawberries, I've licked it all off," he sighed. "Perhaps I should go downstairs and find one of your new pots of jam? Now, what a good idea is that? And you can stay here and calm down a bit and restore your temper."

"Whaaat? Nooooo, don't you go away... Eddie..." but she heard the swish of material as he pulled on his dressing robe and then the door banged shut as he disappeared, leaving her swearing into thin air. Eddie limped slowly along the corridor, down the grand staircase and then below stairs and made his way into the pantry off the kitchen and scullery. Rows of newly-made jars of strawberry jam greeted him, their labels immaculately written in Elise's neat hand. With a grin, he helped himself to one, undid the lid and like a naughty child he dipped his forefinger into the newly-set conserve and put it in his mouth. Sweet and delicious, just like his wife upstairs. Helping himself to a teaspoon on his way out, he left the quiet and deserted kitchens. On impulse, he diverted to his wine cellar, picked up another bottle of champagne and returned upstairs.

A torrent of abuse greeted him as he walked in and he laughed; she was getting completely venomous, totally unlike her, and his painful arousal throbbed as he stared at the tousled hair, the swollen lips, the engorged nipples and then downward as she writhed and tried uselessly to pull away from the bedpost. She managed to kick the stool away but it hadn't done her frustration any good. Eddie limped over to her and started to kiss her but to his amusement, she bit him and he reared back, tasting blood on his lip. "You Wicked Woman," he chuckled. "I ought to spank you for doing that."

"WHAAAT?" she raged at him, "I'll murder you if you DARE. I'm not some naughty child. I've had enough, let me go," she demanded, yanking at the tethering cravat.

"Not at all." He lifted the lid of the pot and dug a small spoonful of jam out and smeared it across a breast, standing back to admire his handiwork. He licked his lips and bent forward and started to suck and lick it off and Elise raged.

"What the HELL are you doing? What have you put on me? Oh… AAAAAAAARGH!" she cried as he bit her nipple, hard.

"Strawberry jam, *Chérie*, my favourite, and note I don't bite quite as hard as you, well unless you want me to do that to you as well. You only have to ask, another form of mastery or torment to discover. Maybe another night, hmmm?" and he watched her cheeks pinken. He wasn't sure if it was anger or arousal at the thought.

She suddenly sniffed. "My jam, you've smeared jam on me?" Elise appeared in disbelief and she sniffed again as the warm smell of strawberries surrounded her. "You're deranged, completely out of your mind, cook and I spent HOURS making that this afternoon, HOURS. Have you any idea how many labels I had to write?" on and on she raged, quite irrational, seeming more annoyed he'd stolen one of her precious new jars than the fact he'd smeared it all over her breasts and he chuckled.

He loved strawberry jam, especially when it was freshly made, and he spooned, smeared, licked and completely ignored the torrent of abuse that poured on his head. But when he smeared some between her legs and then kneeled again to lick that off, laughing to himself at his erotic creativity, her anger went stratospheric... and his lust veered near it. He couldn't deal with it any longer, deciding he'd spontaneously erupt if he wasn't careful.

Eddie got to his feet and kissed her hard and roughly then undid the cravat that tethered her to the bedpost, pulling her away from the bed into the centre of the room. He spun her around until she was confused then left her seething and muttering while he went and washed the jam off his sticky fingers and brought back a wet flannel to wipe her breasts and thighs clean. Then he yanked off his dressing robe again, removed his silken trousers and, taking her with him, went to lean himself back against a bedpost and addressed the woman now in front of him.

"On your knees, Elise," he ordered.

"I beg your pardon?"

"On your knees, you heard me."

"I most certainly will not."

He sighed, he knew it would be difficult. "Do as you're told, or I'll simply leave you here like this, all night, and go to bed in your bed and sleep blissfully peacefully."

"Nooooo, you wouldn't dare!"

"Try me."

"I don't believe you."

"You should. Do I ever make empty threats?"

"You never make any threats. Full stop."

"All the more reason to believe me when I do. On your knees, Elise."

"Why?"

"You told me you wanted to be mastered, so that's what I'm doing. Do as you're told."

"No."

"Goodnight, Elise," and she heard him walk off and a door bang shut. It had been a very short and abrupt conversation.

"Eddie? Eddie?" silence hung in the room and Elise swore venomously. Ten minutes passed while Eddie impatiently wandered around the room next door, debating how long it would take to make her compliant. He made a bet with himself and went back into his bedroom.

"On your knees, Elise. I won't tell you again."

"Go to hell."

He went back into her bedroom, deliberately slamming the door hard, grinning to himself, having won his own bet. He looked at the little ornamental gold clock on the mantel over the fireplace, a wedding gift from Cat, and tried to decide how long to leave it this time, knowing Elise would have no idea how long it was or what the time was. Imagined visions of her on her knees, pleasuring him, overwhelmed his plans and he went back into his bedroom.

"What do you want me to do?" she asked angrily.

"You're an intelligent woman, I'll give you one guess."

"I hate you," she seethed.

"No, you don't. You told me how much you love me and loved doing it last night."

"I lied."

He burst out laughing. "No, you didn't. I'll give you another glass of champagne if you're good," he cajoled.

"I don't hate you, I LOATHE you," she said feelingly.

"And I loathe you too, *Chérie*; on your knees," he led her back to where he'd stood before.

He watched as she slowly sank down in front of him and licked her lips, and his head nearly blew off with lust. "I can't see you, I don't know where you are?" she complained.

"I'm not helping you, you just do as I order. Move forward, I'm right in front of you," and she shuffled forward until she felt his hands on her shoulders.

She licked and sucked and he watched. It was so erotic, depraved and perverted, Eddie could barely contain himself, and it didn't take long as he held her head and erupted down her throat, leaning back against the bedpost to support himself, he was so overcome as he'd suspected he would be. He helped her to her feet and kissed her immediately, lasciviously and sensuously, tasting the residue of himself in her mouth and licking it off her lips. It was so intimate and erotic, she gasped softly.

"You're so beautiful, Elise, I love you so much," he whispered. "Thank you. And you DID enjoy doing that, Ma Chérie, I could tell; so, why did you fight me?"

"I don't like being ordered around or humiliated."

"But you asked me to master you!" She could hear the amusement in his voice.

"Not like that," she tutted.

"How then?" he chuckled. "Tell me, and I'll do it again."

"Ooooooh, you're impossible!" and her foot stamped in frustration and he burst out laughing.

"I'm so frustrated, Eddie. What time is it? How much longer are you going to torment me like this? I never did this to you," she wailed plaintively.

"Hours. Captives get no information, you should know that."

"That is such a tasteless joke, but irrespective of that, I'm going to kill you, so slowly, you'll wish you were dead."

"You're getting even more irrational, that's a good sign. Now come along, I think we need to lie down," and he pulled her gently down on top of the covers and rolled over to start to kiss her again.

Vertical or horizontal, Elise's passionate torment continued and she writhed and squirmed in abandon on his big bed as he rolled her back and forth and kissed and caressed her up and down the length of her body. His knowing fingers and mouth enticed and teased her until she was begging and pleading with him to give her the satisfaction she craved, but all she heard in return was his soft laugh. He started to talk to her in French, most of which she could now understand, but some of it she couldn't but got the gist, the sensual words sounded even more seductive in French as he whispered in her ears and she went beyond blushing with what he was telling her, she was so hot and frustrated she thought she would melt. He wound her up and stopped so many times she lost track of time and space and eventually he sat her up and she drank thirstily of the champagne he plied her with, the alcohol making her dizzy and even more abandoned than she'd been before. He encouraged her to talk to him, tell him what she was feeling, what she wanted him to do to her, and Elise simply let go and gave vent to a torrent of demands and pleas, even partly in French, much to his amusement.

Eddie could see she had lost herself totally in the game they were playing, the self-possessed woman he knew now completely absent; a passionate, demanding, extremely sensual woman now in her place and he decided to go a bit further. He led her off the bed and across the bedroom, encouraging her then to investigate his body as he leaned against his small desk. She gradually sank to her knees with no demur as she licked and kissed her way downwards and took him in her mouth again, taking her time to tease and torment him as best she could, just as he'd been doing to her, but he eventually pulled her off him with a low sigh and merely chuckled at her continued muttered frustration.

After he helped her to her feet and kissed her deeply, he bent her over the desk and spread her legs and sank down to return the favour but as she moaned and pleaded, his fingers began to explore her buttocks and she went rigid with shock and cried out as they intruded where they hadn't been before. Leaving her for a moment to come to terms with yet another new experience, he went and rummaged among the bottles and jars in her dressing room and returned with some scented bath oil which he drizzled on her upraised bottom and his fingers, and continued his investigation. As Elise grappled with what he was doing and the intense, new feelings it created, together with other caresses deep inside her with his other hand, she thought her head would blow off at the sensations Eddie was creating, shocked to her very core, but unable to deny the pleasure it gave her and shaking her head with low moans when he asked her if he should stop.

"So, you like that, *Chérie*? You see, there is no end to the pleasure I can show you, give you; you had no idea, did you, Elise?" he whispered. "The experience is so different to the written word and an illustration; now, are you sure you want me to continue? Just say and I'll stop. It's not to every woman's pleasure."

"I… oh… oh Gooooood. I can't believe I'm letting you do this to me.

How will I be able to look myself in the mirror in the morning?" and he laughed softly.

"You'll look exactly the same, but what you see in your mind is another matter entirely. Just give in and enjoy it. I won't hurt you, I just want to give you another level of pleasure; a different way, a different experience."

"Does this give you pleasure?" she groaned as his fingers continued to caress her.

"*Chérie*, giving you pleasure is my pleasure, just as you discovered for yourself last night. I want you so much, I can barely contain myself."

"Then take me, Eddie, for the love of God, I can't bear this. Pleeeese," she begged, "put me out of my misery."

"It's not misery, really, is it, *Chérie*?" he laughed. "You never knew you were capable of feeling so much, did you? I've never seen you so uninhibited or abandoned," he chuckled softly as he leaned over her, running his tongue down the centre of her back, making her shiver as he started to kiss her and then, as his finger went inside her bottom again, he spanked her and she shrieked with shock.

He laughed as he held her down and did it again and again, and the maelstrom of feelings that exploded inside her was almost more than Elise could deal with: anger, frustration, humiliation and pleasure whirled together as she yelled and screeched at him and he had to stop and put a hand over her mouth, worried the servants would hear and come running.

He hauled her back to the bed and tossed her on it as she completely and finally lost herself totally. She raged at him, trying to kick him, so confused and aroused by the sensations careering around her body and mind she had no idea what she was doing, and Eddie knew then neither he nor she could take any more. He threw himself down on top of her and held her down as he kissed her wildly and her response overwhelmed him. She bit and writhed and kissed him like she was a starving woman just emerged from a desert. Her body was hot and sweating and he watched rivulets of perspiration trickle down into her cleavage. He undid the lacings on her corset, pulled it away and caressed and kissed her all over her now exposed torso, looking down on the abandoned woman just left in a pair of saucy shoes, stockings and garters, and lust, love and desire took over. He couldn't wait a moment more and slithered back off the bed and hauled her backwards to bend her over its side and as she tried to fight him, yelling and swearing, expecting to be spanked again, without a word he spread her legs wide, quite roughly, and finally thrust inside her ruthlessly with a triumphant cry.

Elise cried out as waves of pleasure and relief coursed through her, even as he spanked her once again, driving into her hard and forcefully, almost like a man possessed, as he grasped her upper arms to hold her firmly and she was incoherent as she yelled at him: "Oh... oh... God... harder... harder..." she screeched, writhing to increase the sensation and finally satisfy her frustration. "Harder... don't stop, faster, dammit, harder... don't stop... I'm, I'm..."

It was torrid, coarse and wild as they both let go of their emotions and gave into their basest needs. As he felt his release rising Eddie pounded even harder and as one hand scythed between her legs the other went firmly over her mouth, just in time as a muffled screech tore out of her and she jerked and screamed and screamed as she was overcome by her climax. He felt the strong, orgasmic contractions surround him and his own release erupted and went on and on, like an unstoppable torrent. The room went round as blackness threatened and Eddie gasped for air as the pair of them collapsed forward onto the bed, a duet of thundering hearts and unsteady breaths.

Chapter Twenty-Six

Elise was virtually unconscious, her brain dead, her body reeling; she didn't know who she was, what she was or where she was. She thought she was dying at the rate her heart was pounding unsteadily as she gasped for breath, her whole lower body numb yet on fire and throbbing.

Eddie felt like his heart was going to burst out of his chest at any moment, hardly able to breathe and with almost trembling hands he gently shook Elise, trying to lift her slightly as her head was buried, face down in the coverlet.

"Elise? *Chérie?* Speak to me. Are you all right?"

"*Je suis morte…*" Finally, an almost incoherent whisper wafted up to him from underneath the blonde hair that was now covering her face.

He smiled in relief. "*Moi aussi*, but probably not quite as dead as you!" He shook his head in bemusement. "That was unbelievable, *incroyable*," he murmured.

"I think I'm having one of those strange experiences that people have when they almost die; are you sure I'm alive?"

"You sound it," he chuckled as he heaved himself out of her and started to undo the knotted cravats and unwind the sash from her eyes.

With a feeling groan, Elise blinked several times as her eyes adjusted to the candlelit room, rolled over on the bed, flexing her hands and stretching her arms before looking up at the amused man, casually leaning against a bedpost, arms crossed and looking exceedingly pleased with himself. "Don't you look at me like that, Edouard de Mornay. That was the most SHOCKING thing I have EVER experienced. In fact, I'm so shocked I don't believe it was me at all, it must have been someone else and I was having an exceedingly inappropriate dream."

"Is that so, *Chérie*? Tell me, was that what you wanted? Did it meet the expectations of your dirty little fantasy?" his lips curled wickedly. "Did I wind you up like a clock? Was I rough and wild enough? Did you feel like a prostitute or whatever inappropriate type of woman you wanted to be?"

"That, *Monsieur le Baron*, is completely privileged information," she huffed and he threw back his head and guffawed with laughter and toppled onto the bed next to her and pulled her into his arms.

"Oh Elise, I do love you, you are so funny, so wonderful," and he kissed her. "You are the absolute light of my life."

"Am I really, Eddie?" she looked up into his eyes, now sparkling with humour and love.

"You are, you know you are."

"So you don't think any less of me because of what we just did? It was so disgracefully inappropriate and quite perverted."

"Did I look or sound like I disapprove? I was participating, doing it, enjoying it. My Love, you have made me the happiest of men, but, tell ME, *Chérie*, you're not cross with me because of what I did to you, are you? I know you weren't expecting all that, but I wouldn't have done it if I thought you wouldn't either like it or couldn't deal with it."

"No, I wasn't expecting all that, You Appalling Man," Elise tutted, trying to keep a straight face despite her twitching lips, "but I suppose nothing should surprise me given the family I've married into."

"What's the matter with my family?" Eddie asked innocently.

"Well, apart from the fact you are all quite eccentric and definitely half-mad, with uncontrollable children and pets, a more disreputable group of people I have yet to come across."

"Disreputable? Oh, come now, M'Dear; Francis is a Duke, a veritable pillar of Society, he socialises with the Prince Regent and the Prime Minister."

"Him? Our nefarious smuggler? He's the worst one of the lot of you, with Nicky, our other Duke, not far behind. Francis Granville should have a sign around his neck, never mind on the gate of his house in Berkeley Square, he's a danger to ALL women, old and young," she tutted with a grin. "And now I've just spent an evening in your hands, you're most certainly up there with the pair of them. Some of those things you were whispering to me in French a while ago were so mind-boggling, I couldn't believe what I was hearing, never mind imagining people doing that."

My, my, *Chérie*, your French must be improving," Eddie grinned. "Do you want to try some of them then?" he teased.

"Dear God, I haven't recovered from what you've just done to me, and now you're suggesting we do things like THAT?" Elise goggled at him.

"People do, you know," he chuckled. "As I inferred before, when you asked me if people played games in their bedrooms. Even if it's not discussed openly, a lot of them do, and frequently, all over the country, everywhere between here and China, and have been since the dawn of civilisation. But you have to tell me how you found out what I was talking about. I'm sure some of that vocabulary isn't in the dictionary or French grammar books."

"Well, socialising for months with your sister, and I do not mean Severine or Rose, especially when she's been on the brandy, not to mention going shopping with her in Paris, is somewhat illuminating," Elise said tartly. "She and Francis are a fine pair, and when you three men get together over the brandy and don't keep your voices down, it's enough to make my hair curl. Even if things like that aren't mentioned in polite society, you three are beyond the pale. Heaven knows what the servants must think, especially if any of the young maids heard you, not that if you do it over here the English girls can understand you if you're speaking French, thank goodness. I had to ask Cat what you were talking about a couple of times that made you all laugh so disgracefully, and of course, she illuminated me in enormous detail. Filthy jokes have nothing on you three. I was appalled and she thought they were hilarious."

Eddie burst out laughing. "Really? That's too funny, *Chérie*, and how would you know about m'sister and Francis, pray?" and Eddie watched Elise go bright red. "Have you been peering through keyholes at Firle?" he teased.

"Most certainly not," she huffed. "Take what happened when Bernheim threw his dagger into Francis's shoulder in Richmond. While you went off to find the soldiers, I tried to sort out the wounded as best I could and Francis was making out there was nothing seriously wrong with him, as usual, despite it being obvious he was trying not to pass out. When he wouldn't take any notice of me, I told him in no uncertain terms I would get Cat to take him in hand and make sure he stayed in bed and behaved himself until he'd healed properly, and the wretched man just gave me the most scandalous look, and then informed me he NEVER behaved himself in bed and in fact he was getting worse as he got older... and his wife could take him in hand whenever she liked and he certainly didn't need to be in bed for that!" I was soooo appalled, I didn't know where to look or what to say. Miles Ashcroft heard him too and you should have seen HIS face; I've never been so embarrassed."

Once again, Eddie burst out laughing. "And what's more," and Elise quickly regaled him with the story of what had happened when both she and Cat had tried to stop Francis getting up and going to work in his study before he'd recovered properly "...and I was so mortified, I didn't know where to look and ran out his bedroom as if I had the hounds of hell behind me," she finished pithily. "And as for Nicky and YOUR daughter," she warmed to her theme, "I KNOW you noticed that evening when we were all having dinner the night before Nicky left to take up his posting on Wellington's staff. Sitting there, innocently consuming your soup and discussing the weather as if there was nothing untoward going on around that table. She's your daughter, Eddie; those marks on her wrists and on her neck, and Nicky's just the same... and deliberately showing Cat to wind Francis up. What a disgraceful lot they all are," her lips twitched despite her struggle to sound appalled.

"You don't miss much, do you? I knew you'd noticed those marks, but I didn't know you well enough to comment on it afterwards as we'd not long been engaged; but she's a married woman, with a child, and all that business at *Le Lion d'Or*, which we're not supposed to know about," he chuckled, "and with Nicky for a disreputable husband; what should I expect? And her mother was a very passionate Spanish woman…"

"And look who her father is a very passionate French man, and a disreputable one as well. It's obviously the French influence and it's rubbed off on Francis because he spent so much time there," Elise added pithily, making Eddie chuckle, "and please note, I hadn't been living in a nunnery," she huffed

"Obviously not," he smirked, "as I've just discovered," he grinned.

The pair of them lay quietly for a while, both contemplating their conversation, as Eddie idly twirled a lock of long blonde hair around his finger and mindlessly stroked a hand over Elise's soft skin.

"If I ask you something very personal, would you mind? Would you tell me?" Elise suddenly turned to ask.

"Not my mistresses again?" he joked.

"No, this is serious, Eddie, and I would like to know."

"I don't have any secrets, *Chérie*, not like Francis; but I've told you, I won't discuss affairs that happened with other women a long, long time ago, they're in the past."

"This isn't about what you did with your mistresses," Elise hesitated, "it's… it's about Carlotta," she whispered. "Would you tell me? Did you do with her what you did with me tonight and last night?"

The stroking hand suddenly stilled and the hair fell from his fingers and he lay silent for a moment. "She's dead, Elise, that's all in the past too, I don't want to discuss it."

"I know… but… I need to know. Please, Eddie, just say yes, or no. I don't want the details."

He was quiet for a while and Elise could have bitten her tongue out, frightened she'd overstepped the mark and touched a very raw nerve which he might not forgive, but she simply had to know.

Eddie was an extremely perceptive man and suddenly, a lot of things became clear and made sense. "This is what last night, and tonight, was really all about, wasn't it, Elise? Carlotta. It wasn't about you... or me. You've got a thing about her, haven't you?" he said very quietly.

"I... no..." Elise took a deep breath, deciding she'd have to have it out with him once and for all and make her final stand, before she became even more obsessed than she was, and there seemed no better time for an intimate conversation now he was more open and relaxed with her, uncaring of his disfiguring body scars as he lay naked on the bed. "Yes, I have, and just so you know, last night WAS about you and me as well... but... oh Eddie, she's everywhere in this house, this was HER house. Her pictures hang in virtually every room and she inhabited this bed with you. She's like an invisible presence everywhere I turn..." she gripped his hand and rolled around to look deeply into his eyes. "I'm sorry, Eddie, I love you so very much and I don't want to upset you, but I have to tell you how I feel. I know I'll never replace her in your heart, and I'll never be the woman she was, no matter how much I try, but I want to try to be a bit more like her because I know she was everything to you. You said last night a part of you died when she did. I understand how terrible it must have been for you to lose her, to lock yourself away in grief for so many years. You loved her so very much, didn't you?" she whispered, an agonised look on her face.

Eddie lay silent and still for a long time and Elise didn't know what to do. Eventually, without a word, he pulled away from her and got up from the bed and went to put on his dressing robe, then poured himself out a glass of brandy from a decanter that always stood on the top of a chest of drawers, succour for the cold, damp, winter nights when his pelvis and leg ached intolerably and he didn't want to resort to laudanum.

He went and stood in front of a big bay window and stared out into the moonlit night, deep in thought, and a couple of distraught tears slipped down onto Elise's cheeks at the distance now between them when they'd been so close. He turned suddenly and looked at her, staring almost. "Cover yourself up, Elise. I can't talk to you looking like that." His tone was brusque and firm and she cringed. She rolled off the bed and disappeared quickly into her bedroom. She came back a short while later, her hair combed and neatly plaited, her face bare of the remains of the coquettish cosmetics and a plain, dark velvet dressing robe covered her from neck to feet. She was back to the Elise everyone was familiar with. She looked calm, impassive, composed and in command of herself and she sat down on a chair, hands in lap, and waited.

The minutes ticked past and the clock on the mantel chimed. Eventually, Eddie tossed back the remains of his brandy and went to stand in front of her. He gazed down at her, a strange expression on his face and the words he uttered were the last she'd expected to hear, and her mouth dropped open in stunned shock.

"Carlotta was a common prostitute, but I never did ANYTHING with her like I shared with you last night, or tonight."

Elise was so taken aback, she was speechless... so simply got up and went and helped herself to a glass of brandy and tossed it back in one gulp before returning to sit down again, the silence in the room now palpable.

"What I am going to tell you is only known by two people: Cat and Francis. You are therefore NEVER, EVER, to breathe a word of this to either Nicky or Bella. I think Nicky may have an idea of some of it, but he doesn't know the details and Bella has absolutely NO idea and it has to remain so because she idolised her mother. Do you give me your word, Elise, that you will keep what I tell you to yourself?"

She nodded. "Of course. I am NOT a tattletale, Eddie, you well know that," she said icily.

"However, even Cat and Francis don't know some of what I'm going to tell you; Francis knows a bit but Cat doesn't, even though she's m'sister. However, you are my wife now and I want to tell you. In a way, you deserve to know, given what we've just done, because I can now see it will affect us and our relationship going forward and I am not prepared to allow that."

His tone was so terse, Elise almost reeled, but outwardly she sat calm and serene and watched as he returned to stand in front of the window with his back to her and started to talk.

Chapter Twenty-Seven

"I became crippled and disfigured in my early adolescent years and as you can understand, that had a major impact on my whole life thereafter. As I grew older, I tried to socialise normally as my boyhood friends did, but young girls took one look at my scarred face, and the scar was much more livid and pronounced then, and I watched them cringe. I could see them react with horror and distaste... mainly the latter, and of course, I was also a cripple."

"Oh, noooo," Elise said softly. "That's terrible. How cruel, how can people be like that? It must have been tragic for you?"

"Don't interrupt me, I don't need your pity," he rasped. "Just sit and listen."

"I'm sorry," she whispered, cowering from his withering tone, wondering what other shocks she was about to hear; he was now in a strange mood.

"It took me years to recover from the attack that caused my injuries, and get to the point where I could walk again without crutches or a stick, and during that time I had no alternative but to sit and read or study, otherwise I would simply have run mad. I even contemplated suicide for a while, I was so angry and depressed at what the Fates had decreed for me, but I could never bring myself to pull the trigger, coward that I was," and Elise put her hand over her mouth in distress. "I couldn't join in the usual youthful pursuits of m'friends, such as riding, fencing, anything energetic, but one thing I could do was shoot. One only needs an arm and a good eye for that. I practised constantly until I became a crack shot, and I killed several men in duels who insulted me about the way I looked and walked. I was very sensitive, and bitter, as you can imagine, and took out my bitterness at the world in any way I could." Elise put a hand over her mouth again to stop herself from gasping out loud.

"You killed people? YOU?" She couldn't help herself as she whispered half to herself in shock. "How many men did you kill?"

"Too many, double figures, leave it at that. Just because they called me a cripple, or 'scarface', or other worse names I won't mention. I'm not proud of what I did and no one else knows, especially not Cat. I told you earlier, I'm no saint, even if I don't like killing harmless mice."

"Good God!" Elise muttered to herself, stunned; so much for her kind and gentle, mild-mannered man.

"But of course, as I just said, I couldn't ride, hunt, drive a curricle or dance, not that anyone wanted to dance with me. They could barely bring themselves to carry on a conversation, they would just stare at my scars or make excuses and go off and dance with someone else. So I gambled." His tone was so rife with bitterness, Elise's heart went out to him.

"Our family was comfortable, not particularly rich, but not poor; we had a title but it was nothing special, and we lived quietly in Normandy and you've now seen our old mansion. Nothing palatial or like Valenciennes, but it was a lovely country manor house and had been in the de Mornay family for generations. There was myself, my parents, Cat and our two younger sisters. I had a small allowance from m'grandmother's estate, she was the daughter of a Duke and rather proud of her lineage. Sadly, she was murdered in the self-same attack that did this to me." Elise watched as his hand felt down the scarred side of his face, "And I naturally had a small allowance from m'father, but between them, they barely covered my tailor's bills and accommodation when I visited Paris, and it wasn't nearly enough for my needs. I had expensive taste in clothes, I wanted to dress well to make up for my lack of looks, and I wanted to live somewhere easy to access with no steps or stairs for those times my leg played up; and I had other expenses to cover. With nothing else to do for years, I'd read all sorts of odd literature and became fascinated with training my memory, and I obviously had a talent for it, and also for cards and other games like chess, so it seemed, and I became a consummate gambler; mainly cards, for obvious reasons. I was very careful, I didn't want to become a pariah to my male friends, most of whom accepted my looks without thought, apart from the odd few who I've just mentioned, and also I didn't want to be banned from clubs and gaming establishments. But I made quite a bit of money on top of my allowance. As you know, Cat's godmother is Lady Harriet Aubrey, and once she was old enough, Cat came to spend time every Season, or sometimes a summer as well, in London with her, and I would often accompany her; that's how come we learned to speak English so well and why we weren't at home when Bernheim's father decided to call on the parents and demand money to keep them from being arrested, 'for treason' as he put it. M'father might have been a bit old-fashioned and conservative in some respects but actually, he had quite progressive and liberal views in others; like ensuring m'sisters were properly educated as well as me, and he cared about the welfare of his retainers and tenants, unlike a lot of his neighbours, and other aristocrats like Nicky's father, and it was a good enough excuse for that bastard to try and blackmail him. M'father refused to pay and so ended up in Rouen Fortress with m'mother and sisters… and you know the rest of the story." Elise sat silent, absorbed and fascinated with his early life and merely nodded. However, Eddie kept staring out the window as he continued with his story.

"Apart from visiting London with Cat, and gambling and entertaining myself there where I wasn't known at all, I spent a lot of my time in Paris. It wasn't far from Normandy, but far enough. It was before the Revolution and aristocratic life was one long round of enjoyment at Versailles and the other palaces and mansions of the nobility, a life of excess and pleasure if one had the wherewithal to indulge in it. I made enough money from my gambling to entertain myself royally with a wardrobe of the finest clothes and a stream of beautiful, willing women. First dancers and the like, then I kept a succession of mistresses, demi-mondaines accepted in a man's world but not respectable Society. If you pay a woman, invariably she ignores your looks and any disability," and Elise could hear even more bitterness in his tone and she cringed. "Therefore, that was my life. No genteel, nicely raised woman would look at me, but I enjoyed myself with my mistresses and they fulfilled whatever fantasy I wished to experience and enjoy, and I tried and pleasured myself with most. M'father obviously wanted and expected me to marry, but no suitable young girls from our social circles would look at me unless they were ugly and desperate and I didn't want them. I always liked the beautiful ones who didn't want me... so I became even more resentful and bitter and never socialised in Polite Society unless I had to, and hid myself away in the gaming rooms when I had to attend balls and parties with m'mother and sisters. You see, Elise, there is very little I haven't tried or done with a woman, especially when you pay, and I learned and was entertained by experts."

"Oh God," Elise whispered to herself, cringing even more now she knew the truth, feeling like a worm.

"And then the Bastille fell and Paris became a dangerous place. God knows why so many aristocrats ignored the warning signs even before that; I could sense the unrest but most blithely carried on with their lives there, or didn't think their own peasants would rise up against them. I didn't like what was going on and believed it was going to get nasty, so I gave up my life in Paris for a while and returned to Normandy, and hoped all the political upheaval would pass us by, out in the sticks as we were. As luck would have it, Cat had been invited to her godmother's earlier in the year as Lord Aubrey was in the Diplomatic Service and had gone abroad again on some mission or other, and she'd got lonely so asked Cat over after Christmas while the Season was in full swing. I escorted her over, as I usually did, and intended to spend some time in London too, as Lady Harriet was always very welcoming, and Edgar Bernheim struck while we were away."

"We got a message from a faithful old retainer and hurried back to Normandy. We didn't dare show our faces at home or anywhere we were known, in case Bernheim found us - he had spies everywhere - so I acquired an old gypsy-type caravan and Cat and I kept on the move in that, only staying over in inns and hostelries in out of the way places where we reckoned we would be unrecognised and safe. You see, Cat had had this ridiculous idea that we had to break our family out of the Fortress. You've just said we're half mad, and you're right, as no one had ever escaped from the wretched place. It was so terrible in there: rife with disease and rats, cold, dark, damp, fetid; people were lucky if they kept alive to be released, never mind escape, but few ever got to be released, unless they paid heavily and bought their way out. Edgar Bernheim and his second-in-command, Pierre Dupont, were a pair of the worst bastards the Devil has ever spawned. It was Dupont who did this to me, I think Cat has told you the story?" Finally, he turned to look at the silent woman, sitting listening to him in her chair, and Elise nodded.

"But you know m'sister; nothing, but nothing, would deter her. She was absolutely determined to save our parents and sisters and she drove me insane to come up with some plan to do it. I'd no idea, other than realising we would need help, and that is where The Shadow came in. We'd both vaguely heard of him, most people who lived near the coast in Normandy had, in gossip and tattle, a bit like people here in England had all heard of Robin Hood in his day, I suppose, and The Shadow's fame as one of the few men to avoid Bernheim and continue to cock a snook at him, and make him look a fool, privately fascinated and amused everyone... except Bernheim and Dupont, of course. They were disliked and feared in equal measure by everyone in Normandy, whether you were a noble or a commoner or a criminal. But The Shadow was no Robin Hood, robbing the rich to help the poor; the man was a smuggler and pirate with a reputation for complete ruthlessness and very successful in his criminal endeavours. It was said he cut off the noses and ears of those who crossed him, then cooked and ate them; all ridiculous, of course, another of Francis's mad ideas, but at the time people believed it and really did fear him."

"Anyway, Cat got this maggot in her brain to try and find The Shadow and persuade him to help us. She swore she'd sell the house, and herself if necessary, and give him every penny we had if he would, and that's why we were trundling around the Normandy countryside in a ramshackle caravan, and up and down the coast, looking for him. Why the hell Cat thought we could find him when Bernheim and all his spies and militia couldn't, God knows. But you know Cat now, there was simply no dissuading her. I tried to persuade her it was an impossible task and she should go back to the safety of London and Lady Aubrey, and make her home there with her, and I would go to Paris and petition the King, or those with some useful influence, to release our family as it was a trumped-up charge. I personally thought greasing the palms of the right people in Paris would see a better return than trying to find some elusive smuggler fellow who came and went mysteriously, and no one knew who he was or what he looked like. I was determined to go to Paris and stake everything I had to earn the money to buy my family's release, but Cat simply refused to budge and go to England, and I was frightened to leave her by herself in Normandy, or take her to Paris and leave her to her own devices there, while I spent my days and nights gambling, knowing how hotheaded she was; and believe me, she was in those days, far worse than now. I thought she'd do something reckless and end up being taken by Bernheim and join our family inside the Fortress as well. I was at an impasse and so it was we were at the end of our tether. We'd trailed the length and breadth of Normandy, asking in hamlets and villages, anywhere we thought he might be holed up. We could, of course, find no trace of this wretched villain to hire him and his dangerous crew to help, that was the plan, a force of mercenary fighters to attack the Fortress, and we had virtually given up hope. Cat could sleep quite happily in the caravan but I loathed it; you know me, I do like my creature comforts and a bath and a comfortable bed, especially where I can stretch out as I can't bend my bad leg and pelvis easily; that's why my bed in here is so big, in case you hadn't realised," he sighed sadly, "not for any salacious purposes, I can promise you." But he didn't smile his usual charming grin.

"Anyway, we found ourselves in some out-of-the-way hamlet, literally a cluster of run-down cottages with a local smithy, and some smallholdings nearby, and there was a small inn, just perfect to spend a night or two instead of the caravan, and get some decently cooked food. We ordered our dinner and as we were sitting, rather morosely contemplating what to do with ourselves, having exhausted all avenues looking for this wretched, elusive smuggler, there was a bit of a disturbance at the bar and a small troupe of gypsies appeared. Just a handful of swarthy men with guitars and violins and a dancer. The usual itinerant entertainment, but at least it took our minds off our predicament for a while. The men played and then the woman started to dance with her tambourine, using it to collect a few coins from the patrons. She was quite striking to look at, long black hair to her waist and flashing dark eyes, and the most wonderful dancer; the way she twirled her hands and fingers, I was entranced. She was also eyeing up the men in the bar for a potential customer for the night as she danced around the small floor space, and even though Cat and I were dressed very plainly and simply, she obviously could tell we were Quality, and better off than the rest of the rough clientele in the tavern, and she made a bee-line for me, even with my scar. As I said, when you pay, women don't appear to notice it. I'd abandoned my lightskirts in Paris the year before, and there'd only been the odd high-class whore, or courtesan, in London who I'd picked up at some licentious parties I frequented now and again. So it had been quite a while since I'd been with a woman and this dancer took my fancy, even though I was usually quite particular and kept away from common tarts, not wanting to pick up any disease, even though I used to protect myself with a sheath."

"She was quite some woman, there was something about her that fascinated me, and it was an amazing night. In the morning, we were just chatting, making small talk as one does in these situations, and quite by chance, as she had no idea who I was or what I was doing at that out of the way hostelry, she told me she and her troupe were staying nearby at some gypsy encampment as there was a big gathering taking place and they were providing entertainment at it on some nights. I don't know quite how we got round to it, but I vaguely mentioned in passing I was on the lookout for this smuggler fellow, known as The Shadow, as I had some potential business to discuss with him, well away from the ears of the law. She must have decided I didn't look like some spy for the authorities, and was a decent sort of chap, so she told me she'd overheard a conversation between a couple of gypsies who had said some smuggler, possibly The Shadow himself, was due in the camp for the gathering as he was expected to collect some goods for onward transportation; apparently he had regular dealings with some of the gypsies who brought goods from the east or south to sell to the smugglers on the northern coast."

"Talk about amazing coincidence. Needless to say, Cat was beside herself when I told her what I'd discovered, and so, of course, we went to the gypsy camp with the dancer, and that's where we finally caught up with The Shadow, who actually was there in person. That's how Cat met Francis again, for their paths had crossed for a short few hours in their youth, I think you've heard that tale... and I suppose you've gathered by now that the gypsy I picked up, and paid to spend the night with in that tavern, was Carlotta."

Elise HAD gathered that and was completely dumbstruck by his story, never having the least idea of her predecessor's occupation. She was staggered.

"We remained in the encampment for a few days until it broke up, and I stayed in Carlotta's caravan and our passionate affair continued. She offered to help us with our plan to rescue my family as she wanted out of the life she was leading, and she privately asked Francis, as The Shadow, to give her passage over to England if we succeeded in our rescue attempt. She told him her history and that's how he knows about her. At first, I thought she'd latched on to me as a Good Thing, given who I thought she was, but then she told me the truth as well, and a lot about her suddenly made sense. There was something very aristocratic about her at times, her mannerisms, her accent and just the way she was, which I'd found deuced odd, and she was quite well educated; well, not like you, or Bella, or even m'sister, as she was brought up in a convent in Spain, but far more than any itinerant gypsy would be, and besides that, I realised I'd fallen for her and she told me she'd fallen for me, and I actually believed her, cynic though I was. She was beautiful, feisty and passionate, with creamy skin and dark eyes and a glorious figure with long legs, dancer's legs, and she didn't seem bothered about my face or my body. For obvious reasons I wasn't carrying a lot of money around with me, so I hadn't paid her after the first couple of nights. I just told her if we got my family out, we would simply be penniless *emigrés* from the Revolution and would have to live on charity, or I would have to find work to support them. At the time, Cat was talking about finding a place as a governess or a lady's companion, can you imagine that, knowing her? Francis thought it hysterical, and I had my doubts as well, she of the plate and vase throwing and unladylike language… anyway, I digress," he paused to finish his brandy then continued his convoluted tale.

"So, Carlotta risked her life to help us and my family, and she saved Nicky, along with Cat and Francis. I think it was because of the child she'd lost, and that was how she'd ended up selling herself," Elise looked confused, "I'll get to that in a minute… I'm sorry, it's a long, complicated story and I'm not thinking very straight."

Eddie paused again in his tale to go and get another drink and absently he did the same for Elise, simply handing over another glass of brandy to her without asking. She took it in now slightly shaking hands.

"Carlotta was the only daughter of an old, aristocratic Spanish family who lived on an estate in the countryside not far from Seville. I gather she'd always been quite a headstrong child and hated the local convent where she was educated. She loved to dance, apparently, even as a little girl. She was about fifteen or sixteen when a friend of her older brother came to stay for a few weeks over the summer, and he seduced her. She was so naïve, I understand she'd hardly conversed with a boy, having spent most of her time in that convent, or been kept strictly at home as girls were down there, so she was fair game. She thought she was in love and presumed he'd offer for her, her head full of silly, romantic notions. But he was already affianced to another, apparently, a long-agreed and established match, and having dallied, he disappeared off home. When she discovered she was pregnant, he denied all responsibility and said she'd thrown herself at him and wasn't a virgin but was a little trollop. Knowing how rebellious she'd always been, her parents actually believed him, and he refused to take responsibility saying he was already promised elsewhere and inferring it might not even be his child. Horrified at the shame it would place on them if anyone found out about her condition, and the claims of this youth that she was a little trollop to boot, her parents decided their only option was to send her off to a distant convent, permanently. Carlotta was distraught; the thought of being locked away in a convent, forced to become a nun, was her worst nightmare. But she wasn't some compliant young girl like her peers, and so, seeing no other alternative, she ran away from home and found herself in Seville."

"It was an enormous thing to do for a young girl of her age with no experience of the world at all. She was so naïve, not even understanding about being pregnant and having a child. She made some money at first by dancing in the streets, but as her figure expanded, that became difficult, and so was her pregnancy. Inevitably, because she was starving and desperate, even though she was *enceinte*, she finally sold herself. I never got to the bottom of what happened or what caused it, lack of food probably, sickness, or an infection she picked up, or maybe simply what she was doing, a rough man," he shrugged, "but she miscarried and became quite ill. Some gypsies found her in a gutter, more dead than alive, and saved her. I've no idea why, maybe they thought she was one of them," he shrugged again, his face impassive as he recounted his late wife's history. "Anyway, she recovered, and stayed with the gypsies and travelled around with them, earning her keep by dancing. They travelled up through Spain and into France and she eventually left them to try and earn her living in Paris, seeing no future in what she was doing, trailing around the countryside, always on the move. She'd lived with them, but they and she knew she wasn't a gypsy by birth; however, she had no training to be a lady's maid or a governess, or a shop worker, and her temperament didn't suit that either. All she could really do was dance... and fuck, if you'll excuse my language... and her French was basic then, another hindrance in anything but the bedroom or a tavern. So, she made the best of herself and for a few years she made her living, first as a better class of prostitute and then, as she got enough money to dress herself properly, she moved up in the world and became a courtesan. She already had the deportment and manners for it and knew how to mix and socialise with people of Quality, so it was easy. But she didn't like what she'd become, hated demeaning and selling herself to anyone with money, and she could see trouble was brewing in Paris. After the Bastille fell she decided she'd had enough and gave it all up, thinking she would rather be safe elsewhere, and dance, and choose a man that appealed to her from time to time when she needed money, rather than put up with old goats pawing her and forcing her into acts that made her sick, never mind the risk of being strung up on a lamppost or having her head chopped off simply because she was the mistress of some uncaring aristocrat, something that actually nearly happened to her I gather."

"She left Paris with what savings she had, not knowing where to go. She toyed with going home, but was frightened her parents would pack her off to a convent again, never mind if they would even acknowledge her or take her back after what she'd done, so, with little other choice, she finally tracked down her old gypsy friends and rejoined them. She lived off her savings, trying not to sell herself anymore, but the money ran out and so that was what she was doing the night I met her in the tavern in Normandy. I only spent a few short weeks with her between then and our adventure in Rouen, but by the time we left for England, I realised, for the first time in my life, I'd fallen in love with a woman. She said she loved me too, and I had no reason to disbelieve her as by then I had no home, no clothes nor belongings to speak of, nor any money, so it had to be more than that. Knowing no other nice woman would even look at me, especially as I was now some impoverished *emigré* until I could start gambling again, having left all my savings in Paris, such as they were, and had presumably lost them as, regrettably they were in cash, not in a reliable bank, I proposed to Carlotta and said we would make a home together with Nicky. We'd no idea who Francis really was, other than a wanted smuggler, so thought we'd be on our own when we got to England. We told everyone she was a Spanish aristocrat, which of course she really was, and I'd met her as she was fleeing Paris and the Revolution, as WE were, so they believed us, and my parents were simply delighted I'd finally found what they considered a suitable woman to marry. It was a chaotic time in Paris and France in 1790, so all sorts of strange things were happening to people and no one took much notice of our story as it sounded so plausible. Now you understand why Carlotta was so desperate to adopt Nicky and give him a home. Apart from his terrible plight, he was a replacement for the child she'd lost. I was happy to adopt him too, he was such a brave, self-possessed little boy, not even five, and he was French, like me, and it was the least I could do given where we'd found him and what had happened to his parents. He'd had a traumatic time in his childhood, just like I'd had, albeit I was older and the circumstances were different, but I oddly identified with him and my heart just went out to him."

"Anyway, Carlotta and I married soon after we got to London and as well as generating an income through gambling, I went to work for Francis who by then I'd discovered was not only a wealthy Duke, but ran quite a considerable business empire out of the public eye, as well as his various estates. I'd always thought there was something deuced odd about him, from the minute I'd met him. I knew he wasn't some common smuggler, he was far too aristocratic when he forgot himself sometimes, just his clothes, his attitude and the way he carried himself and spoke; there was, and still is, such an air of command about him, a presence, even though he was thick as thieves with the gypsies and never had any airs and graces with them or other common folk he mixed with. I'd always enjoyed and been interested in commercial matters, even though m'father disapproved and wanted to retain the old ways of his father and grandfather, and Francis and I just hit it off, our minds were in tune when it came to business, and between us, we've made a lot of money over the years. Francis was always rich, but I've made a fortune and am far more wealthy than m'father's family ever was, or he could have dreamed of. Francis gave me this estate as a thank-you for helping to save his and Cat's lives in Rouen… and even though I've argued, pleaded and threatened him for the past twenty-five years, and it wouldn't even dent what I'm worth, he refuses to let me pay him back. But that's beside the point, and I'm digressing again, but I just wanted you to know that. Smuggler, pirate or not, Francis is the most generous and kind-hearted man I have EVER met, and don't ever listen to a bad word about him, because whatever the stories are, I know better."

"So Carlotta and I settled down and we were very happy. But she was an outgoing person and wanted to socialise and she refused to let me wallow in my own reclusive corner, so she dragged me, kicking and screaming, into social life in London. She forced me to confront my issues about my looks and disability, and for the most part, she was right. Some women still shuddered when they looked at me, but Carlotta, or Cat, let loose their wrath on them, and no mistake, and strangely, having a wife, and a beautiful one to boot, made me seem more acceptable to a lot of women; idiotic isn't it? So, in the main, after a while, people and London Society came to accept me. That Scarred French Emigré, they called me, and I got used to it all, and go out and about now and don't care a damn. If people want to stare, I let them get on with it. I suppose, as one gets older, things like looks don't matter to one so much, and of course, I'm not nearly so sensitive as I was in my youth and early twenties."

Eddie limped over to stand in front of Elise for a silent moment before he carried on speaking, gazing down at her with an impassive expression. "My joints ache when it's cold and damp, and it gives me hell, and sometimes I can barely move, especially in winter, that's why I keep the house so warm with fires everywhere, day and night. I HATE it that I'm awkward and clumsy in bed, never mind so disfigured. Have you ANY idea how that made me feel when I first made love to you? Now you understand why I keep those silk trousers on. I blindfolded you tonight, partly because it would indeed heighten your senses and some people find it extremely arousing and erotic... and I like to think you did and perhaps you'll tell me sometime... but also because I frequently did it with women I fucked years ago, because I was so self-conscious about myself, my awkwardness, the scars, everything. And pardon for the language but I fucked them, I didn't make love to them. They are two different things in my book – one merely a physical release or entertaining diversion with someone I didn't care a jot about, the other a true expression of my feelings and emotions with someone special. Anyway, as I said, when one pays, one calls the tune, and the women complied, thinking it a mildly perverted idiosyncrasy of mine which was harmless."

Having made his confession, Eddie hastily turned back to the window before speaking again. "And I actually understand how Nicky feels with his arm, but he won't listen to me at the moment when I've offered him a sympathetic ear. However, hopefully, he will talk to me when he's ready."

Elise saw he had his hands in fists and she realised what the confession had cost him, how wound up he was, but apparently he still hadn't finished. "There, Elise... now you know what I did with my mistresses, and I frequently tied them up, and wound them up and made them beg me to fuck them, just like I did to you earlier, because somehow it made me feel more like a manly man, and paid back all those women who shuddered when they looked at and rejected me. However, be assured, I am no de Sade. I didn't want to hurt them, merely master and humiliate them. Just as unpleasant for an independent woman like you, however. So, tell me, Elise, do you still want to be like them and indulge my little quirks and weird perversions?" he asked facetiously.

"Oh God," Elise whispered, the shocks continued as she stared at his back. "Is that why you laughed at me, why you found my request so funny?" she could barely speak. Was there no end to his bitterness and personal torment?

"Yes, ironic isn't it?" his facetious tone made her cringe again. "I thought I'd finally found myself a lovely, respectable wife with whom I could have a normal, prosaic love life and escape from my past. And you were special to me, Elise, because you were barely touched by another man, the nearest I could ever get to a virgin, unlike EVERY OTHER WOMAN I've ever been with, and now what does she ask me to do? Why, the very thing I wanted to put behind me."

"Oh noooo, you must hate me," Elise whispered. "I... I'd no idea. I'm so, so sorry."

"Don't be. I had so much pleasure tonight I'd forgotten what it was like to feel like that. I thought it would be the same as with the others, but it wasn't. I didn't have to pay you, to my astonishment you offered, and you genuinely enjoyed it. You didn't pretend to, which some of them did, although most found pleasure, but with you, it's because I love you and desire you all the time, and only want to please you; it makes a difference, Elise. And because Carlotta made me confront my issues, I don't NEED to fornicate like that anymore. I don't hate women these days, don't want to get back at them and make them pay in some sort of perverse way. I'm quite normal now, I give you my word. In a way, those years and the women were a bit of an aberration, like the duels and the men I killed. Those days are all in the past and I've moved on. If you hadn't offered to do what we did tonight, I'd never have asked you and our life would have continued exactly as it was. But you did offer, and we did do it, and I enjoyed it enormously and so did you. Therefore, if you are still speaking to me after what I've told you, if you want to do it again, you only have to ask and it will be my pleasure, and yours, too, I hope; but, I assure you I can live without it as much as I would enjoy doing it again. However, YOU will have to ask ME. You do appreciate the reasons for that?" She was sitting with a hand over her mouth, eyes wide with shock, trying to take it all in. "Don't look at me like that, Elise, with pity in your eyes, I can't bear it. I'm baring my soul to you in the hope you understand."

"It's not pity, Eddie, it's love. I LOVE you. Nothing you've said makes the slightest difference to what I feel, it's just I'm completely staggered. I wasn't expecting all this, never dreamed..." her hand waved vaguely in the air, "even if you killed a dozen men, you're still the gentlest, kindest man I know and although what you did to me tonight did shock me, it was only because I wasn't expecting it, not what you actually did. I wasn't offended or upset as I know people do it, even your half-mad family, apparently. I enjoyed it, a lot, as you well know. It was one of the most amazing experiences of my life, ALL of it, well, apart from giving birth to Harry, and I want to do ALL of it again, with you. So I WILL ask again, when I'm ready." She paused, then added, "Did what I did to you last night bother you? Given what you've just told me... letting a woman master you?" she asked quietly.

"Not at all, it's not the same. You didn't want to humiliate me, or master me in some perverted way, you simply wanted to give me pleasure, immense pleasure, so of course I enjoyed that too. In fact, Elise, you can do whatever you like to me if you want," he shrugged. "I enjoy fornicating and playing bed games in all their forms and variations, but I'm clumsy and awkward, Elise, and I STILL CAN'T BEAR IT!" He suddenly sounded agonised and his fists clenched and unclenched. "Now you've seen the scars on my body, how puckered and hideous they are, I can just about deal with that, but other things… I don't want to feel inadequate in bed with you and there are a lot of positions and actions I can't manage. Christ, tonight I had to struggle to get to my feet after kneeling down to pleasure you… I just can't endure being disabled, a useless cripple!" he rasped agonisingly as he thumped a fist into his other palm in frustration.

"You are NOT disabled, nor a cripple. If it makes you feel better, less self-conscious, you can blindfold me whenever you like, but I think you should just forget doing that from now on, UNLESS you want to do it for erotic reasons and because I DID enjoy it; there, now you know. And, if you also don't know by now I simply don't care if you limp or not, have scars or not, or it takes an effort to get up off your knees, you're as mad as the rest of your family. I struggle to get up sometimes after I've been weeding in the garden, so what? And my back aches as well, even sitting too long at my desk does that. I'm not twenty anymore and we're both past the first flush of youth, even we don't feel it sometimes. How you are is all part of you, Eddie, the man you are, the man I love. If you roll over in bed because you lose your balance, we should just laugh, because it will be funny, not a tragedy. Like me tripping over the paving slab on the terrace, falling over, getting my petticoats in a tangle and exposing my nether regions, and throwing all my paints over myself, in front of the Vicar when he came to tea. You were doubled up and howling with laughter when you saw that and I felt enormously embarrassed and a complete fool… especially as the Vicar obviously didn't know where to look… so what's the difference?" her voice was stronger now, more like her usual assertive self.

"I've no idea where all this heart-searching and confession came from, Eddie, not that I'm not hugely relieved and pleased you've felt you should finally tell me, as I think it will make you feel happier to get it all off your chest, especially as I don't care a jot about any of it as you obviously thought I would. You should have more faith in me, knowing how much I love you. But, all I asked was whether you did what we did tonight with Carlotta. You still haven't answered that properly, despite denying it vaguely, although, I have to assume you did, given what happened to her? Which was absolutely tragic and I give you my word, not a mention of any of what you've told me will ever pass my lips, to anyone. Did she make it up with her family, by the way? I thought Bella told me she inherited some money years ago from her mother's family?"

"You're right," he sighed, "I should have had faith, it's... it's just been difficult for me, please understand, Elise. And, I couldn't tell you about Carlotta without explaining all the rest, because it's all connected one way or another... and just so you also know, she never knew about the women and what I just told you. You are the only one I've EVER told."

"Oh, Eddie," she whispered.

"I had ten blissful years with Carlotta and she ranted and raved at me about my scars and limp and forced me to live like a normal man again. Like you, she always said it didn't matter a damn to her and it didn't. But, you want to know whether I did with her what I did with you, and the answer really is no," and yet again Elise gasped. "Not because she was obviously far, far more experienced than you, and I assume she did far more perverted and strange things with the men she serviced, but because I didn't dare suggest it, thinking it would remind her of what she'd been and wanted to forget; and because, as I've just explained, I wanted to leave that part of my life behind, too, and move on. And she never suggested it to me either. I think because she didn't want to remind me of what she'd been. Isn't it all quite bizarre in a strange way? I've already told you what we did, and my body was as familiar to her as hers was to me, just like the two of us finally are, but that is as far as we went. I refuse to discuss the matter any further because it is private and I hope you respect that, but does my answer satisfy you?"

Elise looked at him, horribly embarrassed and nodded mutely, wishing she'd never, ever, brought up the whole subject. "I'm so sorry," she whispered again.

"Don't be, and for God's sake stop apologising," he grated. "We've gone way beyond that. I understand now why you needed to know, I'd no idea what a complex you had about her, but most of it is all in your mind, Elise. She's dead and she died a long time ago and you have to deal with your issues just as I have to deal with mine. Carlotta and I never discussed our pasts and our activities in bed were fairly ordinary. Not that they weren't passionate, because she was a very passionate woman, demanding and insatiable sometimes, and she often wore me out; but what we did never strayed from what I suppose you would call normality, well perhaps a bit creative, and a bit more than some conservative people do, but as I said, nothing like what we did tonight. And there's something else you should know, while we're on the subject, about my children, Bella and Nicky, and why you think Lizzie and Terrie are wild."

"Bella was a complete hoyden when she was a little girl, as you've heard, but Carlotta just let her run wild as she wanted, because of the repressive upbringing she'd had. She never wanted Bella to feel so constrained and naïve as she'd been, and I let her get on with it as I thought it was harmless, and she was only running around with either Nicky, or Cat and Francis's boys, all of whom would look after her; and she was a studious little girl too, when she wanted to be, and absorbed her lessons like a sponge, everything from mathematics and science to history, geography and the Classics, nothing was beyond her; she loved nothing more than to bury herself in a book in the library on rainy or cold days; so she wasn't completely wild, now do you understand? Nicky was also a little tearaway, always into mischief, but it took him a good two or three years before he let go enough to be totally like that. As I said, I've never seen such a quiet, composed and self-contained child as he was when we first brought him to England. I gather his father was a cold fish and his mother much the same, and that explained some of what he was like, such as not being allowed to get dirty, or play outside, and to be on his best behaviour the entire time and do nothing but study with his tutors; but most of it was because of what he went through in that Fortress. God knows what he saw and experienced, and I have my suspicions, but he's never talked about it, ever, and I have tried to ask him, but he's just buried it. I know, because I watched him over the years with some of our male friends and family," and Elise gasped in shock as she grasped what he was inferring.

"Oh, not people like Francis, who he always idolised and did things with him that I couldn't do, like teaching him to ride, drive a curricle, and fight and swim, and generally be the bane of my life and naughtiness itself, just to annoy me, and the Dowager who of course loved him to death. And not silly buggers like Ricky Ambrose who was wonderful with him too, worse than Francis if that's possible, in encouraging him to come out of himself and be mischievous. No, it was others, men who think little children should be perfectly behaved, seen and not heard, or who tutted when he got a bit saucy or was running amok, being a soldier or pirate, or bringing strange creatures in from the garden to show people; men like one of my brothers-in-law, or Francis's sisters' staid husbands. I don't think anyone else noticed, not even Carlotta, but I did. He would go quiet, or cringe slightly, I can't really explain it, especially if the man was a bit over-bearing. It was almost imperceptible, but I'd stake my life it was there. Anyway, I was thrilled when he gradually came out of himself and I never raised a hand to him, not that I would normally, though Francis paddled his backside countless times, and so did Cat, and he didn't have a problem with that, because I watched at first, just to be sure. So Bella ran around with him and her Granville cousins, who she could always outshoot I'm delighted to say, having taught her myself, and in a way, it was good for her as she's never had a problem dealing with men of all sorts and she's a perfectly normal, well-balanced woman now and I'm perfectly happy with the way she lets Terrie run about, just the same, not that I should interfere, and Nicky obviously encour-ages her because of his terrible, unloved early years at Valenciennes which I know he's never quite forgotten."

"Francis was also brought up in a lonely household surrounded by indulged, frivolous and brainless sisters and a neurotic mother who resorted to smelling salts if he so much as went '*en garde*' with a toy sword, and all of them were always having the vapours and wailing about something or other; and his father was a drunken sot who virtu-ally lived in his club as he couldn't be doing with a house full of silly women and an extremely wilful son, not to mention his overbearing mother. The Dowager ran everything from Hertford Street, being such a strong personality, and she'd mellowed a lot by the time you met her, believe me, so Francis doesn't want Lizzie to grow up in a home like that and that's why his boys are also slightly wild, though they're settling down as they grow up and mature. Bella is perfect for Nicky as she grew up with him and won't stand for any of his nonsense as she knows him so well, and vice versa. They played practical jokes on each other, fought and comforted each other and now they're so in love, it's wonderful. So that is why all our children are uncontrollable, or that's what you think, but now you might understand why, and believe me, when it's important, they do what they're told and behave perfectly; and also, remember what I said about Nicky. His past is buried inside him somewhere, just like all our pasts, and maybe it still haunts him, so be sensitive to that, Elise, if the occasion ever arises."

"Oh my God, Eddie, that's so terrible. Are you sure?"

"Positive, well as much as I can be, but you must never say anything, Elise, promise me?"

"Of course not, and I'm so pleased I know now, and you know I was only joking about the girls. I just wish Charlie would be more of a tomboy, believe me, and I'm so glad you've let him go to your sister's for the summer, it will do him so much good. Our little Harry can be the biggest hooligan in Sussex for all I care, as long as he's a good little boy when it counts, and if he's going to socialise with his cousins, Marcus and Herring, I've no doubt he will be, so, go back to whatever you were saying about Carlotta, you lost your thread when you started talking about Bella and Nicky."

Eddie had got another drink in the meantime but continued, "Carlotta had a terrible time when she gave birth to Bella and the doctors warned me she shouldn't have another child. She was apparently carrying twins, but one died and the doctors think that's possibly what caused the complications. I often wondered if she had a problem anyway and that was why she miscarried her first child. So I was very careful after that not to cause her to conceive, and I either withdrew or used protection, both of which didn't lend themselves to a hugely satisfactory love life as far as I was concerned, but it didn't really bother me because other than that we were very happy, as I said, and I never doubted for a minute that she really did love me. I was busy working with Francis and often went overseas for months at a time, out to the East Indies and even to China once, and also to the West Indies and the Americas, and I never went with another woman while

I was away, not that there weren't plenty available, but I'd moved on and wouldn't dream of being unfaithful to Carlotta, despite my past, any more than I'd dream of keeping a mistress now, Elise," and he gave her a tart look. "But then she started. You see, she knew I wanted a son to inherit the title and she nagged and nagged and nagged, and one weekend, she parcelled Bella and Nicky off to Cat and Francis over at Firle, gave most of the household servants, except the kitchen staff, the weekend off, and she got me very drunk, and more to the point, also put something in my wine or food, she never would tell me after. Whatever it was, I lost most of that weekend and we did it without protection countless times, mostly up here but also in the dining room, my study and the library. Hence the absent servants. I was insatiable, I do remember that, and couldn't sleep either, and it was quite a couple of days, which is why I suspect there was definitely something more at play than just the alcohol. Whatever it was, wine and herbs, or probably some aphrodisiac concoction from an apothecary, I was constantly aroused and incapable of withdrawing I was so out of it, and could barely remember half of what we did the Monday after; however, unbelievably, she did conceive, and you know what happened. Charlie survived but she simply bled to death, and there was nothing the doctors could do to stop the haemorrhaging. It was the worst day of my entire life. I felt so helpless as I sat and held her hand and watched her get weaker and weaker and drift away from me. Her last words, as she kissed my hand, were that she loved me more than anything, how happy her life had been with me and she was thrilled she'd given me a son and heir. But I never wanted a son THAT much, not at the risk of her precious life, but of course she didn't care. So I'm sorry I was so frantic and crazed and drove you and the doctor mad when Harry was born, Elise, but perhaps now you can understand why."

Eddie started to walk around the room and Elise watched him, wondering what else he was going to divulge after the rest of his tragic and traumatic story.

"After we married and Bella was born, I took it upon myself to find out more about and write to Carlotta's parents and inform them of our marriage, as I felt it was the right thing to do, and I didn't tell Carlotta at first, suspecting she'd be cross and want nothing to do with them.

However, it turned out they were relieved their lost daughter wasn't lost or dead after all, and said they regretted they'd caused her to run away. They were more delighted, I think, to hear she had apparently married well, even if she was living in England with a Frenchman. They were very impressed she had a Duke for a step-son, even if he was also French, and also that m'sister was married to a Duke, even if he was English. I've no idea whether they eventually believed Carlotta's version of events that caused her to run away in the first place, or wondered what she'd been doing to support herself between her disappearance and her marriage, as they never mentioned it nor enquired. I had concocted a story for them in readiness, but they never asked. I suspect they simply didn't want to know. Anyway, as a result of my intervention, I'm pleased to say we went to see them down in Seville, with Bella, before Europe went to war and they and Carlotta made their peace. They were very taken with Bella, she was about four at the time, and very appealing and amusing, especially as she could prattle a bit in Spanish and she looked just like her mother at that age apparently, and I assume that's why they left her an inheritance, either that or residual guilt, who knows? Unfortunately, because the war in Europe started and I was concerned to sail any distance, even down to Spain, the correspondence between us was sporadic, and we never got to visit again before Carlotta died and they never came to London. But obviously what happened with her must have influenced them, and when Carlotta's father died there was a stipulation in his Will that Bella could only inherit if she married before she was seventeen. The letter about his death and the bequest and conditions got delayed because of Boney's wretched Continental System, the war in the Peninsula was starting, and the ship carrying it got damaged. By the time the letter arrived in London, her birthday was mere days away and so that's why Nicky offered to marry her and we always intended to get it quietly annulled so no one outside the family would be any the wiser. But of course, Bella was in love with him, had always been, and flatly refused to co-operate and sign papers. She was convinced that Nicky really did love her in return, even if he denied it and said she was his sister and so he couldn't possibly stay married to her, not to mention the fact he had no money, other than his army pay and the paltry income from his overseas interests, which were indeed nothing much, because he flatly refused to take any money from either Francis or myself. Well, you know what happened, so I won't go into it, and thank the Lord they seem happy now, and I'm sure this thing of Nicky's is just a temporary spat and they'll sort themselves out, because they really do love each other passionately, we can all see it."

"Anyway, back to Carlotta. After she died I was lost, and for years I decided it was MY fault for letting her do to me what she did, losing control of myself and the situation, and the longer I went without a woman, the less it bothered me, no matter how much Francis nagged it wasn't healthy or normal. And then I met you, and you know what transpired. We were friends and became very close, and then that Christmas happened and I kissed you properly. I've never known a woman like you, Elise. I can talk to you about absolutely anything, like I talk to a man, quite straight without having to mind what I say... look at tonight, you simply take even intimate and sordid information in your stride and don't resort to hartshorn, even if you do still blush a bit when I tease you, but I actually think that's lovely."

Eddie then paused for a long moment before taking a deep breath and continuing. "I loved Carlotta, she was a wonderful, selfless, caring and very loving woman. You and she are so very different in some ways, yet so similar in others. If the pictures upset you, take some down; but please, just leave one or two up, after all, she is Bella's mother, and Nicky's, and I don't want to upset either of them and I would like a couple to remain as well... because I loved her. I can't and won't deny it, but she's GONE, and has been for a long time, and I'm over it and have moved on because I love YOU now. Remember that. I wanted to get your portrait painted anyway, but what with being at Valenciennes all last summer, then the baby and then the worry over all this Bernheim business, I just haven't got around to it. Redecorate the house, it's yours now, YOU are the Baroness de Mornay. Ironically, Carlotta never was as she died just before m'father. If being in my bed disturbs you, throw it out and buy another, I simply don't care. And neither would she actually, she was an extremely practical, understanding woman and she isn't your enemy, Elise. I actually think the pair of you would have got on well if you'd known each other. I also know in my heart she wouldn't want me to moulder away on my own for the rest of my life and would want me to be happy with someone else to care for me, and I really do believe that, and Cat agrees with me as she was very close to her. There will always be a corner of my heart that is forever hers, and you have to understand that, and I hope you now can, having heard about all our family secrets as well as mine, what my life was before I met her and how she changed it, or forced me to come to terms with it... but you, Elise de Mornay, are everything to me now. You are like my soul mate, everything I always wanted in a wife and never believed I would ever have. To me, you have everything: You're a beautiful woman, a genteel and aristocratic Lady, you have a brain and a sense of humour, you're practical and capable, you're a wonderful mother, my family love and respect you, and... I now discover you want to enjoy yourself in bed as much as I used to and would still like to, if you don't mind about my past, which you say you don't." Elise simply stared at him as he prowled around, listening to the emotion that was now pouring out of him, almost choking as she heard his words.

"Carlotta made me confront my problems, but unlike her, you have never once mentioned my scars or disability to me, until it came up last night and tonight, and you make me feel like a whole, normal man in your own inimitable way, a man who could go out and conquer the world. I love you SO much, Elise, and if, after all I've told you, you can still love this damaged man back the same way, it would be simply wonderful," and he stopped in front of her and looked at her with hope and love in his eyes.

"Oh, Eddie, My Precious," tears ran down her face as Elise rose and threw herself into his arms. "I do love you, I'll always love you, you're the most wonderful man. I want to be your everything. I'm so sorry about all those things I've said and done, I bear no grudge against Carlotta, I never did, I was just so jealous of her, but if you truly love me as much as you loved Carlotta, that is all I want."

"I do love you, Elise. When I saw you in Bernheim's clutches, I couldn't bear it. I killed him for you, not for Francis or Nicky, or Miles and Jack, though obviously it was to save them all as they're everything to me too now, my closest friends, especially Francis, and Nicky who I'll always consider my son, even if he isn't my blood. At the time, I simply didn't think. I'd had enough and he had you, so I just shot him."

"You are a very deadly man, under all that mild, calm exterior, I know that now. In your own way, you are also The Shadow. No one takes much notice, but you're always there, seeing everything, and at the end of the day, you saved us all; the only one of all of them to shoot straight."

"Not bad for a scarred cripple after all, eh, *Chérie*?" and he finally kissed her. Deeply and tenderly, committing himself to her and treasuring her, savouring the fervent response he got back as she sighed in his arms and he breathed an enormous sigh of relief. It had been one of the most traumatic hours of Edouard de Mornay's life as he poured out his soul and deepest secrets to her, gambling and praying she would accept them and him, still, and be everything he'd always wanted and dreamed of.

"Are we going to be all right again, Eddie? I couldn't bear it if I couldn't be close to you still. You're my best friend as well as my husband. Say you forgive me for starting this whole dreadful business, please?"

"You did me a favour, Elise. There's nothing to forgive and now I do truly have no secrets from you and I feel so much better for it. I couldn't bear it if I couldn't talk to you and be close to you again either. I just want to kiss you and love you and forget everything; can we do that?"

"Consider everything forgotten, and kiss and love me this instant," and she hugged him tight and kissed him with all the love in her heart until he was smiling at her again and the haunted look had disappeared.

"What 'appened to ze frilly gartairs an' stockeengs, *Chérie*?" he lifted his head and, slowly, his lips curled, his eyes danced and he smiled wickedly down at her as he put on the thick French accent that he knew tantalised her so much.

"I took them off, you were angry with me," she looked at him in amusement.

"No, I wasn't, I just couldn't talk to you looking like you were; it was far too much of a distraction and the subject matter was very serious," his lips twitched.

"I could always put them back on again, if *Monsieur* would like?"

"Are we still feeling frisky, Baroness? I said you would be. I was going to make love to you again, but I got a bit thrown by your questions, and don't you dare start apologising, I told you," he tutted with a smile.

"Again? After all that trauma you put me through? Can a woman nearly die twice in one night?" she grinned saucily.

"I think you'll find, if you go and get back into bed and stop thinking about former wives, complaisant mistresses and too many paintings, and put your mind to current husbands and what they want to do to you next, you might find you're in the mood for all sorts of things, *Chérie*."

"Does that mean, after what we did, I'm your mistress now?" she wrinkled her nose at him and grinned.

"Only if you mean to be extremely salacious, perverted, accommodating, inventive, uninhibited, enthusiastic, available at any time, day or night, and of course with a very interesting wardrobe," he teased.

"That is a very disgraceful and extensive list of demands," she tutted. "It will come with an EXTREMELY high price tag."

"How high?" he grinned. "Oh, *Chérie*, I meant to buy you some jewellery as well as organising the portrait. I'm getting very forgetful in my old age," he chuckled. "Hmmm, I think sapphires would go well with those beautiful hazel eyes of yours and your colouring, and maybe some emeralds. Mistresses always demand a LOT of jewels, y'know."

An amusing thought of Isabelle popped into Elise's mind for a moment and she almost burst out laughing, but merely grinned. "We could go to Paris. We never did have a proper honeymoon. You could go jewellery shopping and I could extend my wardrobe, and reading matter," she winked at him. "And you'll need to take a wagon to the jewellers to carry it all as that list is actually more than disgraceful, the originator must be someone extremely depraved and demanding."

"Depraved and demanding? How on earth did you guess? And he's also extremely strange."

"Strange?"

"Can't deal with dead mice in traps," and Eddie threw back his head and laughed loudly, "but going to Paris is the best idea you've had today, Baroness. I happen to know there's some extremely interesting shops in Paris, or at least there used to be. I wonder if they're still there…you've NO idea what they sell in them."

"Do I want to know?" she gave him a wicked look.

"Probably not beforehand, it will make your lovely hair curl," he chuckled. "But you WILL find out. I think you rather like surprises," his hand roved over her bottom as he pulled her hard against him, "as well as everything else I did to you," he whispered.

"Oh Lord, does that mean I'll be dead again at the end of our visit?" her lips twitched.

"Very probably. I intend to make dying a regular occurrence, if you're willing, that is? And don't forget, you have to ask me if you want to die very badly."

"Only if you get to die sometimes too. Equality for women."

"In your dreams, *Chérie*," he laughed, "but, actually, I feel absolutely suicidal," he threw back his head and burst out laughing. "When can we leave?"

"I'd go tomorrow, but I can't go anywhere until I know Nicky is all right again."

"I quite agree, My Love, me neither."

"We could call our next child Versailles, or Louvre," she mused.

"Whaaat? Not that nonsense again, I'll never live it down. Francis gave me such stick after we called Harry, Hertford."

"Well, he could be Louis for short, or… hmmm, what's short for Versailles, Eddie?"

"I've no idea. Stop thinking about that and go and put your stockings on again, and nothing else. I've a half pot of jam to use up."

"MY LOVELY JAM! You Villainous Frenchman, I'd completely forgotten about that. How dare you raid my stock; have you any idea the hours it all took to make?"

"Well, it tastes a damn sight better on your nipples than a scone, I can assure you. Hmmm, how long will it take you to put your stockings on? I could go down and see if there's any cream left in the pantry. I could spread that elsewhere..."

"Edouard de Mornay, behave yourself, whatever are you thinking?"

"Ah, *Chérie*, in the words of someone very famous, or rather, infamous... I never behave myself in bed; in fact, the older I get, the worse I behave," and the pair of them collapsed into fits of laughter.

Chapter Twenty-Eight

Bella prowled around the house in Hertford Street in the early hours. She couldn't remember when she'd last slept properly, it had been bad enough while Nicky was recovering from his injuries down at Arlington, withdrawn one day and bad-tempered the next, until she was in despair, but now he was by himself at Litlington, supposedly recovering from some sort of breakdown according to her Uncle Francis, she couldn't bear it.

She was convinced his retreat to their country home had been her fault, her and her temper, and it had been weeks and the silence from Litlington was deafening. She'd given her word to her uncle she wouldn't go to him, even though her heart and mind cried out to her to do so, but she was at the end of her tether, sure being by himself couldn't help him. Loving care and tenderness was what he needed, surrounded by his family, especially the children. She tossed back the remains of the glass of wine she'd been drinking, anything to make her sleep, and morosely made her way back to her bedroom, looking in on her sleeping son and daughter on the way, envying Terrie as she lay, sprawled in abandon in her small bed, cuddling the large but softly stuffed lion she always slept with, an amusing gift from Benjy for her first birthday, claiming he'd designed and made it all himself. Lions!

Even the sight of the toy made Bella shiver and the images haunted her day and night: Daisy being eaten, torn apart limb by bloody limb; her abject terror at being thrust into the cage with them snarling at her and about to pounce; and then Nicky, left alone with the big one. Her nightmares were terrible, feeling herself being slowly ripped apart and eaten, with a smiling Bernheim watching from a distance, and she'd wake up in fright, shivering and covered in sweat, with no Nicky there to comfort, reassure and love her.

She missed him like she'd lost half of herself and she couldn't concentrate or do anything. She'd called into her gaming saloons but even the little problems there that needed solving couldn't distract her. Nor did the shops, nor Almack's where she'd gone with some friends, nor a couple of routs and parties she'd called into briefly. Jack was still away in the country, apparently going from one house party to another, courtesy of school friends, and her house was deserted and quiet after Terrie and Herring went to bed. She couldn't even sit and write in her diary, the empty pages staring up at her from before the episode in Richmond. She simply couldn't bring herself to write about any of her life since, it was all wound up inside her, unable to find an outlet.

She'd eventually gone to bed but simply lay there, frightened to go to sleep and decided she couldn't stay in London any longer. She needed to talk to her uncle, maybe get her aunt to persuade him to let her visit, so she determined to leave the following day and call in at Firle on her way back to Arlington. She had half a mind to simply take herself to Litlington and ignore her uncle, but although he was always wise and right with his advice to her, and she wasn't frightened of him and his undoubted anger if she disobeyed him, she'd given her word and she'd never broken it… but there was always a first time.

She pitched up at Firle to find, ironically, her uncle had ridden over to Arlington to see her father. As her aunt welcomed her with open arms, Terrie ran off with an excited scream along with an equally excited Lizzie, to find Bubbles and have a tea party with their dolls, and Marcus's nurserymaid took a frazzled Herring off to the nursery to fuss over. Bella followed her Aunt into her little sitting room and sank into a soft sofa with an exhausted sigh.

"Oh, Bella, My Love, you look simply terrible, completely done in; whatever have you been doing to yourself? I've heard it all from Francis and I know you must be out of your mind with worry, but still…" Cat sat down next to her niece and pulled her into her arms for a big hug and cuddle. "Come along, My Pet, tell Auntie all about it and we'll have some tea, then I'll tell you the latest news from Litlington, not that there's much to tell," she sighed.

"You look wonderful, Auntie," sighed Bella as she surveyed her aunt. "So slim… so… so blooming. Uncle Francis must be being extra nice to you," she giggled.

"Hah! I TOLD that man I looked better now I've lost some weight, much he knows about anything, expecting me to believe he prefers me fat. Once a bumpkin, always a bumpkin," she tutted with a smirk.

"Oh, definitely," Bella rolled her eyes at her aunt's comments. "Perhaps I ought to start calling him Uncle Bumpkin instead of Uncle Francis," she giggled again.

"Ah, that's better, My Love, you're laughing again. Now then, while The Bumpkin is out, and The Devil's Spawn are making mischief elsewhere that I don't want to know about, we can have a good gossip and catch up. It's been an age since I've seen you and I want to know all about EVERYTHING," she grinned.

They sat and talked for a long time and Bella poured her heart out to her sympathetic aunt about Nicky and how much she missed him, not knowing what to make of the updates that Francis had had from Litlington. Carstairs reported Nicky got up late, simply sat for hours in the library every day, dozing or ostensibly reading, but Carstairs doubted he took in a word and the newssheets that arrived regularly from London looked like they hadn't been touched. If it was fine, he sat and slept in the sunshine on a chaise on the terrace, sometimes down in a quiet, remote corner of the gardens where he'd take all his clothes off, so Carstairs had banned the maids from going outside on sunny days. He'd sent his secretary away with the polite order saying he couldn't give a toss about work and to refer himself to the Baron for any instructions. Most days he'd go to the stables and stand or sit morosely in Shadow's stall, talking to him, before returning to the house and the library again where he often played chess with himself, or solitaire. He ate little, only had the occasional glass of wine, and then went to bed. Some days he hardly exchanged a word with anyone, other than the cat or the horse. However, Carstairs said he didn't sleep and often prowled around the house at all hours, carrying a large candle, smoking and drinking brandy, but thankfully not to excess he was at pains to report, and then he'd go into the library and play chess with himself again. Carstairs said it was like living with a strange recluse and this had been going on for nearly a month.

"I simply don't know what to make of it either, My Love," sighed Cat, "and when Francis went over himself last week, it was exactly as Carstairs had described. Nicky was quiet and they sat and chatted a bit, and they had a game of chess. But he refused to go out for a drive and Francis said he hardly ate anything when they had dinner. However, he said Nicky was calm and he thought he was looking better, less haunted, and he noticed he was using his right arm perfectly well and managed to cut his food with his left, as normal, but Francis didn't mention it to Nicky as he didn't want to draw his attention to it, so there we are. The servants fuss over him so he doesn't want for anything, and I'm glad he sits in the garden and dozes in the sunshine, the fresh air will do him good. I'm sure that's much better for him than hiding away inside in that dingy library. It's nice and cosy in winter, but terribly dreary in summer, if you don't mind me saying so, My Pet."

"He does love the sunshine," sighed Bella, "and he always looks so handsome when he has a bit of a tan on his skin, like when he came back from Spain on leave and last summer in Valenciennes. Oh, Auntie," a tear rolled down her cheek, "what shall I do? I want to see him so much and I miss him so much. If I promise not to raise my voice or lose my temper, do you think Uncle Francis will let me go back there?"

"I really don't know, Bella. In a way, I understand and agree with what your uncle says about Nicky needing time and space to get well again, but, on the other hand, I do agree with you too; it's been a bit long now for our Nicky to be by himself, and I think he needs a jolt to get him back into the real world. The longer he drifts, the more he'll just sink into apathy; all this sitting around every day just doesn't sound like him at all. He never was one for sitting quietly, always restless..."

"That's what I think," sighed Bella. "He's normally such a fidget, and I'm sure having Terrie around would bring him out of the doldrums, he's so besotted with her. It was so unlike him to shout at her about nothing, back at Arlington; I was stunned."

"Mmmmm, well I think he's over that now from what Francis says, but it'll take more than Terrie to get him back riding again, or driving his curricle, or fighting Jack. Francis says it's almost like he's frightened of his own shadow, if you'll pardon the joke. Oh, and another thing, I nearly forgot. What do you think? He's taken off his lion necklace. I simply couldn't believe it!"

"Whaaaat?" Bella gaped at her aunt.

"He was only casually dressed when Francis called, although he had bathed and shaved apparently which is a relief to know, and wearing just an open shirt, buckskins and boots, so it was the first thing Francis noticed. When he asked where it was, Nicky said he'd broken the chain, but he wasn't bothered about the necklace anymore."

"I don't believe it." Bella was astonished and concerned. "There must be something wrong, Auntie. I know he didn't care for his father, but that necklace is all about being *Le Duc et Le Lion de Valenciennes*, not so much the fact his father gave it to him in the Fortress."

"Do you think it's because of Bernheim and the whole lion thing? That's the most plausible excuse; I simply can't believe the chain broke, can you? I mean, it's not as if he's doing anything, other than sitting around all day."

"That chain most definitely didn't break, unless he deliberately broke it himself," tutted Bella. "Actually," she mused thoughtfully, "now I come to think of it, the last thing I remember before we argued at Arlington and he disappeared back to Litlington was him fiddling and pulling on it; YESSS," she breathed, her eyes suddenly widening, "he told me he was trying to break it and he was swearing because he had no strength in his arms to do it, and when I remonstrated with him about it he told me he wanted to break it and take it off because he wasn't *Le Lion de Valenciennes* any more, he was just a useless man, and Bubbles was more of a lion than he was. Auntie, no matter what Uncle

Francis says about him getting better, he's taken his necklace off and I just know he won't put it on again until he really is better or has got over whatever maggot he's had in his brain that caused this strange breakdown."

"Oh no, oh Bella, how awful. That's not our Nicky at all. He was always so proud of his name and title, obsessed with it almost. What's happened to him?"

"I don't know, Auntie," and Bella promptly burst into tears.

"Now, now, My Love, he'll get better, I know he will. Oh, men are SOOOO stupid!" Cat seethed. "Such morons, so brainless. They sneeze and think they have one foot in their coffins, you should have seen Francis last time he caught a cold. He convinced himself he had the influenza and was on his way out each time he blew his nose. Useless man! How can Nicky possibly think because his arms were injured he wasn't a man anymore? It's just typical! Those poor beggars on the streets in London who lost limbs in the war would soon put him straight," she tutted. "I think I should go round to Litlington and give him a piece of my mind. I'd soon tell him to get over all this maudlin behaviour and get a grip," and she cuddled Bella in her arms and swore under her breath at the vagaries of the male sex in general.

"Oh, Auntie," Bella sobbed and half laughed, "that's just what Uncle Francis is scared I'll do, or Elise, and he thinks that's not the way to deal with Nicky. He thinks we need to go slowly and as his arm gets stronger, he'll realise it all for himself and come around naturally."

"Well, he's not realising very much at the moment, is he?" said Cat sarcastically. "Francis said his arm is definitely stronger as he can cut his food now quite normally, and he was using it subconsciously and it's been weeks, no months now, since it was injured, so it MUST be getting better. Oh, men! They can't see what's right under their noses sometimes; look at your father and Elise. How long did it take him to get round to marrying her? Good job she got *enceinte* is all I can say, or he would still be dithering, and how happy are they with little Harry?" she said tartly.

"They're like two peas in a pod," sighed Bella. "I'm so happy for him, and Elise is lovely and so funny sometimes, and she's determined to make Charlie more sociable and less of a bookworm. He's gone to

Hertfordshire to stay with Aunt Severine for a few weeks. I agree with her, running around with all his cousins and their friends will do him a power of good, and I heard Elise tell Papa to tell Aunt Severine to lock their library door to keep him out of it," and she smiled at Cat who laughed.

"I'd be surprised if there's anything in there worth him reading; Severine and her family aren't exactly academic, are they? The last time I looked in there everything was covered in dust; I've no idea what the housekeeper is doing to let it get like that, but that's beside the point, even if I don't think anyone uses the room from one year to the next, unless the children are playing hide and seek," Cat chuckled. "Anyway, you get my point," she sighed. "Even your uncle can be as dense as mashed potatoes sometimes. I remember years ago, just after you were born, he got some maggot in his brain about something and it took me and your dear Mama an enormous amount of plotting to give him the shock of his life to bring him back to his senses," and for a moment a huge smirk covered her face as her mind roved back to the incident in his study soon after she and Francis had married.

"Remind me to tell Uncle Bumpkin he's not only useless, but he's also as dense as mashed potato," Bella laughed, her aunt always managing to make her feel better. "That'll make The Shadow's day," and Cat chuckled at her niece before her eyes suddenly lit up.

"That's it!" she suddenly announced, sitting up straight and nearly knocking the tea tray over.

"What's it?" Bella looked confused.

"What we need to do to shake Nicky out of this lethargy he seems to be in, not to mention make him realise he's not a cripple."

"You mean, we can go round and give him a piece of our minds?"

"Ooooh no, My Girl, something much more subtle and Machiavellian than that," Cat smirked. "After all, haven't we promised Uncle Bumpkin none of us will go to Litlington until he says so?"

"Well, he did say to Papa and Elise and I when he came over to see us a few weeks ago that if Nicky hadn't recovered himself by the end of the month, then we could drag him kicking and screaming over here to try and sort him out, *en famille*."

"Ah, but it isn't quite the end of the month yet, is it? And we keep our promises, don't we?" and a wicked smile lit Cat's face. "Tell me, Poppet, if something really dire happened to you or the children, like another Bernheim suddenly appearing and threatening you, or carrying you off again, what do you think Nicky would do, in the normal scheme of things, if he wasn't out of sorts like he is at the moment?"

"What a terrible thought," Bella shuddered. "But that's a silly question, Auntie. He'd go completely insane and run after us and kill the man, just like Uncle Francis would if the same thing happened to you."

"Precisely," said Cat slowly as her eyes narrowed and she smiled evilly. "And I'm willing to stake my new fur pelisse that no matter what condition your Uncle Francis says Nicky is in, and necklace or no necklace, if he thought something was threatening you, something really dire that frightened the life out of him, a matter of life or death, he'd forget his own personal problems and just react subconsciously and follow his instincts and run after you, like a knight in shining armour, St George to fight the dragon," and Cat laughed at her wicked suggestion.

"Oh, Auntie, you've no idea, I actually did something like that to Nicky last year," sighed Bella, and she related to her aunt how she'd played her joke on Nicky to get him to Valenciennes to see her for a few days. "But I'd no idea what he'd really been doing behind the French lines and he was so angry with me, rightly so, despite the fact it was obvious he was worn ragged. I gave him such a fright though, he apparently just dropped everything and rode hell for leather from Wellington's camp over to Valenciennes, enemy lines or personal risk were completely irrelevant to him."

"That was very naughty of you, Bella, and I'm glad Nicky took you to task," Cat tutted, "even though you obviously didn't know what he was up to, spying on the French, but it just proves my point. Do you think he'd fall for something like that again?"

"Oooh, Auntie, he'd be so furious, I think he'd explode, given what I did before; but of course, I'd stake my life he'd do it if he thought I or the children were in any danger. Whatever have you in mind?"

"Well, you see, Bella, that's precisely what we want him to do, and given you actually did something like it before and he was angry, it will make him doubly angry, which is wonderful. When your Uncle Francis gets really, really furious, not that that is very often, thank goodness, he completely loses the plot. Do you know he even tried to strangle me once, a long time ago?" she mused with a reminiscent smile.

"Noooo? Really? What on earth did you do, Auntie? Not that you aren't much different. How many cups, plates, ornaments and vases have you broken over the years throwing at him?" giggled Bella.

"That is quite beside the point, My Girl," Cat tutted, then grinned, "and my aim is perfect, I usually manage to hit him with at least one missile."

"Poor Uncle, but why did he try and strangle you? That's a bit drastic, even for Uncle Francis."

"He thought I was having an affair with someone; Ricky Ambrose, to be precise."

"Uncle Ricky?" Bella gaped, then burst out laughing. "That's completely ridiculous."

"I don't see why, he's a very handsome man," tutted Cat, "and I can assure you, if I had given him the least encouragement, he would have behaved quite inappropriately. It was long before he married Sophy, of course, not that that man has ever stopped behaving outrageously, consummate charmer that he is."

"Oh, Auntie, that's too funny; he's Uncle's oldest friend. He'd never do anything untoward, even if he did find you hugely attractive, which I'm sure he did."

"Of course not, you know that and so do I, but your uncle was being completely irrational, and I mean IR-RATIONAL. Benjy and Clara saw him do it, frightened the life out of both of them, it did; anyway, that's beside the point, it just demonstrates what Nicky will do when he finds out."

"But I don't want to be strangled," laughed Bella, now somewhat recovered from her tearful outburst.

"Don't be silly, of course not, but he'll be so cross, he's likely to be totally irrational too. Tell me, has he ever put you over his knee, Bella?" Cat asked with an amused expression on her face. "I won't even ask if he's hit you as I simply know he'd never do that to any woman, he's just like Francis, no matter how mad you make him."

"AUNTIE! Really!" Bella tutted, not knowing where to look, "What sort of a question is that?"

"Come now, Bella, after some of the conversations we've had, you can tell me. That's nothing to some matters we've discussed," Cat smirked at her niece.

"Yes, he has," Bella muttered with twitching lips, "after my little joke at Valenciennes, actually, and on a couple of other occasions."

"Aha, wonderful!" grinned Cat. "And I won't ask if you enjoyed it, suffice it to say, he'd need TWO hands to do the deed if you resisted him, never mind if we can get him to ride to your rescue, and if we get him cross enough, I'd bet he'd spank you without a moment's thought... *et voilà*, problem solved!" she laughed, throwing her hands in the air in a very French fashion.

"You are soooo conniving, Auntie, you should be working for Ashcroft," chuckled Bella. "Where do you get these ideas? I think it's wonderful, but how on earth are we going to arrange it? It's all very well having the idea, but putting it into practice is a whole other matter, given the circumstances."

"Hmmm, let me have a ponder. Why don't you go and find out what The Two Terrors are up to, it's been very quiet, too quiet," she said thoughtfully, looking up at the clock on the mantel over the fireplace, "then I suggest you stay for dinner and overnight, so we can carry on our discussions if I can get rid of Uncle Francis after dinner. If he's been with your Papa most of the afternoon, he's bound to have work to do. If not, we can resume tomorrow morning and decide what to do next. How's that for a strategy? Miles Ashcroft will have nothing on the Duchess of Firle, take it from me. Madame Nefarious is my other name."

"You're so wonderful, Auntie," Bella hugged her. "I don't know what I'd do without you sometimes. Oh, he's going to be soooo angry, my bottom is twitching already," she giggled.

"You lucky girl," Cat smirked back, making Bella giggle all the more. "Now, off you go and heaven help those two if they've been up to mischief. Do you know, your uncle and I went off on a picnic a few weeks ago when he came down here to join me, and we stayed away overnight, and a certain Little Person who was very cross she wasn't allowed to come as well, decided to go and find a cow and bring it into the house as she wanted some cream on her jam tarts that she'd been making with the cook. The nanny thought she was having an afternoon nap. Hah! Idiot girl, doesn't she know who she's dealing with? How on earth she found it, or got the animal into the house, I'll NEVER know, never mind into the dining room. And where were all the servants? I've NO idea, drinking tea below stairs I gather... but poor Browning nearly had apoplexy, apparently, not to mention Mrs Potter and the housemaids and footmen, and the terrible aroma of cow dung that hit your uncle and I when we got back into the house was beyond belief. You know cow dung, it had gone all over a beautiful Aubusson rug and ruined it, and another very loose deposit sunk into the floorboards and we had to get some workmen in to lift a few where it had seeped through the cracks. You've simply NO idea the chaos she caused. Needless to say, your useless uncle had hysterics, doubled up he was, he literally cried he laughed so much; he didn't stop laughing for the rest of the day, whereas I had to spend MY day getting the house fumigated. I swear you can still smell it now in the dining room, and if you DARE mention it to your uncle over dinner, I shall never speak to you again. I'm so cross with him, he didn't say a word to her, never mind punish her, he just laughed and laughed. Heaven only knows what she'll try to bring in here next. Chickens? Pigs? Horses? It's all HIS fault, I tell you. She's HIS daughter..."

Bella had convulsed in mirth at this ranting tale of woe, not in the least surprised, and she was rolling around on the sofa, holding her sides, when Francis strolled in. "Hello, Poppet. Browning said you'd come to visit on your way back from Town. I've just come back from visiting your Papa and Elise. How lovely to see you. Are you staying... er... what on earth is so funny?" he sauntered over to the sofa and bent to kiss his niece, looking slightly nonplussed. She merely looked up at him, still laughing, and with a wicked look at her aunt went, "MOOOOOOOOOO!" and dissolved into further giggles as her aunt tutted venomously in French and her uncle burst out laughing.

"Aha, catching up on our latest visitors I see," Francis chuckled. "I wondered where she was, I take it the pair of them are making mischief while you're busy gossiping over tea? Well, if they've blown up the nursery while you're discussing reticules and bonnets, don't blame me," he joked.

"I was actually just going to see what they were up to," Bella sighed, wiping her eyes as she recovered from her laughter. "I didn't realise what the time was and they're VERY quiet, and Bubbles is on the missing list too, not like him to miss out on the opportunity of a pastry when he knows tea is being served, so if you'll excuse me, I'll go upstairs and investigate then tidy myself for dinner. I'll leave the two of you until then?" she quirked her brow at her aunt.

"Of course, My Pet, as you know, I have some matters to go over and we can carry on nattering after dinner as I'm sure Uncle Francis will be busy with more of his interminable paperwork for hours... isn't that so, You Disreputable Pirate? And don't I get a kiss hello as well?" she gave Francis a saucy, intimate look which made Bella's lips twitch.

"Oh, definitely, My Twiglet," Francis chuckled back at his wife and winked at her as he bent to give her more than the peck on the cheek he'd given his niece.

"You two get worse as you get older," laughed Bella, rising rapidly from the sofa, feeling like a gooseberry. "If you will excuse me, I definitely feel slightly *de trop* in here," and she hurried out the sitting room with her aunt's amused laughter ringing in her ears.

Bella spent a quiet hour with her uncle in his study after a relaxed and gossipy dinner, but he simply reiterated what her aunt had told her about Nicky and counselled patience for another couple of weeks. Since her aunt appeared to have retired by the time she escaped, she took herself to bed for another restless night, punctuated by her usual nightmares.

Chapter Twenty-Nine

The following morning Cat sent Bella a message with her morning hot chocolate, telling her to meet her in the stables after breakfast as they needed to go for a ride for further discussion on a certain matter, and on no account to mention anything to her uncle if she should bump into him. The three people sat and discussed the weather and their children over breakfast, and after Francis disappeared to his study to secrete himself with his estate manager, and various secretaries who had followed him down from London, eaten up with curiosity, Bella hurried off to the stables to see what her aunt was up to.

"Aha! It's all arranged," Cat grinned at her niece as they mounted up. "It came to me about three o'clock this morning while your uncle was snoring for England. Come along, My Pet, Auntie to the rescue. I've come up with the most wonderful plan and you need to come and see where the dastardly deeds will take place," and with that and a wicked laugh, she wheeled her spirited mare and took off out the stable yard with Bella in hot pursuit.

They finally pulled up at the bottom of the little track that led to Cat's hidden cottage and Bella looked at it wide-eyed as they trotted up to the entry gate. "Good heavens, Auntie, where on earth are we? I never knew this little house was here. Are we still on Firle land?"

"Oh yes, My Pet, just about. This used to be an abandoned game-keeper's hovel, many years ago, back around the time you were born, but Francis had it renovated and we used it as a little hideaway over the years when we wanted to escape from the formality of the house and the servants, not to mention the boys. I had it extended and refur-bished over the last year and it's just perfect for my idea. It actually occurred to me as somewhere suitable when you 'moooo'd' at your uncle yesterday afternoon."

"You were here when Lizzie brought the cow into the house?" Bella gaped at her aunt. "But I thought you said you were away?"

"We were away, we had a picnic and then we stayed away here," grinned Cat with a knowing look.

"Auntieeeeee," Bella tittered with a smirk, "that is so appalling, I don't wish to hear any more."

"And I've no intention of telling you any more," Cat tutted, "but actu-ally, I just wanted to spend some time talking to your uncle in private."

"Of course you did, as if there was nowhere private up at the big house," said Bella facetiously.

"Yes, well, never mind about that," said Cat airily as she dismounted and started to lead her horse towards the new stables, indicating Bella to follow. Having seen to the horses, she led Bella back towards the cottage and unlocked the front door with a key she pulled from her pocket and the two women went inside.

"Oh, Auntie, this is absolutely lovely," exclaimed Bella as she peered out into the back garden and the riot of rambling flowers and the little pond, then wandered around the downstairs rooms, admiring the big open fireplace and hearth in the main sitting room.

"Isn't it?" Cat sighed. "And no one ever disturbs us. It's so quiet and peaceful, there's not a soul around, not another cottage for miles. We can just be ourselves here. Francis is not allowed to bring any work and the children are banned. I cook and tidy up and he potters about outside or chops wood for the fire and brings in coal for the furnace out the back to heat the water. Fortunately, there's a little spring at the bottom of the garden, hence the pond, and your father came up with the complicated system to channel the water in for drinking, or to heat it up for a bath or washing, then drain it away carefully in a different direction along with the contents from the privy, into a cesspit, so it doesn't get mixed with the fresh spring water. It's so complicated I can't begin to understand it with all these endless pipes everywhere, but it does work, provided you keep the furnace lit. It's a simpler version of what he's done at Arlington and for Nicky at Valenciennes."

"You TIDY UP and COOK?" and Bella burst out laughing. "Oh no, I don't believe that for a moment," she giggled.

"I most certainly do, well, while we're in residence," Cat huffed. "I'm not completely useless, you know. Mrs Potter sees to the place herself and keeps it in order and stocked with essentials and clean linens and so forth, as we don't want any nosey servants knowing about it, and if we come we either bring a hamper of fresh food and drink with, although there's always wine and brandy here, or Francis goes hunting and shoots birds or rabbits and I cook in a pot on the range. Anything tastes good if you pour enough wine around it," she winked.

"It all sounds too bucolic for words," said Bella sarcastically. "Mr and Mrs Granville, local yokels," she giggled, "or should I say, what a PAIR of country bumpkins."

"Very funny," tutted Cat but then laughed, "anyway, don't you think this is the ideal spot to lure Nicky to? I think it's absolutely perfect. He can yell and rant at you to his heart's content and no one will hear, and what you get up to afterwards to make it up is totally your affair, and no one will hear that either," she smirked. "There's a bedroom with a nice big bed upstairs if you feel like staying and making use of that as well, and there's a bathing room next door, my pride and joy. I could barely drag your Uncle Francis out of the big bath in there last time we came here; he'd wallow for hours with a bottle of brandy and his cheroots.

"Oh Lord, Auntie, you're so disgraceful," Bella giggled.

"No, My Sweet, just practical, with a very clever brother!" she laughed. "Now then, the range isn't lit, so we can't make tea or coffee, but if you'd like to go and rummage around in the pantry out the back of the kitchen, I think you'll find some bottles of wine and I'll get some glasses and we can sit and I'll tell you my idea. There's nothing like a nice glass of wine to stimulate my creativity," she chuckled.

The two women sat and, amidst much giggling, Cat explained to Bella the plot she'd had running round in her mind since the previous evening and all night "...So you see, if we borrow a couple of tots from somewhere to run the errands and hand over the messages, Nicky will never raise a hand to them, unlike if we tried to hire someone, or got Jack or Alfie to dress in disguise and risk being discovered. What do you think? Aren't I a clever French yokelette? And, of course, we'll have to think up something really outrageous for you to wear. The crosser we make him, the angrier he'll be..."

"He'll kill me, I swear he will," Bella chuckled, "but if it works, it will deal with all the issues Uncle Francis seems to think he still has. Now, what on earth can I put on that will annoy the hell out of him?"

"Well, My Love, you know him better than me, so I'll leave that little decision to you. I'll deal with finding some children. They'll be pleased to earn some coins and Nicky will throw money at them if they look really pathetic. I'll tell them it's a big practical joke and they won't give a fig provided they earn some money."

"So, when are we going to carry out this nefarious plot?"

"Hmmm, that's what we need to decide. You heard your uncle last night, Nicky is still wallowing in some sort of lethargy and scared of his own shadow, but I do heed your uncle, Bella, even if I think we need to take matters into our own hands to break the impasse. How about next week? I can get the cottage prepared for you, stocked up with some food and drink and the water heated, and the children organised which is the key part, and that will take me a few days to sort out and rehearse them, and you can get your head around something to wear and an explanation of where you're going. I suggest you say you're coming down to visit me and your uncle again as Lizzie is getting bored. That sounds quite plausible, doesn't it? And if, by some miracle, Nicky suddenly gets a grip of himself and reappears in the

317

meantime, no one will be any the wiser and we can simply forget all this. It's just perfect, isn't it?"

"What if Papa and Elise decide to come with me?"

"Just make it a last minute decision. You could say you're coming for a few hours, say for tea, and then we'll just send a message back saying you've decided to stay over; it's easy."

"Machiavellian, totally Machiavellian," Bella laughed, "and who is going to write the threatening letters, you or me?"

"I think that needs to be a joint effort, and I'll write the final version as he's less familiar with my scrawl and I can disguise it better than you. How about we open another bottle and make a start? We've got to be very plausible, but really frightening in a subtle way," and Cat got up and went to a dresser to pull out some paper, a quill and some ink while Bella went to open another bottle of wine and the two plotters sat down at the table and set to.

They finally returned to Firle late afternoon and almost fell off their horses, obviously tipsy, and Francis strode out of the front door to greet them. He didn't look happy. "Where the HELL have you been all day? I was about to send out a search party," he yelled at them.

"'Ello Uncle, we got slaightly dee-layed," Bella swayed and giggled up at her irate uncle.

"Good God, are you DRUNK? You could have fallen off your horses, had an accident… and why didn't you take a groom with you? How many times have I got to tell you?" he turned to rant at his wife.

"Oh, do be quiet, You Bumpkin," Cat giggled and tried to swat Francis's bottom with her riding crop, much to the amusement of the watching stablehand who'd come round to collect the horses. "We were EX-TREEEMELY bizz-eee. We had a lot to dis-cussss and we stopped for some ree-fresh-ments on the way. It was all per-fec-telly harmless. Nenny-one would think we'd been up to no good," she replied airily and weaved, tottering slightly, in through the front door.

"Oh God," sighed Francis as he shooed a giggling Bella in after her, "have I got to put up with drunken abuse from the pair of you tonight? There's no way I'm sending you home to your father in this state, Young Lady, so I suggest you go and have a lie down and drink some coffee before we have dinner. And in case you'd forgotten, you left me in charge of those two anarchists while you were out carousing round the countryside all day, and you have NO idea what they got up to while I was sitting in my study trying to do some work; that governess is completely useless, worse than the nanny..." and with a stream of amused grumbles, wondering what they'd been up to, certain it was mischief of some sort, he followed the pair of them as they climbed up the stairs unsteadily, staring at his wife's suggestively wriggling bottom as he did so, wondering if she was doing it deliberately and followed her into their bedroom and shut the door, promptly forgetting to ask her any more curious questions...

Chapter Thirty

One day drifted into the next, and he'd lost track of the days and weeks as time passed in his own little reclusive world. He'd shut his mind to everything and everyone, trying not to think of Bella, how much he loved and missed her, and his children, and his family. The less he thought, the further away they all seemed, and he'd mastered the art of sitting for hours, almost in a trance, simply to while away the day and periodically dozing off. It was easier if he could lie outside in the sunshine, feeling the warm rays seep into his skin as he lolled on a chaise longue and slept, or just lazed in the grass, on hot days, out of sight of the house where he could strip off his shirt and breeches, not really caring who saw him as he lay and dozed naked in the summer sun. He wasn't hungry, wasn't even bothered now to drink himself to oblivion, he'd gone past that, distanced as he now was in his own little sphere of nothingness. He didn't want to talk to people: Carstairs, his valet, or the servants, as they just fussed over him; so he talked to Duchess, or went to the stables and talked to Shadow, telling him he'd be Jack's horse in future, when he got home from school, and he would be his new master, take him out riding and galloping across the Downs because he couldn't do that anymore.

He couldn't sleep at night, of course, the nightmares his perpetual enemy; he could hear hungry lions growling in the darkness, waiting to pounce on him somewhere, along with all his other fears, so he'd wander round the house, always with a large candle to keep the darkness at bay, and try and read or distract himself with cards or chess. Walking round and round the table as he'd play himself into the early hours. Somehow, if he dozed during the day the nightmares didn't come so it was easier all round if he didn't sleep at night.

And so one day merged with the following one, and one week merged into another and he lost track of time, days and dates. He vaguely recognised his right arm and shoulder were better as his valet helped him on with his jacket occasionally, but he never thought about his left arm, didn't want to think about it. It was crippled and he didn't want it cut off, and if he didn't do anything with it, apart from eating, it wouldn't get damaged again.

Sometimes, as he lay and dozed in the sun, he'd dream he was in Spain again, thinking about *Lionesse* back in her gambling salon in London and the things they'd done, or he'd dream of his former life as Leo, or León, or Nico. So many aliases, so many women in his past, but it was always *Lionesse* he fantasised over and he'd wake, hard and wanting like a randy youth. But he'd always caressed and relieved himself with his left hand, strangely, not his right; and now his left arm was useless he didn't even want to try and discover if it was something else he couldn't do, so he'd roll over and think about the darkness, cellars and rats, and torture, and hungry lions, and the hardness would quickly go away.

Francis came and Francis went, and he was like Carstairs and the servants, fussing, cajoling, pity in his eyes, and he didn't want to deal with it, so he just sat quietly, said yes and no, and eventually Francis left him to his peace and quiet again and time simply continued to drift by.

Nicky was sitting in Shadow's stall late one morning. It was grey and overcast and a cool breeze was blowing off the sea, so not warm enough to sit outdoors and inside the house was chilly. The weather matched his mood: grey, cool nothingness. The big horse nuzzled him as he lolled in the straw, searching for an apple or a carrot he usually had in his pocket. Nicky felt in an odd mood as he watched the horse munch the apple, he was unsettled, restless and miserable. He'd been like that for days. He hunched over and put his head in his arms, feeling the urge to cry, and a couple of tears leached out his eyes as he sat in the quiet stall, the warm, horsey smell comforting somehow as he tried to retreat back away from the reality his brain was pushing him towards.

The stables were quiet, not many horses in the stalls, only Shadow and the matched greys that pulled his curricle that Francis had sent for to tempt him out in, but was still lying idle, plus a couple of older horses the groom and stablehand used for errands, and a couple of ponies the servants used to go to the village in the trap. His coach and horses had gone back to Arlington for Bella to use and he could hear the horses shifting and stamping in the straw, restless, needing exercise. The groom and stablehand had made themselves scarce, as they always did when he came to talk to Shadow, so the little boy wandered into the stables, peering warily into the stalls and the big horses dozing there.

"Er... ello? Is th' Guv'ner 'ere? "Ello...?" a small voice spoke apprehensively.

Nicky ignored the voice.

"'Ello...? Is sumwun 'ere? Theys said ter cum look in th' stay-buls; I needs ter find th' Guv'ner, th' Dook. 'Ello...?"

Nicky looked up as a scruffy, dirty urchin, a child of about six or seven, stuck his head warily into the dimness of Shadow's stall, looking at the big horse fearfully. "'Ello... is, is you a groom?" he peered at Nicky and looked him up and down, then almost jumped out of his skin as the big horse whinnied and he backed out the stall in fright.

"Who are you?" Nicky sat up and looked at the unkempt child, wondering where he'd suddenly appeared from, assuming he must be from the nearby village.

"I's no-wun. I's lookin' fer th' Guvn'er, th' Dook. Is 'e 'ereabahts?"

"Why do you want the Duke? Who are you?"

"I's... I's carnts tell. I's gots a lettah fer 'im, is all." The child stared at the big man with a couple of bits of straw in his hair. He was only wearing a shirt, breeches and boots, and although they looked clean and quality clothes, the man must be a groom as he was lazing around in the straw, probably having a quiet nap while his master wasn't around, the shirt and breeches were probably his cast-offs.

"Why didn't you leave the letter up at the house? The butler or a footman would see to it," Nicky assumed it was a begging letter from some local worthy charity, probably for homeless orphans or similar, given the messenger.

"Nooooo, I carnts do that, 'tis urjint an' very pry-vit. I's bin told ter only 'and it ter th' Dook. Do yer knows where 'e is? I's in an 'urry, I's bin lookin' fer 'im everywheres this mornin'."

"Really?" Nicky was suddenly fascinated with this strange child.

"Yers, I mus' find 'im, an' quick. I'll gits a thrashin', I will, if'n I donts find 'im an' 'and over me lettah raight quick; afore noon, theys said."

"Whaaat? Who's going to thrash you?" Nicky looked at the thin, grubby little boy in alarm. He was dressed in almost rags and had a fearful, frightened look about him as he stared around.

"I's... I's carnts tell. I mus' find th' Guv'ner. Pleeeease, Mister, duz yer knows where 'e is?"

"No one is going to thrash you, I promise you that. How old are you?"

"I's six." The little boy stuck his chest out.

"What's your name?"

"No, Mister, I's carnt tell, pleeeeeease, I's gotta finds 'im, really I gotta," he pleaded, looking worriedly at Shadow who was pawing the ground. "Is 'e all raight? 'E won'ts kick me or nuffin', will 'e? 'E's bloody big..." the scruffy little boy looked up at the big horse and shuddered.

For the first time in weeks, Nicky actually smiled. "No, he won't hurt you, he just doesn't know you. His name is Shadow. Here," he pulled another apple from his pocket and held it out to the little boy. "Do you want to give him this? He's very partial to apples."

"Oooooh, er... nah... I's don'ts fink so, 'e'll 'ave me 'and orf," and his dirty hands quickly disappeared into his pockets in fright.

"No, he won't," said Nicky softly. "Come, you give him the apple, and I'll tell you where the Duke is. How's that?" and he took hold of one of the boys's arms, gently pulled his hand out of his pocket and put the apple in it.

"'E'll bite me, jes' look at 'is big teef," the urchin cringed away as Shadow, spotting the apple, whinnied and shook his head.

"He's seen his treat and he won't bite, I promise. He's only interested in his apple, here, let me show you," and Nicky crawled forward out the straw and crouched down behind the little boy, carefully putting his arms around him and making him hold his arm and hand out with the apple sitting on it. "There, see? Keep still, let him sniff and don't move your hand, just keep it flat like that."

"Ooooooh... er..." the little boy was obviously scared stiff but watched with big eyes as the horse merely leaned down and took the apple off his outstretched palm and suddenly the child laughed.

"It tiggled," he giggled, snatching his hand back and looking at it and then up at the horse.

Nicky smiled tenderly, "I told you he wouldn't hurt you. Do you want to give him a carrot too?"

"Oooh, can I?"

They went through the same performance again as Nicky broke in half the carrot he produced from his pocket and the little boy fed it to the big horse, giggling each time as Shadow snuffled into his palm. "There you are, did you enjoy that?" and the little boy nodded. "Do you want to pat him on the nose?" and he nodded again, completely engaged with the big, gentle man. Without thought, Nicky swung him up into his arms as he stood up and the wary little boy ran his small, grimy hand down the horse's muzzle, as Nicky showed him, patting Shadow with his left hand. The child laughed in glee as Shadow whinnied and then threw his arms round Nicky's neck in fright as he tossed his head and his long mane went flying and he stamped on the floor of his stall. "Don't be frightened, he's just restless. He won't hurt you... see?" he crouched down again and put the little boy back on his feet and encouraged him to pat as far up as he could reach on his flanks.

"Is 'e th' Dook's 'orse?" the child asked. "Um... duz yer looks after 'im?"

Nicky's lips twitched. "Yes, here and there."

"Can yer shows me where 'e is then? I's really gotta give 'im this lettah, real quick laike."

"I'm the Duke, actually; what's your name, Lad?"

"Nah..." the child shook his head as he stared up at Nicky. "Yer nots a Dook," he laughed, "yous gots straw in yer 'air, an' yous woz sleepin' in 'is stall, I's saws yer," he grinned suddenly and winked and showed a couple of gaps where some of his teeth were missing.

"I am the Duke, really I am. Shadow is my horse and I come to see him every day, to give him a little treat." Nicky crouched down in front of the child. "Give me this letter you have to deliver and I'll take you indoors and get you something nice to eat; would you like that?"

"Nah. Yer nots th' Dook. Dooks don't loll abaht in stay-buls," he shook his head, "'sides, I's needs proooff afore I 'ands it ovah, an' yous ain'ts gottit, I's can sees that."

"What?" Nicky looked confused and wanted to laugh. "Look, Lad, I promise you I really am the Duke. If you come up to the house with me, they'll all jump to attention when I walk in, you'll see. What more proooff do you need?" and he tried not to laugh as he spoke like the urchin for a moment.

"Yous ain'ts wearin' a neck-liss. I's woz tolds ter ask ter sees it; theys said th' Dook al-ways wears this neck-liss wiv a li-on on it. Yous ain'ts gotta neck-liss, so yous ain'ts th' Dook. Look, pleeease, Mister, yer seems a naice bloke an' all, but I's 'ave ter see 'im quick. I's in so much trubble, I's so late, I don'ts wanna 'ave th' belt on me back agin."

"No one is going to raise a hand to you. Christ, you're a small child. Who is this bully that thrashes you if you don't deliver something on time? I'll have his liver, who is he?" Nicky's face had registered his anger at the child's words.

"Nah," the boy danced away from Nicky in alarm, "pleeeease, I's gotta see th' Dook. I'S GOTTA. I's gotta sees a man wiv a neck-liss an' a li-on," he looked really agitated and frightened now.

"Look, er... oh, for God's sake, what IS your name? I AM the Duke,

I am Nicholas de Bresancourt, the Duke of Valenciennes. Do you want me to speak to you in French to prove it?"

"Yer a FRENCHIE?" the boy suddenly looked terrified and cringed. "Dids yer knows Boney?" he whispered.

"Yes, I am French and no, I didn't know Boney. For your information, I left France when I was your age and grew up here. Now do you believe me?"

"Nah," the boy still shook his head. "No neck-liss an' li-on, theys saids yous 'ad it on all th' time, nevah takes it orf, so yous carnts be 'im. Look, pleeeeease, I gotta deliver me lettah. It's desprit, urjint, if'n th' Guv'ner, th' Dook, don'ts git it on time, 'e'll go mad, I's tellin' yer, yer'll be's in so much trubble too, 'e's laike ter kill yer."

"I could just take it off you, you're only a little boy; oh, this is all a bit ridiculous," Nicky sighed. "Look, I broke my necklace, it's up at the house, that's why I haven't got it on. Come with me, you look like you could do with a glass of milk and a proper meal. I want to know where you've come from and who's threatening to beat you. I don't hold with ANYONE mistreating a child. Come along, Lad," he held out his hand, "come with me, give me the letter if it's so important and I'll read it on the way, and if you insist, I'll show you the necklace while you have something to eat."

"I's 'ids it," the boy backed away as he whispered, "I's not stoopid. Go an' git th' neck-liss an' shows me, an' I'll git th' lettah. No neck-liss, no lettah. If'n yous really is th' Dook...?" he looked at Nicky doubtfully.

"Oh, for God's sake, what the hell is this all about? If this letter turns out to be some sort of joke or a plea for a donation to charity, I'll have serious words with whoever sent it, not to mention threatening you, and I will get to the bottom of that, M'Lad."

"Go an' gits yer neck-liss an' meets me back 'ere in ten minits, an' don'ts be bringin' no-wun wivs yer, or I'll not 'and it ovah. I tolds yer, 'tis urjint an' pry-vit," and to Nicky's complete astonishment the boy turned and raced towards the door of the stables. He turned as he paused in the doorway, "Ten minits. Laife or deff..." and he disappeared.

"What the Devil?" Nicky stared after him, nonplussed, and slowly walked to the stable doorway and peered around. All was quiet and deserted and there was no sign of the mysterious little waif. He couldn't make it out at all but there was something a bit disturbing about it, and, not quite knowing why, he walked purposefully back to the house and up to his bedroom. He went over to a box on the top of his dresser and lifted the lid. He rummaged amongst various stick pins and watches and fobs and finally picked up his necklace... and for a moment he stared at it. It had been mended, his efficient valet no doubt, and he sighed. He would have completely ignored the child if it wasn't for the mention of his necklace, it was very strange and an odd feeling suddenly ran down his back. He grasped the chain in his hand, picked up a handful of gold coins from a bowl on the dresser and hurried out the room and almost ran back to the stables, rushing past an astonished Carstairs on the way. The boy was waiting nervously. Nicky held out the necklace. "Here you are, one li-on neck-liss. I am the Duke, give me the letter," he ordered as he held out his hand.

"'S'not broke? Whys arnts yous wearin' it?" the boy looked up at him.

"My valet had it mended, I didn't realise, but I... I didn't want to wear it anyway."

"Whys not?" the boy stared. "Theys said th' Dook nevah takes it orf, it woz pre-shuss, spe-shul..."

"It was, it is. It's a long story. Look, it's not important and none of your business. Give me the letter," once more he put his hand out.

"Nah," the child shook his head, "puts it back on. I's 'ave ter gives th' lettah ter th' man 'oo's wearin' a li-on neck-liss."

"Oh, for fuck's sake..." Nicky swore, his temper and some rising niggle of concern increasing by the minute.

"Go on, puts it on," and he watched as Nicky struggled with the catch, pulling it round to his chest, swearing and muttering as he tried to do the necklace up.

"Oh, cum'ere, lets me do it fer yer," the boy sighed. "Crowch dahn, I carnts reach up there, yous too big, laike yer 'orse," and as Nicky sank in front of him, the boy fiddled briefly and the little lion hung once more to nestle in the tawny chest hair. "Izzit gold?" he asked.

"Yes."

"Why'd yous wear it? Blokes don'ts wear neck-lisses, usual laike?"

"My father gave it to me, a long, long time ago, in France, before he died," Nicky said quietly.

"Oooh. Dids 'e 'ave 'is 'ead chopt orf wiv th' king an' queen an' uvver dooks?"

"You know about that?" Nicky raised his eyebrows, obviously the waif had had some basic education or had picked that bit of history up from somewhere. "No, but he died in the *Conciergerie*. That was the prison they kept some of the aristocrats in before they went to be executed, a bit like the Tower of London, if you know what that is… but he didn't lose his head like all the rest of his peers. They hadn't got the guillotine going when he died."

"Oooh, er…" the boy pulled a shuddering expression at the mention of the guillotine, obviously knowing what that was as well. "Whys a li-on?" he lifted the little charm and peered at it.

"Because, our family, all the Dukes, were known as *Les Lions de Valenciennes*, The Lions of Valenciennes. Valenciennes is a place in northern France where we come from, and we got the nickname because of our unusual colouring. Look at my hair and eyes; it's a bit silly, but there you are…" he shrugged.

The child cocked his head on one side, stared at Nicky's tawny hair, tanned skin and his strange golden coloured eyes with the black flecks in them. "Yer do's looks like a goldin li-on. I's seen a pic-ture of wun once, on a postah it woz. Theys 'ave 'em in The Tower o' Lonnon. Sees, I's do knows abahts that. 'Ave yer seen one, then?"

Had he seen one? Nicky almost blanched with the memories, he'd pushed them all away, deep into the recesses of his mind for the past weeks and months, except when they reappeared in his nightmares or he heard the growling in the darkness of his mind. "Yes, I've seen one, a real one," he whispered.

"Is yer as fierce as a real li-on then? Rawwwrrrrrr…" the little boy clawed the air in jest. "Yer a very naice bloke, fer a Dook," he cocked his head the other way.

"Thank you, and no, I'm not fierce, I'm not a li-on. Not anymore. Will you give me the letter now?"

"Well, I finks yous is a li-on, yous an' that 'orse o' yers, big'an' fierce... 'ere' yer go," and finally, he pulled out a creased and grubby folded package from inside his torn and ragged shirt and handed it over.

Nicky dug in his pocket and pulled out a handful of gold coins. "Here you are. Look, I want you to take these and stay away from whoever is beating you. Don't you have any parents who look after you or is it one of them who beats you? Where do you come from? If you don't have a loving home, you can stay here and we'll look after you and find you somewhere kind and caring to live. I promise. I'm a Duke and when I give someone my word, I never break it. So would you like to stay here with me?"

The little boy just looked at him, a strange expression on his face. Suddenly, he leaned forward and kissed the crouching man on the cheek. "Takes care, Guv'ner; laike I's saids, yer a good bloke an' a li-on fer sure. Thanks fer lettin' me feed yer' 'orse an' keeps yer neck-liss on in future," and with a cheeky smile, he darted round Nicky and scampered out the stables and raced off.

Nicky turned, watched the ragged child disappear and shook his head. He still didn't even know his name. Slowly, he rose to his feet and turned the package over in his hand. It was simply addressed:

URGENT & CONFIDENTIAL:
  The Duke Of Valenciennes

and sealed, but with no insignia in the wax. The writing looked strange and unfamiliar and was scrawled by someone not very well educated, he surmised. He broke the seal and unfolded the parchment, and a small gold chain dropped to the stable floor. He bent to pick it up and recognised it instantly. Holding a separate folded sheet in one now shaking hand, as the hairs on the back of his neck rose, Nicky read the main letter and slowly, his tanned face went white. He reeled back against the side of Shadow's stall as he took in the words that had taken Cat and Bella, with several bottles of wine, backed up with only some hard cheese and crackers Cat had found in the pantry, all through a progressively drunken afternoon to create... amidst much giggling, laughter, and many drafts and screwed up pieces of paper which had been burned in the grate before they left the little cottage.

Sir,

I have your Wife. As Proof, you will find her Lion Charm Necklace enclosed. I gather, as with yourself, she never takes it off.

I was one of the Group of Men who worked for the Frenchie, Mr Bernheim, and was in charge of the Band that was supposed to take your Ward, Jack Vallance. As you know, he was Delayed returning to London from Eton, so we Waited, but it all went Wrong and the Dog survived and got back to Berkeley Square and the Alarm was Raised. Therefore, we had no chance to Have Him, and the same Happened to the Men who were to Take your Daughter and the Duke of Firle's Daughter. We were on our Way Back to Richmond for Further Instructions, but got held up, so by the time we Arrived at the Farm, we saw the Military were there and knew the Game Was Up, and Scarpered, Quick.

You would never have heard from me, but Somehow, the Authorities have traced me and are on my trail. I know the Runners and Other Men are now after me as the rest of my Small Band have Disappeared.

I thought I was just doing a Kidnapping, and your Family would simply be held to Ransom as I know how Rich you are. I didn't like that Business with the Lions, it was a Sickening and Evil Joke, and Mr Bernheim was undoubt-edly mad, but I had already had enough of my Life here and wanted to Get Away and make a New Start and not get my Neck Stretched. I am therefore off to the Americas. I have Some Learning and there are Opportunities there for a man like me, on the Right Side of the Law, for a change. I have managed to Escape out of London and am on my way to take up my Passage. However, the Pressing Situation means I had to Leave in a Hurry and thus find myself Short of Funds.

Your Wife was by herself again at Le Lion d'Or, so I am afraid I Took Her once more and brought her with me as Security in case I was followed. All I want is 500 Guineas to pay for my Passage and to get me Started in the New World, surely a Pittance to pay for a Man of your Wealth and Standing? I had Difficulty tracking you down as you were not in Hertford Street and not with the Rest of your Family at Arlington or Firle, and then you were always Indoors at your House in Litlington and Never Went Out. I have No More Time to wait now as have to Leave the Area Today. I know those Men will catch up with me Shortly if I do not Keep Moving.

If you want Your Wife back, Untouched and Unharmed, follow the Instructions on the Enclosed Map. If you do not concur, I will simply Take Her With again, and can Sell Her in Portsmouth or Bristol or Liverpool on my way. I know Men there who will pay a Large Amount for such a Hot Tempered, Beautiful and Spirited Woman who they can Subdue and Collar and Pimp Out around the Docks for a Nice Profit.

So, Your Grace, the Choice is Yours. I am not a Cold Murderer like the Frenchie and Some Others in his Employ, and am sure you will Trace Her anyway, in whatever Port I leave her at, and Retrieve Her in due course, but you Might Not Like where she has been In The Meantime, provided no one else has Bought Her, of course. Surely 500 Guineas is Cheap at Half the Price?

You have until the hour of FOUR, Today. Otherwise, She and I will be gone.

PS: Do not bother Questioning the Boy. He knows Nothing, and is only a Gutter Urchin and Lazy Wretch.

It was a complete masterpiece and Cat and Bella thought it plausible enough, given what had come to light in the aftermath of that dreadful day. They well knew Ashcroft was leaving no stone unturned to find any more of Bernheim's accomplices, and make sure his whole nest of vipers was dealt with. As far as Francis knew, and as he'd told Cat when they'd adjourned to their little cottage, Ashcroft hadn't traced anyone as it appeared they had all been killed, including the four Francis had come upon in the farmhouse who had been tasked with taking the little girls, and they'd realised it was a sheer twist of fate that had saved Jack... but of course Nicky didn't know the updated information so the story would all seem quite credible to him.

The letter seemed believable and the underlying threat was there, from a man who was conniving and desperate, obviously educated enough to write a menacing letter, but also a hardened criminal who was happy to kidnap anyone for money, even if he didn't like what was going to be done to them. The two women had pondered over the peril Bella would be in, deciding that threatening to kill her was far too simple, and they'd come up with all sorts of terrible and salacious ideas to wind Nicky up, worse than a gothic novel, before deciding to 'sell' her in the docks of Portsmouth or Liverpool, having no idea if that sort of thing went on, but assuming it did in the alleyways and dark streets near the wharves, warehouses and moorings, where no sensible people roamed alone or unarmed. Nor had they any idea of how much money a man like they'd invented would want, so they'd taken a guess, Bella having no idea how much ready money Nicky kept locked away at Litlington that he could lay his hands on at short notice.

After she'd left Firle the following day, her own precious necklace safe in her aunt's jewellery box, Bella had returned to Arlington and casually mentioned she'd called into Firle to see her aunt and uncle on the way back from London, and Lizzie was desperately upset that Terrie had left again so soon. She'd therefore promised to take her back the following week for another visit and dollies' tea party with Bubbles. In the meantime, she'd realised she'd left some extremely important documents about *Le Lion d'Or* unsigned, so she'd HAVE to make a quick journey back to Town to deal with the matter.

Her father and Elise seemed unusually distracted, but Bella's head was so full of her own plans and schemes she didn't take much notice, and they were indeed so engrossed with each other they vaguely dismissed Bella's stories about returning to London and return visits to Firle, only being delighted to have the house to themselves again for a few days.

Bella left Terrie behind and hurried to London to investigate her wardrobe and come up with some sort of enticing or outrageous outfit that would tip her enraged husband over the edge when he caught up with her. Her head full of suggestions made by her drunken aunt as she'd got to the bottom of her umpteenth glass of wine, she eventually ran Benjy to earth and, having fortified herself with a couple of glasses of brandy, told the bemused couturier she wanted something 'very special' to cheer up her husband who was in the doldrums and discussed her ideas. Highly entertained, and allowing his salacious side full rein, the creative and camp Benjy tittered and set to, and Bella returned back to Arlington knowing if what she was going to dress herself up in didn't have the desired impact on the former rake and womaniser, she might as well consign herself to a convent.

Chapter Thirty-One

Nicky read the missive once more and felt as if he'd been shot, again. He opened the second piece of paper with shaking hands. It was a map with instructions, telling him to bring the money to hand over at a deserted folly marked on the map, and then he'd be told where to find his wife. He was to come ALONE, or else, as he would be watched. He immediately knew where the folly was, he'd been there and knew what it hid underneath. It was on the borders of the Firle Estate, miles from anywhere on a hillock amid deserted fields. It was always deserted there, so an ideal place for an illicit rendezvous with no chance of an ambush, either from the kidnapper or from his side, if he did take anyone with him.

He just reacted, he didn't even stop and think, images coursing through his mind of his precious Bella being bandied about and abused by the dregs of humanity who inhabited the dockyards. He turned and ran, yelling and shouting for a groom or stablehand to saddle up Shadow as he raced towards the house. All was quiet as he burst into the hallway and bumped into Carstairs. "I'm going out, get Shadow saddled and brought round in five minutes or you're all dismissed," he yelled and shot up the stairs, two at a time, leaving the astonished butler with his mouth hanging open. To his credit, Carstairs galvanised himself and started shouting for a pair of footmen to get to the stables, saddle up His Grace's horse and bring it to the front door immediately, or they'd find themselves out on their ears.

Nicky charged into his bedroom and over to the fireplace and pressed a brick in the surround. Just as in her apartment at *Le Lion d'Or*, and where it had been copied from by the assiduous Bella, the stone slid back and he grabbed several bags of coins which he tossed haphazardly on the floor as he pressed the switch again. He threw on the nearest jacket to hand from his armoire, picked up the bags and stuffed them in the pockets then raced out and downstairs again. He burst into his study, somewhere he'd not been since he'd arrived at the house weeks before, and went to a cupboard there. He pulled out a brace of pistols, checked they were loaded, and stuffed them in the waistband of his breeches and then picked up a stiletto which he shoved down inside one of his boots. Finally, he picked up his rapier from where it was resting in a stand in a corner and sprinted back to the hall, buckling the belted scabbard around his waist as he went. Carstairs looked from him to his rapier, noticed the pistols and gasped. "Is everything all right, Your Grace? Whatever is the matter? Is there a problem? Where are you going? Do you need assistance...?" All sorts of frightening thoughts raced round the concerned butler's head for a moment; ever since the 'lion affair' as he privately referred to it to himself and Browning, he was wary of everyone and everything, especially strangers, and especially back in London. He'd been shocked to his very core at the events he'd witnessed and doubted he'd ever get over terrible memories, not to mention the tragic consequences they seemed to have had on his brave young master.

"I'm absolutely fine, Carstairs. Is Shadow ready?" he and a concerned Carstairs headed out the front door to look towards the stables and they both spotted a groom riding the big horse up towards the house. "Ah, wonderful. Efficient as ever," and he ran down the steps of the house towards them.

"But... Your Grace... where are you goinggggg?" Carstairs shouted after his retreating back.

"I'm going to get my wife," was all Carstairs heard as he watched the groom slide off Shadow's back and Nicky instantly leapt up in his place and grasped the reins, pulling on them and turning the big horse in the process as his boots settled in the stirrups, and within seconds, horse and rider were galloping down the drive as if the hounds of hell were after them.

"Well, I never did..." muttered Carstairs to himself. "Mad; absolutely, raving mad. But he's on the horse so that's progress, and he thought nothing of it by the looks of things, and there's nothing the matter with his arm either... but where the devil is he going?" He shook his head as he spoke to himself and turned back to the house, pausing for a moment to look skyward. "Oh, Your Grace, life was so much more NORMAL when you were with us. I DO miss you..." and with a shake of his white-haired head, he headed back inside the front door, issuing orders to the hovering maids to go and air the Duchess's rooms and make them ready, and those of Lady Thérèse, and the nursery for the little Lord, as they were apparently all on the verge of returning at last

Leaning low over Shadow's neck, Nicky raced along, horse and rider in perfect accord. They sailed over hedges, gates, walls and fences, across fields and ditches, completely ignoring the map. Nicky was taking the shortest route he knew to get on to Firle land and reach Francis's Folly as he pulled out and glanced at his pocket watch. He toyed with stopping to get Francis, assuming he was still at Firle, but it would be just his luck he'd be out somewhere, even gone up to London for a few days, and the threat of something happening to Bella was too much of a risk to justify the diversion and delay... besides, dealing with a single man would be no problem for him.

Bella's chain was wrapped around his wrist and he kept looking at it, his mind full of her and the danger she was in; he loved her so much, his heart couldn't deal with the idea of something happening to her. Deep down, he admitted to himself he'd missed her beyond anything: her sauciness, her bossiness, her temper, her laughter, her all-consuming love and devotion to him; and he wanted her. The idea of another man taking her, maybe doing what Bernheim had done to her, was almost agony. And this was all His Fault. He should have been with her, protecting her, not wallowing in self-pity in Litlington, hating the world and retreated from it. On and on he berated himself, praying the love of his life was still safe and he'd get to her in time, wondering what she might already have suffered at the hands of one of Bernheim's thugs, even if this one appeared to have a smidgeon of intelligence. Whoever he was, he'd discovered his captive was no meek and obedient woman by the comments in the letter, so had he knocked her around to subdue her, or had he done more than that???

Round and round in his head it all went as the big horse ate up the miles, pounding across fields, scattering grazing cows and sheep in its wake and trampling unheedingly across crops.

Bella had been slightly apprehensive at the thought of Nicky riding hell for leather; she herself also worried about his arm, but Cat had been adamant. She said she'd never seen such a good horseman as Nicky, nor one who had such empathy with animals, especially horses... and now lions!! He'd been riding since he was five when Francis had bought him his first pony and taught him to ride it, and had even let him ride Nero, his own big black stallion, now very old and even more crotchety, but still in the Firle stables where he was cossetted and indulged by Francis, and of whom Nicky had never had the slightest fear, even at five years old; which was more than could be said for the grooms and stablehands who had tended to give the big, temperamental beast a wide berth, and still did. Cat said Nicky had such a way with horses, he could ride anything, with his eyes shut or his hands behind his back, and he'd never fallen off or been thrown, ever, as far as she knew; therefore, as far as she was concerned, it wouldn't be an issue.

And she was right. As horse and rider slowed when the little temple came into view, Nicky pulled on the reins and patted Shadow's heaving flanks as he pulled up, coat sweating and flecks of foam at his mouth. Nicky leaned over and crooned to the animal, tugging on its ears and scratching between them, which the horse loved. He sat back, breathing heavily himself, and looked around, but all he could see were fields of sheep between him and the hillock, and the heavy grey clouds out over the distant Channel. He kicked the exhausted horse again and set off for the folly, arriving there and sliding down off Shadow's back, rubbing his nose as he looked around warily. He drew out a pistol as he slowly climbed the handful of steps up into the odd little edifice that was Francis's Folly. There was no one there, all was silent. So, with nothing else to do and sending up a silent prayer, he sat down on the solitary marble bench to wait and fret.

Back at Litlington, the little boy ran as fast as his legs would carry him around the back of the stables, down through the orchard and then disappeared into some light woodland. A woman was sitting on the trunk of a fallen tree, reading a book, her horse cropping some grass nearby as he skipped up to her, a big grin on his dirty little face, holding out his hand. "Looks wot I gots, Yer Majisty: TEN GUINEAS!" His eyes were as round as saucers.

"Hello, Bertie. Didn't I tell you he'd give you some money as well?" Cat laughed and ruffled the hair of the little boy. "Did you give him the letter? I was beginning to think he was never going to come to the stables today."

"Yers, Yer Majisty, an' we wents frew all that kerfuffle wiv 'is neckliss," he grinned. "S'bin mendid an' 'e cudn't doos it up 'isself, but I's dids it fer 'im, so 'e's gots it on agin nah, good an' propah."

"Good boy. You obviously said all the things I told you, and you practised too, to get it right, that's why you got ten guineas. Always a soft touch, our Nicky," she sighed with a loving smile.

"Oh yers, laids it on good an' propah I's dids; said me mastah wud take 'is belt ter me back agin if'n I didn'ts give 'im th' lettah quick, an' 'e'd thrash me good. Th' Dook didn'ts laike that much, 'e's a naice bloke, ain't 'e? Not laike a Dook. Minds yous, yer Dook ain'ts much laike a Dook, neivah," Bertie opined thoughtfully.

"No, he's not, though he does have his moments," chuckled Cat, only imagining the conversation that must have gone on, wishing she could have heard it herself.

"'E gaves me an appul an' a carrit fer 'is orse, big buggah t'ain't it? Shadder 'is name is. D'yer knows I's only founds 'im lollin' in its stall in th' straw; bin asleep there I reckins, 'e 'ad bits in 'is 'air. Didn't fink it woz 'im at first as 'e didn'ts 'ave 'is neck-liss on, but 'e woz jes' as yer tolds me, all goldin 'air an' funny eyes; 'e duz looks like a li-on, after all, jes' laike them there pick-chers theys showeds us in skool. Li-ons lives in th' jun-gul in sumwheres called 'Frica, dids yer know? 'S'all 'ot an' sticky there wiv lotsa trees an' monkeys an' big fings called ellee-fants, an' li-ons is verry fierce an' danjerus, wiv big teef, an' goes RAWWWWWWR..."

"Is that so? Well, I don't think I'd like to meet one then. Just as well we don't have them here in England, isn't it?" Cat nearly choked, trying to keep a straight face, the irony of what she'd said known only to her. "And, I'm glad you were paying attention for once, You Little Imp," Cat tutted with a smile. "My, you do look dirty. I almost overdid the ragged look, so we'd better get you cleaned up before I take you home. Mrs Baker will have a fit if she sees you like that... and have you lost another tooth since last week? That makes you look even more wretched," and Cat chuckled, wondering if Nicky had presumed some villain had knocked the missing teeth out.

"S'not much diff'rint from when's I's were in th' tenemints," he shrugged.

"Yes, but you're not in those terrible tenements anymore, are you? You're Mr and Mrs Baker's pride and joy. Now come along, up on my horse with you and you can tell me EVERYTHING you said to him and what he said to you, on our way back, before I die of curiosity," and Cat heaved the little boy up on to the back of her horse.

"That there Dook, the goldin wun, 'e pickt me's up an' let me pat 'is 'orse; I's fort yers woz big, but that Shadder is 'nor-mouse," he waved his hands in the air descriptively.

"He picked you up?" Cat grinned, enormously pleased with that bit of intelligence.

"Oh yers, even tho' yer saids 'e 'ads a bad arm. Didn'ts seem much wrong wivs 'it ter me, onlys a bits ov a fiddul wiv th' catch on 'is neck-liss, but thats woz jes' a fiddulfaddul, needs littul fingies likes mine," he grinned wickedly, waggling his fingers in the air as Cat mounted the horse behind him, using the tree trunk to help, sitting astride, wearing a tight pair of men's breeches under her hoiked-up skirts which had caused the little boy to giggle when he'd first seen her do it.

"Hmmm, yes, nifty fingers, which you DON'T have any more, do you, My Lad?" Cat tutted, putting her arms round the boy and pulling on the reins.

"Oh noes, Yer Majisty, nots since I's bin 'ere in th' cun-try wiv Ma, Missus Bakah. I's promissed, didn'ts I?"

"Good boy. Now then, are you ready for another gallop? Hold tight, Bertie, I've got to get back to Firle, get you cleaned up and home again, and then I've got another errand to run. Do you think Maisie will be all right down at the folly?"

"Piece o' cake," Bertie turned his head to look at the woman behind him, the woman who'd dragged him out of a filthy tenement in London where he'd been living with a gin-sodden aunt after his mother had died, and who sent him out on the streets begging or thieving, and then spent his meagre collection on more gin for herself, instead of feeding him. He was another of Cat's waifs and strays and was now living with a warm and loving couple who'd lost their own child to a fever a few years before and were now delighted to give a home to another little boy, to replace the one they'd lost. They'd also adopted a little girl, so he now had a sister. Maisie was slightly older but from similar circumstances as Bertie, and they all lived over near the county town of Lewes.

"Right then, off we go, then bath and a couple of cook's nice cream pastries you like so much with a glass of milk. Then one of our stable-hands will collect Maisie and you can go home in that nice big coach you like, how's that? And remember, this is all a secret. A special big joke for the nice golden Duke. He's going to be soooo surprised, and everyone will laugh a lot when they hear about it afterwards."

"Yer sure tis a nice s'rprise, Yer Majisty?"

"Look, Bertie, I am NOT the Queen," Cat chuckled. "I'm only a Duchess, you know that, so it's proper to call me Your Grace, but I don't like that much either, so just call me Mrs Granville, how's that?"

"Yous is funny, yous an' th' Big Dook." Bertie shook his head. "Duz yer Big Dook sleep in a stabul as well sumtimes? Dids yer know, 'e tol' me's, t'othah day whens 'e fahnd me's in yer gardin wiv yer fuff-ee dog, an' e' tiggled me's, I's arsked 'im 'ow cums 'e woz so big an' strong, an' 'e tolds me's it woz coz 'e woz ree-lee a pie-rat in diz-guyz, but that's stoopid. 'Ow can a dook be a pie-rat?" and he shook his head.

Cat burst out laughing. Bertie reminded her so much of a younger Jack sometimes, with his cheeky grin and humour, and she made a note to find someone to help him with his terrible gutter accent. "He's the stupid one, and exactly, how can a duke be a pirate? But it has been known for him to sleep in a stable, and a lot of other odd places, for he is a very unusual duke too. But he is wonderful and the very best of dukes, big or small, I promise, and I wouldn't change him for the world. Now then, tell me what happened back in the stable with Nicky, our other duke?"

Chapter Thirty-Two

Nicky sat, and sat, periodically getting up to stalk around the little pavilion, constantly pulling out his watch, reading and re-reading the menacing letter, out of his mind with worry, anger, and a host of emotions that roiled around his stomach until he felt sick. It was now gone three o'clock. He had less than an hour to get to wherever Bella was being held and he'd no idea where that was. He didn't want to fight the bastard, no matter that he wanted to throttle him with his bare hands; five hundred guineas for Bella's life was cheap, a mere nothing for him, just as the man had said. He'd have given his fortune to save her from what the bastard had threatened to do with her. It was chilly in the open-sided folly, a strong breeze blowing in from the sea, but despite that, perspiration ran down the sides of Nicky's face as he sat in turmoil.

In a stand of shrubbery, in a hedgerow at the side of the field of sheep, a little girl was looking at the watch the Lovely Lady had given her, telling her to wait until the hands were both on the three and then to take off her dress, shoes and stockings, ruffle her hair, put on the ragged, dirty dress, put some mud on her face, hands and feet, dig her nails in the dirt, and then go and give the letter to the man who would be waiting in the folly and collect the bags of money he would give her and to follow the Lady's instructions about that. She was then to run back and hide in the hedging as best she could, until he rode away, then change back into her clean clothes again and go and meet the nice young man in the little trap from the big house at Firle, who would be waiting to collect her on the road where she'd been shown, take her back there to collect her step-brother, wash herself clean again, have some tea and go back to her adopted parents in Lewes, with a bag of money all for herself and her family. The Lovely Lady, Mrs Granville, although she'd heard she was really a Duchess, which was very strange, was the one who'd taken her away from the dirty whorehouse where she'd been born and brought up as no more than a slave to the coarse women who lived and worked there, after her mother, another prostitute, had died. She'd do anything for her, and to help her play a practical joke on one of her family was no problem at all, anything to pay her back for what she'd done for her, and little Bertie. She rehearsed her lines, smiled mischievously to herself and carried out her instructions.

Nicky turned from his contemplation of the distant view of the sea as Shadow whinnied and he watched as another ragged urchin ran across the field towards the folly. He got to his feet and looked around; no one else was with her, but who might be observing them from a distant hedgerow with a spyglass? The child neared and then ran up the steps. "'Ello. Is you th' Duke?" this child's accent was much better, but still had the twang of the gutter.

"Yes, who are you? Have you a message for me?"

"Show me yer neckliss?"

Once again, Nicky fell to one knee and pulled out the chain and little lion from inside his shirt. "Good," the little girl announced, "'ave yer brought money wiv yer?"

"Who ARE you people?" Nicky grabbed her shoulders angrily, shaking her roughly, and she flinched. "Oh God, I'm so sorry," he rubbed them gently, berating himself as he grappled with his extreme anxiety. "I forgot myself, you're just a little girl, I'm sorry. Look, do you have a letter, a message, anything? I was expecting to meet a man here..." he sounded fraught and desperate.

"'E's watchin'. Yer can't see 'im, but 'e can see yous, us," she

343

cringed. "'E'll beat me if'n I don't do as I's told, an' me little bruuvver. We're not bad, like 'im, I promise."

"Hell's teeth," Nicky seethed. "What sort of a bastard is he, using children?"

"'E bought us," the little girl answered quietly. "'E owns us, but 'e's goin' away an' 'e said 'e'll give us sum money so we'll be free, an' rid of 'im when we do this."

"Good God, he's abandoning you? How old are you?"

"I's eight," she puffed out her chest proudly, "but I can look after Bertie. I can work. I can clean privvies an' chamber pots, an' sweep floors an' set fires. I used ter work in a cat 'ouse. I can do that too. When I's nine or ten or when I gets me tits, I'll earn enuf ter keep us bowf. I's watched, I knows 'ow ter do it. I knows 'bout all sortsa fings: 'ow ter use me 'and or git on me knees an' suck a gent, an' I can do..."

"ENOUGH! That's obscene," Nicky raged under his breath, his golden eyes flashing with fury. "NEVER! Over my dead body," which was exactly what Cat had said when she'd come across the little girl who'd said much the same thing to her.

"Did yer bring th' money?" the little girl thought she'd better get back to why she was there.

"He has my wife. Have you seen her? Is she all right? Do you know where she is? I'll look after you and Bertie, you'll never want for anything again, never have to look at a chamber pot, never mind clean one, and certainly never go near a man until you're properly grown up and know what you're doing, or married, preferably, to a kind and decent man." Nicky held the little girl's shoulders tightly and stared into her face, "But pleeeease, you have to help me find her."

"Yer've got gold eyes," she stared back at Nicky, "wiv black bits in, like a lion, an' yer 'air is all gold like. Is that why yer 'as a lion on yer neckliss?"

"Oh God," Nicky cringed. "I am NOT a lion, what is it with everyone? For Christ's sake, I just want my wife back."

"Did yer bring th' money? If yer gimme th' money, I'll 'and over th' messij."

"How do I know I can trust you? I couldn't care about the money, I just want to know where she is. I'll do anything to get her back, anything."

"'E's watchin' us. 'And over th' money an' I'll gives yer th' messij; 'e says she's there. 'E's goin' away, that's all 'e wants, th' money. If yer pay 'im, 'e'll give sum ter me, an' me an' Bertie, we can run away as well."

"You don't have to run anywhere, I'll look after you. I can't bear to see abused children, you've no idea; besides, I doubt he'll give you anything, you shouldn't trust him."

""Ow do I knows I can trust YOU? That's wot 'e said ter me, that 'e'd look after us."

Nicky swore. "Do I look like a bad man?"

"Sum o' th' nicest lookin' gents 'oo came ter th' cat 'ouse were bad; nasty 'abits they 'ad an' all. I woz glad one ov 'em didn't want me like in sum uvver places wiv girls my age or smaller," the little girl shrugged then pulled a distasteful face. Nicky had a good idea of what the nasty habits consisted of and seethed at the idea of abusing such small girls. He knew all about abuse of very young children; boys and girls; he'd been there himself and the rage inside him knew no bounds as he thought of how it had affected him all his life and he'd never forget it until he was in his coffin.

Nicky almost threw the money at her. "Here, take it," he looked around, wondering where the bastard was, feeling murderous. "Just give me the message, and when he goes, come to Litlington Manor House and ask for me. Tell Mr Carstairs, he's the butler, 'the Dowager would approve' if he's a bit difficult and I'm not there. Just tell him, 'Nicky told you to say that'." He smiled his killer smile, "NO child I know gets beaten or used as slave labour, or pimped out as a whore at the age of eight or younger, not if I have anything to do with it, and I've changed my mind. I AM a lion. Rawwrrrrrr," he growled play-fully, the smile suddenly lighting up his handsome face. "Remember that. You have to be strong and fierce sometimes, Little One, to fight bad people."

Maisie stared at the big, stunning man in front of her, she just knew he really was a Good Man, just like the Lovely Lady, and she wondered what the joke was she was playing on him, then shook herself and told herself to get on with her instructions. "How much is 'ere? I 'ave ter count it, e told me ter."

Nicky looked at his watch. "Five hundred guineas. Look, he said he was going by four, I haven't got time for you to count it, Sweeting."

"I 'AVE ter count it, 'e's watchin'. Do yer want 'im ter beat me when yer've gorn? Or Bertie? Yer should see th' stripes on Bertie's back."

Feeling murderous to the unknown man, Nicky did as he was told. "Hurry up, be quick," he poured the golden coins on to the floor of the folly and started to count them back into the bags with the little girl, casting his eyes over his watch.

"Wot's th' time, Sir?"

"What? Half three, come along, hurry up."

"Four 'undred an' ninety-eight, four 'undred an' ninety-nine... Oh Lordy, we's one short." Maisie looked at Nicky innocently, he hadn't seen her quietly pocket one of the coins.

"I don't believe this, it's a bloody nightmare. Who cares, it's just a guinea. Give me the message," Nicky was almost out of his mind, eyes going wild. "WHERE IS SHE?" he shook Maisie again. "You know where she is, don't you?" his voice rasped with the stress of the situation.

"I need anuvver guinea, then I'll give yer th' messij," she cringed.

Nicky was almost screaming with frustration, looking around, wondering if someone was really watching. "'E's watchin', yer 'ave ter believe me," Maisie whispered.

Nicky scrabbled around on the dirty floor, looking for the missing guinea but no little gold coin could be seen. He swore long and hard and hit a pillar with his fist, then finally, grappling with his temper, he dug around in his pockets and to his relief, he pulled out a small handful of loose coins and found... one golden guinea. He tossed it at the little girl, "NOW GIVE ME THE DAMN MESSAGE!" he yelled, and she reared away from him, cowering in fear. Slowly, she pulled a small letter out from inside the bodice of her ragged dress and handed it over with trembling fingers.

Nicky was appalled with himself. She was a little girl, innocent and a victim of circumstances. "I'm sorry, I'm sorry..." he swept her up into his arms, cuddled her and kissed her cheek. "I didn't mean it, I didn't mean to shout and frighten you, but I love her so much. I just want her back; you promise she's here?"

Maisie shrugged. "I fink so."

"Go... go and give him the money," and he gently set her on her feet again. "I hope it bloody chokes him, then go to my house, Litlington Manor House. It's a bit of a way from here, but not that far. Promise me? Promise me? We'll look after you, I give you my word, we're good and kind people," and for the first time in his life he just let go and spoke of something to an absolute stranger that he'd always kept bottled up and hidden away. Jack knew some of it and Francis was the only living soul who knew it all, but they weren't strangers, they were close to him. "I know what it is to be beaten, and abused and used by rough men, made to perform lewd acts and perversions, and to be starved," and he crouched down to look her in the eyes, "it happened to me when I was a child, just as small as Bertie is. No one will do that to you again, I promise, or let you live in fear," and he kissed the little girl on the cheek again and hugged her gently then rose to his feet, tearing open the folded message. It contained another map and one line:

We leave at four o'clock.

Nicky looked at his watch, it was nearly 3.40. He turned and ran down the steps, threw himself on Shadow's back, and took off once more, shouting at the horse to go like the wind. Maisie stared after him, completely bemused. They were all very strange, she thought, and if she didn't now have a lovely home, she would have gone to his, because he did seem so very nice and caring, not like the crude, coarse, sometimes vicious or drunken men in the cathouse. But she smiled to herself as she slowly counted out one hundred guineas into a pile and put it to one side. That was for her and her family and she'd never seen so much gold in her entire life, staring at the guineas in complete amazement. It was a fortune to her. She was to tell Mr and Mrs Baker it was from the Duke of Vall-on-see-enz, to help pay for her and Bertie to go to a good school, as he was the nephew of Mrs Granville and he was a generous donor to the Lovely Lady's charities, especially for children. Then she rose to her feet, put the money in another bag she had stuffed under her skirt, and happily skipped off back to the woodland, changed her clothes and made her way to the crossroads where there was a little trap waiting for her, as promised.

Cat had ridden back and forth from the folly to her little cottage, timing her rides, so she knew just how long it would take, even if she hadn't ridden like a man possessed, as Nicky now did. That was why she'd told Maisie not to appear until 3.15, and also told her to delay the man as much as she could, if possible, after 3.30, and not to let him go until she'd counted out the money and pinch one of the guineas surreptitiously, knowing it would all take time and wind Nicky up even more.

She'd borrowed the rescued children from the Bakers for a couple of days the previous week, which was when Bertie had bumped into Francis while he was peering curiously into the fishpond, something he'd not seen before as he'd stared at the golden fish and spotted a frog. And the day before, telling the couple she was going to take them on an outing into the country first, and then show them the new baby animals on the home farm, and they'd happily acquiesced. She'd told the children she was playing a prank on her nephew and niece, promised them a reward, and rehearsed lines with them, fed them up with good wholesome food, let them play in the home farm among chickens and baby animals, and they'd been looked after by one of the kindly Firle tenants. Francis had merely thought Bertie the child of a gardener, playing truant from the village school, and hadn't been the least bit concerned as he'd strolled through the gardens on his way to the stables and teased the mischievous little boy he'd come across wiggling his fingers in the water of the pond, seemingly fascinated by the fish swimming about while Bubbles rootled around in the nearby shrubbery. Both the children had had a wonderful time and it had been a whole new world to them.

Nicky followed the map, got lost a couple of times, swearing and yelling to himself in his frustration, until he eventually found the little track that led to Cat and Francis's secluded hideaway. He jumped down off Shadow before the horse had come to a standstill and was about to barge along the path and through the gate when sense, former training, and experience got the better of him. He paused to catch his breath, his body covered in sweat, pulled out a pistol and cocked it; he crept silently up towards the pretty little cottage, listening for any sounds. It seemed peaceful and deserted as he stared at it, never having known it was there, and wondered if he was still on Firle property. He didn't know precisely where the Firle estate stretched to exactly, its borders having always been somewhat higgledypiggledy, but did know Francis had made it his business to acquire small pieces of land or fields, here and there, wherever he could, ever since he'd got into the smuggling business, all the way down as far as the coastline, with its intermittent flat beaches, high chalk cliffs and the sea, and of course Nicky knew why he'd quietly done that. But now, he didn't care whose land he was on, all he was concerned about was who was in the cottage.

Holding the gun in his right hand as he usually did, he pulled back bushes with his left, pushed open the heavy gate and used his left arm, completely without thought, just as he'd been doing all afternoon, his entire focus on finding Bella and potentially confronting her kidnapper, wondering if the man had been watching him after all, or had he been waiting here all the time, readying himself to leave and possibly ambush him. Nicky had wondered, but decided he couldn't take the risk and the little girl had seemed so certain, so frightened.

He crept around the perimeter of the cottage, trying to see in the windows, but the curtains were all drawn. There were no horses or transport in the stables and he looked at his watch. It was five minutes past four and his heart was in his mouth. Supposing he'd missed them and they'd already gone? Still holding his pistol, he couldn't wait; he went up to the front door and banged on it with his left fist. "OPEN

UP! OPEN UP! I'M NICHOLAS DE BRESANCOURT," he yelled. "BELLA? SOOTY? SOOTY? ARE YOU THERE?"

All was silent. Perspiration ran down his face as he thumped again. "SOOTY! SOOTY… for the love of God, open the door, someone…"

Did he hear a woman's voice distantly calling his name, or had that been his imagination? He rattled the door violently and, not expecting the doorknob to turn, he was amazed when it did, and he stepped into the silent interior. Senses on full alert, every nerve alive, it was like when he'd broken into Bernheim's house outside Madrid. He stood still for a moment, his eyes adjusting to the dim interior. With the curtains drawn over the windows, it was dark and seemed potentially dangerous. He crept around the ground floor, peering in through open doors, discovering nothing. There was a small staircase leading to the upper storey and softly he went up a couple of steps. "Sooty? Sooty? Are you there? Dear God, was that you?" he called, his nerves now strung out to their limit.

Heart thumping, he crept up the remaining stairs, one by one, until he reached the small hallway at the top. There were two doors. He peered inside the open one, there were no curtains over the windows and it proved to be a bathing room and he was amazed for a second at the pipes, taps and equipment, as well as the huge bath, but he quickly turned and crept back to the second door. Slowly, he turned the handle and, pistol raised, he burst inside…

Chapter Thirty-Three

"Good afternoon, Your Grace. Late again. Can't you be relied upon to EVER be on time?"

Nicky stared at the woman sprawled across a chaise in the light and airy bedroom, her long legs akimbo in an extremely provocative position. She was smoking a small, thin cheroot and holding a glass of champagne in her other hand.... and he saw crimson red.

If her appearance and suggestive position weren't enough, her outfit was the final straw. Her long, thick black hair was loose, tousled and frothed up, and she had what appeared to be a pair of furry lion's ears sticking up from the mass of it on the top of her head. Her face was part covered by a lion-themed mask, just over her eyes this time and the lower half had white paint and black whiskers artistically drawn on it and her lips and the tip of her nose were black. She was barely wearing anything, mainly a tawny, fur-covered, low-cut corset affair that left her breasts and rouged nipples bare since there was no shift underneath; she had short, tawny fur, fingerless gloves on and there was matching fur circling her ankles; as she moved and rolled over slightly, he could see what appeared to be a lion's tail dangling from the bottom of back the corset. Her lower body was denuded of hair and otherwise bare. As the red rage roared through his mind and body, he took in the furry collar she had around her neck which had a golden ribbon lead attached to it.

"Well, Androcles..." Bella indolently put down her glass and cheroot and waved the end of the lead in the air and twirled her tail with the other hand, "wouldn't you like to take your lioness for a walk? I'm very good on my hands and knees, but of course you know that," and the lion-painted mouth opened and she emitted a filthy laugh as she grinned at him.

If Nicky had been of sound mind, he would have doubled up with raucous laughter at the ridiculous sight before him, and Bella's outrageous words, but as it was, a tide of fury such as he'd rarely, if ever experienced, tore through him and his face flared bright red, as red as the mist in front of his eyes. He felt like shooting the woman in front of him but, in such a rage, merely threw the pistol at the window near her head where it crashed through and fell to the garden below in a tinkling of broken glass, then he stormed up to Bella and without a word, slapped her hard across the cheek, dislodging her mask slightly and making her head rock back and her body jerk.

Quick as a flash, Bella sprang to her feet and walloped him back. She'd been expecting anger, but not violence like that, and her face stung from the viciousness of his blow. "You ANIMAL! How DARE you!" she yelled, putting her hand to her flaming cheek.

"You EEE-VIL witch," he virtually spat at her, "I swear to God, one of these days I really will kill you!" and he slapped her again on the other cheek... with his left hand.

With a feral shriek, Bella launched herself at him, her nails in claws, and like the wild cat she was dressed up as, she scratched him down the side of his face and tore out of the room with him hot on her heels, yowling with pain and anger, his hand feeling the blood on his cheek. Down the stairs Bella ran and Nicky chased her hither and thither through the downstairs rooms, swearing at her venomously while she screeched abuse back at him until she ran into the kitchen and bolted through the little scullery, out of the back door and into the gardens. Up and down and around the lawns and flower beds and trees they ran, the tail above Bella's naked bottom seeming to enrage Nicky even more, if that was possible. Finally, they faced each other on either side of the little pond, their chests heaving and panting, Bella's naked and enhanced, voluptuous breasts rising and falling above the tight corset, taunting him as he stood and watched her pant.

"I TOLD you, you were NEVER to do that to me again," he yelled at her, hands in fists, wanting to strangle her.

"And you expect me to sit and wait forever while you moulder away in your own little well of misery, ignoring your wife and children, and your family, who all love and care for you? Don't you think every single one of us hasn't been affected in some way by what happened in Richmond?"

"You've no idea what I've been through."

"If you talked to me, perhaps I could understand, instead of losing your temper all the time or ranting at your little daughter for nothing."

"You don't want to be talked to. Look at you, you just want to be fucked like some desperate tart," he sneered venomously.

"How would you know? You won't talk to me, you haven't been near me for months, you told me to go away. So here I am, back to being *Lionesse* again; only this time I'm looking for a proper lion."

"Is that where you've been, scrutinising your clientele? Did you find a suitable 'lion' to entertain you in your apartment? Weren't they perverted enough for you that you had to come back down here and play your depraved games with me? I know what you like now, Arabella; the more perverted, the better," he jeered lewdly.

"Don't you dare speak to me like that, you know that's not true, but at least you've woken up. It was a JOKE, or are you still so lost you can't even see that?"

"A JOKE? Is that what you call this? I could have killed myself haring all over the countryside, out of my mind with fright, just like you did to me in Normandy last year, except there aren't any marauding French around this time."

"Oh nonsense, you were just riding back and forth between Litlington and Firle. That's hardly the same as going through enemy lines between Brussels and Valenciennes, unless you were scared of being attacked by a herd of woolley sheep and mooing cows."

"You evil, THOUGHTLESS bitch; you've absolutely NO idea what that letter did to me, HAVE YOU?" he yelled, undoing his sword belt and throwing his rapier carelessly aside together with his other pistol, and so incensed and wound up, and now unencumbered by both, Nicky tore round the edge of the pond and threw himself at Bella's retreating form, catching hold of the swinging tail which he yanked and the pair of them tripped and fell into a large flower bed where they wrestled, Bella kicking and screaming for all she was worth as he tried to get a hold of her flailing limbs. Bella kneed him in the groin viciously, wriggled away from him as he howled in pain and she took off again up the garden, her bare feet hurting from where she'd trodden on all sorts of stones and twigs. He caught up with her yet again and with another flying tackle he brought her down and slapped her on the jaw with the back of his hand and for a moment she saw stars. In seconds, he was on his feet and hauled her up and over his shoulder like a bag of flour, and then walloped her viciously on her naked bottom as she screeched and screamed invective at him and drummed her naked feet against his body, beating and scratching him viciously on the back as he carted her inside the cottage.

Outside on the pathway to the cottage, a curious woman came upon Shadow, idly cropping grass from the verge. "Oh dear, abandoned you, has he, You Poor Boy? You must be gasping for a drink?" She slithered down off her own mare and tethered her to an overhanging branch and went up to Shadow and stroked him on the nose as she gently led the big stallion down the track, in through the gate and into the small stable where she showed him a big bucket of cool water and a net of fresh hay, and then retreated back outside. Hearing nothing for a moment as she stood and listened, she went back into the stable and loosened his saddle, letting it drop to the floor, and removed his bridle. Then, leaving Shadow to his own devices, she crept out and went to hide in the bushes and continued to listen. She'd been watching, hidden, from a vantage point a short way away and seen Nicky ride like the devil towards the cottage with a pleased smile on her face as she'd consulted her watch. As she stood, the sudden sound of breaking glass made her look up to the first storey, but she realised it was round the back. Muted sounds of shouting reached her and she caught the odd words, smirking to herself. Oh dear, he was VERY cross and she grinned. It went quiet for a few minutes and then she heard it again, screeching and yelling as the pair erupted into the back garden and Cat doubled over, trying not to laugh out loud as she crept a bit closer and tried to eavesdrop...

"... Put me DOWN! You ANIMAL, you CRETIN... you're such an oaf, OWWWWWWW...!" the faint words drifted over to Cat and then it went silent. Well, he'd managed to pick Bella up - so much for being half a man with no use in his arms! Cat smiled to herself in triumph and with a big, satisfied smirk on her face, she strolled out through the gate to her little hideaway, shut it behind her and made her way back to her horse and cantered home in time to wash and change for dinner with her husband, looking as innocent as the day she was born.

Meanwhile, back inside the cottage, the Battle of Waterloo was being fought all over again. Nicky tripped over the doormat as he went back inside so his grip on Bella loosened for a moment and she slipped in his grasp and tumbled to the floor. She was on her feet in a minute and grabbed the first thing that came to hand, a large copper pan which she swung and caught him on the side of the head.

"Hah! Hit me, will you? How DARE you hit me like that, you're worse than Bernheim," she screeched and dodged out of his grasp and tore through the scullery and kitchen, tossing cooking implements and plates behind her as she went, anything that came to hand. Nicky ducked and dodged and followed her into the sitting room where Bella retreated to the large inglenook fireplace and started to toss chopped up logs in his direction, uncaring of the damage she was wreaking to her aunt's furniture and ornaments, but as Nicky threw one and then another back at her, she screeched and picked up a pair of fire irons and stood and confronted him with her weapons, eyes alight, snarling venom at him, brandishing her poker and toasting fork. Any man, other than her husband, uncle, father or Jack, and possibly Miles

Ashcroft, would have been exceedingly wary of the sight that confronted him. Her uncle would merely have asked for a toasted crumpet, her father would have sighed in despair, Jack would have made a dreadful joke about playing 'poker' with cards, not iron implements, and her husband, if he'd been his normal self, would be rolling around in mirth, she looked so ridiculous given what she was wearing.

"You don't frighten me, You Vicious, Selfish Bitch," Nicky snarled, feeling the side of his face which was still sore and bleeding, "I'll have you; I'm worse than Bernheim am I?" he seethed. "Why I EVER thought I wanted you, I've NO idea. When I've finished with you, you can go back to Arlington and I NEVER want to see you again. NEVER!"

"You ABUSIVE FRENCH BASTARD! Is that how you get your real pleasure, hitting women? I'll be bruised all over my face now, what the hell am I to tell YOUR daughter and YOUR family? Look what my husband did to me? Well, I don't want you either, You Callous Excuse For A Man. You can go back to London and whore your way around Town to your heart's content, just like you used to, and see if I care; it seems you've finally turned into a replica of your delightful father."

"At least the whores I knew or half the women in the Ton who want me, don't treat me like you do," Nicky snarled, "and I'm no bastard. Like my father, I am a duke and proud of it, and my father was very careful to ensure the line was pure." His facetious, icy tone cut through her, "But after what you've no doubt been up to, how will I know any child you produce will be mine?" and he launched himself at her.

Bella had always revelled in Nicky's big, muscled, tall physique, finding his strong arms and chest a haven of safety and security when she was younger, of comfort and protectiveness as their relationship changed, and then luxuriating in it once they became lovers... but she was no match for his powerful strength when he chose to exert it. Tall, determined and feisty though she was, as he attacked her, she was no match for him, and he pulled her to the floor even as she hit him with her poker and tried to stab him with her brass toasting fork. He tore the fire irons from her grasp and loomed over her, his golden eyes wild as he finally mastered her, holding her flailing wrists in a grip of steel above her head and he glared down at her, ripping the mask off her, staring at the decorated face beneath, the big, black, painted eyes, just like a lion. "You're no better than a common trollop, you know that?" and he tore open his breeches, violently shoved her legs apart and thrust into her making Bella shriek as she felt herself brutalised.

Her earlier pleasure as she'd anticipated Nicky's arrival long gone, Bella screamed and whimpered as her husband drove into her relentlessly, not knowing this man who was now attacking her like a rough and coarse soldier, or uncivilised thug from the stews and backstreets. She screeched and pulled her arms free to beat his shoulders as she tried to push him off, but she was helpless against his brute strength.

Suddenly, as the tears now poured down her face, he pulled out of her. "I'm not here to give you pleasure, you BITCH," and he roughly tossed her over, grabbing her hair to pull her head back hard to control her, making her scream in pain, then he grasped the ribbon on her fur collar with his other hand and hauled backward. He thrust into her again, driving forcefully and violently, a torrent of abuse raining down on her ears as she couldn't move, fearful he'd strangle her he was pulling so hard on the collar.

"Ni... ni... Nicky... pl... please..." Bella begged, choking, hardly able to speak.

"Isn't this what you asked for, *Lionesse*?" and he yanked her hair viciously, making her scream again as he thrust remorselessly and suddenly yelled out as he erupted deep inside her, and half-collapsed across her back.

"Oh God," Bella whimpered as she crumpled, in disbelief at what had happened, what Nicky had done to her.

But it wasn't over. Nicky was still in another world: anger, frustration, desire, lust and all sorts of emotions roiling around inside him and he heaved himself out of Bella's limp body, part did up his breeches and hauled on the ribbon on her collar. "Come along, You Bitch, I haven't finished with you yet," and he yanked Bella to her feet as her hands tugged on her collar to try and undo it but he merely slapped them away and grabbed her hair again. "Upstairs with you, you know your place, to serve me in bed."

"Nooooo, no, what's the matter with you, Nicky?" Bella whimpered. "This isn't you… it was a JOKE."

"I don't happen to appreciate your jokes. Come along, You Tart," and he half dragged, half pushed Bella up the stairs to the bedroom.

"Not again, Nicky, please… you hurt me," Bella whimpered, backing away from him as best she could.

"Ha, don't like being treated like the trollop you are?" Nicky seethed, tossing her on the bed and finally tearing off his jacket and ripping his shirt over his head and he looked her up and down, lust and anger still overriding all his other emotions as she crouched there like a cornered fox. He went and sat down on the side of the mattress and reached for her and they wrestled, Bella not willing to give in to him again. But it was a useless and unequal fight, no matter how she hit and battered him, scratched and bit as they wrestled over the covers; he overwhelmed her once more, swearing and muttering at the damage she'd wrought on him. He pulled her over his knees as she alternately screeched and pleaded with him, and he held her firm as he slapped her buttocks, hard and viciously. On and on he went until they were red and bruised and his palm was sore, and then he pushed her to the floor and stood over her, looking down on her angry and tearful face as he undid his breeches again. "Pleasure me," he rasped, tugging on her hair yet again.

"NEVER!" Bella screeched up at him as he yanked on her hair. "I don't know who you are, but you're not the Nicky I know. I'll never give in to you, NEVER!"

"DO IT, or I'll beat you, so help me."

"You can threaten, beat or do what you like to me, but I'll never submit to you, NEVER!" she screamed up at him. "Bernheim never got the better of me, he did what he did because I LET HIM, no other reason, and you certainly won't better me, nor any man," she seethed and actually spat at him.

"Oh no? I'm more of a man than that bastard ever was, and you're my wife, Arabella, your lord and master, so you will do what I order you, whether you like it or not, with or without your permission, like wives are supposed to."

"NEVERRR!" Bella screeched and surged to her feet, heedless of the hold Nicky had on her long hair and punched him in the face. Gentleman Jack would have been proud of her.

"OWWWWWWW!" Nicky howled as he put a hand to his bloody nose and spat a stream of obscene language at her and Bella shook her head to escape his hold and backed away, eyeing up the door, wondering if she could make it and escape the nightmare she'd now found herself in.

But he backed her into a corner, eyes wild, nose bleeding, cheeks red and scratched, breathing hard. "You BITCH," he seethed and he grabbed her. Yet again they fought but she was no match for him and he tossed her back on the bed and followed her down, surging out of his breeches, alive with a lust he'd rarely experienced and once again he spread her legs and impaled himself deep inside her.

She yelled and screamed and writhed. He pulled and tugged at the top of the corset in frustration, finally loosening the strings and freeing up her breasts and torso totally, and the tantalising nipples as he bit them hard, making her shriek, and held her arms down on either side of her head, pounding into her.

At some point, Nicky reared up over her and stared down into Bella's face as her big green eyes burned up into his manic golden ones, alive with anger and hate... and something finally broke inside of him. Without thought, he lowered his head and kissed her. Kissing the artfully painted lion's face and black lips as hunger for her overwhelmed him: passionate hunger, incendiary lust... and love. A deep, desperate, all-consuming love and he let go of her wrists and took her head in his hands and lost himself as he ate her, his lips and tongue feasting like a starving man as he assaulted her mouth; his need of her overtaking every other sense and emotion.

Bella reeled, emotions swelling inside her, love and hate combined as he started to kiss her, never having experienced anything like it as she finally responded to him, unable to help herself. He groaned as his body surged into hers, slower now, tantalising, finally encouraging and eliciting a response.

"Sooty, My Sooty," he breathed and a stream of erotic French poured out of him in an impassioned torrent as he bent and now nibbled her nipples and caressed the body he loved and fantasised over endlessly, finally removing the furry corset. They rolled together on the bed and Bella moaned as her body responded and a soft scream of pleasure finally filled the silent bedroom as she exploded with an intense and agonised climax and Nicky erupted deep within her with a groan as his eyes closed and he swore in French.

They lay together on the big soft bed, their breath mingling, hearts thundering, as they slowly returned to reality.

"Sooty, oh God, Sooty, what the hell did I do to you?" Nicky rolled over and pulled her into his arms, mortified as he recalled the past hour, horrified as he remembered hitting her and the appalling way he'd acted, and he buried his face in her hair, not knowing what to say or do, remorse consuming him. He'd never lost control of himself like that in his entire life, it was as if a different person had taken over his body and mind.

"Oh Nicky, Nicky, have you come back to me at last?" Bella breathed softly, still bemused at what had happened, in disbelief at how they'd both behaved, but just happy to be held in his strong, loving embrace once more; her haven, her home.

"But I hurt you..."

"It doesn't matter. Well, it does, You Moron," she tutted lovingly, feeling her bruised chin and cheeks, "but I suppose I deserved it. No, actually I didn't, not that. Oh Nicky, I'm so confused, but I only wanted to find you again. I missed you so much," and emotion overwhelmed her again as tears leached out her eyes.

"Oh God, Sooty, I can't bear it," and emotional tears ran down his face.

"Nicky? Nicky... oh no..." Bella was in disbelief at his tears. "Nooooo, I'm so sorry, it was a joke, I never meant to hurt you, I would NEVER do that. I just wanted to find you, to make you believe in yourself again."

"I thought I'd lost you. I thought you'd be raped and abused, sold on to a ship... transported. I thought... I thought... I couldn't bear it."

"Shhhh, I know, but it was all imagined. You came, I knew you would," she whispered. "I knew you loved me, just as much as I love you. I'd follow you to the ends of the earth and I knew you'd come for me, just like you came into the lions' cage after me."

"I love you, Sooty," and he hugged her close to him again and kissed her, all his tormented emotions and angst going into it as he felt at home once more in her loving embrace.

They lay quietly and, as all the trauma of the terrible day caught up with him, the torrid fighting and sex, and the endless weeks and months without proper, peaceful rest, Nicky turned in Bella's loving arms and fell into a deep, exhausted sleep. Bella lay and looked at him, her heart bursting with love. She stroked his beloved face and his hair, missing him so much, and then grappled with the coverlet on the bed and pulled it over them. She settled down into his loving, protective arms, and, with a smiling thanks to her aunt, she, too, drifted off to sleep.

Chapter Thirty-Four

Bella woke a few hours later, disoriented at first, then she remembered where she was and the events of the day. She looked down at the sleeping man beside her, the moonlight through the broken window illuminating his face. She noted the bags under his eyes, evidence of lack of sleep, and the lines of strain on the so familiar features, and she leaned down to kiss the sensually curved lips that she'd missed so much. She'd missed everything about him... he was her other half, she was nothing without him, never had been since she was a small girl, totally entranced with her big older brother, the brother who wasn't her brother. He was all-encompassing: her hero, her torment, her comfort, her refuge, her confidante. He was everything. He always had been and always would be.

She lay back on the pillows, watching his deep breathing and considered everything about the previous day. He hadn't had a care about riding across country on Shadow to come to her rescue; he'd fought, wrestled, carried and subjugated her without a thought to his weak arm and, as she reflected, he'd never even winced if using it had hurt him. He was a fool and her aunt was right, as ever; he just needed a shock to bring him out of his lethargy and prove there was nothing the matter with him and he had nothing to be frightened of.

Idly, as she lay musing to herself, Bella wondered what on earth had gone on between her mother and her aunt that they'd done to her uncle to catapult him out of whatever maggot had been in his brain so many years ago, and she was determined to ask her aunt and get to the bottom of it, a naughty smile curling her lips. Her aunt was simply disgraceful, the more she heard about her and her uncle, the worse it got, but that they loved each other to distraction and still lusted after each other was obvious; The Great Love Affair she'd written about in her diary was just that. Even after twenty-five years. And her aunt had been proved right about Nicky, but in the meantime, she had the reality of him to deal with. Had he realised he was quite normal now? Had he got over whatever maggots were in HIS brain about his injuries and his arm? Bella wasn't prepared to let it go, having come so far, gone through so much. She wanted him back, back to the man she knew and loved and desired. She had to be sure, prove to him, once and for all, there was nothing wrong. He was her man, her lion… and she wanted more cubs.

She got out of bed, pulled the covers over the deeply unconscious man and silently stole out of the bedroom.

Bella crept downstairs and surveyed the destruction they'd caused, her lips creasing at the thought of her aunt surveying the mess and broken furniture and ornaments. She would need to put all that to rights before anyone came there again, especially Mrs Potter; the poor housekeeper would be shocked to her core. She padded into the little kitchen and helped herself to a large glass of cool water and went back to the sitting room. She drew back the drapes from the windows, letting moonlight flood the room and she stood, deep in thought, as she stared out into the gardens, grinning ruefully to herself as she looked at the destruction of the plants and pots. She pondered for a while, wondering what to do, until a naughty smile curled her lips. He would go mad again, she knew, but it was the only way, if she could do it.

Bella lit an oil lamp and wandered around the sitting room picking up the shattered ornaments and upturned furniture, her mind turning on what to do with the sleeping man upstairs, and how to carry out her plan. Eventually, lamp in hand, she crept back up the stairs and went into the bathing room. She stared at herself in the glass, her painted face now something of a mess. She retrieved the bag she'd brought with her earlier in the day which was lying on the floor, repaired the painted decorations on her face and straightened the ears in her hair and she washed, refreshed and perfumed herself as best and quietly as she could. Silently, she crept into the bedroom, checked on the sleeping man, then went back to the bathing room to put to rights her amusing costume which she'd retrieved from the bed. With a considered look at other contents of her bag, Bella picked out some further items and then went back into the bedroom. Her aunt had done as much as she could; the last play of the dice of *La Lionesse*, owner of still the most topical and sought-after pair of gaming saloons in London, was now totally in her hands.

Nicky was deeply asleep. Bella crawled up the bed next to him and he didn't move. She gently picked up a hand and it flopped limply against hers. She smiled to herself. She crawled down the bed and carefully pulled off his boots. He didn't move. She tugged down his breeches, smirking to herself that there was nothing on underneath, not that there was anything unusual about that as she well knew, and she also knew her uncle was of the same inclination, having overheard her disreputable aunt occasionally comment rather salaciously about it to her husband over the years, not realising little ears were listening… and she tossed them on the floor. He was now totally naked, but still in the depths of slumber. She looked at the naked body in the moonlight: taut, muscled, slightly thinner than before but still formidable. The scars on his body, irrelevant as far as she was concerned, and the mass of scars on his injured left arm, in no way detracting from the torso she was surveying. Any woman who was a connoisseur of men and who enjoyed carnal pleasure would salivate over his well-endowed naked-ness, want to explore it, want to experience everything it had to offer.

Bella sat back and surveyed her husband. She loved him, she desired him, she lusted after him in the most inappropriate ways… ways that would make most ladylike women blush, but which had brought them closer as he'd introduced her to all avenues of fornication and making love. He was everything to her and she would never let him fall prey to any other lecherous, avaricious woman. She'd kill them first. She loved him beyond anything possible and he was HERS.

Bella looked down at the wrist she was tying a ribbon around and the scars above it. Gently she secured the ribbon to the bed-post and looked at the arm it now tethered. It wasn't in an awkward position and she couldn't see how it would strain or pull on the muscles unnecessarily. Obviously, Nicky would pull, but he'd spent the previous afternoon pulling on reins, guiding Shadow, undoubtedly galloping pell-mell and jumping over obstacles, also pulling her, fighting her, lifting her, spanking her, and this was the only way to make him consciously think about it, what he'd done, and focus on her, and them together, putting their relationship to rights without matters potentially going awry again, and the risk they'd argue and he'd storm off once more.

Nicky stirred restlessly, wanting to feel the woman he loved against him, tight against his skin, close to him, loving him. But she wasn't there. He tried to roll over, but he was constrained somehow, and he pulled as he tried to move. He went nowhere and consciousness impinged on his dreaming fantasies. He lifted an eyelid…

"*Bonsoir, Monsieur le Duc. Comment ça va?*" Bella looked down into confused, golden eyes.

"Bella?" Nicky was half asleep

"Oh, no, *La Lionesse*, Nicky, *Mon Cher*," Bella purred as she sat above him, straddling his lap, a curling smile on her decorated face, her mask now back in place, as was her furry corset.

"Bella?"

"I don't know that person. *Je m'appelle La Lionesse*," Bella purred again, running a fingernail down the chest below her.

"Bella?" Nicky shook his head, trying to clear the mists of deep sleep, something he was lately unfamiliar with.

"Hello, Nicky," Bella smooched, "are you awake?"

Nicky went to sit up and realised he couldn't move, because his wrists were tethered to the posts of the bed. "Bella? What the hell are you up to?"

"It's been a while, Nicky; not since you were last in my apartment at *Le Lion d'Or*, do you remember?" Bella leaned over and pushed a couple more pillows under his head and shoulders, propping him up a bit.

"Bella? What are you doing?"

"I keep telling you, there's no Bella here. I am *La Lionesse*, and you are my prisoner. Don't you remember me, Nicky? What we did?" Nicky shook his head again, slightly bemused still. "Look at me, Nicky, what do you see? Am I not *La Lionesse*?"

Nicky surveyed the woman above him in the soft lamplight. She wasn't *La Lionesse* who had originally seduced him, but then she was; this one was more familiar and her enticing figure entranced him in her costume, so much more alluring than before. Despite two children, she was still tall, slender and lithe, but more voluptuous; she was tempting, virtually naked... now her face wasn't masked, just painted, and those ears... so silly, so appealing ... and her breasts... delicious. This woman was a black-haired *Lionesse*, not a tawny lioness, and he wanted her, she was the fantasy he dreamed about.

"Bella..."

"Tut, tut, I am DEFINITELY not this woman, Bella. Bella is the mother of your children, your wife. She bores you sometimes, she irritates you frequently, she organises your home, your life and your days. I," she tapped her chest, "am *Lionesse*; your mistress, your lover, the purveyor of endless erotic pleasure to your nights... as well as the provider and producer of little cubs."

Nicky just lay there, getting his mind into some sort of order, trying to make out what Bella was up to now. He pulled on the ribbons but couldn't move as he watched Bella lean over him and start to lick and kiss his chest.

"Bella, what are you doing?"

Bella just ignored him and started to enjoy her exploration, it had been such a long time. Up and down his torso she roved, licking and kissing, nibbling on his nipples, sucking, then biting, knowing what he liked, what drove him wild, but restraining herself for the time being.

"Let me go, Bella. My arms, my injured arm..."

"What about them?" Bella didn't even raise her head, she just shrugged and momentarily bit a nipple, hard, and Nicky suddenly groaned and squirmed and yanked hard on his tethers but didn't wince, and for a moment he looked at his tethered left arm, slightly bemused. Bella noticed but said nothing and carried on her erotic torture.

"Bella..." he breathed, eyes now closed, head thrown back.

"I'm *La Lionesse*, remember? I don't answer to Bella. Look at me, Nicky," she ordered softly and bit his nipples hard again.

"CHRIST!" he jerked and pulled hard again and Bella was satisfied.

"How very biblical; now, do you remember what we used to do?" Bella slowly licked her way up his chest, nibbling on the join at his neck and shoulder, making him shudder, then advancing up his neck, sucking and biting as she'd done before, so long ago.

"*Lionesse*," he whispered, eyes closed again, lost, as Bella kissed him.

She sat back, watching him like a hawk, wanting him, wanting to torment and love him and drive him wild, make him forget all his imagined failings. "Ah, finally you remember who I am," she breathed.

"I've never forgotten, you haunted me, every time I tried to escape the nightmares, you were there," he spoke, almost to himself.

"I'm always there. Look at me, Nicky,"

Golden eyes now blazed up into green, sparkling ones. "Remember me? Remember who loves you?" and Bella pulled a long black sash out from under a pillow with a salacious smile.

Nicky looked at it, knowing what she was going to do and his whole body froze. "Noooooo," he gasped and then shivered slightly.

"No?" Bella laughed, thinking him playacting. "Whatever do you mean, no? You know what happens when we do this, we procreate cubs, My Handsome Lion," she purred

"I'm not a lion. Don't do it, Bella, I'm telling you, ordering you...!"

"Whaaat? Don't be silly," and she leaned forward again, playfully brandishing the blindfold and tugging on his chain to remind him.

"NO! No, Bella, please, don't. You don't understand. DON'T DO IT," he rasped.

"Nicky, this is me, *Lionesse*. We did this for a week almost; I drove you insane, you privately love it... admit it."

"NO! No, Bella, please. I beg you, don't put me in the dark...." his tone changed to one of pleading.

"What nonsense, you're playing the fool again. I know what this does to you," and Bella leaned forward with a wicked, knowing chuckle and wrapped the long black sash around his eyes. "There, just like we were in *Le Lion d'Or* and you are my prisoner, again. Now, what tortures can I inflict on you this time?" she mused teasingly.

Nicky tossed his head, his whole body breaking out in a sweat. "Bella, please, take it off. I can't deal with it. The darkness... PLEEEASE..." he cried brokenly.

"Nicky? Are you joking? What game is this? You love it, you get so aroused, I can torment you and drive you wild."

"NO! Bella, I beg you," and Bella suddenly looked at him, taut, frightened, unaroused ... terrified; if she'd been asked to describe it.

"Nicky? Whatever is the matter?" she leaned forward and kissed his cheek softly, confused.

"TAKE IT OFFFFF!" Nicky almost screamed, pulling on his tethers.

"Nicky?" Bella was dismayed. "Talk to me, what is it, what's going on?" she leaned over and kissed him lightly on the mouth this time.

"I... I... can't deal with the darkness. Please, Bella, take it off, quickly."

"What do you mean, you can't deal with the darkness? Since when?"

"Since Nice, since always actually, but not so bad. Please, Bella, don't argue. Take it off," and he yanked on his tethers and swore.

"What nonsense, we did this last year. You got so aroused, and look what happened: Herring!" Bella laughed softly.

"Bella, PLEEEASE," Nicky thrashed against the ties on his wrists, "TAKE IT OFF!" he yelled, tossing his head back and forth.

Bella was stunned at what she saw. Nicky wasn't scared of anything, what was he talking about? Then her aunt's words came back to her about his apparent fears, and how he roamed the house with a candle at night, never sleeping.

"Nicholas de Bresancourt, are you frightened of the dark?" Bella leaned over him, kissed him softly as she asked.

"Yes, take it off."

"Is this because of Bernheim?" Bella whispered.

"Yes... pleeeease."

"Talk to me, Nicky, is this something he did?"

"TAKE IT OFFFFFF!" He was almost hysterical and Bella was shocked.

"It is," she breathed. "NO!" she suddenly declared, frightened at her decision. "He won't win, this is ridiculous."

"TAKE IT OFFFFF!" Nicky screamed and writhed on the bed, tugging and pulling on his arms, his head tossing to and fro.

"NO! I won't. Deal with it, Nicky. This is you and me. Bernheim is dead and I'm going to love you... think about that. This didn't bother you last year so deal with it now," and without any further words Bella kissed him and, getting no response, started to kiss down his body, reaching his belly and going lower, teasing and licking. She got no reaction from the tortured man, apart from epithets and tormented pleas; not like him at all.

"Nicky," she rose up to stare into his face, knowing he couldn't see her and determined to force him to confront whatever fears he had. "This is me, Bella... *Lionesse*. You're in Sussex, not Nice or Richmond, or anywhere else that bothered you. Whatever Bernheim did to you, you didn't give in and you're not going to give in now. I'm not taking your blindfold off until you're hard, out of your mind and begging for release, just like you were before when I did this to you. You can beg, scream and threaten me, but I won't listen. You're a lion, not a mouse. It's a harmless item of my clothing, not those terrible needles. Forget them, think of ME, revel in the pleasure I'm going to subject you to: pleasurable torture, not painful torture. And you're NEVER going to be afraid of the dark when I've finished with you. Bernheim will NEVER get the better of us. NEVER, NEVER."

"Bella... I beg you..." Nicky whispered, completely terrified at her words.

"NO. You can beat me black and blue after, do whatever you like to me, but I won't let you give in to this. I'm a lion too, well a lioness, and I don't give in to anything."

Silence reigned in the dim bedroom and Nicky writhed his body, pulled on his tethers and tossed his head, all to no avail. He was now lost in his tormented darkness, unable to escape, forced to fight his demons. While lions growled threateningly around his head, visions of his cellar in Nice were vivid in his mind, feeling the rats on his feet, remembering the obscene torture: dangling for hours in agony by his manacles, not quite able to stand properly; the silent Turk beating his body black and blue with his club; the flail of Bernheim's vicious whip; and worst of all, the Chinaman with his needles; all with the uncertainty if that day would be his last, not knowing where he was, how long he'd been there, totally disoriented.

And then other memories, deeply buried memories: a small, frightened boy of only four, apparently abandoned by his father in preference to some golden fortune; a father who had impassively watched first his wife be brutally raped and beaten and then his little son suffer a similar fate. After that, the child had been left for a time he had no concept of, listening to his mother moan, cry and scream as she painfully miscarried and bled to death in the darkness of their shared cell as a result of her treatment, with him shivering, starving and abandoned in the deep, cold and dank dungeon with no light. Then going for days and weeks with the dead and stinking carcass of his mother rotting beside him; knowing nothing; confused, hurting, hungry, thirsty, terrified, only hearing the scuttle or occasional squeak of rats in the stygian, fetid blackness, and the drip of water occasionally as it ran down the damp walls... until HE came. The big, fat, smelly and vicious man who hauled him out periodically to make him perform more depraved acts on his stinking, gross body and then be sodomised, abused and beaten again, always being asked about gold, before being angrily slung back into the terrible darkness to sob his heart out until he had no tears left to cry, and to curl up in a foetal ball and wish he was permanently asleep like his mother; and then he'd finally been moved up into the light at the top of a high tower, to face yet more depravity and abuse, and had ended up locked in a small cage which he couldn't get out of but the rats could still get into...

It had seemed like a nightmare with no end. And then, yet again, there was the dank cellar in Richmond, feeling helpless once more, not knowing what it was all about until he was led into the barn and heard the snarling of the lions... positive he was going to die for sure this time... the sheer and utter helplessness and fear... the darkness. Always the darkness...

Bella had no idea what was going through his mind as she watched his sweating body, but she was determined not to let him give in to whatever nightmares were plaguing him. She couldn't believe it: a year ago he'd laughed, sworn and pleaded with her, but it had all been in erotic pleasure, not this terrible torment he seemed to be enduring. She bent and kissed him, she kissed down his body, caressed and teased him, her mouth tantalised and licked and sucked but didn't get any response. She persisted, berating him, feeling like she was battling Bernheim again herself in some strange way and not wanting him to get the better of her. After what seemed an age, finally, she began to feel something. Nicky started to sigh and jerk as she bit his nipples; he moaned out loud as she licked down his body; then groaned and cried out as she took him in her mouth, teasing and winding him up until he was pleading for release. She sat back and looked at the restrained and sweating torso and crawled back up to lie on top of him.

"Nicky." She whispered, elated. "Finally, this is the Nicky I know. Any last requests from the condemned lion?"

"Fuck you, *Lionesse,*" was the response she got and she almost crowed with pleasure and triumph.

"THAT, will be my pleasure, but when I'M ready. Blind prisoners get no privileges," she whispered in his ear with a chuckle.

"Wait until I get my revenge. You'll lose your voice from begging and screaming so hard, you've no idea what I can do to you, what I did before was nothing. Don't you remember I warned you at Valenciennes? I can get SO perverted, SO tormenting, SO depraved, your mind won't be able to deal with it; deal with what you're participating in; deal with what you'll feel; like your body is on fire and the tormenting and painful but extreme pleasure, loving me and loathing me for putting you through it, all inextricably linked until you feel your body and mind explode with everything; the pleasure when I've finished, whether you've finished another matter..." the whispered response made her shiver with expectation, fear and hot arousal, and she knew she'd won. Bernheim was consigned, yet again, to the depths of Hell. She impaled herself down on top of him, riding him hard until they both jerked and cried out with an earth-shattering release.

Bella pulled off the sash and looked into the golden eyes. "We won. Bernheim lost. Lions are still kings of the jungle. I WILL do this to you again, frequently, just to remind myself, and you, there is nothing the matter with the dark."

"As often as you like, *Lionesse*, but just remember what I'll do to you back, in spades. Think of the clamps, and there are so many other toys I can use; you won't know yourself. You'll become the most depraved woman in the Ton."

"Promise? It'll take a special lion to capture and better *La Lionesse*... a man with two arms." It was the critical comment and she held her breath.

"Release me. I'll show you."

Apprehensively, but somehow sure of herself, Bella undid the ribbons fastening Nicky's wrists to the bed-posts and he looked at and flexed his left arm then immediately rolled over and gripped her hands in each of his as she battled with him playfully.

"Try and escape me now, You Witch," his self-satisfied smile made Bella crow.

"Amazing recovery, Androcles; just like Lazarus," she giggled. "Apart from being tethered, you do realise you must have ridden like mad, and you wrestled, you hit, you fought, you picked me up and had your wicked way with me. I don't see anything wrong with you. Does your left arm ache?"

"As if I'd tell you, that's between me and my lions," and he bent his head to kiss her. "I am going to punish you suitably for what you did to me. How is your delectable bottom feeling? That was nothing to what I'm going to do to you now."

"Oh no," Bella tutted, waggling a finger at him, "and extremely sore. How's your face, and head?"

"Shocking, no one will lust after me anymore, scarred and clawed as I am, but I can take my grief out on you," and he kissed her again, at length, deeply, full of lust and love, feeling alive again, confident, big and strong once more, like a lion...

"Where are we?" he rolled over, catching his breath, his body thrumming with desire again. It had been so long and he lusted after and loved Bella so much.

"Auntie's little hideaway," Bella giggled. "Are you going to tell her about the mangled flower beds and smashed china, or shall I?"

"This is Cat's house?" Nicky rolled back again to look at Bella in astonishment. "She knows about this plot of yours?"

"Um… somewhat," Bella muttered, not wanting to give her aunt's involvement away for the time being. "I gather she and Uncle Francis come and retreat here when they want to get away from it all, and they play house." She quirked a brow suggestively, "Auntie says it's very private, no one to hear or interrupt their peace and quiet."

"The dirty bugger!" Nicky guffawed. "No one to hear indeed, and how long has this been going on? I never knew this was here and I thought I'd explored all of the Firle Estate."

"Years, apparently, and your explorations were inefficient, as to be expected; how you were ever a dastardly spy, heaven only knows," she giggled. "Besides, I think it's very romantic," Bella huffed.

"So, there's no reason why we can't stay here for a day or two? No irate yokels to come and demand their property back?"

"I don't think Auntie would mind, why?"

"Good. Apart from picking up broken china and repairing the flower beds, you and I have time to make up and cubs to procreate. Are you in season?" he looked at Bella with a wicked smirk. "It's been a long time since I've had you to myself with no interruptions and punishment to administer… and you owe me five hundred guineas, by the way. How are you going to pay that off? I wouldn't mind taking it in kind of course, but I would have to be very specific…"

"You Cheeky Sod!" Bella giggled. "Your money has gone to a worthy charity, well part of it, and I don't deserve any punishment, I was an angel of mercy," she tutted, "bringing you back to the land of the living."

"Is that so? Angel of torment more like. No, you definitely need to be punished, and I know how you love being punished," he smirked again. "Did you bring your little box with you by any chance?" his eyes danced evilly.

"What sort of question is that?"

"*Lionesse*, if you go around dressed in nothing but bits of fur and a corset, what sort of questions do you expect to be asked? Is there a proper lead to that collar, by the way?" he grinned.

"Disreputable Wretch! It was a joke, just like the letter; a means to wind you up so you'd be cross. As if I'd let you at me with a collar and lead."

"I don't know, I think it's a fine idea. I could walk you around the garden for some exercise in the sunshine; as you said, you are a very interesting specimen on your hands and knees, and you've already experienced what I can do to you with a collar on... and if you play about and don't follow my orders, I suppose I'd have to hobble you in some way, tether your paws and claws, then we'd see who was master in this establishment..." and his lips twitched.

"Nicholas de Bresancourt, you are the most disgraceful, depraved, perverted and lecherous man I have ever met. I completely ignored your former commentary about turning me into the most depraved Lady in the Ton, since you were otherwise distracted, and I made allowances. HOWEVER, I am an independent woman, a rarity in this world, I know, but mark my words, our day will come, and I have absolutely NO intention of going anywhere with you on a lead, EVER!"

Nicky yanked on the collar, still around her neck, and she tumbled down onto the mattress again. "Only words, my lioness. My name is Androcles, by the way, and my lions do EVERYTHING I ask of them."

"Not this one," she giggled up at him.

"Oh, very definitely this one," and he yanked her up to kiss her lasciviously, "and I am renowned in lion circles... look," he twitched his chain in front of her, "my own calling card. I am a lion in all but name. Indeed, I've been told by two people very recently I look just like a lion. Rawwwwwrrrrr," he growled playfully, and nuzzled Bella in the neck making her giggle again.

"Well, since I'm a lioness, I suppose I had better follow the leader of my pride. I thought I'd lost him, but it appears I might have found him again. Do you think you fulfil all the necessary criteria?"

"I suggest you come and inspect, closely, and find out for yourself,

Lionesse, and we WILL go for a walk tomorrow, as I've just described; in fact, I can't wait."

"Over my dead body."

"That, too, can be arranged. I'm extremely hungry, I haven't eaten all day…"

"That is the MOST appalling, tasteless joke."

"I know, but it's the only way I can deal with it. Blow out the lamp, *Lionesse*."

"But you don't like the dark?" the bedroom suddenly went black.

"Not any more, interesting things happen to me in the darkness."

"Where's my necklace, by the way?"

"Come and find it."

"Androcles, what ARE you doing?"

"Procreating more cubs. Actually, I have a secret. My name is Leo, I'm a lion, and that's what we do, entertain all the lady lions and then go off and enlarge our pride with the most special and best lioness in the entire jungle…

"I love you, Nicky, I always have, I would never give up on you, I knew you'd come back to us again."

"I love you, Sooty, so much. I don't know why I ran away from you, you're my whole life, my rock, everything…now where's your lead? ……………OWWWWWWWOH!!

Epilogue

PART 1

The Little Season was well under way as Parliament was sitting and autumn was giving way to winter with Christmas not far off. The Ball at St James's Palace was a very grand affair, visiting Royalty from across Europe meant everyone who was anyone wanted to be there and be seen.

No one had seen the extended Granville family for months, most of the year in fact. All sorts of lurid stories had abounded around Easter time of kidnappings, gruesome murder and all manner of tall tales involving wild beasts, but the famously scarred Baron de Mornay, his second wife, and his daughter, the Duchess of Valenciennes, had appeared briefly, after Easter, at various balls and parties and seemed nonplussed at the gossip, especially nonsense tales of wild beasts, so it had all died down and no one thought much of it. Rumours of the involvement and serious injury to the Earl of Keswick had also circulated, but he had appeared with his wife at a couple of parties, his usual elegant and insouciant self, and Society concluded it was all an immense Storm in a Teacup. All the same, the absence of the entire family for so long was strange, especially the Duke of Firle. Always elusive and reclusive since he'd inherited the title, he did generally put in the odd appearance, here and there, either at his club or the odd ball, as if he wanted to remind people he did exist… but he, and especially his beautiful, eccentric, French wife hadn't been seen for nearly a year. The gossip that had died down, started to rear its head again as the Ton returned back to London from their country estates as the winter weather drew in and the entire family was conspicuous by its absence.

The great and the good were there. The famous and even some infamous had managed to wangle an invitation. Leaders of the Government and across politics and the Establishment and Military were there. Foreign Royalty and their advisers and acolytes were there, and members of the English Royal Family were also gracing the occasion with their presence. Jewels and gowns were on display, all the ladies ogling each other, commenting cattily on the designs and styles and the accompanying jewellery: everything from tiaras to brooches to hair decorations.

It was a dreadful squeeze, the world and his wife being there, and the heat from the candles and lamps almost overwhelming. And then they arrived. All eyes turned as everyone goggled to peer and inspect.

The Baron and Baroness de Mornay appeared first. The Baron didn't often mix in Society, well, one knew why with his terrible scar and limp, one understood, and he normally disappeared quietly into the card room as he NEVER danced. The current Baroness, so different from her foreign predecessor, was a tall blonde. Serene, calm and normally somewhat reserved, she could be quite beautiful if she put her mind to it. She was always elegantly understated in her dress, however, and tended to melt into the background.

Elise descended into the ballroom on Eddie's arm as he limped slowly down the grand staircase and all eyes were on her appearance. Her blonde hair was elaborately coiffed and she looked quite radiant and vital for a change. There was colour in her cheeks that didn't appear to be cosmetic, although her eyes and lips definitely appeared suspiciously enhanced, and some women tutted, but she looked quite strikingly lovely. Her gown was a stunning royal blue with elegant trimmings, but her whole appearance was heightened by the glorious set of sapphires she was wearing. A sizeable tiara, drop earrings and an amazing necklace of sapphires and diamonds covered her chest, with matching bracelets and rings; the assembled multitude stared and gossiped. They'd no idea the Baron was so wealthy, and he looked his usual tall, slender, elegant self but beaming with delight over his wife's appearance. He'd disappeared for years from the Society social circuit, mourning his first wife everyone said, but he seemed well over that now as he continually gazed at his second one with an almost besotted, sensual look on his face, kissing her hand and whispering in her ear, making her laugh up at him flirtatiously, batting him playfully with her fan. The Baroness looked alive, restless, enjoying herself enormously, her eyes sparkling as she moved around and almost fidgeted when she stood still.

Everyone had just got over that, when the Baron's daughter entered with her husband, the Duke of Valenciennes and a good-looking young man following. All sorts of stories had always abounded about the lethally handsome and charming Duke. Some said he had no money, others that he was hugely wealthy. Some said he'd bedded half the ladies in the Ton, others that he was completely infatuated with his wife. That he'd been in the army in the Peninsula and had served Wellington was no secret, and with honours too, it was said, and he'd been badly injured at Waterloo, but had miraculously survived. The man had always turned heads, tall and well built, his unusual colouring and looks were stunningly attractive and made him stand out in any company and most women went weak at the knees if he turned his charm on them; but now he only had eyes for his wife, and all could see why. She'd had a Spanish mother, the Baron de Mornay's aristocratic first wife, and it was obvious she took after her and tonight she'd dressed accordingly. Amidst her elegant but restrained coiffure, slightly Spanish in style, instead of a tiara, a large, elaborate, golden Spanish comb stood up high from her black hair and rubies and diamonds glittered in it. More large rubies and diamonds hung in her ears and around her neck, and her wrists and fingers were covered with the same. Her gown, in a Spanish-style design with layers of flounces in the skirt, was a dark crimson, almost fitting indecently to her tall, slenderly voluptuous figure. She stood out amidst the other women, not only because she was stunningly and darkly beautiful, but the unusual red dress and the enormous rubies were a statement in themselves. The Duke could barely keep his eyes, or his hands, off her, it was almost but not quite inappropriate as the pair whispered and laughed with each other, obviously much in love and lust!

No one knew who the youth was until a whisper went around he was the Duke's ward, lately down from Eton. He was extremely elegant and aristocratic in the way he carried himself and sported a very large diamond stick-pin in his elaborately tied cravat, and people assumed he must be French, perhaps a distant relation of the Duke who'd survived in the mess that was France, another refugee presumably now given a home in England.

The trio strolled off to join the Baron and the Baroness, who were talking to the Earl and Countess of Keswick and Lord Ashcroft, something in the Government people understood, a tall, spare man with receding grey hair and grey eyes that seemed to see right inside one, which people found most disconcerting, along with his facetiously cutting wit.

And then They arrived. The elusive and reclusive Duke of Firle and his wife. As ever, he sported diamonds instead of buttons on his otherwise immaculately tailored black jacket, but it was the Duchess that everyone goggled at. The Duke was extremely tall, well-built and imposing, a charismatic man and still darkly handsome. There was an indefinable quality about him that made him stand out, apart from his physique and striking looks. He'd appeared and disappeared in and out of Society in his younger days, spending time in France people said, before the dreadful Revolution, and had been a terrible rake at one point, he and the Earl of Keswick. He had made female hearts flutter for years and been the despair of his old battleaxe of a grandmother in his refusal to select a wife from all the loveliest and eligible young women in the Ton, but then he'd suddenly upped and married a Nobody. Even though his French wife was an exceedingly beautiful woman, extremely eccentric people said, with a temper, a predilection for giant hairy dogs, and odd ideas of equality, it was also said she carried a knife under her petticoats, which was ridiculous of course, as if. But then, she was French, so what did one expect?

The Duchess of Firle descended the stairs on her husband's arm and the assembled crowd simply gaped and a collective gasp went around the room like a giant wave. Men and women together. They'd rarely, if ever, seen such diamonds. The Firle Diamonds were well-known, but even they were nothing like this spectacle. A large tiara sparkled in her thick, light golden-brown hair and her fingers, wrists and ears dripped with large, glittering stones, but it was the necklace that drew all eyes. She was wearing black, as was her husband, and the dress bared her chest and shoulders, almost, but not quite, indecently, and was covered in little jet beads which flickered in the light and the whole ensemble enhanced her slimly voluptuous, still youthful figure. She certainly didn't look her age and a lot of older men stared at her lasciviously, especially the creamy breasts that oozed out of the front of her gown.But all eyes were gaping at the necklace, if one could call it a necklace. That wasn't like any necklace anyone had ever seen; it made the Crown Jewels look positively nondescript. Tasteless, some tutted jealously, as from the top of the Duchess's elegant neck, just under her chin, row upon row of the finest, sparkling diamonds descended like an enormous, tiered collar. The rows increased in size right down to her collar bone and then there were scallops of more diamonds that covered her upper chest and back... and if that wasn't enough, a single short rope of the finest stones hung in a line from the top of the collared rows to her cleavage, at the bottom of which the most enormous, giant diamond glittered and sparkled. The necklace was outrageous in its concept and extravagance, totally over the top and ostentatious, and only a woman like the tall, elegant Duchess could carry it off with such aplomb. People goggled, stared and gasped at the diamonds and while women discussed the strange and unusual style of the decorative necklace, their husbands whispered about its value. Everyone knew the Duke was rich as Croesus but even so, the necklace's value was simply mind-numbing.

The pair seemed totally oblivious to the stir they'd created and sauntered over to join the rest of their family and friends.

"Nice necklace," Nicky whispered into Francis's ear. "However, a trifle understated if you ask me. Amazing what one can mine out of the ground in Sussex these days. You can't see a glimmer of any scars, not that anyone would be looking, they'd be too riveted on the bird's egg at the bottom of the rope."

"Mmmm, I wondered if it wasn't big enough," Francis whispered back with a straight face. "And there's STILL a pile left in the bloody box. Are you sure you don't want some for Bella?"

"I beg pardon? If I want my wife to have a diamond necklace, I'll go and sink a couple of treasure ships myself, and have you seen the hoard your grandmother left her? She could wear a different bauble every day for a year. Do YOU want a giant gold lion statue? I've got one going spare…"

"What are you two whispering about?"

"Francis has some spare diamonds, do you want some for Elise?"

"What? That lot in your cave? I'm a respectable citizen, since when do I receive stolen goods? Whatever next, what do you think I am, a fence?"

"Brandy, tobacco… diamonds. Same difference," Francis chuckled. "That ghastly, enormous, solid gold epergne and candelabra, plate and cutlery on your dining room table doesn't count, I suppose?"

"What, those trifles? Can I help it if I happened on some random knives and forks and other dining accoutrements in the middle of a field full of sheep, obviously dropped by some nefarious individuals on their way somewhere," Eddie said airily.

"Obviously not. Ah well, I'll leave them be. Maybe Lizzie might want a pretty necklace of her own or something when she's a bit older," Francis sighed.

"She probably will, a woman can never have enough diamonds," chuckled Nicky. "That's what your grandmother told me one day, and Lizzie certainly won't want to wear that monstrosity of her mother's. Good God, Francis, are you trying to announce to the world you've found Blackbeard's hoard or something?"

"No, I told someone I'd inherited a diamond mine in the Americas, from a distant relation of my grandmother's, several times removed," Francis said. "People will believe anything, the more far-fetched it is, the more they believe it. It'll be around this ballroom in ten minutes flat."

"You should have told them you were a smuggler and pirate then," chuckled Nicky.

"I did actually. I told that fat old bat over there, the one with the green feathers in her hair and that dreadful puce gown, and she just giggled at me and swatted me with her fan and said "*Là*, you're SUCH a tease, Your Grace. You wouldn't know a smuggler if you bumped into one on Brighton beach at midnight." Francis's imitation of Lady Fanwick's arch tones had Eddie and Nicky in stitches.

"What are you reprobates laughing at? As if I couldn't guess," Ashcroft joined the three chuckling men.

"Smuggling, would you believe?"

"Why does that not surprise me," sighed Ashcroft. "Your wife looks quite stunning tonight, Francis, if I may say so. Interesting jewels she's wearing..."

"Aren't they? I inherited a diamond mine not long ago, y'know."

"And I'm the King of Scotland. I don't want to know, actually," Ashcroft sighed yet again.

"Good, the less you know, the less your conscience will trouble you." Francis winked at him.

"You're too kind. My conscience isn't big enough to deal with what I suspect you could tell me, all three of you," Ashcroft looked at the three men whose faces were masks of innocence.

"Why don't you go and dance with Bella?" chuckled Nicky. "You know you want to. Isn't she looking spectacular tonight? If you ask her nicely, she might teach you a few steps of the fandango. I'm sure you'd be a riveting exponent if you put your mind to it."

"I'm SO desolate you've left my service," Ashcroft tutted. "You've NO idea how much I've missed your delightful conversation and repartee."

"Likewise, My Lord, your charm always did overwhelm me. Would you like me to come back again? I could be Chalmer's Assistant, imagine that? You'd see me every day..."

"If you will excuse me, I think I need to go and dance," and with a disgusted glare in Nicky's direction, Ashcroft bowed and sauntered over to the group of women as all three men burst out laughing again.

"What ARE we going to do with all our ill, or not so ill-gotten gains?" Nicky sighed.

"I've not the remotest notion," sighed Francis. "I've been grappling with the problem for the past twenty-five years and still not come up with a useful solution."

"I keep telling you," tutted Eddie, "we should start our own Bank, that's where the money is. Nicky, you could put your statues in as collateral, either or both, and Francis could simply melt down all that foreign gold in those chests of his, and I've got so much sitting in Rothschilds now, I don't see why they should profit from it when I could do just as well for myself."

"As if we haven't got enough money," sighed Francis. "What the hell do I want more for?"

"One never knows what's around the corner. Wars, revolutions... if you'd been French like me, you wouldn't be so blasé."

"But I lived through The Revolution as well, I was back and forth to France when it all began," Francis interjected.

"Yes, I KNOW that, but you were still the Duke of Firle as well as The Shadow, you weren't French. Have you ANY idea how much money I lost in Paris when we fled? It was all appropriated by those bastards just because I'd squirrelled it away somewhere quiet. If I'd left it in a proper international institution, like Rothschilds, it would probably have been safe," Eddie sighed feelingly "more fool me, it was a very expensive lesson."

"Well, you've made more than a pile now, why worry about what happened so long ago?"

"Because it was hard won back then, for a variety of reasons, and I'll NEVER forget. You've no idea how many friends I lost to The Terror and those who survived, so many were ruined, mentally as well as financially. One or two actually killed themselves, it was so appalling. And look at Nicky, I doubt he'll ever get his Valenciennes lands and holdings back, any more than I'll get the de Mornay ones, no matter how much money I throw at those idiots in Paris."

"All right, all right, point taken. Look, we can't discuss all this here, how about we all sit down quietly at Christmas, away from all the madness and children, and put our heads together again."

"What will we call it?" Nicky mused. "We've got to have a good name. Granville, de Mornay and de Bresancourt? Or Granville, or Firle, de Mornay and de Valenciennes? It doesn't exactly flow. My names, in particular, are damn awkward, and I don't think people will like the French connection either, memories of Boney are still too raw."

"Good point, I'll have a think. Hmmm, Granville, Monsewer and Growler?" and the other two rolled their eyes at his absurdity. "Fine, you don't like your nicknames, so how about Granville, Mornay and... er... Nicholas?" Francis grinned.

How about Granville & Mornay, or I think you could get away with Granville & de Mornay. I'm part of the de Mornay family, I'll throw my bit in with Papa, I'm not bothered about having my name involved, but we could have a growling lion as our insignia, that could be my input," Nicky chuckled. "I wonder if Bella would like to invest her gambling ill-gotten gains too? It's all mounting up in a tidy pile, I'd no idea those places were so lucrative. I was in the wrong business, why the hell did I join the army?" he sighed with another chuckle.

"Because you wouldn't listen to any of us, as ever, but at least it kept you out of trouble, female trouble," Francis winked at Nicky knowingly.

"That's what you think," he grinned back. "Talking of females, I was always one for an interesting and beautiful older woman. I think I'll go and give Cat a whirl, show Miles what he should be doing," and with a playful dig in Francis's ribs, Nicky sauntered off to find his adopted aunt.

"I can't leave Elise by herself," mused Eddie. "Doesn't she look lovely tonight?"

"Stunning. Very... ah... perky? Also, a trifle flushed, if I may say so?" Francis looked at Eddie with a pleased smirk and a curiously raised eyebrow.

"She just needed me to bring her out of herself."

"Obviously," and Eddie ignored his playfully facetious tone. "I'll dance with her if you like, then you can disappear off for your usual game of cards and find some unwary fool to fleece; there appear to be plenty of foreign ones dotted about."

"I've had enough of playing cards, I want to dance with my wife," Eddie announced, and Francis was so stunned, he was momentarily speechless. He watched, completely bemused, as Eddie went and found Elise, who was quite happily making small talk with another woman who was eyeing up her sapphires with an avaricious gleam in her eye. He limped over, picked up her hand and kissed it, whispered something in her ear and she gazed at him with such surprised pleasure and no little adoration that Francis almost beamed as he watched them move to the dance floor and slowly circle into the swaying, twirling throng. They didn't swirl round and round as Nicky was doing with Cat, and Ashcroft was doing with Bella, albeit more sedately, but Eddie seemed to have mastered moving on his stronger leg and they swayed and turned slowly, gaining more momentum as they went, no one taking the slightest notice of them. Francis felt a lump in his throat as he watched, thrilled to see his close friend come out of the shadows at long, long last; all due to Elise, Francis was sure. They twirled and spun and Eddie leaned forward to whisper in Elise's ear and she smirked back at him and whispered in his ear, making Eddie smile. Francis watched it all, his mind half on his brother-in-law and half contemplating the whole idea of the family bank, yet again. It seemed the perfect place to 'lose' his ill-gotten gains once and for all... and no one knew there was more, stashed away in another hiding place over in Brittany, the remainder of Marcus Bonaire's golden treasure hoard, waiting to be relocated back to England now the long, long war with France was finally over.

"Penny for them. Good lord... is that Eddie? DANCING?" Jack came up behind Francis.

"It certainly is. Do you know, I've waited twenty-five years to see that. Not even Carlotta could entice him onto the floor and she could entice most men to do anything. God, I miss that woman, it was such a tragedy to lose her so young. I used to have such a laugh with her... but whoever said love doesn't happen second time around is utterly mistaken, and it couldn't happen to a better man."

"Well, good for him, and Elise. You know, the more I get to know her, the more I like her."

"Mmmm, me too. There's far more to that woman than meets the eye, take it from me. My grandmother was no fool, she wouldn't be friendly with anyone who didn't have something about them, else they'd have bored her rigid; either that or she'd have walked all over them and she could never abide obsequious or toadying individuals. Carstairs told me they used to get on like a house on fire, he often heard the pair of them cackling with laughter."

"I wish I'd known your grandmother," sighed Jack. "Everyone says what a remarkable woman she was, even if she did frighten most of them to death. Some of the servants down at Firle still talk about her even now, as well as the ones in Hertford Street. I swear old Carstairs was more than half in love with her."

"She was an amazing woman and I still miss her so much. She frightened ME at times, but she was as soft as butter underneath."

"Sounds just like you," chuckled Jack.

"Enough of your nonsense, but what have you been up to since we arrived? What do you make of your first formal ball at a Royal Palace then?"

"I've never seen so many rich and important people together, in one place, in all my life."

"Mmmm, and more than half of them are complete idiots. One featherbrained matron came up to me with a spotty daughter in tow and asked me if you were a displaced French aristocrat looking for a rich English wife. Another one asked if you were Nicky's younger brother, and a third told me I wouldn't know a smuggler if I bumped into one carrying a cask of brandy on his shoulder, walking up the beach on a moonlit night..."

"Of course you wouldn't," grinned Jack. "Estimable pillar of the Establishment that you are, and how could I be his younger brother when he came over here as an orphan of the Revolution? And do YOU think I look like a displaced French aristocrat?"

"Yes, actually." Francis looked the younger man up and down with the eye of an expert. "Benjy has done you proud and your mannerisms are something to behold. You've been spending time with Ricky I take it, I recognise the gestures and affectation a mile off. A pair of deadly popinjays, according to Ashcroft. Nice stick pin, by the way," Francis winked at him.

"I can't believe you gave me this, it must be worth a small fortune. I'll take such great care of it and whenever I wear it, I will ALWAYS think of you." Jack looked at Francis with hero worship on his face as he fingered the enormous solitaire diamond that was sparkling in his cravat.

"Stop looking like a puppy with its tongue hanging out," Francis chuckled. "You deserve it. You could have been killed at Richmond, what you did that day was more than brave. If you hadn't jumped his horse, he'd have got away before Eddie arrived and shot him."

"I didn't want a reward," grated Jack angrily. "Besides, I should have killed him."

"So should I, and so should Nicky, and so should Ashcroft. Even Ricky is annoyed as hell he didn't anticipate Bernheim's intentions. How do you think we all feel? Especially Nicky and I? Don't berate yourself, Jack, the bastard's dead and we're all here, right as rain, enjoying ourselves while he's finally six feet under."

"I suppose."

"You came out of it better than most of us, despite taking him on personally, and no one at school suspected a thing with your injury, did they?"

"No, I just kept my head down and got on with my work."

"Mmmm, you certainly did; your end-of-year exam results were exemplary. I can't say I wasn't amazed, and you well deserved your little holiday at Marguerite's," Francis winked at Jack again. "Though compared with your end-of-year, final Report from your teachers, I've no idea how you managed it. If I didn't know better, I'd think it all rather odd, wouldn't you, Jack?" He quirked a curious eye at the innocent-looking youth beside him, sure something wasn't right somewhere, but he'd no idea how to get to the bottom of it.

"I just told you, I worked bloody hard all through the last term. In fact, you've no idea how many hours I spent in the library, swotting up and reading and preparing for the exams, knowing it was my last chance to make the most of the education I was getting."

"Well, that makes a change from the many hours you spent in the local tavern," quipped Francis facetiously. "One serving wench, plus one scullery maid, plus the local trollop, plus x numbers of bottles of wine, plus y flagons of ale, divided by one bed, times one randy youth, equals not enough attention in class, was about the extent of your algebra and mathematics, according to Nicky," and Jack choked slightly. "But your education is far from finished, My Lad. Eddie has the bit between his teeth now, and he'll keep you at it when you're home, filling in the gaps and covering things they don't cover at school, no matter how extensive the Eton syllabus."

"I know, I know, and don't think I'm not grateful. Eddie is a far better teacher than those old farts at school; that's the last time anyone threatens me with the cane, that's for sure."

"That's not what I heard from Marguerite; talk about prostrate with shock at what you've been up to there, but I think we'll leave that for the time being, not QUITE the time and place for such an illuminating discussion," chuckled Francis archly. "Anyway, enough of that, your future is a conversation for another time. So, Jack, what else have you to say about this motley gathering here tonight? It's quite a turnout, even in my experience."

"I've never seen so many jewels in one place," grinned Jack.

"Well, mind you keep your fingers to yourself," Francis tutted with a knowing look. "Is there anyone you know here? I gather you went to stay with some school friends at some country house parties over the summer? That's partly what Eton is all about; you'll soon learn it's not always about what you know, but who you know. Meeting people at those sorts of gatherings is always useful, you make acquaintances of individuals who might not come to London much, or socialise in Town, but there are some very wealthy and influential people up north, industrialists, all sorts, not all aristocracy, some have very ordinary backgrounds, but each one could be a useful individual to know."

"I only stayed with two or three," Jack shrugged. "Only those who I actually liked and who didn't try and bully me."

"Mmmm, you weren't at the Bassenthwaites up in Yorkshire, then?"

"Er... no. Definitely not there. Couldn't stand Ernest, he's over the other side of the ballroom actually, in that far corner with his father, on the left, can you see him? Tall, red-faced, vaguely gingery hair, no taste in cravats; supercilious, vicious arse," he muttered venomously. "Why?"

"Oh, nothing. Lady Bassenthwaite had her famous emerald necklace stolen over the summer, so I gather. She swore someone took it at one of their weekend get-togethers, didn't you hear? She made an almighty stink about it, called in the Runners, wrote to the Home Secretary and no doubt would have bent the Regent's ear given half the chance. She's here tonight with her husband and Ernest, moaning she had to wear her lesser rubies instead." Francis looked at Jack with a quirked brow.

"Don't look at me like that. I never stayed there, hated the bastard. What the hell are you implying?"

"Absolutely nothing, Jack; absolutely nothing," Francis said airily. "Glad to know you weren't near the place. Now then, would you like me to introduce you to that lady in puce over there. She's looking for a nice young man to introduce her daughter to. She has twenty thousand a year, I hear."

"Whaaat? That's obscene!"

"Not as obscene as her daughter," Francis grinned. "Takes after her delightful mother: fat, frizzy hair, thick as two short planks, and with the addition of spots."

"Urrrrgh," Jack pulled a face and shuddered. "Heaven help me. But what on earth do I want a wife for, I'm only eighteen?"

"I merely thought I'd ask. She's after Alex, of course, or one of my other boys. Idiot woman." Francis tutted. "She's the one who told me I wouldn't know a smuggler if I bumped into one."

"Like daughter, like mother, as you say," Jack chuckled. "Now, that blonde minx in pale pink over there, she's much more my type."

"Ah, Netherington's daughter. No use to you, pittance of a dowry, her mother's hoping to use her looks to find her a good match."

"I'm not interested in other people's money, I'm going to make my own fortune. I'm going to be like you and marry for love," Jack grinned. "I want a wife like Cat or Bella, someone beautiful and feisty."

"Love? *Moi*? The estimable Duke of Firle? I'm the most henpecked man in London. Under the thumb, that's me. Ask Ricky. I'm so hard done by, I do what I'm told or I get a vase thrown at my head. I just pay dressmaker's bills, that's all I'm good for. I don't ask questions. I daren't, you know what a coward I am. I know my place in life, married to that eccentric French harridan."

Jack guffawed quietly. "You Silly Bugger, you're still so besotted. I just hope I can find a harridan like that who loves me like she does you; the way she threw herself in front of that giant Indian to save you, mad she is, completely mad."

"You do that, Jack," Francis's expression suddenly went serious. "Always remember what a very wise old woman once said. All the money in the world counts for nothing if you have no one to share it with, and by that, I mean someone who loves you selflessly, for your-self. I searched all London and farther afield and never found anyone I could face spending the rest of my life with, and then, BANG, one day, there she was, in the most unexpected place, and I was instantly smit-ten, completely bowled over. And as you said, I've been smitten ever since. I've never looked at another woman, no one compares to her in my eyes. She's risked her life for me, and nearly lost it as a result, more than once, and I'd do anything for her, give her the world if I could, not that she's remotely interested. If you find a woman like that, Jack, you'll be a very lucky man. Capture her and never let her go. Best nefarious pirate's advice I can give you, as one Shadow to another."

Jack was stunned by the heartfelt, softly serious words. "You really mean that, don't you?"

"Of course I do, Jack. One day, hopefully, you'll find that out for yourself. In the meantime, enjoy yourself, sow your wild oats exten-sively and then you'll recognise a good woman when you find one."

"Just like Nicky did. He followed your advice, didn't he?"

"In a way, yes, but it took him a while, and the circumstances were different. She was under his nose all the time, it just took some terrible situations to make him see it, but you know how devoted he and Bella are now, because they truly love each other."

"The pair of you are just a lot of hot air with your advice about the ladies. Some role models you are. Rakes? Hah!" Jack chuckled.

"Oh, I wouldn't say that, we've both had our moments over the years. I still look and appreciate and have the occasional harmless conversation…"

"Once a dirty bugger, always a dirty bugger," Jack smirked. "And what, exactly, is your idea of a 'harmless conversation'?"

"Now you look here, You Puppy, any more sauce from you and I'll go find my cane. Your teachers and the girls in Marguerite's cathouse aren't the only ones who know how to use one."

"I told you, no one is brandishing a cane over my backside, least of all you. Well, unless they've got long blonde hair, a small waist, long legs, a saucy mouth… and other interesting attributes, far too delicate to mention to a Gentleman of your advanced years. Remember, I'm The New Shadow," and he smirked at Francis who rolled his eyes at his cheek and nearly burst out laughing.

"Is that so, My Lad? Well, there's still life in the old one, make no mistake. Remember Nicky last Christmas?"

"I was being careful, but I've learned my lesson, I dare you to try and cane me now."

Francis turned to him with a curling smile. "Really? Come and find me tomorrow morning at dawn, in Hyde Park, and we'll see who has the biggest mouth."

"You're on. Canes or rapiers?"

"Your choice."

"Rapiers it is. I wasn't just sitting in the library, y'know, and I wasn't just farting around country houses all summer."

"I didn't think so, somehow."

"Dawn it is. The Old Shadow versus The New Shadow."

"Less of the old, thank you. I'd put you over my knee except it sounds like you'd probably enjoy it! Be waiting at the back door, I'll pick you up in my carriage at dawn."

Jack saluted saucily. "Yes, Sir. Just you and me? No seconds or audience this time?"

"Just you and me. This is between us, master versus apprentice. If I win, you can tell me what you really got up to last summer," he gave the handsome youth a knowing look, "it takes one nefarious Shadow to know what the other nefarious Shadow must have been up to."

"Shadows never reveal all their secrets, do they, oh Master?" Jack looked at Francis knowingly.

"Insolent Whelp, dawn it is!" and with a chuckle and a wink, Francis sauntered off. Jack watched his tall form disappear into the throng, still turning heads, even at his age. He thought about the lessons he'd acquired over the summer and was continuing to have, from a little Chinaman he'd run to earth in the burgeoning community in the alleyways of Limehouse, down by the docks in the East End of London, Bernheim's words and fighting skills burning in his brain. The Old Shadow was in for a big surprise the following morning, despite still being a renowned swordsman, and with a huge grin on his face, Jack turned and sauntered off in the direction of the blonde in the pink dress.

"I'd no idea you were such a good dancer, Lord Ashcroft?" Bella smiled at her partner as they waltzed into the throng of dancers.

"I'm a man of many talents, My Dear, as you well know, and please call me Miles, everyone else in the family does and you did once..." Ashcroft smiled, in his element dancing with the woman he'd been in love with since she'd first erupted into his office.

"Have you managed to beat Papa yet? You're the only man who can better him, you know."

"I have actually, a few weeks ago when he got back from Paris. He said he was distracted, lack of sleep I think he said. Obviously ate something nasty, snails were never my thing, slimy creatures, or too much smelly cheese, but more probably something odd in one of their rich sauces. Cover a multitude of sins sauces do... but I've got his measure now."

"Really?" Bella gaped for a moment. "I can hardly believe it, that's amazing," she grinned, "how many times has he beaten you?"

"Only three times, and I was distracted as well at the time. The aftermath of that little episode in Richmond took it out of me a trifle."

"Of course it did."

"Are you all right now, My Dear?" Ashcroft looked at Bella in concern as he spoke softly, "You can tell me, you know I understand."

"It's all stored deep in another box in my attic, Miles; hopefully it will never see the light of day again. I couldn't even bring myself to write about it in my diary, in case I happened on it again by mistake."

"Understandable. Shocking it was, simply beyond shocking, and Nicky? How is he? Oh, he seems his usual facetious self but your father was very worried about him for a while. He wasn't well, I gather?" Ashcroft fished.

"No, he wasn't. Some old wounds flared up, especially his bad arm." Bella waved her hand airily, "But he's absolutely fine now, fighting fit. I know, he fights me all the time," she laughed.

"Is that what you call it?" Ashcroft said sarcastically. "Is it right, a little bird told me you're expecting another happy event next year? What will it be this time, cod or lobster?" he chuckled.

"Who told you that?" Bella giggled. "And we've already decided on a name, very unfishy. I've told Uncle Francis, I'm not going near a ship for months beforehand. He or she will be Leonard, or Leo for short, or Leonora."

"Very leonine," Ashcroft chuckled. "I might have guessed."

"Private joke," Bella giggled again. "Papa has a big mouth, I presume?"

"Well, we have to talk about something over the chessboard," Ashcroft chuckled again. "He's terribly pleased, he dotes on you, on both of you actually."

"I know," Bella sighed. "I look so much like my mother, but he's extremely happy with Elise now, I'm thrilled for him... oh my GOD!" Bella gaped for a moment as her head turned and she tripped over Ashcroft's foot. "He's DANCING!"

"My word, so he is," Ashcroft stared for a moment. "He doesn't do it often, I gather?"

"He NEVER dances in public, never, EVER, and only lately at home within the family, and that's probably because he's likely had too much brandy, at Christmas for instance."

"Really?" said Ashcroft softly. "Well, I never."

"It's Elise, oh how wonderful! I've always wondered why, but then he's always been so self-conscious about his limp and awkwardness. She's brought him out of himself after all these years. Oh, Miles, you've no idea how pleased that's made me," and Miles looked into her big green eyes, glassy, almost on the verge of tears.

"Oh dear, don't weep on me, Bella, please. People will think I've stamped on your toes. My reputation will be in shreds," he smiled jokingly at her, moved by her obvious devotion to her father.

"I'm sorry, it's just such a surprise," Bella sighed. "Miles, you see, that's what love does for you," she smiled tenderly in her father's direction.

"I envy him, I envy you all. I wish I could find a woman I could settle down with. I've thought about it a lot lately," Ashcroft sighed and Bella raised her eyebrows in surprise, they all thought he was a confirmed bachelor, married to his work.

"Really? Well, if Papa can fall in love again at his age, after all these years, I don't see why you can't find yourself a wife, maybe even contrive a little Ashcroft," and she winked at him. "You're never too old…" and she giggled.

"Ah, but that's the problem. I don't just want ANY wife, and you're taken, unfortunately," Ashcroft joked, only he knew how serious he was. "Beauty and brains aren't commonplace, and what has Nicky got that I haven't? Apart from looks, swagger, address, charm, wealth, a Dukedom, being half my age and a complete idiot at times."

"Silly man," Bella laughed. "You're getting as bad as Uncle Francis, there's never been any other man for me, only Nicky, but if Papa can find Elise, we can find someone for you. There are plenty of intelligent women around, you just have to look for them. Men being what they are, they tend to keep their brains to themselves."

"Where do you suggest I look, then? Should I take up a pitch outside the British Museum and inspect the female visitors?"

"Not at all," Bella huffed in amusement. "I tell you what, I'm going to take you in hand. Make you my New Project and I'll enlist Elise. We'll find you the perfect wife, see if we don't," she chuckled. "My Great Aunt Elizabeth, the old Dowager, suggested Elise for Eddie, so I'm going to find someone for you. I'll start first thing tomorrow morning. I could put an advertisement in the Gazette, or

The Times," she mused. "How about. 'Eligible, supremely intelligent, well connected, titled bachelor of independent means, and fond of strange canines, seeks beautiful, witty and equally intelligent Lady. Must be extremely patriotic, able to play chess to a high standard and like men with interesting grey eyes and one-eared dogs," she giggled.

"Has anyone told you, you get more like your idiotic, facetious husband by the minute? Not to mention your reprobate uncle." Ashcroft shook his head in despair, "Strange canines indeed. Nelson would go into a decline if he heard you, and advertisement in the Gazette? Whatever next?" he burst out laughing.

"Well, if you insist on associating yourself with my eccentric family, what do you expect?" Bella winked at him. "But you know me well, Miles Ashcroft, when I make up my mind to do something, I always succeed, as a certain French personage we won't mention, found out to his cost," she tutted.

"He certainly did. Well, Dear Lady, it seems I am in your hands. I might as well try and stop a runaway curricle... er... are you sure you don't have time to work for me part-time?" And as they both burst out laughing Ashcroft whirled her around and into the melee of dancers.

"Will you stop going so fast, you're making me giddy," Cat laughed. "I'm a respectable Matron, not some gadabout girl."

"You could have fooled me. We could show Ashcroft and Bella a thing or two," laughed Nicky.

"OUCH!!" He suddenly stumbled as Cat came to a dead stop in the middle of the floor, her mouth rounding in a wide O, as she trod on his feet and they nearly fell over.

"*Mon Dieu, Edouard,*" Cat whispered in shock as Nicky's head turned.

"Papa? Bloody hell, is he DANCING?" he quickly righted himself and swept Cat into their steps again before too many people noticed who they were staring at and commented.

"Oh, Nicky, your kerchief," tears leached out of Cat's eyes as Nicky fumbled for and handed over a square of fine linen. "I never, ever, thought I would see it, it's so wonderful."

"Well, damn me, she finally did it. Isabelle, I owe you one," Nicky muttered to himself under his breath, an enormous smile on his face as he watched his step-father and Elise glide around the floor, totally engrossed in each other.

"Pardon?" Cat looked at him curiously.

"Oh, excuse me, just talking to myself. I'm so thrilled. Elise has been such a revelation and she's so good for him. He's got a new lease of life, especially since they came back from France."

"I know. I don't know what they did in Paris, apart from shopping and sightseeing, but it's done him the world of good and Elise has got big plans to refurbish our old de Mornay home in Normandy next year, so they can go and spend the summers there. It will be so good to have the old house back to what it used to be," she sighed. "It seems so long since I last saw it. I wonder if the old tree I used to climb up to get in and out of my bedroom unseen is still there?" she mused for a moment, her eyes far away.

"It's nice for him to spend some of that money he's made, instead of just leaving it to moulder in Rothschilds. Those sapphires are quite something, and they suit Elise perfectly, and I have it on good authority there are more where those came from."

"Mmmm, I always had faith in him, though I never expected him to become quite so rich. My dear Papa would have been staggered. He always thought Eddie's ideas were slightly mad and we knew he was gambling a bit to make some money in excess of his allowance, even before we left Normandy. He'd disappear off to Paris for weeks and weeks, then come back looking shockingly pleased with himself and dressed in the height of fashion. I was just happy to know he was getting over his injuries, he was terribly bitter about them, you know. When he was in his late teens and early twenties, girls would grimace at his scarred face. I could have hit some of them," she grated and Nicky grinned at her vengeful tone. "I'm not sure what Papa would have made of Eddie making such a fortune from trade, he was very conservative and old fashioned about things like that, but the world has changed." Cat sighed again, "Papa was so delighted when I married Francis and discovered just how wealthy he was, though of course he and Mama had NO idea of the truth," she giggled. "Mama hasn't seen this latest donation to my jewellery collection, she was goggled-eyed when I first wore some of the Firle diamonds, she'll have a spasm when she sees these," she smirked.

"I have to say I need some shades for my eyes, dancing with you in those sparklers," grinned Nicky as he whirled Cat around and around again.

"They are outrageous, aren't they." sighed Cat. "Are you sure you can't see any scars?"

"I can't see anything but diamonds in front of my eyes. They're blinding, and those scars have almost faded to nothingness, as you well know."

"Not completely, though. Beady-eyed, nosey parkers would see them and I wasn't prepared to take the risk, no matter how much Francis nagged me. How on earth would I explain them?"

"Nonsense, you need spectacles. Look in the mirror, You Silly Woman, a blind man would be pleased to see them, and if you and Francis couldn't come up with some plausible story between you, I simply give up on you. How about, you've acquired a pair of deranged cats and they scratched you, or Francis came up behind you and went 'BOO!' while you were sewing one day, and you accidentally scratched yourself?"

"You are sooo stupid, I don't know how Bella puts up with you," tutted Cat with a laugh. "Me? Sew?" Cat chuckled, "And deranged cats indeed, what would Bubbles have to say about that?"

"He'd leave home, come and live with us. It's all peace and tranquillity in our houses, and we can manage a plentiful supply of cold chicken, cream puffs and brandy."

"Peace and tranquillity? Is that so? What about all my broken china down at the cottage? Not to mention a broken window?" she quirked an eyebrow.

"We had the window replaced, and those vases, and the plates and glasses, and don't forget the new flowerpots and urns," Nicky grinned wickedly.

"Hmmm, shocking behaviour. I was absolutely appalled," she tried to keep a straight face but gave up and smirked.

"Talking of which, I meant to ask, where DID you find those enticing brats? Were they really ill-treated urchins or just budding child actors? I've never had a quiet moment to ask you since the summer, I've been so busy with Alfie looking for some breeding stock to ship over to Valenciennes and overseeing the building of my new stables."

"What, Maisie and Bert? Aren't they sweet? No, they really were ill-treated urchins, or they used to be. I found them a lovely new home with a childless couple near Lewes. Mr Baker has an ironmongery shop there and they'd given up on ever having more children of their own after their first child died."

"Ah, I might have known, more waifs and strays like Jack, hmmm?"

"Oh Nicky, you've no idea. Maisie's mother was a low prostitute and she was consumptive. When she died the dreadful madam in the cathouse kept Maisie as no better than a child slave and was grooming her to sell as soon as she got big enough, unless a better offer came along from some depraved cretin who had a predilection for children, which fortunately hadn't happened but was undoubtedly on the cards. I've never been so disgusted and shocked when one of the girls in the house mentioned it. I came across Maisie quite by accident, dragging a huge bag of coal down an alley to the back of the house. The bag was almost as big as she was and she was so thin and dirty, I couldn't believe what I was seeing. I went into the house and remonstrated with the woman, it was so dreadful in there, you can't imagine. The men..." Cat grimaced and shuddered, "I swear if I hadn't had Maisie out, she really would have been abused shortly after, she was barely seven at the time. What she must have witnessed doesn't bear thinking about. She used to empty the chamber pots and take the waste out, it was all too sordid for words. I ended up buying her out as the madam insisted she was her legal guardian and I couldn't be bothered to investigate or argue the toss, but I punched the bitch on the nose before I left, I was so incensed," Cat said forcefully, "I hope I broke it," and Nicky laughed even though he was also appalled at the story.

"How did you find Bert? In the same place? And where was it?"

"Don't ask, The Dials, near The Rookery," Cat whispered and Nicky's eyes widened in shock. "He was in a tenement further down the alley. His mother was also a prostitute, she worked in the house from time to time but she died. She shared a room with her sister, a drunken sot, I think she had the pox too, and she sent Bertie out onto the streets to beg or pick pockets. Poor little lamb, he was scared to death of her and he was virtually starving. He only made a few pennies and she would beat him if there wasn't enough to buy her ration of gin. I found him begging outside the same cathouse, haranguing the men as they went in and out. After the episode with Maisie, I kept half an eye on the place in case she'd replaced Maisie with another child; well, I wasn't having any of that nonsense, and no mistake. The Bakers are such good-hearted people and they always said they wanted more than one child, so they were delighted to take in Bertie as well. And of course, I organised a small regular allowance for them too, to help pay for things, like clothes for the children and extra food, as they're not very well off... well not financially, but in my opinion, being loving and caring is a much more important attribute when it comes to parenting," she said forcefully.

"Good God, that's a terrible tale, but Cat, what on earth were you doing wandering about in The Dials, let alone The Rookery? Does Francis know? St Giles Rookery? I can't believe it, he'd go completely ballistic, surely, if he did."

"Of course not, and don't you DARE tell him. Well, after that episode when I found Jack and the children, I made it my business to wander around there from time to time to seek out other poor children. Francis knows I sit on endless committees to raise money for charities and that's what he thinks I do all the time; but I wanted to go and see for myself, not just sit and talk to other do-gooders."

"But Cat, The Dials, The ROOKERY, it's the most terrible, dangerous place. Please don't tell me you go there by yourself?"

"Of course not, I'm not THAT stupid," Cat tutted. "I always dress very plainly, even in old, worn-out clothes sometimes, and take a brawny groom or footman with me who I always stay close to, and I always have my pistol or stiletto handy, of course."

"Oh God, you're mad, you know that? Madder than ever, if that's possible."

"No, I'm not. If you saw what I've seen, you would understand. You've seen Maisie; imagine some perverted beast forcing himself on her, or even Bertie. I'm sure if the madam had seen him outside, she'd have had him in and made available. You know what these places are like, or I think you do, it's too ghastly for words. Just imagine Lizzie or Terrie in that situation."

Nicky blanched. "God forbid. Look Cat, next time you want to go for a walk around there, just let me know. I'LL come with and look after you. A single groom or footman isn't good enough, no matter how brawny they are, and if I'm not around, take Jack, for heaven's sake. At least he knows what he's doing around there, and his way around, so you won't get lost."

"Thank you, My Love, but you promise you won't tell Francis? He doesn't mind whatever I want to do for charity, how much money I give away, but he'd never approve if he knew I went out and about around The Dials and The Rookery, or The Stews, they're just as bad," she muttered to herself.

"You're telling me," Nicky tutted and then mused, "so they were telling the truth, then? Maisie and little Bertie. I wasn't sure, but there was something about them..."

"Well, I don't know precisely what they said, of course, but if they were referring to their former lives, then yes, they were. Terrible, wasn't it?"

"Appalling. I can't abide to hear of small children being abused like that," Nicky said forcefully, his mind suddenly full of his own long-ago memories.

"They said you were shocked. Bertie couldn't believe you gave him ten guineas," Cat chuckled.

"I'd have given him far more if I'd had it on me; I wanted them both to come back to Litlington with me, to look after them. Isn't it strange? I was going to ask you if you could find homes for them," he shook his head as the irony of the situation struck him.

"Nicky, why don't you get more involved in this and help me? I know you loathe all the endless paperwork you do, business isn't in your blood like it is in Francis and Eddie's, you're far too much a man of action, a bit like me in a strange way. If this sort of thing concerns you, why don't you support my charities too? There are so many poor children out there, something should be done. We have so much, and they have nothing, except starvation and abuse. I just want to help as many as I can, to get a better start in life, take them away from the crime and poverty, and people are so cruel, especially around there. You've no idea the satisfaction it gave me to punch that woman on the nose."

"I can well believe it, I know what you're like when you lose your temper, and you've just had a go at ME about your broken vases and window! What do you want me to do? Go around beating up more whorehouse owners and drunken women?" he joked.

"If it makes you feel better, go ahead. But there's far more dangerous and nasty people who could do with a thrashing, believe you me, and I can't think of a better person to do it. I'm only a woman and most of the people on my committees think I'm slightly deranged, but you're a man, a titled one, and a forceful one, you could make such a difference, Nicky. You can still breed your horses and oversee your estate affairs, but this would give you such a sense of doing something worthwhile, really it would."

"Cat, My Love, you have no idea how empathetic I am to what you've told me and what you do. You've just found yourself a willing and enthusiastic recruit to your army. Are you going to order me about like Bella does if I become your assistant?"

"Absolutely," chuckled Cat. "Just like I order Francis about, useless oaf that he is. Now, when I disappear out of the house in my old clothes and he looks at me suspiciously, I can tell him I'm off to a secret rendezvous with a tall, handsome young man. That should wind him up a real treat."

"And I can tell Bella I'm off to an assignation with a stunningly attractive older woman. She'll have my liver," Nicky chuckled.

"I think we'll make a wonderful team. *Vive La France!*" she announced.

"Hush, keep your voice down, have you been on the brandy again? I don't think that sort of expression would go down well here," he chuckled. "But it'll be just like when I was a young boy and you taught me to fence. We did have fun then, didn't we?" he mused as they continued to sway around, deep in their quiet conversation.

"Mmmm, Francis never did understand what we were laughing at half the time."

"Do you know, it was years before I realised that little girls didn't all wear stilettos under their petticoats or want to swordfight with me?"

"You Shocking Boy, as soon as you found out what little girls DID have under their petticoats we all know what you did do with them, and it certainly wasn't swordfighting," Cat huffed with a smirk.

"And that's when YOU didn't understand what Francis and I were laughing about the other half of the time."

"Was that all twenty-five years ago? Where have the years gone?" Cat sighed.

"I don't know, they seem to have flown past. But you're still as lovely as the day I first laid eyes on you in the Fortress. I'd never seen such a strange nun or such a beautiful one. I've never forgotten it..."

"And I'd never seen such an angelic-looking little boy, even if you were filthy and ragged. So brave, so self-possessed, you refused to run away, even when I ordered you to."

"What, and leave you to that bastard, Dupont? He was such an evil, brutal man, and such a pervert, Cat, you've no idea what he did to me. It's because of him that I understand about Maisie and Bert," Nicky said softly. "If I can stop one single child from being abused or experiencing some terrible depravity, I'll be happy, but maybe I can help plenty of them now."

"Nicky? Oh no, Nicky, My Love; I thought I'd saved you from such a fate? Don't tell me he'd already done it? That is beyond belief, you were four..." Cat gripped Nicky's sleeve in horror, her green eyes wide with shock.

"I'm afraid so, frequently, not to mention beating me and bandying me about like a toy amongst some of the other sods who worked for him there who were as perverted as he was. I could never forget it, nor being incarcerated in a deep, dark, unlit cell with the rotting carcass of my mother for I don't know how long. It took me years to confront it all and come to terms with it, but I have now, and I can finally talk about it. It was all part of what happened to me when I went a bit insane for a while last summer at Litlington."

"Oh God, You Poor, Poor Man, I'd no idea. Francis was very close-mouthed about it all, he just said all the terrible things that had happened to you in Rouen, then in Spain and France, and then the Richmond business with Bernheim, and your injuries, especially your arm, had all caught up with you and you simply needed time and space to deal with it in your own way "

"Well, it was that too. I was in a very strange place for a while, quite lost. But Francis ranted at me, worse than I've ever seen or known him, and he even hit me, really laid into me, black eyes and the rest, would you believe. But once he breached the dam, as it were, it all started to come out and once that happened, I gradually got better. I owe him a lot, Cat, as always."

"Hit you? Black eyes? Good grief he never mentioned that; but it was nothing, Nicky, what is family for? And as long as you're back with us and recovered, that's all that matters, and with another little fish on the way now too," she grinned. "Never mind your pride, you're breeding a shoal!" and she burst out laughing at his affronted expression.

"Over my dead body, and I'm emigrating before the birth, someone else can deal with it. I NEVER want to go through that experience again, it was the MOST horrendous and frightening thing I've ever done. She was in such pain, screaming and yelling, the whole crew could hear her, even above the storm, and I thought she was dying; as for the bloody mess..." he shuddered theatrically and Cat smothered another laugh. "It took me weeks to look at Bella again as I had before. I'd no idea women went through so much to give birth, the process is simply ghastly!"

"Oh, You Poor Man," Cat said sarcastically. "Perhaps now you'll accept we definitely are NOT the weaker sex. Put you off procreating a large pride of little lions or shoal of fish, did it?"

I couldn't face anything like that for weeks and weeks," Nicky's expression made Cat burst out laughing again, getting her more curious looks from other dancers passing by.

"Oh dear, what a trial. Perhaps I should get Francis to introduce some legislation in the House suggesting all men be present at the birth of their offspring. That'll soon make them think twice about their lecherous appetites."

"Where DO you get these ideas from? What with Elise muttering on about there being a female Prime Minister one day, or women fighting in the army, and Bella insisting women should have equal rights to men in everything, I think next time Francis threatens to emigrate to China, I've a good mind to go with him, or we could go to Africa and I could teach him how to be a lion tamer."

"You see, you're completely useless, just like him, running away from assertive women. You simply don't know how to deal with us. You wait, My Boy, one day... one day..."

"One day, my foot. There's only one way to deal with assertive women or plate throwers," and to Cat's huge amusement and shocked expressions from other dancers, Nicky kissed her, quite lasciviously, albeit extremely quickly and then looked as if he'd done nothing of the sort as they twirled around the floor.

"You DISGRACEFUL Lout, whatever are you doing?" she spluttered and laughed, licking her lips.

"Well, I always did have a thing about older women," Nicky's arch look was pure wickedness. "That was very nice, I'd always wondered, and it's not as if that's the first time a swashbuckling man has kissed you in the middle of the dancefloor in here, now is it? And don't you faint on me..." and as people around them stopped dancing and stared for a moment, the pair of them simply laughed at each other and merely carried on and the rest of Society tutted, as it always did when the eccentric Granville family gave the gossips something to talk about.

"Good God, whatever are Nicky and Cat doing?" Elise gaped as she spotted Nicky kissing Cat and turned her head at the gasps of people who'd noticed.

"What?" Eddie turned his head too, just as the couple quickly pulled apart, smirking at each other. "Oh Lord, it's like Francis and Cat all over again," he sighed with a grin, "though nothing is ever going to outdo that little episode. That boy is the absolute limit!"

"He's hardly a boy," giggled Elise.

"He'll always be a boy in my eyes," sighed Eddie again. "But it's good to see him back to his normal, disgraceful self."

"Like father, like son," whispered Elise in his ear and smirked at him.

"Well, I do beg your pardon," Eddie chuckled. "And since when are we so prim and proper?"

"WE, behave ourselves at all times in public," tutted Elise.

"Is that so? Hmmm, tell that to the caretaker who found us in the gardens at Versailles."

"He was a nosey parker."

"Voyeur, more like," Eddie smirked.

"You led me astray," giggled Elise.

"And didn't you enjoy it?" It was a statement, not a question, and he laughed with enormous satisfaction. Between dancing with his wife and pleasuring her as he had on their belated honeymoon in Paris, and not only in their hotel bedroom, he felt like he was a re-invented man and hardly knew himself. She made him feel like he could conquer the world and his love for her grew with each passing week. "And speaking of enjoyment," he leaned to whisper in her ear, "we really must do something about all the noise you make, you must try not to cry out quite so loudly; the strange looks I got from the concierge when I settled the account at our hotel when we left were very knowing."

"And that is MY fault?" Elise whispered back.

"Is it my fault you're so demanding and get carried away?"

"Speak for yourself," Elise huffed then laughed saucily.

"God, you look so lovely tonight, those sapphires suit you perfectly; I'm going to make love to you later in just them and your stockings. I can barely keep my hands off you as it is."

"You didn't in the coach coming here."

"Just putting you in the mood, and I wanted to see if your little balls were having the desired effect."

Elise went bright pink. "Ssshhhh! Those little Chinese things are simply dreadful. I should never have let you try them out on me in Paris, it's given you all sorts of erotic ideas."

"They'd been sitting in my dresser's private drawer for nigh on twenty years, it was about time they saw the light of day."

"Now I know why Francis says he wants to emigrate to China. The entire population must spend their time fornicating and not getting any work done," she giggled as she whispered in his ear.

"He's absolutely no idea. I told you, that's what you get from sending people there in your stead to investigate new trading opportunities," Eddie smirked.

"Carlotta didn't know what she was missing," Elise sighed.

"I don't know why I brought them back; I told you I only bought them on a whim when I heard about them. I suppose I had a vague idea I might give them to her one day, but at the end of it, I just didn't dare to."

"It's such a tragedy, all those wasted years. I know you loved each other but you were so wary of her, and she of you," she sighed sadly.

"But you get to reap the benefit," Eddie whispered in her ear. "You know, you've been looking a trifle flushed ever since we arrived. Even Francis noticed. He said you were looking… ah… perky."

"Nooooo. Oh God," her blush deepened and Eddie chuckled.

"I said you were feeling the heat in here. I have to say it is a terrible squeeze."

"Feeling hot is an understatement. You know what happened when you made me ride down to the village with them in. I had to go and sit down and have a glass of water when I got there, I was so overcome."

"I'd have given anything to see that," Eddie laughed wickedly. "Oh, Elise, *Ma Chèrie, je t'aime…* so very much," he leaned and whispered in her ear followed by a stream of eloquent French which she now understood and her heart tripped in her chest.

"It's so wonderful to dance with you, I could do this all night," she sighed.

"I hope not, I've got far more pleasurable ideas in mind. I've never made love to you with them in, I'm told it's extremely arousing, not that I can quite get my head around the geography, as it were. Nevertheless, I'm expecting some spectacular results. I can hardly wait to experiment."

"Bad man," she tutted with her own wicked smile, "is there no end to your lecherous suggestions?"

"Elise, My Love, you've absolutely no idea. But if you're willing to experiment then so am I. Who cares what we do, no one knows except us, and if it's pleasurable to us both, that's all I care about. Besides, there's nothing much else to do before we go to sleep at night, or after dinner, especially down at Arlington, and experimenting is a damn sight more interesting and entertaining than reading yesterday's news sheets," and Elise chuckled as he grinned.

They glided round in circles for a while, whispering to each other, and Elise leaned in close and asked, "Eddie, are you sure your leg is holding up, you're not in any pain are you?" she looked at him closely.

"No, I'm absolutely fine. I'm so glad I found that little Chinese man in Limehouse who practises acupuncture. It eases the ache amazingly. I'd almost forgotten after I tried it when I was in China all those years ago."

"Strange how putting needles in you can ease pain, yet when they did that to Nicky in Nice, it had the opposite effect," Elise mused. "I have to say I find it all extremely bizarre."

"It certainly is, and I don't understand it at all. I can barely talk to the man, but he obviously knows what he's doing. I was going to suggest Nicky sees him when his arm twinges, but it's a bit close to home and I don't think he'll be able to deal with it. The last thing I want is to resurrect any of his nightmares again."

"Mmmm, I quite agree, but you must say when this waltzing gets too much for you."

"My Darling Girl, I know I won't see fifty again but as long as I'm fit enough to make you cry with delight when we get home, that's all that need worry you."

"Fifty, fiddlefaddle," Elise tutted. "But be warned, Husband Dear, if we keep waltzing around like this, something rather inappropriate might happen to me in the middle of the floor that will make Nicky's kiss seem quite mundane," Elise winked at him.

"Perhaps we'd better go and sit down then; I'm not going to spoil my fun," smirked Eddie. "Oooh look, who is that lovely girl in pink Jack's dancing with? She looks quite overwhelmed, and doesn't he look quite the thing tonight? Young devil, you'd never know where he came from, he's got such an aristocratic air about him. Y'know, I've no idea how he did so well in his exams. It's deuced fishy if you ask me. When I was tutoring him in the Easter holidays, before he went back for his final term, he was struggling no end."

"He told me he worked like stink, day and night," mused Elise. "Maybe it all came together, you know how it is…"

"Hmmm, and I'm Napoleon," chuckled Eddie. "But it doesn't really matter now he's finished with Eton. Francis and I think he'll do well broadening his horizons, travelling a bit, he's definitely got a head for haggling and trading, even if the finer points of algebra, geometry, chemistry and physics seem beyond him. The only thing that really fascinated him in that department was making something that exploded, like gunpowder, and I don't even want to think about why he was interested in that!" and Elise rolled her eyes at that bit of information as Eddie nodded at her with another amused sigh. "I gather Francis is going to send him over to the Carolinas on one of his ships after Christmas and see how he does; but God only knows what mischief he'll get up to over there, away from our supervision. I'm telling you if he's half the lad I think he is, he's definitely going to out-shadow The Shadow. He's so obsessed with Francis and his past, not to mention Nicky's work for Ashcroft, I hope America knows what's coming."

"Oh, leave the boy alone, he's such a lovely lad, why do you all think the worst of him? It's the girls you should be worried about, I swear he's worse than Francis and Nicky and you put together. He could charm his way into anyone's petticoats, take it from me," Elise now sighed with a laugh as they watched Jack flirt with the blushing girl he was dancing with.

"See, he's even got you wrapped around his little finger," Eddie chuckled. "You mark my words, that boy has nefarious written all over him, just you wait and see," and with that, he swirled Elise over to the side of the ballroom floor and they disappeared off to find some refreshments and sit and watch the gathered throng.

Epilogue

PART 2

J ack sauntered across Horseguards and into the back entrance of the nondescript Government building. He was stopped by the official on the door. "Can I help you, Sir?" he looked the youth up and down, noting his elegant, expensive clothes but he wasn't taken in; the tall lad couldn't be more than eighteen, nineteen at the most.

"Actually, no, My Man, but thank you for asking. I'm quite familiar with the place, I have been here before. I'm merely on my way to see Lord Ashcroft," Jack pulled out his gold pocket watch and tutted. "In fact, I'm frightfully late; Miles will be most displeased."

The uniformed official looked the young man up and down again with a disdainful eye, "Do you have an appointment, Sir."

"Of course I have an appointment. Do you think I just stroll in and out of Government buildings at random because I have nothing better to do with myself?"

"Quite possibly. There are a lot of radical elements around, Sir; we cannot be too careful," the man tutted officiously.

"Of course not, one should expect nothing less here in Whitehall, but, I ask you, do I look REMOTELY like a Radical? Or some anarchic riffraff? Not that I'd know what either look like, never having actually met one of the species." Jack quirked a brow and flicked an invisible piece of fluff off his immaculate jacket with an aristocratic and disdainful hand, the jacket one of Benjy's finest efforts that fitted and complimented his slender torso to perfection. The whole act was a complete imitation of Ricky Ambrose at his most sarcastic and superior. Both that man and Francis would have doubled up if they'd been witnessing this exchange.

"Possibly not, Sir, but it takes all sorts."

Jack was fed up with the difficult official and considered just brushing past him, but he didn't want to make a scene, so he sighed. "Look, My Good Fellow, much as I appreciate your dedication to keeping the occupants of this building safe from harm, would I be going around with this causing a bulge in my pocket, which my tailor would have a complete turn at if he saw how it spoiled the entire line, if I wasn't on my way to see Lord Ashcroft?" and he half pulled something wrapped in a kerchief from the inside of his jacket.

The official reared back. "Is that a pistol, Sir? Are you threatening me?"

"Oh, for God's sake, what sort of a man are you? You can't possibly have been a soldier despite your uniform," Jack tutted in disgust. "This is a bone for Nelson, You Fool," and he poked the bulge back into his pocket, "Now look here, I've had enough of this nonsense. I'm later than ever because of you and I will tell Lord Ashcroft why, so get out of my way," and with a slight shove and considerable aplomb Jack pushed the officious individual aside and headed off towards the flight of stairs and hurried upwards as the doorman just watched him go, telling himself the lad did seem to know where he was going and if he had a bone for that scruffy dog, he presumably DID know that facetious icicle, Lord Ashcroft. He was a different official from the one who'd been on duty that fateful afternoon earlier in the year, or he would have remembered the demanding young man who apparently always kept a bone in his pocket for Nelson…

Jack smirked to himself as he headed down the long corridors, looking for the Department of Information, the small pistol he now always carried, back deep in the inner pocket of his jacket. Never again would he be outsmarted by the unexpected, he'd sworn to himself in the deserted field in Richmond.

He got to the door he was seeking and without a knock, simply opened it and sauntered inside. "Morning, Chalmers. I'm here to see his Lordship,

if you would be so good as to announce me."

"Master Vallance, isn't it?" Chalmers never forgot anyone. "You don't have an appointment, Sir, and his Lordship is rather busy at the moment."

"He won't be too busy to hear what I have to tell him," Jack looked knowingly at the grey man, "...and it's Mister Vallance now. I am not a schoolboy. I mean, look what happened last time I was here."

"Heaven forbid," Chalmers shuddered. "I trust you are not on such critical business this time?"

"I'd be in his Lordship's office already, and not passing the time of day with you if I were," tutted Jack. "Now be so good as to announce me. I can assure you he won't be cross."

"Well... I..." but Jack was in no mood to be put off and headed over to the door to Ashcroft's sanctum looking expectantly at Ashcroft's right-hand man.

"Oh, very well, just a moment, let me announce you," Chalmers tutted back and went and knocked on the door to Ashcroft's office.

"Come." They both heard the summons and Chalmers was about to head in before Jack, but Jack merely brushed him aside and walked across to Ashcroft's desk with a large grin on his face. "Good morning, Lord Ashcroft, it's been a while. We didn't get a chance to talk at the Ball at the Palace, did we?" and he turned to dismiss a bemused Chalmers with a flick of his hand.

Chalmers raised a brow at an astonished Ashcroft who merely nodded at him and the grey man withdrew with a glare at Jack's back.

"If it isn't Master Vallance," Ashcroft rocked back in his chair, "and to what do I owe this untimely intrusion? Not another crisis to put my life, never mind my nerves, at risk, if you're involved?"

"Ah, now, there's the thing," mused Jack, his lips curling upward, "and as I just told Chalmers, it's Mister Vallance now. Oh, hello Nelson," and he pulled a small biscuit from the pocket of his exquisite

ANTOINETTE GEORGE

pantaloons and fed it to the dog now sitting expectantly at his feet. Nelson gobbled up the treat in seconds and pawed Jack's boots for another. "Oh dear, never satisfied, just like your Master." He ignored the indrawn breath that emanated from the other side of the desk as he bent down and picked up the scruffy dog. "So, how are you, My Dear Admiral? Is Hardy treating you well? We all know who rules the roost in your household," and he laughed as the ugly mutt proceeded to lick his face enthusiastically and he fished another treat out for him as he returned him back to the floor.

Across the desk, Ashcroft sighed. Here was another individual from the Granville household who had seduced his dog. What was it about those men who could charm him and he ignored virtually everyone else? Ashcroft didn't even bother to answer his own question. "When you've QUITE finished? Unlike you and other people of your acquaintance, I do have work to do," tutted Ashcroft. "I trust this is NOT a social visit, so what do I owe the dubious pleasure, Jack?"

Jack sat himself down on the other side of the desk and smirked at the aesthetic man across from him. "How's the leg, Lord Ashcroft? Still have your stick, I see. Is that for practical or show purposes?" Jack eyed the stick that was leaning against the wall behind Ashcroft.

"Purely practical, I do assure you, my leg has healed nicely." However, Ashcroft swivelled in his chair and grasped the stick, turning back to Jack. He pulled the handle slightly and Jack could see it was in fact a swordstick before Ashcroft put it down to lean against the desk.

"Expecting more trouble, or are you going hiking in more muddy fields?"

"One can never be too careful, we're living in difficult times. The last thing we need is a repeat of what happened in France in 1789," said Ashcroft icily. "And don't you think assassinating the Prime Minister a few years back gave us all a sharp reminder of the reality of how little respect some people have for their leaders, even here in England?"

"Well, I feel considerably more reassured knowing you're looking out for us," smiled Jack, his dry tone making Ashcroft tut.

412

"Precisely, which is why I am so busy. So, MISTER Vallance, what can I do for you?"

"Well, you see..." began Jack, rocking back in his chair, "as you know, I have now finished at Eton and am left to my own devices. We, as in The Family, are all agreed that Oxford or Cambridge are not for me, so I am now a Young Gentleman of Leisure, and as I refuse to live on their charity, I need to find myself an occupation. Given my... ah... interesting background, it was felt that working for the Duke's organisation would be an answer, and trading the obvious opening. They think I am very good at negotiating and producing a good deal." He beamed at Ashcroft proudly, "Additionally, Eddie, the Baron, felt I needed to travel and 'broaden my mind', as he put it. So, to that end, I am off to the Americas, the Carolinas I think, after Christmas, on one of the Duke's trading ships, in charge of ensuring the goods receive a profitable price at the other end. Also, that we import back in a similar capacity, as in interesting and desirable goods bought at a low price to turn a nice profit here or in Europe."

For a moment, Jack thought back to the conversation he'd had with Francis a few days before. "... So you see, You Scapegrace, if you aspire to being another Shadow, among many other things, learning to sail would be useful. How to navigate, the stars, the currents... you never know when all that would come in handy, on land as well as at sea... but that, M'Lad, is secondary to learning how to trade; legally, I might add, but as you cross the Atlantic, I suggest you spend time with my captain and learn from him. Willoughby is a good man and patient, and he'll teach you well."

"Like the Chinaman I had lessons from last summer?"

"Yes, well, we won't go into that now, this isn't about you and your extremely ungentlemanly way of fighting," Francis tutted with a grin. He'd been knocked for six as Jack had unleashed the results of his lessons on the hapless Duke early in the morning after the Palace Ball, Francis's rapier flying out of his hand, much to his complete astonishment, as he'd fallen to the soft turf, gaping at Jack.

"So, back to lessons from Captain Willoughby. Is that how you started?"

"Not exactly. My late and much missed French uncle, Gerard, let's just say 'he dabbled', in a bit of brandy and tea to increase his income, and I learned from him when I was about your age, or a bit younger, actually. I used to spend my summers on his estate in Normandy, 'improving my French' as my family assumed, and visiting Paris to gain a bit of polish and... ah... *je ne sais quois*," he'd grinned, "and it went from there."

"Have you ever been to the Americas?"

"No, Jack, not that I didn't want to go, but I only got as far as the Caribbean a couple of times, visiting some of the islands in the West Indies when I was in my early or mid-twenties. What a land of opportunity," Francis had sighed, "and what a vast country; but I've too many responsibilities here and I never got the chance. Eddie was the one who went on the long overseas trips to investigate trading opportunities and new contracts, but now we're no longer at war with America, the time is ripe to capitalise on what the country has to offer, and it's an amazing country, Jack, simply amazing. Resources we can only dream about here. I hope you were paying attention in your geography classes," Francis tutted.

"Oh absolutely, oh Master, absolutely. I got top grades in my exams, remember?"

"Mmmm, wonderful, Jack, and that was well done of you as I've already said. I can't tell you how pleased Nicky and Eddie, as well as I and the family were to see your results. Despite my suspicions, you obviously worked extremely hard, even given everything that happened over the past year or two, and you didn't get too distracted at the tavern." Francis's sly wink made Jack's lips twitch. "Time enough for all that, but your schooling was important so I'm glad our faith in you was rewarded, despite my own misgivings about your behaviour. I just hope some of what you learned has remained inside that big head of yours."

"Oh, it has, and thank you, oh Master," Jack grinned at Francis.

"So, back to your forthcoming little trip, the first steps in what we hope will be a rewarding career for you. The world is your oyster, Jack;

learn and seize opportunities when they present themselves…" and so the conversation had drifted on.

"Well, that is very interesting and commendable, Jack, but I fail to see what it has to do with me," Ashcroft huffed and pointedly got out his pocket watch to peer at the time.

"Oh, but you see, Lord Ashcroft, it has EVERYTHING to do with you…" Jack said softly.

"It does? How so?"

"Well, you see, while I am over in our former colonies, poking around, looking for interesting goods at bargain prices to import back to England and turn a nice profit on, I rather thought I might be of use to you; digging around here and there for intelligence to import back to the Department of Information, or mayhap there are papers you want … er… acquired or repossessed… or messages sent?"

"Papers acquired? Messages sent?" Ashcroft's impassive face covered his rising excitement. "What exactly do you mean?"

"Well, Lord Ashcroft, as one Shadow to another," Jack smirked, "the present and the future, I thought I might as well jump the gun and offer myself to your organisation. A replacement for Nicky if you like, as I know you were going to ask me at some point."

"I was?"

"Of course you were. You've been watching me like a hawk ever since our paths crossed. All those pointed questions when we talked in the gardens at Valenciennes after Waterloo, for a start."

Ashcroft couldn't help himself, he threw back his head and his bark of laughter emanated beyond his office door. It was so rare an occurrence Chalmers hurriedly got up and stuck his head around it. "Is everything in order, M'Lord?"

"Perfectly," smiled Ashcroft back at the man. "Perhaps some coffee, if you would be so kind, for two," and Chalmers withdrew, completely bemused.

"So, You Disreputable Rascal, you think you can come and work for me? And where has this sudden idea arrived from? You've only just left school, and not long before that you were cleaning stables, and before that, you were struggling in the gutters and trying to avoid getting your neck stretched."

"But I think that's a perfect background for your line of work," Jack gave Ashcroft a superior smile, "and you were the one to tell me to come and find you at some point if I was at a crossroads... remember? At the end of our conversation at Valenciennes? You see, I haven't forgotten."

"That may be, but you need a degree of intelligence as well as being streetwise, as the saying goes," tutted Ashcroft. "I need clever men to work for me, men who can fit in anywhere and hold conversations with anyone, as well as understand political matters in some cases. You've only been at school for five minutes, how do I know you can cut the mustard?"

"I passed all my end of year exams with top grades," announced Jack. "I'm NOT an idiot."

"That's quite an achievement, Young Man. Congratulations," muttered Ashcroft, obviously impressed. "You must have worked extremely hard?"

"Well, the Baron spent all the rest of the Easter holidays tutoring and coaching me down at Arlington, while my wound healed, and contrary to popular belief in Berkeley Square and Hertford Street, I did pay attention in class and keep out of the local taverns... most of the time," he grinned mischievously.

"Is that so? I'm pleased to hear miracles are still happening then," Ashcroft's facetiousness belied his amusement. "So, Jack Vallance," Ashcroft rocked back in his chair once again, "you want to be a spy?" he said softly.

"I need the money."

"That is NOT what it is always about. No reward can possibly compensate for the risks my people often take. You have to believe in King and Country. Ask Nicky, you won't make your fortune being a spy, M'Lad."

"I know that," Jack said dismissively, "but I'm not cut out to be a paper pusher in the Duke's organisation, and I have other ideas, bigger ideas, but I thought this type of work might well suit me, and who knows what opportunities it could present."

"Is that so?"

"Absolutely. I've given it a lot of thought."

"Have you now? I know you're a brave lad, I've seen that for myself, but are you devious enough? Are you clever enough? Even nefarious enough? You're still only eighteen, after all... this is all slightly premature."

"How devious, nefarious and clever do I need to be? Nicky is a lot of things, but devious and nefarious? Well, he obviously is a bit, but not that much I wouldn't have thought, and Bella certainly isn't, intelligent and lovely though she undoubtedly is."

"You've no idea, Jack. How do you think Nicky tracked down Bernheim in Spain, and then in France? And what he did for Wellington in the weeks before Waterloo is need-to-know information only; but believe me, it would turn your hair grey." Ashcroft tapped his nose, "Bella is another matter, but she convinced Bernheim in Nice, and no one outside the family knows she still runs those gaming establishments of hers."

"I suppose... I've never thought of it like that," mused Jack. "But I'm so devious, you've no idea," he smirked.

"Really?" but Ashcroft was dismissive. "This isn't the squalid alleys of the Dials or Rookery, Lad, this is a deadly game we're playing here. Often in the higher echelons of Polite Society, among the Establishment or the Military, wherever those in power congregate, socially or officially. Give me an example, and I'm not talking about cutting purses or picking pockets."

"I used to be a thief, a proper thief."

"I know that, but you were only, what, twelve? That hardly counts."

"I was learning to be a burglar, I told you, a proper thief; to break into the houses of the gentry and rich City types, merchants and shops. I could pick most locks then, I could pick anything now."

"And you've been practising, I suppose. When, in between geography and Latin classes at Eton?"

"Need-to-know, Lord Ashcroft, need-to-know," and Jack tapped his nose, smirking back at the man.

"That still doesn't prove anything. You need to be crafty and cunning, to be able to plot and plan and strategise. You need to keep a cool head in a dangerous situation and not panic; you need to be able to think on your feet, all of those things. Give me an example of how you've done that, then I MIGHT consider you."

"If I do that, you give me your word you'll take me on?"

"I give you my word I'll take you on when I think you're ready for it, and NOT before," tutted Ashcroft. "The tail does NOT wag the dog around here. I can hardly believe I'm having this conversation as it is, haggling with an eighteen-year-old. Whatever next. You're worse than Nicky, and that's saying something."

"Well, what do you expect from someone who lived and worked in the Granville household, and then got transferred to the de Bresancourt's? You don't get better teachers than both of the Dukes," Jack smirked.

"Oh, get on with it," tutted an irritated Ashcroft.

"All right," Jack sighed, "but I want you to know I did this, not for myself, because I couldn't really give a damn, but because of both of them, Francis and Nicky; and Bella too. I wanted them to feel their faith in me was rewarded and justified, and I'm not just a ne'er-do-well on the make, who isn't grateful for the opportunity they gave me. I'll never be able to thank them enough for what they did for me."

"You saved their lives, Jack, all of them," Ashcroft said quietly. "They don't want your thanks, they're in YOUR debt. Looking after you was the only way they could repay it."

"They could have just given me some money," Jack shrugged, "that's what usually happens in return for a good deed."

"But they're not like that, are they?"

"No, they're very special, and that's why I did what I did."

"What did you do, Jack?" Ashcroft was suddenly fascinated, not that he hadn't been fascinated from the minute Jack had sauntered into his office and dropped his bombshell on him.

"I cheated," Jack said quietly.

"The hell you did! In your exams I take it?" Ashcroft sat up.

Jack nodded. "I knew, no matter how much I tried, I'd never get my head around some things. I mean, what the hell is algebra for? A plus B equals C over D. What on earth is the point? Eddie spent forever trying to explain it all, but I'm from the gutters, I just couldn't understand. One guinea plus one guinea equals two guineas, or ten times one guinea equals ten guineas; or if you have ten guineas and you spend five, you have five left; that makes sense to me. A plus B?" Jack shrugged. "And then there's Latin. What is that about? No one speaks it anymore, they're all long dead, centuries ago. Who cares what Julius Caesar did in Gaul, writing about building earthworks when he laid siege to somewhere no one's ever heard of? Or the poems Horace wrote? Why don't they teach Italian instead? At least that might be useful to someone. Quite frankly, I'm glad they stabbed Caesar in the Forum, put an end to his bloody ramblings; verbs at the end of sentences, it's all back to front, different endings for every bloody word you read, no wonder no one speaks it anymore and the Empire collapsed... and then there's Shakespeare, and don't even get me started on Chaucer. Why couldn't they write in proper English? I mean, Shakespeare: 'To be or not to be, that is the question.' What question?" Jack shrugged again. "To be what? If he's contemplating doing away with himself, why doesn't he just say so? It's all gobbledegook, lines and lines of it, and HE wrote about bloody Caesar. AGAIN! What is it with that man? 'Friends, Romans, Countrymen, lend me your ears'. Whatever happened to, "Ey, oi, yous there, yer motley lot, listen 'ere. Caesar's popped 'is clogs, bin done in, I've come ter arrange 'is funeral, an' I ain't gonna say more'n a few choice words neiver, as 'e weren't no saint..."

Ashcroft's lips twitched, the lad was too funny. "How did you cheat, Jack?"

"Ah, now then," Jack abandoned his rant about his lessons and eyeballed Ashcroft. "So, knowing I hadn't a hope in hell of doing well in most things, except French possibly, well, you'd understand why I got to grips with that," he sighed, "and fencing, with the teachers I've got at home, and my English isn't at all bad now I've been elocuted... therefore, not wanting to disappoint the family, I decided desperate measures were needed. Hence, I broke into the Headmaster's office one night."

"Reeeally? How fascinating." Ashcroft didn't bat an eyelid, but he was completely engrossed.

"Oh yes. In the early hours. I crept out of my dormitory and it was easy getting into his office, the door was never locked. The exam papers were all locked in a cupboard though, but it was nothing for someone like me to get into that, except someone came along..."

"Oh dear, that was a bit unfortunate."

"It was the caretaker. Evil sod, always patrolling around at all hours, keeping an eye out for wandering boys... off to the kitchens, mostly, though, to find something to eat, if they were lucky. Bane of my life he was when I went off to the local tavern after a hard day in class," Jack grinned for a moment and Ashcroft rolled his eyes. "So, there was I, busily copying out the questions in the exam papers when I heard him coming along the corridor. I snuffed out the candle, shut the cupboard door and dived under the Headmaster's big desk with all my papers, but he must have smelled the candle even though I fanned the air, or something else, as he came into the room, sniffing, and wandered around, helped himself to a glass of Madeira off the sideboard, sly bugger, and then he sat down at the Headmaster's desk, not a foot from me. I thought my heart would burst out my chest I was so sure he'd find me; but he drank his drink, got up eventually, wiped the glass on his stinking shirttails and put it back on the sideboard. Urrrgh..." Jack shuddered in distaste, "then just shrugged and left and carried on his patrol. I finished my copying as quick as I could, put all the papers back in the cupboard, very carefully, in precisely the same order I'd found them, locked it after me and went back to bed just before dawn."

Ashcroft was sitting, completely riveted by this tale of youthful misdemeanours and criminality. "But even with the papers, I STILL couldn't answer all the questions, so I sent them via a fast courier to Eddie, pleading for him to answer them quickly and by return, saying I hadn't been well, had knocked my wound and had had to retire to bed for a bit as it got infected, so had got behind in class and I was at my wit's end. Soft heart that he is, he sent them straight back. He must have been at it day and night, to do it so quickly, but there it was, everything in endless detail and explained to boot. He's far better than any teacher there, believe me... so between that, and some deep research in the library which took me every spare hour, I was well prepared for when the exam days came. *Et voilà,* I passed with flying colours, though I was careful not to answer every question perfectly, I'm not that stupid," he finished with a boyish grin, but his face went suddenly serious. "You have to give me your word you'll never tell ANYONE what I did, please?" Jack begged Ashcroft. "I told you why, and it was the truth. Oh, and you'll like this... they STILL didn't give Eddie one hundred percent for his Latin translation," Jack chuckled.

Ashcroft looked at Jack for a long moment and then, for the second time that day, he threw his head back and guffawed with laughter. "You Misbegotten, Conniving, Thieving Boy," Ashcroft cackled, "that's the funniest thing I've heard since Francis first admitted to me he was The Shadow."

"You're not cross with me? I knew it was wrong to cheat, I'm a Gentleman now and I know I shouldn't do things like that, but I HAD to, you do understand?"

"Jack, there are plenty of Gentlemen who I wouldn't trust from here to here," Ashcroft swept his finger a few inches across his desktop, "and there are plenty of cheats in the London clubs, believe me, but they'd never own up to it. Your secret is safe with me, M'Lad, never worry about that. Oh Lord, and you can't even tell Eddie he didn't get top marks for his Latin." Ashcroft found that even funnier. "It's too much, I'd have given anything to see his face on hearing that," and he doubled up with mirth, much to Jack's bemusement.

"Does that prove I'm devious and clever enough, Lord Ashcroft? I know I wouldn't have passed my exams, but I've only been at a proper school for a couple of years. I'd never even heard of William the Conqueror or algebra til I arrived at Eton, never mind bloody Caesar, his Gallic Wars and the Ides of March."

"You knew who Androcles was, and Machiavelli," chuckled Ashcroft, "that's good enough for me; and just so you know, I could never see the point of algebra either, not much use when keeping an eye out for enemies of the State or more would-be assassins of the Prime Minister or Royal Family," he winked.

"Really?"

"Really. Ah, Chalmers, thank you... perfect timing," his assistant appeared with a coffee pot, cream, sugar and cups on a tray and put it down on Ashcroft's desk and silently withdrew.

Ashcroft sat back, hugely amused and impressed, but his face gave nothing away as he sipped his coffee. "Well, Jack, that's all extremely interesting. But at the end of the day, breaking into your Headmaster's office and copying out some exam papers, isn't exactly breaking into a Government building in a foreign country where you're likely to be shot, at the very least, if you're discovered. You know what happened to Nicky in Nice, not that you're likely to come across many deranged individuals like Bernheim, but over the years I've lost men to torture when they've been taken, and some, unfortunately, are rotting in foreign prisons, despite our best diplomatic efforts to get them out. The worst that could have happened to you at Eton was expulsion; that's not exactly the same, the caretaker was hardly going to shoot you, was he?"

"But the disgrace would have been terrible. I would never have lived it down, it would have ruined me before I'd even started... and I couldn't have faced the family. I've promised faithfully I'd leave my thieving past behind me now."

"So, what are you doing here? No, don't answer that," muttered Ashcroft. "As I said, this isn't about picking pockets, this is King and Country; a whole other matter."

"I don't know what else I can tell you to prove my point," sighed Jack.

"Isn't there something?"

"Why are you looking at me like that?"

"Leopards don't change their spots, Jack, not in my experience. Francis Granville is one of the richest men in England, but I'd stake my life the brandy I drink in his house has come straight up from the beach. It's not that he can't afford to buy it, it's the thrill and challenge, and the amusement to outwit His Majesty's Revenue men; and Lord knows what other nefarious things he gets up to with his brother-in-law, in their business dealings, that also evade taxes. He'll have the smuggler's mentality until he dies, Jack, you mark my words." Ashcroft rocked back in his chair as he put down his coffee cup, "Whereas you, Mister Vallance, are a thief. It's in your blood and although I'm not a gambling man, I would bet your fingers will itch for a long time to come, if they haven't been itching already. You must have been out of your mind with frustration at all the baubles on show at that ball at St James's." Ashcroft's brow quirked and his lips twitched. "But I also think, like Francis, your heart is in the right place. I'd also bet you've never touched so much as a penny or a piece of paper that wasn't yours in any of the family homes, have you?"

"Of course not," Jack bridled, "what do you take me for?"

"A thief, Jack, but a principled one," said Ashcroft softly. "That's what you're here to offer me, after all, your skill at breaking into places and taking things that don't belong to you, for the greater good. Just like the reason you cheated at Eton. You see, Jack, if I thought you didn't have a conscience, I wouldn't touch you with a bargepole, and you would be out of this office on your arse before you could say 'shadow,' because I could never trust a man like that. Everyone has their price, Jack, everyone. Even Francis and Nicky. But their price is love for their family. You saw what happened in Richmond. Bernheim was expecting a struggle to get his money, based on what happened with Nicky in Nice, and Francis with his father, not that we think he actually knew the details of what really happened in that little episode, but the pair of them were on a different page this time. Before, their pride wouldn't let them concede, because it was a personal battle, them versus Bernheim, senior or junior, but this time, Cat and Bella were there, and Eddie and Elise, and that made a difference, so they simply caved in. Other people have different values, but few can resist money, it's what motivates most of us, and a lot of unprincipled people would sell themselves out for a few guineas; just like Judas and his mere thirty pieces of silver."

"What's YOUR price, Lord Ashcroft?" interrupted Jack.

"Me? I've never really thought about it. Not money, I can assure you... but who's to say if I was in the gutter and my life was at risk what I would do? Until you find yourself in that situation, one can never be one hundred per cent sure. But to answer your question, probably the people I care a lot about and my country. I couldn't have stood an abomination like Bonaparte overrunning England, although, I have to say, some of the measures he brought in while he was in power make a lot of sense, but then again, the country had gone to hell and France has always been a mess, in my opinion. However, now he's wallowing in misery on St Helena, I have other enemies of the country to deal with... internally and internationally. It is never-ending, Jack, never-ending. So, that is MY price, keeping our country safe."

"Very altruistic," muttered Jack.

"Don't be facetious with me, Boy, I won't have it," rasped Ashcroft. "Didn't you see that gruesome guillotine machine when you went to Paris with Bella? Right in the centre of the city? How would you like it if they set one up here, in Piccadilly, or outside St Paul's, and started chopping people's heads off, EVERY DAY, by the wagonload, just because they happened to mention they didn't like something the Prime Minister said, or because they were accidentally related to someone who had a title or some money, or was an intellectual, a Papist, a Jew or a prostitute. Have you any idea how many people were killed in Paris during The Terror alone?

"Thousands, tens of thousands across France in the Revolution alto-gether, my teacher reckoned," whispered Jack, "he said no one knows."

"I'm glad you were awake in your history classes," tutted Ashcroft. "Do you think I'm prepared to let that happen here? And believe me, there are plenty of radicals and all sorts of anarchist elements, racists and bigots running around who'd like to see that, so if you want to work for me, NEVER let me hear you mock love of your country and the sensible rule of law and order. We're not perfect here, by any means, but we're a damn sight better than a lot of other places. Once you've travelled a bit and seen for yourself, hopefully, you'll understand."

"I'm sorry, Lord Ashcroft," Jack hung his head. "I wasn't mocking you, truly. I know you've given your life to the service of your country, and Francis and Nicky think extremely highly of you. You're one of the few men they trust outside of the family, especially Francis, and you well know they trust very few people."

"That's all right, Jack. Apology accepted. I just wanted to make a point." Ashcroft liked that Jack readily apologised and didn't try and excuse himself. He went up in Ashcroft's estimation another notch. "Now then, back to what I was saying, about leopards and spots. So, you were a thief. Are you going to sit there and tell me, hand on heart, you've not thieved ANYTHING, since the Duchess hauled you out of the Dials?"

"No, Sir."

"I thought as much. Will you tell me what?"

"No, Sir."

"Why?"

"Because… because it's my secret. Just like Francis has his secrets."

Ashcroft sighed. "I need to know, Jack."

"But I can't."

"You mean, you won't?"

"No… yes… you wouldn't understand."

"Try me," Ashcroft said quietly, steepled his fingers, sat back and waited patiently. He refilled his cup of coffee as he waited and watched the youth in front of him grapple with himself, wondering what was so difficult to admit to. He actually wondered why he was asking, but he was curious. The more he got to know young Jack Vallance, the more the boy fascinated him… and he'd be perfect working for the Department of Information. He was clever, despite the gaps in his education; he was cunning; he could thieve, and he could fight, and he could mix with the lowest of the low, where he'd come from, and the highest in the land, with whom he now lived and socialised. Ashcroft was expecting a confession about some stolen money from school, or an ornament from the house of a friend, maybe even a shop or tavern he might have burgled for their takings, but he wasn't expecting Jack's sudden explosive confession, and it took his breath away.

"I'm the thief who stole Lady Bassenthwaite's emeralds. There, is that nefarious enough for you?"

Ashcroft's cup stopped half-way to his mouth. "Good God! That was YOU? YOU stole the Bassenthwaite emeralds?"

"Yes." Ashcroft could barely hear the whisper and he was absolutely stunned. There'd been an enormous hue and cry about it; Lord Bassenthwaite had connections in the Government as well as the City, and he'd called in all sorts of favours to find the burglar and recover his wife's famous jewels. The lady herself had been incensed and had written personally to all sorts of powerful individuals, bemoaning the lack of law and order now apparent in the country where people obviously couldn't sleep safe in their beds. It had been the talk of Society all the previous summer.

"How the HELL did you do that? And, I have to ask, WHY?"

"Because they belittled me, and Ernest Bassenthwaite is an evil, vicious bastard... and they're so rich, they won't miss them."

"Tell that to Lady Bassenthwaite. She was ranting on and on at that ball, wanted her servants hung, drawn and quartered as she was convinced it was one of them. She took the loss of her baubles as a personal affront."

"She's as bad as her son; horrible woman, foul-mouthed and foul-natured. Obviously where he gets it from."

"Good heavens, Jack, what on earth have they ever done to you? I didn't know you even knew them. I doubt Francis or Nicky socialise with them, they're not their type of people at all."

"I was at Eton with Ernest."

"Ah..."

"Oh, you've NO idea."

"Tell me, Jack, what did he do to you?" Ashcroft ordered softly.

Jack sat for a short while, his mind going back over the recent past, only a couple of short years, to his first term at Eton. He'd put on a swaggering, brave, laughing face when Francis and Nicky had left him there, complete with a cover story and ensuring people saw and knew their young protegé had been delivered by no less than TWO Dukes; but he'd felt bewildered, frightened, alone and totally out of his depth, in an upper-class world that was like another planet. He hadn't known the angst the two men who'd left him there had suffered as they'd departed and driven back to London, but Francis had maintained if Jack could survive a term, or even two, it would be the making of him; he wouldn't look back and nothing in the world would challenge his aim to be a Gentleman. Nicky was more worried, he'd had his own problems there in his time, being French. But he was a Duke, not a stableboy, and he'd had his own demons that wouldn't let any older boy or master abuse or beat him again, so he'd kept his head down, fought back at the right time and place, and won the respect of his peers. Jack wasn't a Duke and he'd had little schooling, and he'd walked into an utter nightmare.

"Ernest was in my year and a few weeks after I'd arrived, a little late as the term had already started, he found out I was an ex-stable-hand. I gather he got it from one of his grooms who'd got it on the servants' grapevine, and then he dug deeper, and somehow, he found out I'd come from the Dials. God knows how he discovered any of it, especially as we were cloistered away in school, but I reckoned he must have paid someone to ask questions and investigate my background. I've no idea why, as, on the face of it there was nothing to make me stand out, and I was a Duke's ward; I NEVER spoke anything except perfect English and I watched my mannerisms. I was so careful, but I must have done or said something, or maybe it was just that no one had ever heard of me in connection with the family. Anyway, whatever caused it, my background wasn't a secret when I first arrived at Firle, so I suppose I shouldn't be surprised someone said something. From then on, however, once he knew the truth, Ernest made my life hell, he and his supercilious, bullying friends and then his family. They were all as bad as each other, but he was one of the worst, actually THE worst. I didn't have blue blood or an ancestral line, or was even remotely related to the aristocracy, and that's what counted. Nor was I from a rich or powerful, or influential family, even if I was a Duke's ward. He was also venomous about Nicky, called him a dirty French bastard and more. He called Cat a French whore and Eddie an ugly French cripple. I know we'd been at war with France, but they've spent half their lives here, and look what Nicky did for his country."

"Unfortunate, but some people are so bigoted," tutted Ashcroft, disgusted despite himself, "what did he do to you, Jack?" his voice whispered into the quiet room.

"I got set upon and then beaten up. The first time I could barely walk, bruised or cracked ribs and everything. I don't actually know how bad it really was, though they were very careful not to mark my face so the teachers wouldn't find out, and don't you ever tell the family, they'd go mad. Nicky would do something rash like calling him out and killing him. When I got home for Christmas, I'd just about recovered and Francis, Cat and Nicky gave me some fencing lessons. I said I needed to be able to fence, but I think they suspected I'd been bullied, and although it helped with other boys, and believe me, that place is full of bullies, it didn't do much against Ernest and his coterie of like-minded friends. I went back again the following term and they beat me up again and again; they weren't so fussy about my face the second and third time but the teachers merely turned a blind eye, the bastards," he muttered, "then they really went to work. They stole my clothes, my belongings and my books; they made my life utter hell on earth. I would frequently find horse manure and straw in my bed, or among my clothes, and when I could get into bed, they'd deliberately wake me up, again and again throughout the night... sling cold water over me, tip up my mattress so I fell on the floor, rip off the covers and hide them, they even set my bed on fire once. Jack lifted his head and his deep sherry eyes looked directly at Ashcroft, "Francis and Nicky think it amusing I spent so much time at the local tavern, and thought the money they gave me, which I had to keep well hidden or that disappeared as well, went on wine, ale and girls. But the reality was, I was in and out of a local doctor who strapped me up and tended my wounds, and do you know why I ended up keeping a room at that hostelry? Because at least the bed was clean and I could sleep and keep my clothes and belongings there, and it was only because I was so used to creeping around in my time at the Dials that I could get in and out of school without being found out. And if I couldn't get out sometimes, it wasn't difficult for me to sleep on some bare floorboards somewhere, or in a cupboard, or even outdoors on the grass on warm nights. Bare floors were nothing new to me, and I've slept in enough doorways or streets in my time. Never mind drinking and fornicating, I was so bloody tired and sore, all I wanted to do was sleep." The sherry eyes narrowed and grew hard, "And Ernest Bassenthwaite was the ringleader of it all. I tell you,

Lord Ashcroft, Eton is no better than the Dials in some respects," he grated.

"You poor boy. I know public schools are bad, but they do tend to make men out of boys. Nevertheless, why on earth didn't you tell someone? I can't believe the Headmaster would turn a blind eye to all that? Good Lord, if Francis knew half of what you've just told me, he'd create merry hell there. Never mind the guilty teachers, the Headmaster would be out on his arse, and deservedly so."

"I couldn't, WOULDN'T tell anyone. I'm not a sneak or a wimp. I survived in the Dials and I was damned if I was going to give those bastards the satisfaction of driving me out of Eton," Jack snarled. "I got my own back, my way."

"Oh dear, dare I ask how?"

"I cut him, with my knife. Bernheim had nothing on me."

"Good God!" Ashcroft actually gaped.

"I waited and waited until I could catch him alone, and I did, one night when the senior boys were out having a quiet drink locally over the weekend. I attacked him when he went to have a piss and hauled him off down an alleyway in Windsor. He was no match for me by himself, without his cronies. He's now got a long scar down his chest and abdomen to remind him not to mess with former citizens of the Dials, and I cut the tendons behind one of his knees in payback for what he said about my family. I told him to see how HE liked being an ugly Yorkshire cripple. That's why you didn't see him dance at the ball, he's still recovering, and he'll never run or walk properly without getting a pain in his leg, if it heals that much. I told Ernest Bassenthwaite if he and his evil friends came near me, ever again, I'd cut his bollocks off, literally, castrate him like a stallion, and that's what you get from tampering with horse manure, which is how they referred to me, amongst other things of an equine nature I won't sully your ears with."

"My God, talk about retribution..." the goings-on Jack related at what had happened in the country's leading school made even Ashcroft's eyes widen.

"Exactly. Ernest left me alone for a long time after that, he told the school he'd had a riding accident to explain his leg injury, and gradually, the other boys got the message, but I never had to do anything so drastic to anyone else. The worm had turned and I fought a lot of them, and cut one or two, but nothing serious. After a while, some of the other boys who were also being badly bullied came to me and I helped them. They were the friends I went to stay with over last summer. Unfortunately, but you won't be surprised to hear, Ernest tried to have his revenge on me when I got back to school after Easter. He thought since I was injured I'd be fair game, but I was very wary and slept with my dagger and a pistol under my pillow, when I wasn't working in the library, and mostly slept in the tavern. It was like an exhausting game of cat and mouse, but I managed to avoid him, thank heaven, and I had the last laugh to boot. I wasn't going to let him get away with everything he'd done to me and insult my family."

"Dare I ask?"

"What I didn't tell you, Lord Ashcroft, was that I broke into the Headmaster's study a second time. I found all the exam papers waiting to be marked and I made a mess of Ernest's, and one or two others I wanted to pay back for various reasons. I tampered with them, just enough, and their marks were abysmal. It was petty, they had no idea what went wrong, and there was little I could do with essays and the like, but other papers weren't so difficult to alter. They were confounded, but I knew, and I got a lot of satisfaction from it."

"That, Jack, is quite an extraordinary story. But if you did all that, and you more than got your revenge, why on earth did you steal his mother's emeralds?"

Jack got up from his chair now and started to pace around the room as he talked, in full flow as he finally confided in someone what he'd done. "As I said, I went to stay with two or three school friends over the summer. Unfortunately, the Bassenthwaites turned up at one of the house parties. Ernest must have told his mother and father about me, though ironically not what I'd done to him; I still don't know how he explained that as any doctor would know his knee had been cut, and it was no riding accident, but it matters not. The point is, Ernest has a sister, Anne. A nice young girl, nothing special to look at, terribly timid and bullied by her mother, but away from her, she was very sweet, nothing like her dreadful older sibling. When her mother caught Anne merely talking to me, soon after they arrived, she went absolutely ballistic and caused a terrible scene, and that's what set her off. The woman made it her business to treat me like a pariah, the entire time we were there. She told everyone who would listen that I was nothing better than a common, thieving beggar, or filthy stableboy, fit only to shovel shit, and tried to get me thrown out of the house. It was so embarrassing for everyone, especially my hosts, but although I suppose I should have done the gentlemanly thing and disappeared quietly to save everyone's embarrassment, I was determined not to leave with my tail between my legs. Therefore, I brazened it out. Not only was I incensed on my own behalf and made to feel like a maggot, and a number of Society people have now heard the truth about me, though whether they believe it or not I'm not sure; however, poor Anne got sent to her room for the duration of their stay, and the next time I saw her, as they were leaving, she was limping slightly and had a livid bruise on her cheek from where her mother had obviously beaten or hit her, just for innocently passing the time of day with me, and she cringed and ran away when I tried to apologise. Not that I'd done anything remotely wrong or inappropriate, but I felt so sorry for the abused girl."

"Well, that explains WHY, but not HOW you thieved the emeralds."

"She'd brought them with her; there was a big ball on the Saturday night of the house party, quite a turnout and all the local gentry from the surrounding district came as well, and she was preening herself all evening, wittering on about her bloody necklace, that's when I first saw the emeralds. I didn't even know they existed before that. Then, as luck would have it, I went to stay with another friend, a few weeks later, who also lives in Yorkshire, though quite a way away from the Bassenthwaites. When I discovered where their house was, I couldn't help it, I just wanted to pay that dreadful woman back. So, I went riding a lot for several days," and Ashcroft actually smirked. "They thought it was over the Dales to look at the scenery, but I went to have a look at Bassenthwaite House. I disguised myself a bit, got some spectacles and greased my hair down, and I went into the kitchens and pretended I was making a delivery, and chatted up a couple of the serving girls about the routine in the house, when people went to bed, and so on. Oh, sweet things, they were so gullible and such gossips. Then I hung around in the local tavern and did the same thing with a couple of footmen, except with a slightly different disguise. No glasses this time, I became a dirty farm labourer with bits of mud on my face and hair. It was all very casual and they'd no idea. It was just like being a servant again," and Ashcroft's lips twitched as Jack shrugged.

"On a couple of my excursions around the Dales, I told my hosts I'd got lost to explain my late return. They were very concerned and said I shouldn't be riding around in the dark, I could get attacked and robbed, how funny is that, and they said I should have put up at an inn and merely sent a message to that effect so they wouldn't worry. They thought I was another harmless and somewhat dim wimp like their son, so that's what I did a couple of times. But of course, I'd been casing up Bassenthwaite House at night, peering in through the windows, watching them all and their routines, and the comings and goings. Then, having laid my plans, I pleaded sickness one day and retired to my room but sneaked out, helped myself to a horse from the stables when all the grooms were having supper, rode hard over to Bassenthwaite House and broke in, in the early hours. I climbed up some creeper at the back of the mansion, where there was an open window, and went into a deserted bedroom. From there, I crept around the upstairs until I found Lady Bassenthwaite's bedroom. She was snoring for England and I searched all her cupboards and in her dressing room. I'd no idea if she kept her jewellery there, or if it was locked away downstairs somewhere, but I struck lucky. I found a strongbox, hidden at the back of an armoire, and made off with it, and no one was any the wiser. It was almost too easy, and I had a perfect alibi, not that I needed one. I was asleep with a migraine, miles and miles away, somewhere completely disconnected from the Bassenthwaite's social milieu; but no one ever asked."

"What was in the box?"

"The emeralds and some other bits and pieces of jewellery, obviously not the rubies, she must keep them in another box somewhere, and I wasn't going to push my luck and hunt for anything else; as I said, it was my lucky night and I wasn't going to push it."

"What have you done with them, if you don't mind me asking?"

"I had to be very careful about fencing them, given all the fracas going on about the burglary, and I know the Runners know a lot of the fences in London, on the quiet, and I didn't dare keep them at home for long in case one of the servants came across them by accident when they were cleaning my room, even though I hid the box under a couple of floorboards I'd loosened and had a rug over them to boot. So I told the family I was going away for another stay in the country with schoolfriends; they were all down in Sussex so weren't particularly interested in what I was up to, and I went over to France."

"Whaaaat? All by yourself?"

"Mmmmm, my French is quite good now, I practise it a lot with Nicky and Bella, and try and talk to Cat and Eddie in French as well when I see them. And when I was in Paris with Bella, you know, when we were looking for Nicky, I went off on my own and wandered around all the more insalubrious areas... incidentally, that's how I eventually found him. But whilst doing that, I'd asked around, knowing the criminal fraternity always tend to know what's going on in those places. So I went back there, disguised myself again with glasses and a false beard this time, and eventually found a fence. I didn't get nearly the value of what I'd get in London, but it was much safer over there, and as you've gathered, this was never about the money anyway. So I've opened myself a little account in Rothschilds, who I gather are one of the best bankers to invest money with, and I now have some wherewithal to buy one of my little half-siblings a commission in a good regiment in the army, as that's what he's set on at the moment, though it's like to be something else next month knowing him. It will also pay for some decent schooling for some of the others, just like I've had. The village school is all very well, but I want them to have better. The girls could then get better work, in an upmarket shop maybe, or train as a high-class lady's maid if they speak properly. Whatever they want. I'll simply say I had a run of luck at the tables if anyone enquires, or I've been saving my allowance."

"Unbelievable, quite extraordinary," mused Ashcroft. "That's quite a story," and he quietly added ruthless to the character traits he'd already identified in the youth. He was like a combination of Francis and Nicky all rolled up in one, with a touch of the flamboyant but deadly Ricky Ambrose added to the mix.

"You have to give me your word you'll never tell anyone what I've just told you. I can trust you, can't I?"

"Jack, you have my word. What is discussed in this room, stays in this room. After all, this is where Francis came and confessed all his misdemeanours to me, and to the best of my knowledge they are still a secret. He's not dangling from a gibbet somewhere as far as I've heard," he chuckled, "and I can assure you I am the repository of so many people's secrets, you wouldn't believe the half of what I know."

"Oh, I think I would," sighed Jack.

"Is there anything else you'd like to confess to, while you're about it, or anything else of interest you got up to over last summer?"

"Isn't that enough?" Jack suddenly grinned.

"Probably, but I thought I'd ask while you seem to be in confessional mode," Ashcroft tone was back to its normal facetious self as his lips twitched.

"Hmmm, well, let me see, what else have I done lately that would recommend me to your service?" mused Jack thoughtfully with an assessing smirk at Ashcroft. "Apart from... commit the burglary of the year; cripple the scion of a rich and powerful noble family; corrupt the exam results at the most well-known educational institution in the country; take part in the rescue of one of the aristocracy's finest families from a murderous plot that has rarely seen its like. You probably won't want to know about the slightly older ladies I've seduced at said house parties and elsewhere?" he enquired with a roguish grin. Ashcroft tutted at him disapprovingly and added womaniser to his ever-growing list. "Well, it's all part of my education according to Francis and Nicky," and Jack chuckled wickedly at the expression on the other man's face. "Aha, I know, I beat that dastardly rogue, The Shadow, at his own game. Fought him and beat him. Finally, I'm ready to step into his shoes," Jack crowed with a laugh and Ashcroft almost goggled.

"You fought Francis? Where and why? And you BEAT him? Good God, he's still one of the best swordsmen in London, if rumour has it from that studio where he practises, him and that popinjay, Ambrose."

"They're a good match, believe me. I've watched them lark about at Firle, but Francis is still at the top of his game, just a bit short on stamina these days. I simply taught him a lesson, something I learned from you, actually, Your Lordship."

"Me? But I'm no hand with a rapier."

"It's got nothing to do with technique, it has to do with something I've taken to heart."

"What on earth is that?"

"Expect the unexpected," Jack smiled softly.

"Aaaaah... and dare I ask what you did to my friend, Francis?"

"We fought a duel."

"The hell you did?"

"Mmmmm, the morning after the ball. Soon after dawn, in Hyde Park."

"Good heavens! Have you argued? What on earth was it about?" Ashcroft looked momentarily shocked.

Jack laughed. "Far from it, I love him to death, think the world of him, as you WELL know. No, he merely threatened to cane me for being a saucy jackanapes."

"I'm glad someone seems to be trying to control you," tutted Ashcroft.

"So I merely challenged him to try. It was just him and me in the early morning dew, master and apprentice, there wasn't a soul around, well, unless you count Bubbles, he was the referee... but he was more interested in rabbits and squirrels than the finer parts of swordplay."

"Come on then, out with it. What the hell did you do to the poor man as it's obvious you got the better of him. Lord knows how."

"You could say that. He's some fighter, I've no idea how Bernheim's thugs overcame him," muttered Jack.

"He forgot the Gospel According To Ashcroft, the one you've obviously taken to heart. Expect the unexpected, even though I'd been nagging him forever to be on his guard. But I dare say, if he'd been thirty, or even twenty years younger, I doubt they'd have taken him."

"Probably not, he must have been quite something in his day, smuggling day, that is. I certainly couldn't better him with a sword, couldn't get near him, he just toyed with me; made me realise how dangerous that big Indian was who he fought at Richmond. Anyway, I, therefore, had to recourse to other means to escape getting my arse coloured black and blue."

"Other means? How ungentlemanly," tutted Ashcroft with a quirked brow.

"Well, at the end of the day, I'm not one really, am I? And The Shadow forgot that…"

"How very remiss of him. Serves him right. What did you do, Jack?"

"Well, you see…" Jack began slowly, as Ashcroft listened, quite rapt, "I never forgot what happened in that cellar in Nice, what that strange Chinaman did to Bella, and Bernheim had obviously learned from him; don't you remember what he said to me when we fought by that lean-to in the field? I suppose it didn't mean that much to you, but it did to me, and that's how he caught me off guard, those strange manoeuvres and kicks. So, I went and poked around in Limehouse, amongst the Chinese immigrants there, and finally found a man who could teach me their way of fighting. I think Nicky saw something like it on some training endeavour he got sent on, years ago. I don't know if that was your doing or not, but he never forgot it; he told me about it one day soon after we got back from Richmond. Anyway, this little man was unbelievable, and it's going to take me years to be as good as he is, but I went, day after day and practised for hours with some of his students, and I'm quite a dab hand at some moves now and still go to classes or practise when I can, even though I'm a mere novice in their terms. However, the little I've learned was enough to catch Francis off guard. Hah! You should have seen his face when his sword went flying through the air and he fell in a patch of muddy grass," Jack cackled and Ashcroft couldn't help but laugh at the vision Jack conjured up, one of the few men who were aware of what exponents of the oriental martial arts were capable of.

"Poor Francis…"

"He thought it was very funny, well, when he got his temper back. Oh boy, was he cross," smirked Jack.

"I'm not surprised."

"He even told Bubbles to attack me," Jack guffawed at the memory, "as if that big lump of fluff would do anything; he just sat there looking stupid, with his tongue lolling out. I swear that dog laughs at us, y'know," Jack continued to chuckle, "anyway, to give him his due, Francis did try and fight me properly when he got up, punch me properly, man to man, but he couldn't get near me, and he got even angrier, it was the funniest thing."

"I wish I'd been a bird in a tree watching it."

"Would you have laughed, you and Nicky if he'd been there as well," Jack chuckled. "I'd have murdered me if I'd been Francis, but he just gave up, sat there in the long grass and simply howled at me, doubled up he was. He said he was abdicating forthwith, going to live in Bath and get wheeled about in a chair by a pretty young thing. I could be The Shadow from now on and YOU, Lord Ashcroft, he named you personally, and the rest of the world were welcome to me and should be warned," Jack grinned at the man across the desk from him.

"How old ARE you, Jack?"

"I don't know precisely; officially eighteen, but I could be seventeen or nineteen, why? What difference does that make?"

"None at all, actually. I've had my eye on you since you rescued Nicky and Bella in Nice. You were always meant to be mine, all MINE, my perfect protégé, my youngest recruit."

"I'm my own man, Lord Ashcroft. I have my fortune to make and I intend to do that, my way. The Shadow will rise again, in a slightly different incarnation, but I will always be available to serve King and Country, for YOU, only for you, because of the respect and high regard I hold you in… and because the same applies to you by the other men whose opinions I also respect, namely Francis, Nicky and Eddie."

"Thank you, Jack, I'm honoured," Ashcroft said quite truthfully and looked at his new recruit, and excitement thrummed through his veins. The spymaster sat and looked at the youth across from him and his mind ran amok with all sorts of missions he could get this resourceful young man to carry out for him.

Jack sat patiently and looked at Ashcroft as the man contemplated him back, his mind floating to the final words Francis had had for him as they'd strolled back across the park to his coach, Francis's arm around his shoulders as Jack had teasingly crowed over him. Francis had stopped walking and pulled Jack up with a suddenly serious expression. Then, without a word, he'd pulled off his casual jacket and dragged his shirt over his head and turned his back on him. "Look at my back, Jack. Look at it really closely," he'd rasped. "I know you saw it when we were messing around in the piggery at Valenciennes, but look at it properly now. Up close. Touch it, feel the scars and weals. I thought I was as untouchable as you when I was your age and then throughout my twenties. I laughed at danger and had never been wounded or captured by anyone. I thought I was cleverer than everyone else, invincible, and everything I wanted would fall at my feet. But I was very wrong, on a lot of counts. I nearly lost Cat, for one, through my own stupid arrogance, but, even more important for you to learn is that one day, I discovered I wasn't clever nor invincible after all. An evil bastard, one Pierre Dupont, who worked for Bernheim's father, had me whipped til my back was in ribbons, and when they'd done that and kicked my body black and blue and cracked half my ribs, he strung me up back to front by my arms and decided to lay a red hot, flat iron across my lower back and gradually burn the skin and flesh off it, bit by bit, until there was none left; his particular speciality I gather... unless I told him where the Shadow's treasure was..."

Jack sucked in a breath and grimaced, tentatively putting out the fingers of one gentle hand to feel the raised weals as they criss-crossed Francis's back, and he shuddered as they roved downwards and they touched the hideously puckered and scarred remains of the once-scorched flesh. He couldn't begin to imagine how agonising the torture must have been or how Francis had withstood it.

Francis's voice continued and it was the very quietness of his impassioned words that disconcerted Jack. "I never knew pain like that existed. I screamed so hard Benjy said it made his blood run cold and he nearly vomited when he heard me, down on the street, outside a tower torture chamber in the old stone fortress I was being held in... and that's how I learned my lesson. I wouldn't be here today if Cat hadn't burst in, in the middle of it all, made them stop, fought them by herself, and then rescued me with help from Eddie, Benjy and Carlotta, Bella's late mother; but that isn't the point of my story."

He turned for a moment and his piercing blue eyes seared into Jack's sherry ones before Francis turned his back once again. "Look at it, Jack, look at the scars and puckered flesh, feel them and commit it all to memory. NEVER forget what I've shown and told you this morning. Look at my back, try and imagine what that felt like, except you couldn't possibly because it's beyond any imagination, believe me; and I'll tell you something else, between you and me, one Shadow to another. They STILL hurt on occasion, ache like the devil at times, especially the burn scars, even twenty-five years after it happened. So remember what you're seeing, Jack, and NEVER, EVER, be cocky and think you've got the better of someone or have every eventuality covered, because Ashcroft is right. The unexpected is always there, waiting for you. Nicky got caught in Nice because he wasn't thinking properly when he went to get his boots mended, though I still don't know what was on his mind that morning, Bella probably; and I underestimated MY enemy because I was distracted by a woman; Cat, of course. We'd parted on the most terrible argument... so whatever you get up to in the future, Jack, be VERY careful. We mock Miles, but he's absolutely right in the way he operates. Just like the consummate chess player he is, he thinks through everything at length, considers it from every angle, before he commits to it and that's what you must do, and DON'T be cocky. I don't know what you got up to last summer, but I'd stake my life it was mischief of some sort, and I don't mean of the female variety, and who knows what you're going to get up to in the future. However, Jack, mark my words well, as Master to Apprentice, as this lesson is more important than ANYTHING. No one is untouchable or invincible, even The Shadow..." and with those telling words, Francis put his shirt back on, playfully cuffed Jack round the ears and continued their stroll back to the coach.

Jack had caught sight of Francis's disfigured back during their summer in Valenciennes while he'd been building his piggery wall and when he taken him swimming in the big lake, but hadn't dared ask what had caused the terrible scars, although he'd gathered it had been years before, soon after Nicky had been rescued from the former Fortress that had stood in Rouen and was connected to Bernheim's father. Now he knew, and he'd been rendered almost speechless as he stared at and touched the terrible scars and tried to imagine the unbelievable pain and suffering Francis must have experienced and endured... and as far as Jack knew, he'd never revealed the whereabouts of his fortune or else the Bernheim he'd been involved with wouldn't still have been after it. It was mind-boggling and a salutary lesson and his adulation of the man went up still further.

As Jack committed the sight of the scarred back to memory, he knew he truly would never forget it and how it had been caused... and the lesson sat alongside Ashcroft's lesson... always expect the unexpected... and now... be prepared, think through every move thoroughly, and don't be cocky.

He raised his eyes to Lord Ashcroft and waited for the man's answer.

"Welcome to the Department of Information, 'Shadow'," and Ashcroft laughed softly. "I think that will be your new codename around here and I think you'll fit in quite perfectly. It's certainly more interesting than Lionel... and I'm sure you know who that was. Now then, tell me, exactly where do you anticipate going on your little jaunt over to the Americas? There just might be some interesting documents Her Majesty's Government would like to have sight of, if we knew of someone who could get to them... and do you think you could get hold of a copy of the floor plans of the new White House while you're about it? You never know when they might come in useful for a nefarious burglar I know..."

THE END....
but Jack's story will continue....

In The Meantime...

The Pride of Lions is the second set in the whole Granville Legacy series, lots more to come, and don't forget, if you're interested in joining my little group and getting advance reader copies of the books to review as they come out, or to hear about special offers, or read my occasional blog, or get a monthly newsletter, go to my website https://antoinettegeorge.com/ and join my lists. You'll find out about all the rest of the Granville Legacy series there, especially the contemporary stories which are being published next, in Spring 2022, starting with **Soldier Banker**, all about Francis Granville's direct descendant, Marcus Forsyth, and after that is the tale of Nicky's descendant, Alasdair Kinross, a Scottish Earl no less, a man with lots of secrets....

This is
THE GRANVILLE LEGACY

Coming soon, the full series of The Granville Legacy

18th and 19th century

The life and times of Francis Granville and his friends

Behind The Shadow

Pride of Lions

Publish And Be Damned

To Catch a Thief

21st century

The adventures of Marcus Forsyth, Francis Granville's direct descendant, and his close friends and family.

Soldier Banker

Lions and Feathers

Matilda's Diamonds

Never Left Behind

The Chameleon and The Swan

The Cat's Whiskers

Pins and Noodles

Acknowledgments

Barbara – thank you for your continued enthusiasm and support, endless useful comments on everything, and of course, the editing.

Zivan – thank you for your graphics and covers and grappling with a coat of arms!

Clare – thank you for the formatting and pulling all the content into shape.

www.ingramcontent.com/pod-product-compliance
Lightning Source LLC
Chambersburg PA
CBHW020923020726
47495CB00002B/316